Quintin Jardine was born once upon a time in the West: of Scotland rather than America, but still he grew to manhood as a massive Sergio Leone fan. On the way there he was educated, against his will, in Glasgow, where he ditched a token attempt to study law for more interesting careers in journalism, government propaganda and political spin-doctoring. After a close call with the Brighton Bomb, he moved into the riskier world of media relations consultancy, before realising that all along he had been training to become a crime writer.

Now, more than forty published novels later, he never looks back. Along the way he has created/acquired an extended family in Scotland and Spain. Everything he does is for them. He can be tracked down through his website: www.quintinjardine.com.

Praise for Quintin Jardine:

'Well-constructed, fast-paced, Jardine's narrative has many an ingenious twist and turn' *Observer*

'A masterclass in how murder-mysteries ought to be written' *Scots Magazine*

'Very engaging as well as ingenious, and the unravelling of the mystery is excellently done' Allan Massie, *Scotsman*

'Remarkably assured, raw-boned, a *tour de force*' *New York Times*

'The perfect mix for a highly charged, fast-moving crime thriller' *The Herald*

'Slick and suspenseful . . . starts with . . . and doesn't let up till the last se

By Quintin Jardine

Quintin
Jardine
COLD CASE

HEADLINE

First published in 2018 by
HEADLINE PUBLISHING GROUP

First published in paperback in 2019 by
HEADLINE PUBLISHING GROUP

3

Cataloguing in Publication Data is available from the British Library

ISBN 978 1 4722 3895 5

Typeset in Electra by Avon DataSet Ltd, Bidford-on-Avon, Warwickshire

Printed and bound in Great Britain by Clays Ltd, Elcograf S.p.A.

HEADLINE PUBLISHING GROUP
An Hachette UK Company
Carmelite House
50 Victoria Embankment
London EC4Y 0DZ

www.headline.co.uk
www.hachette.co.uk

This book, the thirtieth Skinner, is for Jim Glossop,
who will never leave my side.

Acknowledgements

My sincerest thanks to my dream team; Marion Donaldson, my peerless editor, Hannah Wann, her tenacious assistant, and Martin Fletcher, my conscience, for their tireless devotion to the Skinner series, and for putting up with me. I know how difficult I am, but I can't help it.

Also, to my friends Peter and Cherry for showing me the view from their window.

One

'Bob, I'm wondering if you have some time free tonight. The thing is . . . I've got a problem.'

I have one thing in common with Maggie Thatcher: history showed her to be a long way short of being St Francis of Assisi, and so am I. I've never been much good at sowing love to replace hatred, and when it comes to bringing joy to drive away sadness, my record is patchy to say the least. However, since I walked away from the police service and Chief Constable Robert Morgan Skinner became plain Bob to all and sundry, I have noticed that when my friends have a problem, they may choose to come to me for help and counsel.

I've had to deal with a few difficult situations, for my friends tend to be the sort of people who draw problems like tourists draw midgies on a damp and wind-free lochside morning. But if there was one I never expected to make such a request, it was my predecessor in the Edinburgh chief's job, and my principal supporter for much of my career, Sir James Proud.

The thousands who served under his command used to call him Proud Jimmy, a silly nickname I will use only once in this account, to emphasise how inappropriate it was. If anyone ever belied his name it was Sir James. I have never met a man in a command situation who exuded such humility, and who showed less self-importance or pride. The phrase 'public servant' is bandied around at will, but I've never known anyone who grasped its true meaning, and put it into practice, as well as he did.

Jimmy at work was one of those rare people who didn't have problems. He had challenges, and it's a tribute to him, and a reason for his longevity in a job that wore me out in a few years, that he rose to all of them. I've known officers who went into his office to be disciplined and were heard to thank him as they left for the wisdom he had shown them. Latterly, of course, he didn't do too much of that; he delegated it to me. No one who wound up on my carpet ever left feeling better for the experience.

That was why, when I took his call that day, as I was ending a meeting in the Balmoral Hotel, my instant reaction was apprehension. A few months before, he had been diagnosed with testicular cancer, but the last medical bulletin he had passed on to me had been positive. His therapy had been effective and he was officially in remission. It's back, was my first thought, even though he had just told me he was clear.

'Jimmy . . .' I murmured.

'No, no, no!' he insisted. He always could read my mind. 'It's not that. That's fine; I meant it when I said I'm in recovery. I saw my oncologist yesterday and she said I'm in better shape than she is. She's right, too. Poor bugger's a stick-thin midget; I wouldn't be surprised if she's her own patient pretty soon. No, son, this is something else entirely, something completely out of the blue.'

'Something that's worrying you,' I observed, 'from your tone of voice.'

'I confess that it is, son,' he sighed. 'Maybe there's nothing to be done about it. If so, I hope the judge takes pity on me. But if there is anyone that can help,' he added, 'I'm talking to him right now.'

'Jesus Christ, Jimmy!' I had visions of my old boss being caught slipping out of the grocer's with a filched tin of corned beef in his pocket. He had never shown the slightest sign of dementia, but he was in the age bracket where it's most likely to occur; indeed, the variability of Lady Proud's memory had been worrying Sarah and me of late.

'He's involved, in a way,' he said. 'I might need a miracle. This is serious, Bob: the last thing I need at my time of life.'

'Okay,' I told him, 'we can meet tonight. Do you want to come to me or me to you?'

'Neither. I don't want either of us to have to explain anything to our wives. I'll meet you in Yellowcraigs car park, eight o'clock, if that's all right. I'll be taking Bowser for a walk.'

'It's all right, but why don't we meet on Gullane Bents? Why Yellowcraigs?'

'Because nobody can see it from your house.'

TWO

I thought about Jimmy all the way home on the bus.

Me? Bob Skinner? Bus?

That's right. It had been the simplest way to get to the Balmoral given the institutionally baffling and constantly changing traffic management in the heart of the city of Edinburgh. Yes, I could have driven by a simpler route to my office in Fountainbridge and taken a taxi, but I had nothing else to do that day, so I let East Coast Buses take me straight to the door.

I was slightly vexed by my new engagement, because I had been looking forward to spending some time with my younger kids in the evening, once the homework burden had been disposed of – don't get me started on that: I don't believe in it – and then a quiet dinner with Sarah, my wife, in celebration of the successful conclusion of an investigation in which I'd become involved.

When I left the police service, or when it left me, as I prefer to put it, I had no clear idea, not even the vaguest notion, of what I wanted to do with the rest of my life. I'm still not certain, beyond my determination to see all of my children through to happy adulthood. I have six of those: the eldest by far is Alexis, my daughter with my late first wife Myra. She has turned thirty and is building a reputation as the Killer Queen of Scottish criminal defence lawyers, after turning her back on the lucrative but unfulfilling corporate sector. Mark, he's in his teens; we adopted him after he was orphaned by separate tragedies. James Andrew, the first of my three with Sarah, is a hulking lad who is easing his way through primary school, just as his sister Seonaid is starting to make her presence felt there. The youngest, Dawn, was a complete and total surprise, and is still only a few months old.

And then there's Ignacio, the son I didn't know I had, the product of a one-night stand twenty years ago with a dangerous lady named Mia Watson, who left town a couple of days after he was conceived and didn't reappear until very recently, still in trouble and still dangerous.

Ignacio lives with me now, and is embarking on a degree course at Edinburgh University; he's a very talented chemist – too talented, with a couple of things on his teenage CV that will never become public. His mother has found a safe haven – I will qualify that; it's been safe so far – having married a guy from Tayside called Cameron McCullough, known as 'Grandpa' to his associates and on his extensive police file, although only his granddaughter gets to call him that to his face. My side had him marked down as the biggest hoodlum in Scotland, but we never laid a glove on him. He always pleaded innocence, as still he does, and was never convicted of anything; indeed, he was only in the dock once, but that case collapsed when the witnesses and the evidence disappeared, traceless. There is an irony in him being my son's stepfather, one that isn't lost on either of us, or I'm sure on any of the few people who are aware of it.

I didn't think of Grandpa, though, as the X5 bus bore me homewards to Gullane. My mind was too full of Jimmy's mysterious call and what might lie behind it. It wasn't the first of its type I'd had since I'd become a private citizen, and quite a few of those had been the triggers for some accursedly interesting times.

Have I ever doubted my early termination of my police career? In a word, yes, but just the once. The first time I had to drive myself from Gullane to Glasgow, through the dense motorway traffic, I found myself looking back nostalgically on the times when I'd made the same journey in the back of a police car, with my driver in front. He never flashed the blue light; he didn't have to: one glimpse of it in a trucker's rearview mirror and he vacated the outside lane, sharpish.

That was the only time I ever regretted my decision to turn my back on the controversial national police service that I'd always opposed but had been unable to prevent, even though I was married at the time to one of the few politicians who might have stopped it. I'm not saying that was the reason why Aileen de Marco and I split; it didn't help, but we were pretty much doomed from the outset, by the lingering occasional presence of a famous Scottish movie actor, and by the fact that I'd never really fallen out of love with Sarah, Aileen's predecessor.

I knew at the time that I was right about police unification, and I still know that I am, although I take no pleasure from the obvious truth that a great majority of Scots now agree with me, both serving cops and civilians.

There's nothing I can do about it, though; only the politicians who caused the fuck-up can repair it, and there's very little chance that they will. However, I am content. I still have, as an old guy in Motherwell used to say, my feet in the sawdust.

I don't call myself a private detective, but I do accept private commissions from individuals. Also, recently, I have been called in by an old colleague and friend in London to help with a couple of situations. As a result, I now carry a piece of plastic that gives me Security Service credentials; that's MI5 to most people. Nobody outside my inner circle knows about my involvement, that being the nature of the beast. At the moment I'm inactive on that front, but Amanda Dennis, the director general, could ask for my help at any moment.

All that occasional activity sits comfortably alongside what's become my main employment in my second career, my part-time executive directorship of a Spanish-owned company called InterMedia, which operates internationally. Amongst a long list of media outlets, newspapers, radio and TV across Spain and Italy, it's also the proprietor of the *Saltire*, an old-established Edinburgh newspaper that was hirpling towards the press room of history until its star reporter, Xavi Aislado, persuaded his brother to buy it, transformed it and made it the only title I know of that is still maintaining the circulation figures of its printed version. Not only that, he is spreading the readership of the online edition across the English-speaking world, and increasingly into Hispanic territory, for we are translated. Hector Sureda, our digital guru, told our last board meeting that the *Saltire* now has as many Spanish-speaking subscribers in the USA as it has Anglos. Globally, the main Spanish title, *GironaDia*, does better, but we're catching up fast.

I got off the bus in Gullane just as the school crossing patrol woman was seeing James Andrew and Seonaid across the road. Jazz – he's never quite shaken that nickname – does not like that too much; having the traffic stopped for him by a lollipop lady is beneath his dignity, he feels, but I have told him firmly that looking after his sister is a responsibility I entrust to him and that he will do what it takes to fulfil it.

I could see them from my bus stop in the distance, and waited for them. As I stood there, Sir James Proud walked past me, a newspaper under his left arm and a Co-op shopping bag in his right hand.

'Afternoon, Bob,' he said briskly, with the briefest of glances in my direction, then passed me by without breaking his stride.

Three

I pushed the mystery to the back of my mind for a few hours, devoting them to Sarah and the kids as I had planned. Dawn was teething and had given her mum, and Trish, the children's carer, a tough day, but I have experience in such matters, and some skill; pretty soon she was back to her placid best. Smug, Skinner, smug.

I'd hoped to spend some time with Ignacio too, but he called from university to say that he needed to work late on a class end-of-session project and would be staying at Alex's overnight. I didn't mind that; he and his half-sister had bonded from the moment he appeared in our lives. My kid, as Alex has always been to me, is always great with the second family – she is James Andrew's idol – but she liked having a sibling with whom she could speak as an adult. Ignacio, he just liked having a sibling, period.

A set routine is important for all children – when Alex was growing up, it was just the two of us, and that was difficult – but bedtime is a fluid affair in our house; homework is done after supper, and then they have some free time until it's lights out. For Seonaid, that's seven o'clock, for James Andrew it's eight, although often he crashes early. Mark is old enough to set his own limits now, but he's usually asleep by ten thirty.

Jazz had just disappeared upstairs with a mug of hot chocolate when I told Sarah I was going out for a while.

'Where you off to?' she asked.

I grinned. 'I'm going to see a man about a dog.'

She raised an eyebrow, but said nothing. She assumed, I assumed, that I was going to the golf club or to the pub. I imagined her raising the other eyebrow a few seconds later when she heard me start the car.

Yellowcraigs Beach lies just outside Dirleton, the neighbouring village to Gullane; it's also called Broad Sands Bay on some maps, but not many people know that. It's a favourite spot of James Andrew and Seonaid, not so much for the sands, more for the children's play park. It has a pirate ship theme, a reference to Fidra, the small island which is situated not far below the low-tide mark. Legend has it that Robert Louis Stevenson, a frequent visitor, drew inspiration from it in writing *Treasure Island*, which is in my eyes the greatest adventure story ever written in the English language.

Mark would go there too on occasion, but with less enthusiasm. The boy is a natural mathematician, with computer skills that I come nowhere near to understanding, but he doesn't know his left hand from his right, nor does he have any interest in finding out which is which. The climbing frames and rope roundabouts in the playground never offered a challenge to him, only a hazard to be avoided.

That's where Jimmy took me. He was waiting for me when I reached the car park, a couple of minutes after eight; Bowser, his springer spaniel, was still on its lead, tugging. Both of them looked impatient. The light of day was dying, but its warmth lingered. I've known many years when the Scottish summer has been over by the middle of May; I wondered if this would be another.

'Sorry,' I said as I climbed out of Sarah's new car, a big Renault hybrid. She chose it because it has seven seats, a sign of the family times. 'I got caught behind a cycling club,' I added, by way of an excuse.

'No matter,' he grunted. He glanced around. We weren't alone. Yellowcraigs is a popular dog-walker destination in an area where pooches seem to outnumber pigeons. I've never had a dog, but Seonaid is beginning to drop hints about puppies. Since she's known how to push my buttons since she was a year old, I suspected that the household would soon hear the patter of tiny paws.

Sir James gave Bowser a quick tug. 'Come this way,' he said, to the dog and to me. 'There are no kids around at this time of the evening, so it'll be private through here.'

I followed him out of the car park, across the road and down the short tree-lined path that led to the Treasure Island mock-up. Last time I'd been there, four days earlier, I'd watched Jazz climb to the top of the rigging surrounding the tall pole that represented a mainmast, while Sarah called after him to be careful. I don't think he'll ever be that, but I don't worry as she does, because he's strong, agile and he knows his limits, as did I when I was his age. However, I do worry about his determination to join the military when he grows up. I don't like the idea of any of mine in harm's way.

I took a seat on a long, snake-like swing as Jimmy unclipped Bowser's lead. The spaniel shook itself, then found its way through the rigging and lifted its leg against the *Hispaniola*'s mast. 'Piss on you, Long John,' I whispered, then looked up at my friend.

His silver hair was thinner after his course of chemotherapy, and he had lost some weight, but physically he looked okay. His expression suggested otherwise.

'So, Jimmy,' I exclaimed, breaking the silence. 'What precisely the fuck is all this about?'

I must have sounded exasperated, for his immediate reaction was to whistle for his dog and snap his fingers. 'Here, Bowser!' he called out, fiddling with the clip of the lead. 'I'm sorry, Bob, this is a mistake. I have no right to put this on you. You've got enough on your plate with the newspaper, the family and everything else in your life. It was thoughtless of me to call you.'

I glanced across at the simulation of the *Hispaniola*, where Bowser was ignoring his master and having a real good sniff.

'Bollocks to that,' I retorted. 'You've looked out for me more often than I care to recall. If you've got a problem and you took it to anyone else, I'd be seriously, seriously pissed off. So come on, man, out with it.'

He seemed to sag, and lowered himself onto the circular perimeter of the enclosure, wincing as he settled on to it. He'd had surgery as well as the therapy.

For the first time since we'd come together, he looked me in the eye. 'Does the name Matthew Ampersand mean anything to you?' he asked.

I did a quick trawl through my memory; I can't claim to recall every investigation during my career, but most of them left a mark. 'I can't say that it does,' I admitted when I was done. 'Professional?'

'Yes, but this business happened before you joined the force. I thought you might have remembered the name from the newspapers of the time, but no matter. He was a murder victim whose body was found in the old quarry at Traprain Law, here in East Lothian, on a Wednesday three weeks before Christmas. It had been freezing hard for days, otherwise he'd have gone to the bottom of the quarry pond, but the ice was so thick he didn't go through it, just landed on it very hard. At first they thought he was a suicide, but Joe Hutchinson, the pathologist, found injuries that were inconsistent with him having jumped.'

At the back of my mind, something stirred. A vague recollection of headlines about 'The Body in the Quarry' around the time I was completing my university degree. 'Yes, maybe I do recall it,' I murmured. 'Why? Has he come back to haunt you?'

'You could say that,' he snorted. 'I'm being accused of killing him.'

Four

I stared at him, gasped, and then laughed.

'Are we on *Candid Camera* here?' I asked.

'I wish we were,' he said. 'It's the truth.'

'Come on,' I protested. 'You were a police officer for forty years but you never as much as kicked a hooligan's arse in all that time. You're the least violent man I know. Tell me who's saying otherwise, and I'll put them right in a way they won't forget.'

'It's a journalist.' Bowser had rejoined us; he was giving me a funny look, as if he had detected his owner's distress and blamed me for it. Jimmy may have sensed this too, for he reached out and ruffled the dog's ears. 'He's called Austin Brass. Ever heard of him?'

I recognised the name at once. The guy wasn't what I would call a journalist, but the world is changing and most of its definitions are being rewritten. He ran a blog, a website called *Brass Rubbings*; its focus was on the police, but not in a positive way. Its meat was misconduct, and it offered a ready ear to anyone with a complaint, however far-fetched, however bizarre.

During my brief time as chief constable of Strathclyde, before the post became part of Scotland's history, my media people had been kept busy by his pursuit of an allegation by a group of citizens in Argyllshire that their local officers tended to prioritise along ethnic lines, with long-established families being given preferential treatment over incomers, moneyed folk who'd moved out of southern cities in search of a calmer lifestyle, 'white settlers' as they were labelled in those parts. I sent a trusted officer up there straight away; she reported back, very quickly, that the complaint was valid. Her investigation mirrored the journalist's own. The guy was thorough; he had done his homework before coming to us and he knew that his story was well founded. Action was taken, Brass was advised, and his site had a field day. Fortunately for my force, the damage was limited, since the mainstream media were not over-keen on promoting an upstart rival by picking up on his story.

'Yes,' I told Jimmy.

'Do you know much about him?'

I nodded. 'Some.' I didn't want to go into detail about my Strathclyde experience. 'He's not to be taken lightly,' I admitted. 'What's he saying?'

'Best if I start from the beginning,' he said. 'As I told you, when Ampersand was found, it was assumed that he'd jumped, so nobody got excited. Then Joe announced his findings and everything changed. What had been an inside-page story about the sad death of a popular priest—'

'Priest?' I repeated.

'Yes, he was an Episcopalian minister. As soon as the murder inquiry was set up, it became front-page news, nationally. The press went crazy and we were under pressure from the off. Sir George Hume, the chief constable of the day, only liked to be seen announcing good news, but he couldn't duck that one.

He did a media briefing where he announced that "Scotland's top crime-fighter" – he actually used that phrase – would be heading the investigation. That, of course, was Alf Stein, your old mentor. He was a detective super at the time, but Sir George was smart enough to know that the then head of CID, an over-promoted old school pal of his from Daniel Stewart's College, whose name was Rodney Melville, could not find his arse with both hands and a map.'

I smiled at the mention of the name. 'Alf told me about him,' I murmured. 'He wasn't as kind as you, though.'

Jimmy grunted. 'No, he wouldn't have been; he never could stand him. Up until then Alf had only a local reputation, given that Edinburgh didn't have a lot of high-profile crime. He was competent, down-to-earth and popular, and that suited him fine. But as soon as Sir George stuck that label on him before the assembled media, he became a national figure, with huge expectations lumped on him.'

'I'd certainly heard of him before I joined the force,' I admitted, 'but I'd no idea that was why.'

My old boss nodded. 'Oh yes, that was the reason,' he confirmed, 'for he lived up to Sir George's star billing. He made an arrest within a week, and saw it all the way through to a conviction. The fact is that Alf only had two high-profile murder cases in his whole career – and you were part of the team on one of them.'

He didn't have to remind me of the details; I knew well enough. It was a double murder, a businessman and his wife; he was kidnapped and she was held hostage to force the guy to give the gang access to his factory. When they had what they wanted, the captives were killed. It went unsolved for years, and when finally the killers were identified, there had been nobody to arrest, for two of the principals died in a suicide pact, and the third had been seen last heading into the Australian outback without food or water.

As the senior investigating officer, 'Scotland's top crime-fighter' was given all the credit by the media, and it became part of his legend, but the truth was we did nothing to close the case. The answer was brought to us by someone else, a guy who turned out to be almost as big a loser as the two victims, in a different way. Jimmy didn't know that, though, and it wasn't the time to enlighten him.

'How did the Ampersand thing pan out?' I asked him.

'There was an obvious suspect from the start. His name was Barley Meads and he and his family had been members of Ampersand's congregation, until there was a big falling-out. That family included a teenage daughter, name of Briony; she was an active member, went to bible class and sang in the church choir. She spent a lot of time at the church, eventually too much time for her father's liking. He followed her there one night and, he claimed, saw the vicar and his kid in what he described as "a compromising position". Briony was fifteen at the time; Ampersand was forty-two. Barley reported him to us, but there was no corroborating evidence of any kind, and the daughter refused to confirm his story.'

'Was the vicar interviewed?'

'Naturally he was, by a uniformed sergeant. He denied it absolutely; he said that whatever Meads thought he'd seen, there had been no inappropriate behaviour. He said that Briony had helped him off with his dog collar once when it had got stuck, one evening when the lass was in the church practising her solo for the following Sunday, and suggested that maybe Barley had seen that and got the wrong idea. Without an admission from the girl, or a complaint by her, there was nothing for us to do but dismiss Meads's allegation. He took it badly, I can tell you,' he said with a grimace.

His sudden vehemence surprised me. 'How do you know?'

He gazed back at me. 'It was me that dismissed it. I was a chief inspector then, out in Dalkeith, and it landed on my desk for review. I sympathised with the man, for I felt that he really believed what he was saying, but I didn't have any choice. Like I said, he didn't take it well. He was a big, brawny fellow, a farmer; he yelled at me, and for a minute I thought I was going to have to call for assistance, but it didn't go that far. He swore that he wasn't giving up and that Ampersand would get what was coming to him.'

'Did you warn him against approaching Ampersand?'

'Of course I did, man,' Jimmy snapped tetchily. 'He replied that he had no intention of doing that but that he still intended to ruin the man, to put an end to his career. He tried too, using a different channel. He made a formal complaint to the bishop who was the titular head of the Scottish Episcopal Church. Meads didn't stop there. He took it to the press as well; his idea was that the adverse publicity would be enough to have the man kicked out of the charge, but it didn't work out that way. Briony being fifteen, the papers were constrained in what they could report. They couldn't use her name because of the nature of the allegation, and the legal advice was that if they named him or even printed the address of his church, they were risking contempt. When the bishop threw out the complaint and formally exonerated Ampersand, they used that, though.'

'How long was it between all this happening and the murder?' I asked.

'About three years . . . four and a half since the initial complaint. The girl, Briony, she was nineteen by that time.'

'What can you remember of Alf's investigation?'

'Quite a lot. I'd risen in rank, and was an assistant chief when the murder happened. Sir George wanted to keep his hands clean, as he always did, so he told Alf to report progress to me. I protested about that, I said it was borderline improper, but Hume just waved me away and told me to get on with it.'

I was puzzled by that last remark, and quizzed him. 'Why was it improper, Jimmy? CID always report to the command corridor at some level.'

The look he gave me said a lot, but most of it was that he had let something slip, something he hadn't meant to. 'Alf Stein and I were brothers-in-law, Bob,' he said quietly, as if that would lessen the impact of his words. 'He was married to my older sister Peggy; she died of breast cancer in her early forties. You weren't aware of that?' he added, almost as an afterthought.

'It's the first I've heard of it,' I told him truthfully.

He showed me a small smile. 'Then you're not infallible.'

'Alf never mentioned it either,' I retorted. 'Never once in all the time I worked for him. As for you and me, while he was around our paths never really crossed, and when they did, I was hardly going to quiz you about your family background.'

'No, maybe not. We never tried to keep the relationship secret,' he insisted. 'But at the same time everybody in the job who needed to know did. They were our senior officers, and they were not the gossipy type. Still, I'm surprised that you never picked up a hint.'

'You shouldn't be. I learned early on that if Alf wanted you to know something, he would tell you. His boundaries were set, and they didn't include talking about his private life. Back then, I was an acolyte; I knew I was his protégé and I was content to sit there and wait for the pearls of wisdom to fall. Occasionally I thought he was less respectful to the chief constable than most, but I put that down to Alf being Alf.'

'Yes,' Jimmy agreed. 'He had a way about him. Now I think about it, I can understand him never mentioning Peggy to you. Her death crushed him. From then on he focused entirely on the job. When he had to retire because of his age, he had nothing left but smoking too much and drinking too much. He didn't last three years. I had assumed, Bob, that with you being widowed as well, he must have mentioned it to you, but obviously not.'

'No kids then?' I said. 'Not that he ever mentioned any.'

'No.'

'That was a pity for him,' I remarked. 'It was Alex that helped me survive. Anyway,' I continued, aware of the gathering darkness in the tree-lined enclosure, 'back to the Ampersand investigation. Alf made an arrest within a week, you said. I assume it was the man Meads.'

'Yes. It was pretty easy really. Ampersand wasn't the most popular vicar you ever met, but there were no other serious complaints recorded against him, only a few older members who thought he was too liberal in his sermons and too conservative with the blood of Christ, the communion wine.'

I was switching into detective mode, and a question arose. 'Given where and how the body was found, did Joe have trouble establishing the time of death?'

'Yes, he did, but he had help from the victim's housekeeper. She was the last person to see him alive, at five o'clock on a Friday night. He wasn't there when she arrived the next morning and she reported him missing that same evening. That being a Saturday, she was afraid he'd miss the next day's services. Alf was left with a window of around sixteen hours, but that was enough. As soon as he had it, he went to see Meads—'

I held up a hand. 'He and who else?'

'Tommy Partridge. Remember him?'

'Of course I do. Tommy's daughter June is the managing editor of the *Saltire*. He comes into the office every so often. He scrounged a coffee off me a couple of weeks ago, and chewed some fat.'

Jimmy's eyebrows rose. 'Does he now? It might be useful to know that. I'm relying on my memory here, but since Tommy was around at the time, he might back me up. I'd feared he might be dead.'

'No, he's getting on a bit, that's true, but he's as fit as you and me.'

'In that case he'll be fitter than me, son, but never mind. Alf and Tommy interviewed Meads, informally at first. The body was found late afternoon on Wednesday, Joe did the PM on Thursday morning, Hume had his panic press conference in the afternoon, so it would have been the Friday that they went to see him. They asked him for his whereabouts on the night Ampersand disappeared. He said he was at home, and his wife backed him on that. So did Briony; she was at college but she'd been home for the weekend.'

'A double alibi,' I mused aloud. 'The wife you'd treat with caution, but the daughter as well, that must have added weight with Alf.'

'It did make him pause, for he told me that same night he'd have to back off. Then on the Monday he got lucky. The door-to-door enquiries produced a neighbour who said she had seen an odd-looking vehicle parked up the road, close to the vicarage, in the early hours of Saturday morning. That's all she said, Alf told me, an odd-looking vehicle.'

'What was she doing up in the early hours of the morning?' I asked. 'Let alone peering through the curtains?'

'She was elderly. Probably the type that never sleeps. But a credible witness as it turned out. Barley Meads drove a pickup truck,' Jimmy continued. 'They weren't as common in those days as they are now, and his was a big American thing with enough seats for a family.'

'So Alf used that description to get a warrant from the sheriff to search Meads's place?'

'Absolutely. It was always by the book with Alf.'

That wasn't quite true, but I wasn't about to sidetrack him at that point in his story, for the evening was cooling fast and I was beginning to regret not having put on a heavier jacket.

'It paid off,' my old chief added, with a gleam in his eye that was unusual for him. 'The vehicle was impounded, and it did for him. There were forensic traces from the victim on the flat-bed of the truck, and on a folding trolley that was lying in it. Also, there were traces in the driver's seat; they led Alf to seize Meads's clothing and find more evidence on a pair of overalls. At that point he reported his findings to me. With the old lady's statement, and her identification of the truck as the type of vehicle she'd seen, that would have been enough for a conviction, but I asked him – you didn't *tell* Alf, remember, even if you were an assistant chief – to go back to the wife and interview her under caution. He did that; she admitted that Meads was in the habit of getting up at odd hours through the night to check on his livestock, and that it didn't always waken her.'

'But the daughter gave him an alibi as well,' I pointed out.

'He went back to her too, not under caution, but she was interviewed at greater depth, with a woman officer present. She admitted that her accommodation was in the rear wing of the farmhouse, quite separate from where her parents slept. Whatever she said, she was useless as a defence witness, because she couldn't say with certainty that her dad didn't go out, any more than her mother could.'

I nodded. If I'd been Alf, that would have been enough for me too.

'Barley Meads was charged on Tuesday evening, and he appeared in court next morning, exactly a week after Ampersand's body was found in that quarry. Sir George Hume breathed a huge sigh of relief and basked in the glory, but it was Alf's reputation that was set in stone. Meads pleaded not guilty and hired a top QC, your friend Archie Nelson, to defend him, but the trial was a formality. It took the jury under two hours to convict him. He was given leave to appeal, when he might not have been, but it did him no good; his life sentence stood.'

'That all sounds rock solid to me,' I said. 'What's the problem? Has Meads been released, and is he using this police-baiter Brass for revenge?'

'Meads is dead,' Jimmy retorted. 'He hanged himself in Peterhead prison two years into his life sentence. I have no idea who's behind the accusation or what information Brass has.'

'Even though you say he's accusing you of murder?'

'He hasn't quite gone that far,' he conceded 'not yet, but that's where he's heading, the fucker!' He spat out the last word as if he couldn't get rid of it fast enough. Sir James isn't a swearer as a rule.

'What did he say?' I demanded. 'Come on, man, it's getting cold here.'

'He called me, on my home number – the one that nobody's supposed to be able to access, like yours – and he said that he has information that places me at the centre of a plot to falsely incriminate Barley Meads for the murder of Matthew Ampersand, and that leads to the conclusion that I was a party to Ampersand's death. He said he wanted to give me an opportunity to deny the allegations before he makes them public and reports them to the Lord Advocate with a view to obtaining a posthumous pardon for Meads, and criminal charges against those involved in Ampersand's murder and Meads's conviction. He wants to meet me, in a place of his choosing, tomorrow at one o'clock.'

'And are you planning to go?' I asked, warily. 'If you do, it could be seen as lending credence to his nonsense.'

'Well,' he said, then paused, but I knew what was coming. 'I was rather hoping that you would meet him, Bob. You've always been, shall we say, better with the press than me.'

'Where did you get that idea?' I laughed. 'I remember hanging a journo out of a second-floor window once. Is that why you want me to see Brass? To put the fear of God in him and rough him up if I have to?'

'The thought had crossed my mind, I admit.'

'Then forget it. I'm not your heavy, Jimmy. If I did see him on your behalf, it would be to hear what he had to say, no more. I would approach the meeting with no preconceptions.'

Even in the gloom, I could see his face darken. 'You think he might be telling the truth? Is that what you're saying?'

'Don't be bloody silly, man,' I replied impatiently. 'I'm saying I'd be there to listen, not to talk. But there is one big flaw in this proposition. Austin Brass won't agree to meet with me; he'll only want to talk to you.'

'I don't intend to tell him you'll be there, Bob.'

'He'd run a mile as soon as he saw me.'

He shook his head. 'I don't think so. Nobody runs away from you, Bob, in case you come after them.'

'I doubt if I could catch him these days.' I scratched my head. 'Mind you,' I added, 'it may well be that he's assuming you'll send me, or someone like me, along. That's why he's insisting on choosing the venue. You can bet it'll be a public place.'

'What makes you so sure?'

If Sir James Proud ever had a fault in my eyes as a chief constable, it flowed from his lack of exposure during his career to the darker side of humanity. It had bred a naïvety in him that on another occasion I'd have found touching.

'If you were arranging a meeting,' I explained, 'at which you would confront someone you believe to be a murderer, don't you think you'd take reasonable precautions to ensure that you walk away afterwards?'

He thought that over for a few seconds. 'If that's so,' he murmured, as he went on to put my own thoughts into words, 'he really must think he has something on me. Please Bob,' he exclaimed, 'do this for me. There's nobody else I can trust.'

It was dark, there was the possibility of a late frost in the air and I wanted to go home. So I gave in, against my better judgement. 'All right,' I said. 'But I'm not doing it tomorrow. Tell him you'll meet him, agree to him choosing the venue, but he's to make it somewhere convenient for you. After all, you're just recovering from a serious illness and shouldn't be travelling too far. Tell him you've a hospital appointment tomorrow, tell him anything you bloody like, but get me a couple of days' grace. This is Wednesday; don't agree to anything before Sunday.'

'What if he insists on tomorrow?'

'You insist even harder. Fix a hospital appointment for real if you have to. But he won't. He knows the story isn't going anywhere and neither are you.'

Five

I was fucking perishing when I got home.

To warm myself up, I brewed a large coffee and laced it with ratafia, a Mediterranean liqueur that I bring home from my frequent trips to board meetings in Girona. Sarah caught me as I topped it up with milk and gave me a disapproving look. She tries her best to curb my caffeine addiction, and as a rule I let her think she's winning.

'Did the dog run away?' she asked, as I took a sip.

I shook my head. 'No, Bowser was as good as gold.'

'You were seeing Jimmy?' she asked. Her surprise was evident, but I could see that it was mixed with concern. 'How is he?'

'He says he's fine, officially in remission. He certainly looks okay.'

'It took him a long time to tell you that.'

'There was more to it,' I admitted. 'He's got a problem, and he asked me if I'd help him.'

'Bob,' she sighed. 'When are you going to start telling your friends to sort out their own problems? What is it this time?'

'He's being pestered by a journalist,' I told her. 'He wants

27

me to meet the guy and find out what he knows and where he's planning on going with it.'

'Why can't he do that himself?'

'He seems to think I'd be better at it.'

'Which you would, no doubt,' she agreed. 'But why lumber you? What is it anyway? Is it work related?'

'It's something from the dim and distant past.'

'And Jimmy can remember that far back? Bob, if this is a story that relates to his police career, shouldn't he be referring it to the police? They have a huge press department these days. Every time I do an autopsy for them, someone different shows up to help me draft the statement for the media.'

I smiled and ruffled her hair. 'As if you need that.'

'Exactly,' she exclaimed indignantly, batting my hand aside. 'Most of them don't have a clue about the anatomical terms. They try to dumb everything down.'

'Some of the end users they have to service are pretty dumb,' I pointed out, then thought better of what I had said. 'No, as a newspaper executive, let me correct that. A large chunk of the modern media sets out to explain things to its readers in the simplest terms possible, and in the fewest words. Not just in what you do either; life is being dumbed down.'

'That doesn't cut it for me. The police press officers never have to stand in the witness box and be cross-examined by defence counsel about quotes they've given to some bloody tabloid reporter and attributed to me. If I let them get it wrong in a release or a briefing it could affect the outcome of a criminal trial and a guilty person could walk free.' She paused to pinch a mouthful of my coffee. 'Hey, that's not bad,' she admitted. 'It would be better if it was decaf, but I'll let you off this once.'

'How do you know it isn't? You didn't see me make it.'

'You're enjoying it. That's all the evidence I need.' She glanced up at me. 'Is that what Jimmy wants you to do? Put the right spin on his response to whatever this guy's story is?'

'More or less. I'd have promised him anything to get out of that meeting place. Even the fucking dog was complaining about the cold,' I grumbled.

I'd hoped she was done quizzing me, but no such luck. 'What's this journo saying, that Jimmy can't just come up here and talk to you about it?'

'Like I said, it relates to an ancient case, one that he was involved in peripherally. It was a murder where the perpetrator protested his innocence—'

'As most of them do,' she interjected.

'Agreed. In this case, it seems that there was more than enough evidence to convict, even if the circumstances were bizarre.'

'How?'

'The killer dumped the body into a disused quarry pond, without realising it was frozen solid.'

'The Traprain Law homicide?' Sarah exclaimed.

I stared at her. 'You know about it? It happened thirty years ago, just before I joined the police.'

'That's right, but it was one of Joe Hutchinson's classics. He refers to it in a forensic pathology textbook that he published last year after he retired. He sent me a copy, so yeah, I know the details. The body was frozen to the ice when Joe arrived at the scene. Like everyone else, all the attending police, he assumed that the guy had jumped in the dark. When he did the autopsy, the damage was what he expected to find: massive internal injuries, all the organs ruptured, fractures to every limb, face crushed. There was very little blood at the scene, but with an instantaneous death, that wasn't unnatural and so he didn't query it at first. He was on the point of closing and writing it up as a suicide, but just to be thorough, he turned the body over. When he did, he found a massive depressed fracture at the back of the skull, one that couldn't possibly have been caused by the impact with the ice.'

She blagged another sip of my coffee, then decided to fix herself one, and another for me since she'd necked half of the original.

'Joe came under heavy cross-examination from defence counsel at the trial,' she continued when she was ready. 'He tried to get him to concede that everything could have been impact injuries, but all he was doing was setting Joe up with a career-defining punchline. He replied that not even a suicidal acrobat, let alone an Episcopal vicar, could have managed to fracture both the front and the back of his skull in a single face-down impact. Conviction secured, case closed.'

'Maybe not.'

'Is Jimmy's journalist trying to argue that the victim . . . What was his name? Ah yes, Ampersand . . . did kill himself?'

'No,' I told her. 'He seems to be saying that someone other than the man who was convicted did the job.'

'How does that affect Jimmy?'

'Profoundly, if there's even half a grain of truth in what he's suggesting.'

Her eyes showed anxiety. 'Does he want you to scare the man off?' she asked.

'If he did, he knows that's not going to happen. I've promised that I'll listen to the guy, no more than that.'

'What's his name?'

'Austin Brass.'

Surprise supplanted anxiety. 'The man who runs that blog *Brass Rubbings*?'

'That's the one. I've had dealings with him before, from a distance, but I'm surprised you've heard of him.'

'He has quite a following. I have a couple of students who hang on every word he writes,' she told me. 'They are going to fail the course unless they can demonstrate to me that they're able to approach every situation with an open mind, which is not something Mr Brass seems able to do. How about you? Will you be able to do that when you meet him?'

'I hope so, but I'm not intending to walk into the meeting cold.'

'How do you plan to prepare for it?'

'By talking to someone who was around at the time. For all I know, he might be Brass's source. If he is, I'll find out quickly enough.'

Six

'Bob Skinner?' the voice in my ear repeated. 'The Bob Skinner? As in the raw young detective constable that joined Alf Stein's team and went racing past me on the promotion ladder, all the way to the executive corridor?'

'The same one, Mr Partridge,' I confirmed. If we'd been on FaceTime, he'd have seen that I was smiling. 'The same one whose coffee you're very happy to drink every time you come into the *Saltire* office.'

'Fine, but I didn't know you had my home number, hence my surprise.'

'I'm a fucking detective, Tommy. It wasn't hard to find.'

'I suppose not; all you'd need to do was ask my daughter.'

'Exactly.'

'So.' He paused. 'What do you want?'

'A chat,' I said, 'about times past. One time in particular. How are you placed?'

'All my time's my own since Mary died,' he replied. 'Neither of my daughters has seen fit to make me a grandfather, and I doubt it'll happen now. This chat,' he added abruptly. 'Does it affect June? Is it business?'

'Not at all.'

'Is it about Xavi, my stepson?'

'No. Do you still keep in touch with him?'

'Of course I do; always have done. He banished his mother from his life for ever, for reasons I didn't like but I understand, but he and I got on fine from the time we met. I did him a few favours when he was a young reporter on the *Saltire*.'

'So did I,' I admitted, 'but that whole time in his life is blocked off now. Pretty much everything that happened before he moved to Spain is off limits. As I said, though, what I want to discuss is nothing to do with him. He was just a kid when this thing happened. When can we meet?'

'Where are you?' Tommy countered.

'Office.'

'Then I'll come to you. June gave me a pass for the car park, so that's easiest. Around three o'clock be okay?'

'Suits me,' I confirmed.

'Good. When I get there, I'll expect some of that asphalt you call coffee.'

There was a fresh brew waiting an hour and a half later when he strode into my room after the briefest of knocks. I don't know exactly what age Tommy is; by the time I reached the rank that would have given me access to his HR file, he had retired from the service. With many cops, that doesn't happen on the scheduled date, but even so, I knew he had to be in his mid seventies.

He could have passed for ten years younger: his eyes were clear, his back was ramrod straight and there was a breadth to his shoulders that gave a hint of a senior citizen with an active gym membership. There was still plenty of dark in his thick hair, but the two-day stubble on his chin was pure silver.

He caught my glance and rubbed it, grinning. 'Why shave every day?' he said. 'There's nobody to complain about my beard being rough. June never has time to drop in on me, and her sister Nanette's married to an architect and lives in Bath.'

'Yes, I knew that,' I said. 'You're talking as if you've retired from the human race. It's been a couple of years since your wife died; you should be getting yourself out and about.'

He grunted as I poured him a coffee, and as he dropped into a chair. 'This might be hard for a guy like you to understand,' he replied quietly, 'but I don't want to. I loved Mary and I still do, even though she's dead.'

I nodded. 'I understand that. My first wife, Alex's mum, she's been gone for over twenty-five years, but the part of me that loved her still does. It's never got in the way of later relationships, though.'

'I think the whole world knows that, Bob.' He laughed. 'I remember when you were hauling your way up that ladder, and all the time you were a single dad raising a kid . . . except you werenae always single. You and that Alison Higgins,' he glanced up at the ceiling and crossed himself, 'God bless her; the whole bloody force knew about that. Then of course you went and married that American pathologist. And after her—'

I held up a hand to stop his recital of my marital history. 'Exactly,' I exclaimed. 'I think that's the point I'm trying to make.'

'Yes, but I'm no' you.' He frowned, unexpectedly. 'Mind, I wish I had grandkids about my feet . . . not that I could ever say that to June or Nanette,' he added.

'There's Xavi's lass, Paloma, out in Girona,' I suggested. 'She's growing apace. I'm sure that if you took an interest in her, the big fella would welcome it.'

'He's asked me out there,' Tommy admitted, 'but I've always put him off. Given that he had no real relationship with his mother, I'm scared I'd feel awkward.'

'I doubt that you would,' I suggested. 'Xavi would be very pleased to see you, I'm sure. He has very few friends, you know. He's always been a solitary man.'

'Maybe I will, then,' he murmured, then drained his mug. 'Now,' he continued, 'before that stuff gives me palpitations, are you going to tell me what piece of ancient history you want to chat about?'

'The Vicar in the Quarry,' I replied. 'The Matthew Ampersand murder. I'm told that you were involved in the investigation with Alf Stein. Do you remember it?'

'There's not a hell of a lot to remember,' he retorted. 'Yes, I was on the team; I was a detective sergeant then. But it was a stonewall conviction. Motive, tons of forensic evidence, and no alibi that stood under cross-examination.'

'I'm told you sat in on the interviews with Alf.'

'I did. It might seem unusual now, a DS backing up a superintendent, as Alf was then, but the chief constable had lumped all sorts of pressure on us to get a result, and Alf didnae fancy the DI on his team. It was that tosser Greg Jay; his father had a connection to Hume, the chief, and he'd been promoted way before his time, still in his twenties. Alf made him co-ordinator and stuck him in the murder van, even though there was precious little to co-ordinate.'

'You interviewed the principal witnesses twice, is that right?'

Tommy scratched his head. 'Did we? It's that long ago, man. You're asking a lot so just hold on a minute and let me get it sorted in my mind.' He held out his mug. 'Some more of that stuff might help.'

I raised my eyebrows as I poured him a refill. Not even I come back for seconds of that brew. I watched him as he sipped it, leaning back in his chair, frowning, nodding.

'You're right, we did. The chief suspect was a farmer, Barley Meads; an odd name, but appropriate. He told us it had been his grandfather's nickname, the real one being Bartholomew, and his dad gave it to him officially. A big, rough-looking bastard, he was, with a temper to match. The first time we spoke to him, he was just a box we had to tick. We had no specific evidence against him at that point; the only thing that put him on the list was a complaint he'd made against the victim a couple of years or so before, a complaint to the police, mind. He'd accused him of making advances towards his teenage daughter, but it was rejected; not least, if memory serves me right, because the daughter refused to back him up. Anyway, when we reminded him of this and asked him where he'd been on the night the victim disappeared, he blew up at us. At first he told Alf it was no business of his, but finally he said he'd been home with his wife, all evening and all night.'

'How did he react to the news that Ampersand had been murdered?'

'He shrugged and looked away from us, then he muttered something. Alf asked him what he'd said and he turned and yelled, "I said it serves the fucker right!" That was before we asked him for his whereabouts. Looking back, I suppose we started taking him seriously as a suspect from that point on.'

'Was the wife there when he said all this?' I asked.

'No, we interviewed him separately, then the wife and daughter together. It was informal at that stage, Bob,' Tommy explained. 'We had no rights there; he'd let us in and if he'd thrown us out we'd have had to go. We spoke to him in the sitting room,' he continued. 'They'd all been in the kitchen when we arrived, him, the wife and the daughter. Wife's name was Carmel, and her I do remember: Italian descent possibly from her name, but local accent, tall, dark-haired, a real looker, a bit like Sophia Loren. I'm buggered if I can remember what the daughter was called. Meads took us into the next room and they stayed there. They might as well have come with us, though. He shouted so loud, they were bound to have heard.'

'The wife backed him up, of course.'

'All the way,' Tommy confirmed, 'not that it did him any good in the end.'

'And the daughter?'

He made to answer, then paused, frowning as he trawled the depths of his memory. 'That's right,' he murmured, nodding, then continued. 'She never knew Ampersand was dead, not then,' he said. 'It had been in the papers, but she was a student . . . damn it, I wish I could remember her name . . . and she'd had exams, so she'd missed it.'

I found that odd. 'The parents never mentioned it to her?' I exclaimed.

'The mother said she'd hidden the *Evening News* from her. They were afraid that it would be a shock.'

'And was it?'

'It certainly seemed to be. I remember how she reacted. She went white as a sheet, her hands went to her mouth and there were tears in her eyes. But she backed her father up as well. She said he'd been at home all evening and no, he hadn't gone out later on.'

'Did you press her on that; her or her mother?'

'How could we have?' Tommy protested. 'We had no grounds not to believe them, however strong Alf's suspicions might have been – and they were. Apart from that unsupported accusation, a few years in the past, there was no evidence to put Meads with Ampersand . . . not at that stage.'

He paused for a couple of seconds, glancing at me. 'We did ask him about the complaint he made; or rather, Alf did. As you can imagine, he did all the interviewing – you know how it was with him, Bob; I was just there as the legal necessity, in case corroboration was required later on in court. When the question was put, big Barley's face sort of darkened; all he would say was that he'd seen what he'd seen, and that Briony – that was the lassie's name!' he cried out in triumph. 'That Briony had only denied it to save Ampersand from the sack – and to keep him out of jail, I suppose, for any minister caught having sex with a minor would have been put away for a long time, even in those days, when attitudes might have been a bit softer.'

'What did he claim to have seen, exactly? Did Alf press him on that?'

'Oh aye, he pressed him all right; he told me later that he'd a feeling about Meads from the start. At first the guy refused to go into detail. He said nobody had believed him when it happened, so why the hell should he discuss it now? Alf told him, "Because this is a murder investigation, sir, and I need to know every detail of the events that led up to it." Meads protested; he said that it was in the past and had nothing to do with what had happened to the vicar. He said that we should be trying to find out who else's kid he'd been shagging, because likely that's who had done for him, but Alf wouldn't let it go. He threatened to do him for withholding information. As we both knew, and you know Bob, that was an empty threat, without proof that it was directly relevant, but it worked on

Barley. He described seeing shapes through a window that he was passing; it was steamed up, but he could see Ampersand and Briony, tongues down throats and his hand on her bum pulling her against his groin. Alf asked if he was sure it was Briony, with the window being steamy. He blew up again. "D'ye think I don't ken my own daughter?" he bawled.'

I frowned. 'The obvious question is if that's what he saw, why didn't he go in and sort it out there and then?'

Tommy nodded. 'Sure it was obvious, and that's exactly what Alf asked him. Meads said that he was with somebody at the time. There had been some sort of church council meeting and he and this guy were heading for the pub. So he did nothing, but bottled it all up and tackled Briony when they were home. She got hot under the collar, he said, and told him he'd been seeing things, but he didn't buy that. He saw what he saw, he declared, and he went to the police. When we sent him packing, he complained to the Episcopalian bishop, but got no joy there either.'

'So,' I said, 'that was the end of it for the time being.'

'That's right,' he agreed, 'but not for long. As you reminded me, we went back there a few days later, and it was very different then.'

'What made you re-interview them? Can you remember?' I knew the answer, but I wanted to hear it from Partridge.

'Oh aye, I can remember. It's all come back to me now; little wonder, it was the biggest case I was ever involved in. A few days after we visited the Meads family, door-to-door enquiries turned up a sighting of a vehicle in the vicinity of the vicarage the night that Ampersand disappeared. The witness described it as a big muckle thing, a kind of a truck. That rang a bell wi' the gaffer straight away. I'd never noticed it, but he said that he'd seen something like that at the Meads farmhouse. He made me phone the Department of Transport in Wales, and check on cars registered at Meads's address. They came up with four, a Jaguar and a Vauxhall in his name, a Ford Fiesta in Briony's and a Dodge Ram pickup registered to the farm, to the limited company that owned it. I'd never heard of a Dodge Ram; it turned out to be American, a huge thing with four doors and a platform behind. There were no more than a dozen or so in the country at the time. I found the distributor in London, and they faxed me an image.' He smiled. 'Remember fax machines, Bob? Do you think anybody still has one?'

'Most businesses still do,' I replied. 'You can't rely completely on the internet.'

'I suppose,' he conceded. 'It worked for us that time. Alf sent me to show it to the witness, and she gave me a positive response. That was enough for us. We went straight back there, armed with a warrant from the sheriff to search the premises and impound vehicles and other items as necessary.'

'You must have found a right friendly sheriff if that was all the evidence you had,' I observed. That thought had occurred to me immediately when Jimmy had told me about the warrant. In my experience, warrants aren't handed out casually by the Edinburgh judiciary.

'We did. Jimmy Proud sorted that; handshakes were exchanged, if you get my drift.'

I did. You won't find it in Sir James's Wikipedia page, but he's a member of a Masonic lodge in Edinburgh, and was throughout his police career.

'Anyway, we took the Dodge, and everything in it, back to the police garage and set the forensic people to work. It was a fucking gold mine, even in the days before DNA. The victim's blood was all over the platform, and other traces too. It was on a trolley that Meads had left in there, and even on a pair of his overalls that we found hanging on a hook in the barn he used as a garage. The only prints they found in the vehicle were his and those of a farm labourer.'

'Did you look at the labourer as a potential accomplice?' I regretted the question even as it was passing my lips. Of course they had. I held up a hand in apology, under Tommy's withering gaze.

'Naturally,' he replied, with a tone of indulgence in his voice. 'He'd an alibi, provided by everyone else on the package holiday to the Canaries that he and his wife had got back from the day before we took the Dodge.'

'Did you detain Meads straight away?'

'We went back to the farmhouse. Mind you, we'd been keeping an eye on it, and him, from the moment we took the truck. Second time around, we cautioned Meads, arrested him and held him on his own while we re-interviewed the wife and daughter, separately, on the premises. Everything changed then. Alf was still polite, but there was something different in the way he approached the women. You must know what I mean, the way he was when he knew beyond doubt he was onto a winner. Witnesses sensed it and tended not to fuck him about.'

I nodded. Yes, I remembered Alf's 'gotcha' mode. Indeed, I did my best to copy it all through my career, even at times when I was only guessing, snatching at possibilities.

'It didn't take long for the stories to change. Carmel, the wife, she admitted that sometimes Meads got up in the night, just to go and check the livestock, she said, and that she didn't necessarily hear him. Briony, as it turned out, was no more reliable. Alf made her show us her bedroom. It was in another wing of the farmhouse, away at the back. He stayed there with a WPC, while I went back downstairs and slammed the front and back doors as hard as I could. When I got back up, neither of them had heard a damn thing.'

'Why did Barley finally crack? Three or four years is a long time to keep a grudge festering before it explodes.'

'We never got to the bottom of that,' Tommy confessed, 'because he denied everything, and kept on denying it, right through to the end of the trial.' An eyebrow rose. 'And beyond,' he murmured, as another recollection came back to him. 'After the High Court had refused him leave to appeal to the House of Lords, he wrote to the Secretary of State asking for a review. The Scottish Office, as it was then, asked Sir George Hume to respond. He passed it to Alf and he passed it to me. I did a summary of the investigation and its findings. I heard afterwards from the gaffer that the Secretary of State turned him down. A few months later, Meads hanged himself, or asphyxiated himself, however you want to describe it.'

He slapped the arm of his chair in frustration. 'Yet none of that need have happened,' he snapped. 'Nor would it if those sloppy bastards had done their job properly in the first place. If senior CID officers had been assigned to the complaint, rather than a disinterested uniform, it would have been investigated properly, and proved or disproved beyond doubt. Either Ampersand would have gone to jail or Barley would have been satisfied of his innocence. The Episcopalian General Synod could have done more too; even if they accepted his denial, they might have quietly shifted him to another church, in another part of the country. It was a bloody tragedy all round, Bob. The man's death was preventable, but still it happened.'

He finished his coffee, stared into the mug as if contemplating another refill, then replaced it on my desk. 'So,' he continued heavily, 'what's brought this up again after all these years? You're not going to tell me that the family have raised it again, are you? Is your Alex involved? Have they asked her to look into it?'

'No,' I assured him, shaking my head. 'She isn't. Let's just say there might be press interest in it.'

'You mean from the *Saltire*?' he exclaimed. 'It isnae my daughter rather than yours that's put you up to this, is it? There are limits to what I can tell her about my police career – not that the Meads case would be beyond them,' he added.

'No, it's not,' I replied. 'And none of this goes back to June at this stage, please, Tommy. There are sensitivities.'

He laughed. 'Bob Skinner? Sensitivities? Dearie me, that's a first.'

His sarcasm was accompanied by a perceptive glance in my direction. He was a loyal father with his daughter's interests in mind and he wasn't about to be brushed off.

'Okay,' I conceded. 'I'm looking at this on behalf of someone who might have an interest in how it plays out. I won't say any more than that. I'm relying on your discretion here, Tommy, but trust me, I'll be mindful of the *Saltire*'s interests as well, and I won't see its editor embarrassed by being scooped on a story where I had advance knowledge. That's my duty as a director, and I won't forget it.'

'Fair enough,' he said. 'Do you need any help? I've got time on my hands, I'm experienced, and if you have to go digging into the past, I have met some of the people involved, even if it was thirty-something years ago.'

43

He had a point. 'I don't know yet,' I told him, 'but I promise I'll keep your offer in mind, and if I do feel the need for backup, it'll be you I call.'

He nodded and rose from his chair. In the doorway he paused and glanced back at me. 'By the way,' he asked softly, 'how's Jimmy Proud doing these days? I heard he has cancer. You and he are near neighbours, aren't you?'

Seven

I stared at the door for some time after it had closed behind my visitor. Had his enquiry after Jimmy's health been made out of concern, or had he been dropping a hint that he had tied him to my line of questioning?

Either way, I hoped that I had given nothing away in my expression when I replied, 'In remission as far as I know.'

I didn't dwell on it, though, as I sat there musing over my next step. I decided pretty quickly what it would be, but I had a couple of hours to spare before I could act upon it. I filled the first of those with work on a report I had to make to the InterMedia board, then another building up my Catalan vocabulary. In my first few months as a director, Xavi interpreted for me at meetings, but I decided early on that for the money I was being paid, the least I could do was learn the company's business language. I'd picked up a limited amount over the years, on holiday in my Costa Brava house, so it wasn't as formidable a task as it would have been to a newcomer.

When I'd done as much of that as I could for the day, I still needed to kill some time, so guessing that she might have made it back by then from the High Court in Glasgow, I walked the short distance to my daughter's office.

When Alex, my firstborn, gave up corporate law to become a solicitor advocate, specialising in criminal defence, I fixed her up with space in the *Saltire* building, which is owned by InterMedia. I was proud of her when she made the move, but anxious also, although I tried to keep it from her. She had become a partner before she was thirty in her old firm, Curle Anthony Jarvis, the biggest business law practice in Scotland, but found that the astronomical money she was making didn't sit comfortably alongside her social conscience.

The irony of her decision, when it became known, wasn't lost on the media or on the chattering classes in general. 'Bob made a career out of locking them up; now his daughter's devoting hers to getting them out!' That was the usual line of chat in the lawyers' watering holes, of which there are quite a few in Edinburgh. One or two people suggested – wisely, never to my face – that I would be opening doors for her. The fact was, I couldn't have, but as it transpired, there was no need, for she hit the ground running. She's been busier than she'd ever dreamed she would be and now employs a very efficient clerk named Eimear Blake and a paralegal assistant in an expanded office unit. I had assumed that she'd want to move her premises closer to the High Court and the Sheriff Court, but she likes her slightly off-patch location. It gives her clients a degree of privacy when they call on her. Also, the rougher types know I'm close by, and that does no harm either.

'Turned any more hooligans loose on the streets?' I asked her cheerfully as I stepped into her workplace.

She shook her head. 'Not today; my client got two and a half years. The Crown expected five, so he and I were reasonably happy.'

Said client was a hedge fund manager who'd borrowed some of his investors' cash to buy an apartment in Glasgow for his mistress, thinking blithely that they'd never notice. They did, of course, when the business on which he'd gambled the bulk of their money went into administration before he could pay it back. The Justice Minister in the Scottish Parliament is the son of one of the investors, and the Lord Advocate had been leaned on to make an example of the guy.

'You must have offered a pretty good plea in mitigation,' I observed.

She shrugged. 'It worked. I cited disposals in similar cases, then suggested that the accused had been stupid rather than deliberately fraudulent, and that if the prosecution hadn't been subject to political pressure, they wouldn't have pressed so hard for an exemplary sentence.'

I laughed. 'The advocate depute must have loved that.'

Alex nodded. 'Oh yes. She really spat out her dummy. Pauline doesn't like me at the best of times; veins standing out on her neck.'

'Who was the judge?'

'Lord Hardcastle. He's a regular in the Bank Bar, so he's up with the gossip; he knew the score all right.'

'So you've had a good day,' I concluded.

'That wasn't the highlight,' she countered. 'I was on my way back on the train when I had a phone call, from the new Lord Advocate himself.'

I felt a frown gather. Okay, she might have pushed it in court, but I wasn't having any bugger bullying my kid, even if he was the nation's top law officer.

She read my expression. 'No, no,' she said quickly. 'He wasn't bothered about my plea, but the outcome hadn't been lost on him. He told me that Pauline's time is up as an advocate depute. She's being sent back to general duties, as it were. He offered me a place on the Crown Office team, as her replacement.'

Bloody hell, I thought, that was quick. Yes, the Crown Office recruits prosecutors from the general bar, but usually they have more time served than Alex.

'Congratulations,' I exclaimed.

'Not so fast, Pops,' she continued. 'I turned him down. I'm not ready. I'm still building a practice. My dream is to gather a stable of solicitor advocates around me, with Eimear as the clerk; when we've got there, yes, it would be possible for me to spend a couple of years in the Crown Office. If I walked out now, there would be no work for her, and she's too bloody good to be sidelined.'

'Even so,' I argued, 'it's a good career move. It would help you make QC.'

'I'll make QC with or without it.'

'It would help you become a judge.'

'Who says I want to?'

I gazed at her. 'You're my daughter,' I said quietly. 'Of course you want to.'

She looked back at me steadily. 'I'm your daughter, but I'm not your clone. I'm done with climbing ladders as fast as I can. If . . .' She paused. 'If I ever try for the bench, it'll be in my own time, and that won't be for another twenty-five years at least.'

'By which time everyone will have forgotten about me,' I murmured. 'You really want to distance yourself from me, don't you?'

She gasped. 'Don't be daft! First off, nobody will forget about you until long after you've stopped breathing, and that's a while off. Second, have you looked at yourself lately? Since you left the police, you've become just as interested in protecting the innocent as in pursuing the guilty.'

'Bollocks,' I muttered.

'It's true,' she insisted.

And maybe it is, but I didn't have time for a debate, not then.

'Where did you get to last night?' she asked me, suddenly. 'I called to try my plea out on you, but Sarah said you'd gone off on a mystery assignment. What was it?'

I've never been able to lie to Alex, or even dissemble. Besides, I'd already told Sarah. 'A cold case – in every sense of the term – of Jimmy Proud's has resurfaced,' I replied, 'and is threatening to bite him on the arse. He's asked me to help him out by talking to the journalist who's pushing it.'

'Do you really want to get involved in that?' she asked. 'Suppose there's something in it? Not that I suppose for a moment there might be,' she added quickly.

'I've made it very clear that I'll approach the meeting with an open mind. Fact is, I've already started to prepare for it.' I told her about my conversation with Partridge. 'From what Tommy said, there's nothing in it, but to be absolutely sure, I'm going to ask Mario McGuire if he can get me access to all the case files.'

'If they still exist.'

'They will. They'll be archived somewhere but they'll still be accessible.'

'Who's the journalist?'

'A man named Austin Brass. He's a blogger really, runs a website. I don't like to describe those people as journalists,' I grumbled.

49

'Welcome to the modern world, Pops,' she chuckled. 'And don't be so blinkered. Your company – my landlord – does very well out of its websites. Didn't you tell me that the Italian one won an international award last year? I've heard of Brass, and visited his site, *Brass Rubbings*. I can see why you wouldn't like him, but there's a counter-argument that he performs a more valuable public service than the so-called police watchdog.' She smiled. 'All the same, I don't approve of him upsetting poor Jimmy. He's the nicest man that ever wore a silver-braided uniform. I'm exempting you from consideration,' she said, 'because you always hated wearing the thing, and it showed.'

She was right about that. Maybe she had a point about Brass too, but I wasn't ready to concede it.

'If it helps, tell Jimmy that if it becomes necessary I'm ready to fire off a letter to Brass warning him that if he oversteps the legal line, an action for defamation will follow. I know that's not what I do, but I know how to do it. In my limited experience, the threat is usually enough.'

Coming from Alex, it would be enough for me, that's for sure. I felt a twinge of sympathy for Mr Brass as I left her and took the lift down to the basement garage.

Habit made me look around as I stepped among the parked cars. A while ago I wasn't so careful and a misguided thug tried to mug me. He failed, but it isn't an experience I plan to repeat.

The journey to Cramond took me no time at all. Mario McGuire and his wife Paula had moved house in the summer, from their beloved rooftop apartment in Leith to a villa in the city's eastern suburbs with the garden they needed for their increasingly vigorous toddler Eamon. As I pulled into the drive, I was pleased to see that I had timed my unannounced visit well, for Mario's car sat in front of the double garage.

As I rang the doorbell, I wasn't quite sure how I would be received. A little while before, Mario and his immediate boss, Maggie Steele, the chief constable of the Scottish national police service, had involved me informally in a disciplinary matter. It was very sensitive, and it related to a live homicide investigation. They brought me in because I knew the officer involved. Mario hadn't been pleased with the outcome; he thought I'd exceeded my brief and made no secret of his views. He had been a junior colleague and friend for many years, but for the first time, I wasn't sure of my welcome in his home.

I needn't have worried. Big McGuire is one of those rare human beings who will remember an act of kindness for ever, but bear a grudge for around a minute and a half.

'Bob!' he exclaimed as he opened the door, a smile splitting his broad face. 'What the hell's this – and don't tell me you were just passing. Nobody just passes this place. Come on in.'

As I stepped indoors, Eamon came rushing up to me, and I swept him up in my arms. The warmth of his hug may have been related to the fact that when I visit, I always bring him a present; on that occasion, it was a toy car I'd found in a garage on Queensferry Road. He chortled happily as I put him down and handed it to him.

'I'm not interrupting dinner, am I?' I asked his father.

'No, no,' he assured me. 'You're way too early for that. The wee man's just had his, but we don't eat until he crashes. That will be sometime in the next half-hour. How's your Dawn – and all the rest, of course?'

'Dawn is serene, and lives up to her name by waking up around then. The rest make their way through life with all the subtlety of a wrecking ball – including Alex, who's just broken another advocate depute.'

He nodded. 'I heard about that. Good for her; the Crown Office shouldn't be letting itself be pressured by the pols.'

Eamon led us through to the kitchen, where Paula was working on the evening meal. She is third-generation Italian, but with first-generation cooking skills. She's also one of the sharpest businesswomen in Edinburgh. How to describe her? Looks like Cher did thirty years ago, and I predict will have the same ageless quality. Mario? A mountain with black curly hair.

'Where's the fire?' she asked me, grinning.

'No visible fire yet,' I replied. 'Still at the smoke stage.'

Her other half led me outside, onto a deck that overlooked the garden, where Eamon had already staked out his territory with a swing, a slide and a sandpit. He offered me a broad wooden armchair with thick cushions and handed me a bottle of flavoured San Pellegrino.

'So?' he murmured as we settled down.

'Favour, if I still qualify.'

'Of course you do. Shoot.'

'I need to review a case from thirty-plus years ago. I'm hoping that you can dig up all the paperwork and let me see it.'

'Mmm. Were you involved?'

'No,' I said. 'It was before my time. Alf Stein was the SIO, with Tommy Partridge as his sidekick and the tosser Greg Jay in an admin role.'

He grimaced as if he'd just bitten on the killer chilli in a pizza. 'Jay? Bastard.' That was the general view of Greg; Mario had seen him close up, as a young constable, before I'd hauled him off to CID. The guy's transgressions included taking payment in kind from sex workers. The day I got rid of him was one of the most satisfying of my career.

'It was a homicide investigation, swiftly concluded. A farmer killed a vicar he believed had molested his daughter, and made a Horlicks of dumping the body.'

'The Traprain Law killing?' my friend exclaimed. 'That was used as a case study on one of the courses you sent me on. I'll be interested to see you run an eye over that one.'

'Why?' I wondered aloud. 'Did the investigation strike you as questionable?'

'Not a bit. It was impeccable. I'll be interested in seeing you try to take it apart, especially as it was your hero that ran it.'

'Come on,' I protested. 'That's a bit strong. Alf was my mentor, not my hero.'

'That's not how it sounded. You were forever quoting him as if he were the Holy Bible.'

'Maybe,' I conceded. Alf was the formative figure of my early career. He picked me out early, as I'd picked out Mario and others, and it was his teaching that I applied to the job when I reached higher rank. And yet there had been stuff he'd kept from me, as I had discovered – the prime example being his relationship to Jimmy Proud, our chief constable – as he was advancing me through the ranks, until I succeeded him as head of CID. Why had he kept that a secret?

'Any point in me asking you why you want this?' my host asked.

'If it comes to nothing, as I am one hundred per cent sure it will, no,' I told him frankly. I had asked myself that question on the way to his place, and had decided that if Jimmy had come to me, privately, and not to Mario, officially, there was an ethical issue, one that I had to respect.

'If it doesn't, if the case becomes live again?'

'In that unlikely event, you will be the first to know.'

'Not your client, whoever he is?'

'No, you and Maggie, should it become a police matter: promise.'

'That's good enough for me.' He drained his sparkling water. 'Where do you want the stuff? Home or office?'

'Office, please.'

'Okay.' He beamed again. 'You're fucking loving this, aren't you? All this secret squirrel stuff you've got into since you left. McIlhenney told me about the adventure you and he had in London. I wasn't sure whether to believe him until he got promoted to deputy assistant commissioner on the back of it. What did you get?'

Actually, I got a knighthood, but at my request it was never gazetted, and not too many people knew about it. I'd turned the honour down once before, but I didn't feel I could refuse the person who put me forward second time around. In addition to that, I made more friends in very high places; they might be much more valuable down the line than any gong. Neil McIlhenney's accelerated promotion will be worth more too; Mario's soul brother has told both of us that he does not intend to spend one day beyond his fifty-fifth birthday in the police service, and that his only remaining professional goal is to maximise his pension.

'Ten per cent of bugger all,' I replied.

Eight

I'd assumed it would take a few days for the records of an archived investigation to be unearthed, but Mario must have marked his instruction 'Priority'. I was on the fifth tee of Gullane Number One, just after two thirty the following afternoon, when my phone vibrated in my back pocket to signal an incoming text from my secretary, Sylvia.

Big box delivered by police officer, I read. *Signed for and waiting for you.*

I'd started, so I had to finish; the golf course was quiet, but I was playing a competitive round rather than a friendly. My opponent was dogged and the match went to the seventeenth before he succumbed by taking three to get out of one of the big cross-bunkers. Even so, I had time to shower and change before Sir James Proud arrived for the meeting I'd requested.

I was occupying a window table and contemplating the pint of IPA that stood before me when he entered the big room. He glanced around, maybe concerned that we might be overheard, or possibly looking for familiar faces. He'd been nervous over my choice of venue, public even though it's a private club, but I'd told him not to be paranoid, that there was nothing out of the ordinary in two old colleagues meeting for a drink.

As it happened, he did know a couple of the members in a group seated in front of the fireplace. One of them hailed him and enquired after his health. 'Fine, Jo, fine, thanks,' I heard him reply. He nodded generally at the table, murmuring, 'Ladies,' then turning his back on them and joining me.

I fetched him a half-pint from the bar, and settled back in my chair as he fidgeted in his. 'Good game?' he asked, breaking the thin layer of ice that lay between us.

I shrugged, then gave him the classic winning golfer's response. 'Played shite, but I'm through to the next round; that's all that matters.'

'Mm, good,' he said with a half-smile. 'What's your handicap these days, now that you're almost full-time?'

'Four point six; if I really was full-time it would be lower, because I'd have time to practise properly. But I'm not, am I?' I grinned back at him amiably. 'My friends think that all I've done is move service, because they turn up wanting me to put out their fires.'

'And have you?' Jimmy countered, peering at me over his glass.

'I haven't seen any flames yet. I've had one conversation, and nothing came out of that to give me a clue about whatever Brass thinks he has.'

He stared at me anxiously. 'Who did you speak to?' he asked.

'Tommy Partridge. On the basis of what he told me, the conviction's rock solid; it was never in doubt back then and won't be challenged now.'

'Did you tell him—'

I cut him off. 'Don't be daft. Your name was never mentioned.' Actually, that wasn't true, but I decided not to mention Partridge's throwaway line at the end.

'That's a relief.' Jimmy sighed. 'Are you ready to meet Brass now?'

'I will be by the time we get together. This is Friday, so make it Sunday. By that time, I'll have reviewed the case papers and be as well briefed as I can be.'

'You'll have . . .' He stopped in mid gasp. 'Where did you get them?'

'From storage; no problem. Mario fixed it up for me.'

'Bloody hell, Bob. Does he know? Does Maggie know?'

His anxiety was beginning to annoy me. 'He assumes I'm acting for a client, formal or otherwise. He also assumes that if I need to tell him who it is, I will. As for Maggie, he may have told her, he may not, but it doesn't matter. So . . . when do you want to call Brass?'

'Right now.'

'Fine, but not from here. We don't like mobiles in the clubhouse.'

We took another twenty minutes to finish our drinks. I went deliberately slowly, making my friend talk about mundane day-to-day matters: Scottish politics, the Brexit shambles, government by social media and the fortunes of Edinburgh Spartans Football Club, Jimmy's only genuine sporting attachment. Finally, when I was good and ready, I took our empties back to the bar, then led the way down the back stairs and out into the car park.

Once we were out of sight of the clubhouse, I said, 'Okay, get out your phone and make the call. Put it on speaker so I can hear.'

'Will I tell him you're with me?'

'Of course not,' I retorted. 'That's a happy surprise we're keeping for Sunday.'

He nodded and did as he'd been told, scrolling through his recent calls for Brass's number and pressing the trace line.

The ringtone sounded four times before the call was answered. 'Sir James,' a deep voice exclaimed. 'I was beginning to think you weren't taking me seriously.'

I couldn't place the accent. Scottish, but neither Glasgow nor Edinburgh; possibly somewhere in between.

'It did cross my mind to report your threat to the police,' Jimmy boomed back, 'but I don't need the aggravation at my time of life, so before I get to that stage, I'm still prepared to meet with you. Sunday lunchtime, take it or leave it.'

'I'm not sure you're in a position to be dictating terms, Sir James,' Brass said, 'but I'll go with that. Book a table for two in the Waterside Bistro in Haddington, one o'clock Sunday. Do you know it?'

'Yes, I do, but why there?'

'Because it's always very busy on a Sunday. Whether you like it or not, I want people to see us together.'

'You're in no danger from me, Mr Brass,' Jimmy told him, 'but if you're that paranoid, I'm prepared to humour you. Sunday it will be.'

He hit the red button to end the call. 'Happy with that, Bob?' he asked.

I smiled. 'Fine by me. I like the Waterside any day of the week, but even more next Sunday.'

'Why's that?'

'Because you'll be paying.'

Nine

Officially I am a part-time executive director of the InterMedia group, and my salary is calculated on the basis of one day per week. In practice, I contribute more than that, because I enjoy the job even more than I thought I would when I took it on, and also because I like having an office base in the city. I was lost when I left the police service. I knew that I had at least twenty potentially productive years in front of me, but I had thrown myself on what might have been the scrapheap, all on a point of principle.

I might still be there if Xavi Aislado hadn't come back into my life while I brooded over my future, or the lack of it, in Spain, where he had a business problem he needed my help in solving. We sorted it out together, and worked so well that he asked me if I wanted to continue. My whole life clicked back into place then. I had a job that interested me, I had free time to do other stuff, and Sarah and I got back together, having split during what I now accept may have been a slow-motion breakdown on my part.

Alex said to me recently, over an early dinner in Edinburgh after we'd both finished work, 'You know, Pops, I believe you are happier than I have ever seen you.' And I believe she may be right.

I don't usually go into Edinburgh on Saturday, other than to Murrayfield Stadium a couple of times a year, but my delivery of the previous afternoon was waiting for me in the office and I needed to get into it as quickly as possible.

Sylvia, the secretary I share with June Crampsey, the *Saltire* editor, was there also. She looked up in surprise as I waved through her open door on the way to my office. 'Have I got the day wrong?' she asked lightly.

'Maybe I have,' I countered. 'No,' I continued, 'it's Saturday all right; I have to prepare for a meeting I have tomorrow, and I'm best doing it here.'

'To do with the box the cop dropped off yesterday?'

I nodded. 'Yes, but it's got nowt to do with the *Saltire*.'

Sylvia is experienced and discreet; she knew not to press me further about its contents. 'You going to need me?' she enquired.

'No, you're fine. I won't get in June's way. In fact, I was never here.'

The box was waiting for me, plunked in the middle of my meeting table. It had been sourced from whatever catacomb it had been lying in and sent to me so quickly that nobody had thought to wipe off the dust, in which several handprints could be seen quite clearly. I took some tissues from my desk and did the job myself, then used my scissors to cut the security tape that had been used to seal it.

I removed the lid and looked inside; as I had half expected, there wasn't a hell of a lot there. The investigation had taken only a week, and the conviction had been secured on the basis of very simple and straightforward evidence. I lifted all of it out of its container and arranged it on the table.

In a modern investigation, there would be a video record, but the Ampersand case happened in the very early days of camcorders and before anyone in my force had considered their use. Instead, everything that could be photographed had been, I didn't expect to find anything there, but I went through all of it anyway, because it's what I've always done. My middle name is Morgan; when people ask me what the 'M' stands for, I've been known to reply, 'Meticulous'.

The first thing I noticed about the victim when I looked at the crime scene photos was that, as Sarah had told me, he had impacted absolutely face down, splat, arms outstretched on either side. He had either been wearing a greatcoat when he was killed or had been bundled into one afterwards. The way it spread about him as he lay on the ice, it conjured up a vision of his being thrown from the quarried summit of Traprain Law, and of the thick garment acting as a sail. I skipped ahead and checked his measurements: Matthew Ampersand had been five feet eleven and weighed fourteen stone three and a half pounds. Not a giant, but he'd have taken a bit of chucking. I wondered about that, until I saw the custody photos of Barley Meads. He touched six feet five according to the height marker and was built like one of his barns, a brute of a man who stared at the camera in the full-face shot with a malevolent intensity that I have seen in very few people in my career. Yes, I had no doubt that he could have heaved the vicar's dead weight off the Law in the way I'd envisaged, without any bother at all.

I went back to my meticulous review. There were very few photographs of the body *in situ*. I frowned disapprovingly at that, until I remembered that the officers who attended had made the initial, if slightly unprofessional, assumption that it had been a suicide.

On the other hand, Joe Hutchinson's autopsy had been recorded with his customary attention to the smallest detail, and in colour. The body of the deceased vicar had been photographed from head to toe, and its dissection stage by stage, each abrasion and fracture being recorded, each supporting that earlier basic assumption, until the professor had turned him over, when everything changed. All of the previous injuries and insults had been sustained to the front of the body, but Joe had found, after recording fractures to the nose, jaw and right cheekbone, that at the base of the skull, the temporal bone had been shattered, and that fragments had penetrated the brain. Beyond doubt, his report declared, that had proved instantaneously fatal, and all the other injuries had been suffered post-mortem.

His calculation of the time of death was less certain, but he placed it within three to four days before the examination, enough to satisfy prosecution and jury during Meads's trial, as it transpired. I made my way carefully through the rest of Professor Joe's report without expecting anything that would throw new light on the case, or finding it. The forensic evidence was straightforward too; some of the traces found in Meads's truck, on his overalls, and on a folding trolley were all matches with the victim's O negative blood type. The farmer and his family were all A positive, and James Armstrong, the farm worker who was the only other user of the Dodge, was O positive. Most damning of all, the vehicle's tyres offered a perfect match for tread marks found in an icy puddle on the Law, fifty yards from the quarry edge.

From there I glanced at the notes of the door-to-door enquiries; I knew that anything that had come from them would appear later, so reckoned I was safe in skipping them, to save myself some time.

That decision made, I moved on to the witness statements. There weren't many of them; two were effectively precis of interviews with Carmel and Briony Meads, in which they agreed that while neither of them had been aware of Barley leaving the farmhouse around the time when Ampersand was believed to have died, neither could say beyond doubt that he had not. A third was a note of a meeting with a Mrs Esme Royce, age eighty-six, tenant of an upper council flat that overlooked the Apple Tree Vicarage. It recorded that the old lady had been shown a photograph of Barley Meads's Dodge truck and was able to say that she had seen an identical vehicle reversed into the vicarage driveway during the key hours of the investigation. It was signed by Mrs Royce's shaky hand, and witnessed by Thomas Partridge, detective sergeant.

The last document wasn't a statement at all, in any sense of the word. Instead it was a transcript of a recording of the interrogation of Barley Meads. It had gone on for hours, and it took me a full seventy minutes to read it. Virtually all of the questioning, apart from a few interjections by Tommy Partridge, had been done by Alf Stein. The tape was in the box also, but I doubted there was anything in the building that could have played it. I regretted that, for I'd have liked to hear my old boss's voice one more time.

It was patient, it was repetitive, it was remorseless; time and time again, Alf took his suspect through the circumstances of Ampersand's murder. He took him through his allegation that the clergyman had abused his daughter, and he put it to him that he had refused to accept rejection after rejection of his complaint until eventually he had decided to exact what he saw as his own form of justice. I could only read it, but the tape seemed to play in my head as I imagined him cajoling, persuading, insisting, but never threatening; not vocally, that is to say, for Alf's body language could be completely different from his tone of voice when he wanted it to be.

And yet he didn't come close to cracking it. Meads denied everything that was put to him, over and over and over again. He ridiculed his interrogators; both of them, for at one point he referred to Tommy as 'that fucking wooden Indian alongside you'. He abused them, he threatened them with civil law suits, he lapsed into silence for minutes at a time, but not once did he ever concede an inch, or waver in his insistence that while the news of Ampersand's death was 'like Christmas come again', he had had nothing to do with it.

All of it happened in the days before an accused person was allowed to have a lawyer beside him during interviews under caution, so Alf had free rein, but he couldn't crack the man. A part of me admired Meads's fortitude, even though it was obvious from everything I had seen and read that he was as guilty as sin. I asked myself, 'Would you have done any better than Alf did, Skinner?' My answer had to be, 'No.'

It would have been more satisfactory for the guys to have been able to top it off with a confession, but it didn't affect the report that Alf made to the Edinburgh procurator fiscal, the prosecutor whose agent he was in the constitutional framework by which our criminal investigation system has always worked. It summarised everything in two and a half pages and recommended that Mr Barley Meads, of Easterlee Farm, Midlothian, be prosecuted for the murder of the Reverend Matthew Ampersand, vicar of the Apple Tree Episcopal Church, Heatherston.

I gathered all the elements together and replaced them in their cardboard container. Then I leaned back in my chair and thought about what I had just read.

'He did it, no question,' I murmured. 'So what the devil is

this man Brass on about? Jimmy wasn't even involved in the investigation. His name is never mentioned in the papers, nor should it have been since he was an assistant chief when it happened. He'd made it to the command corridor. On top of that,' I reminded myself, 'he spent his entire career in uniform.'

My conclusion was that Brass was probably out to make a name for himself; he'd heard that Sir James Proud was vulnerable, and he wanted to raise his profile by throwing mud at a sick old man. If I felt that was the case when I met him in the Waterside, there was every chance he'd wind up in the river.

Ten

Every time I step into the Waterside Bistro, I think of Myra.

When I moved to Gullane, in my mid twenties, with my young wife and our very young daughter, we assumed we'd be housebound for a while, given that we didn't know a single person in the village. We were pleasantly surprised when we discovered within a couple of weeks that we were wrong.

People think that social media was invented by geeks with an eye to the main chance – 'Beware of geeks bearing gifts,' a friend warned me recently – but I take a broader view. Social interaction has always existed, especially among the young; the internet has given it wings, that's all.

In the days of our youth, Myra's and mine, the prototypes of social media were things called the Welcome Wagon, and the Housewives' Register. The latter is probably too non-PC to exist today, but both worked. Back then it was said that when a new couple moved in, there was a race between the Welcome Wagon and the Church of Scotland minister to be first on the doorstep. I can't remember who won in our case, but in the short term the Wagon was a hell of lot more useful. It introduced us to the village and its institutions – for example, the ballet classes at which Alex showed she would never be a dancer, and the playgroup, a godsend to Myra with me off policing the city for most of the time – it gave us shopping tips and contacts for other essentials, and it helped us meet people.

The Register carried on its work, with an emphasis on the social side, helping us meet even more people, many of whom I count as friends to this day. Also, it operated a babysitting circle with its own currency, consisting of plastic rings, each one worth a unit of time. When you joined, you were given an allocation, and if you maintained your balance at that level, you were a model citizen. Run short and you weren't putting enough time back into the system. Pile up too many, and you were putting it at risk.

Without that babysitting circle, we might never have found the Waterside Bistro. Money was tight in those days, but with plastic rings to spend on childcare, we could afford one good night out a month. We'd been in Gullane for almost a year when someone mentioned a place in the Nungate area of Haddington, so we gave it a try. We had to book four Saturday nights ahead. We took that as a good sign, and on our first visit found that we had been right. The riverside location was attractive in the summer, the old building was warm and welcoming in the winter, and the quality of the food and drink was consistently exceptional – or is that a contradiction in terms?

I got to know Jim, the owner, very quickly. He's a friendly, chatty guy, the ideal host; maybe he focused on me because he knew I was a cop, but I suspect that all of his clients got the same welcome. When Myra died, he was one of the first people to call me. Naturally, my visits became less frequent after that; as a single parent I couldn't be part of the babysitting circle, and when friends did offer to give me a break, I always went to the cinema, because I didn't fancy dining alone.

Instead, I began to take Alex with me, at lunchtime, as soon as she was old enough to have the patience to sit through a meal. As Myra and I had been regulars, so were Alex and I, for as long as Jim was there, until he wasn't, until he sold the business and moved on. It was never the same after that, and we stopped going.

Having done all the preparation for the meeting that felt necessary, I hadn't thought about it since then. The rest of Saturday had been a together day; Sarah and I had taken the younger kids to East Links Family Park, just outside Dunbar. It's one of Seonaid's favourites and there's still enough there to draw Mark and James Andrew. Later we had dinner at home with Alex and Ignacio; neither of them seems to have any love interest at the moment, although I don't quiz them about that. Alex has had more downs than ups in that department, and seems happy focusing on her work, while my oldest son is still at the novice stage.

It had been so long since I'd been to the Waterside that I used my satnav to ensure that I took the correct turn for the car park, which lies in a courtyard at the back of the building. If I hadn't, I'd have got it wrong, for the route was no longer familiar. I'd made a point of getting there early, before the appointed hour, so that I could observe Brass's arrival and mitigate the chances of his doing a runner if he saw me first. We'd never met, but I'd checked out his blog often enough to be confident of recognising him, even from a distance.

I left the car park and walked round to the riverbank. The day was pleasant and wind-free; the 'other Tyne' was flowing smoothly and wasn't over-full. When there is snow melt from the hills where its source lies, it can overflow its banks. There were several tables outside the bistro, most of them occupied, but only by drinkers. Rather than join them, I strolled up and onto the grey-stone pedestrian bridge, stopping halfway across and looking down at the bistro, trying to appear as inconspicuous as a six-foot-two-inch man can, waiting for any sign of Brass: waiting in vain.

It was ten minutes past one before the flaw in my theory dawned on me. Brass had chosen the venue, which meant that he knew it and felt comfortable there. If he was a regular, he would know also that visitors can enter via the back door directly from the car park.

I abandoned my post, trotted down to the riverside and into the restaurant – where I was greeted by none other than my old friend Jim. He was greyer and older, but the years sat more lightly on him than on me. We stared at each other in shared astonishment.

'Bob Skinner,' he exclaimed, breaking the silence. 'There's a surprise. I didn't know you were visiting us today.'

'I didn't know you were here,' I countered. 'Are you eating here too?'

He shook his head. 'No, I'm back. We've taken the place over again . . . that's to say, my sons have. I'm helping them get up and running, that's all. Seeing you again, it brings back some memories. Remember that night when it was chucking it down and you dropped your wife off right at the back door?'

I did.

'Yeah,' I agreed. 'Chucking it down so hard that the river had come over its banks and Myra ran into two feet of water. I can laugh at it now, but back then I got pelters. I should have known in the black dark, shouldn't I, that the Nungate had flooded. I was a cop, wasn't I; we were supposed to know these things. We still ate though, didn't we?'

'That's right. We put you in the upstairs restaurant, and you got in there through the kitchen. Great times, Bob, great times. So,' he continued, 'can I fix you up with a table? We're full, but I'll manage it somehow.'

'I'm booked,' I told him. 'Name of Proud, table for two. There's been a change and I'm standing in for my friend Sir James. The other party is a man named Brass; I'm guessing he's probably here already.'

'Austin Brass? No, I don't think so. Give me a sec.' He stepped away from me and looked into the bar area. 'No,' he said, returning. 'Your table's at the far end but there's nobody there. He's usually sharp, too.'

'Comes here often, does he?'

'A couple of times a month since we reopened. Never alone, but never with more than one person.'

'Same one every time?'

'No, other than his girlfriend. The others tend to be one-offs, and at lunchtime. Business meetings, whatever his business is.'

'He calls himself an investigative journalist,' I explained, then shrugged. 'I thought all journalists were supposed to investigate,' I added, 'but I'm just a cynical old bastard.'

'Not that old,' he laughed. 'How's your Alex? You'll be a grandad by now, I imagine.'

'Hell, no, and don't let her hear you make that assumption. She's still single – not that it's a bar to parenthood these days. I've acquired five more kids since you saw me last. Three boys, two girls.'

We stood there for a few more minutes, running through each other's families, even showing them off on our phones, until I dragged myself back to the reason for my visit.

I glanced at the doors, front and back. 'You know, Jim,' I murmured, 'I'm beginning to think I've been stood up.'

He looked at his watch. 'I think you have. Mr Brass is never late.'

'I'm not going to waste the table,' I assured him. 'I'll still be eating.'

'That's good; come on and I'll show you through.'

'These lunch dates of Brass's,' I ventured as he led me through the bar. 'Did you know any of them?'

As we reached my corner table, he frowned. 'No,' he replied. 'But the last fellow he met, I believe I recognised him. He used to be in the press quite a lot, in your line of work. Much older now,' he tapped the side of his head, 'but once a face is in there, it tends to stay. I'm pretty sure his name is Partridge, Tommy Partridge.'

Eleven

I chose the seat facing the door, in case Brass did confound me by turning up. Who knew, his car might have broken down, or his dog might have died, and he might rush in at any moment, stifling his apologies as he saw me there rather than Sir James Proud.

He didn't, and as I made my way through my excellent lunch, I hazarded a guess as to the reason for his absence.

I thought a lot about Tommy Partridge too; the old bastard had played me, and I do not like that. June Crampsey's dad or not, he was going to answer for it.

Not that day, though. I'd promised Sarah I'd be home by three at the latest. It was a special day in our family, Seonaid's seventh birthday, and she was having a party for all her school friends in the village hall. I was allowed to skip the first hour, but not a minute more. It was a three-liner for all of us, including Alex and Ignacio. Mark and Jazz had been assigned waiter duties.

I made it back with fifteen minutes to spare and spent the rest of the afternoon socialising with the mums of the celebrants and some of the dads. I felt awkward; none of them were any less than ten years younger than me. Indeed, several of the mothers were younger than Alex, which made me old enough to be their dad, never mind that of the party princess.

Happily, Sarah was in her comfort zone; two of the mums were in her age bracket, and they formed a group within a group, my wife carrying Dawn on her hip for most of the time.

One of the mums was a cop; I didn't know that until Sarah introduced her. 'This is Noele McClair,' she announced. 'That's Harry, her little boy, over there.' She pointed to a cute sandy-haired kid with a face-full of freckles, standing beside Seonaid. 'They've just moved into West Fenton.' She smiled. 'I think our daughter may have won Harry's heart. You and Noele have shared job interests,' she added. 'She's a police officer.' She broke off as a child's cry came from another part of the hall, then moved away to deal with the crisis.

My new companion was early thirties, with striking ice-blue eyes. She told me that she had spent the first part of her career in Ayrshire before being moved to Edinburgh on promotion to detective sergeant. I realised that I must have been her chief constable in my brief period as head of the doomed Strathclyde force, but she hadn't appeared on my radar. That was un-surprising, since it had been Britain's second largest, after London's Met, and I wasn't there long enough to meet many people outside of the Glasgow headquarters building.

I looked around the hall, scanning the dads for a face I didn't recognise, but failing to find one. 'Is your husband here?'

'No, I'm afraid not. He's at work today.'

'Where are you based?' I asked her.

'I work out of the old HQ, Fettes.'

'As did I for many years,' I remarked. 'As a building it's as ugly as sin, but I had more good times there than bad. What's your unit?'

73

'They've put me in serious crimes; I'm with DI Haddock and DCI Pye.'

'DI Haddock?' I repeated. I'd known that a promotion was in the wind, but not that it had happened.

'Yes. He's very young for the rank.' She put a hand to her mouth. 'Maybe I shouldn't say that to you.'

'You can say anything you like to me,' I assured her. 'Especially when you're right. Sauce Haddock is very young for the rank, younger than I was when I made DI, but already the jails in Scotland are full of people who underestimated him. You've landed on your feet there.'

She looked up at me. 'Maybe you can answer a question. He keeps mentioning someone I think he calls Cheeky. Have I got the name right, do you know?'

'Yes,' I laughed, 'although I can understand your doubt. She's his partner; her given name is Cameron, after her grandfather, Cameron McCullough; she acquired Cheeky as a nipper and it's never left her. Have you ever heard of Grandpa?' I asked.

'No,' she replied immediately.

'I'm pleased about that, in a way. Cameron McCullough senior was a person of interest to police forces all over Scotland for quite a long time. For Sauce's sake, I'm happy he seems to be leaving it behind him. For someone else's sake too.' I pointed my Corona bottle towards Ignacio, who was deep in conversation with the two youngest dads. 'That big lad over there; he's my son, and Grandpa McCullough is his stepfather. I'm telling you all this so you're fully aware of Sauce's connections, although he and Grandpa rarely meet.'

My abortive lunch engagement was still on my mind. Sometime soon I was going to have to excuse myself and update

Jimmy. I went off at a tangent. 'Tell me, in your career have you ever come across a man named Austin Brass?'

In an instant, her face darkened. 'The swine who writes the *Brass Rubbings* website? I've heard of him – I doubt if there's a police officer who hasn't – but I've never met him.'

'It sounds as if you've got a fairly firm view about him nonetheless,' I suggested.

'He stitched up an excellent cop, Terry Coats, a couple of years ago. Terry was a DI in North Lanarkshire, and Brass accused him of turning a blind eye to a resetter, a receiver of stolen goods. It's reckoned that his source was a colleague, a DS called Charlie Ruiz, who was pissed off when Terry was promoted and he wasn't. Brass published photographs of Terry and the guy together. What he didn't say in his story was that the bloke was a confidential informant and that he'd given Terry a dozen and more convictions. The chief constable – it was before you, when Ms Field was in charge of Strathclyde – she knew that, but she suspended Terry anyway. The complaints people exonerated him, but she still kicked him out of CID and was going to move him up to Argyllshire in uniform, only he resigned. He works in airport security now, in Edinburgh.'

This was ringing bells; I had found the case file in Toni Field's office when I moved in there. I heard another tinkle in my ear, one that had never been publicly connected to the situation.

'What happened to the informant?' I asked, although I was sure I knew.

'Not long after that, he was found in a suitcase in the boot of his car, in a lay-by out beyond Eaglesham. It wasn't a very big suitcase, so he'd been cut up to fit in it. That was down to Austin Brass, all of it; Terry told him to leave it alone, that he could put lives at risk, but he went ahead and published any-way.' She paused. 'Why are you asking about him, Mr Skinner?'

'Let's just say that his name came up in the context of a very old case. I have an interest in speaking to him.'

Her mouth set in a hard line. 'If you do, tell him that Terry Coats says hello. That'll get his attention.'

'And yours, from the sound of it. You still bitter about it?'

She nodded. 'Too right. Terry's my husband.'

Twelve

I called Jimmy in the evening, when the last of the guests had gone. He was disappointed that Brass had no-showed, even hinted that I might have been to blame. 'Are you sure he didn't spot you, Bob? If he did, well, your reputation goes before you.'

'My reputation fades with every passing day,' I told him sharply, 'but I still know how to keep myself out of a subject's line of vision. He didn't turn up, and that's all there is to it.'

'Maybe he's lost interest,' he murmured hopefully. 'Maybe he's realised there's no story after all.'

'It's possible,' I agreed.

He read the doubt in my tone. 'But you don't think so?'

'I don't know. How could I? Look, you have a choice. Either you phone him and ask him where the hell he was, chew his ear about wasting your time, or you forget about him until he contacts you again.'

'Do you think he will?'

'How the hell would I know? All that I can tell you is that on the basis of what I've read in the investigation record, there's nothing to suggest that it was anything other than a safe conviction, nor is there anything to link you to it. And why should there be? You were never within a mile of the inquiry

77

team, too busy breaking in your new ACC uniform. As for your relationship with Alf Stein, if I went through my entire career being close to you both without ever knowing about it, I doubt very much that Brass will turn it up either. If he did, so fucking what? There is nothing in it that's relevant to the case.'

That didn't stop him persecuting Terry Coats, I mused, but I kept that to myself.

'You have a third option, of course,' I continued. 'You could have a very tough lawyer write him a very tough letter explaining the Scots law of defamation to him. My Alex will be happy to draft it for you.'

'That's very kind of her, Bob, but I don't want to sue him; I just want the bugger to go away.'

'Maybe he has.'

Jimmy sighed. 'Dammit,' he decided, 'I am going to phone him. I'll call you back and let you know how I got on.'

'Do that,' I agreed, 'but stay calm.'

I ended the call and left him to it. As I waited, my thoughts turned to Tommy Partridge and to the conversation that he and I were going to have very soon. There was no way he could know he'd been spotted with Brass; I could take him completely by surprise, wherever and whenever I chose. I didn't choose, however, to share my knowledge of their meeting with Jimmy. My main interest lay in keeping him calm and putting an end to the worry that the unscrupulous blogger was causing him. That said, one question kept nagging away at me. Could Tommy be the author of the allegation? If he was, what did he know that he hadn't told me when he visited my office?

My brooding was interrupted by Sir James's return call. 'No reply,' he told me. 'His phone went straight to voicemail, and a message that he was in a meeting. It said if I left a message he'd call me back. I did; I told him what I thought of his non-appearance, and that I wished to have no further communication with him. I didn't manage to stay calm, I'm afraid, Bob. I raised my voice a little; in fact I shouted at him.'

Jimmy never has been one of nature's blusterers. If Brass was for real, I thought, he was hardly going to scare him shitless. That would be down to me.

Thirteen

I didn't give Tommy Partridge any preparation time. June Crampsey had told me, casually, a year or so back, that her father was a creature of habit. He rose at eight every morning, breakfasted, did his household chores and then, at eleven a.m. sharp, went to his local gym and leisure club, for coffee rather than exercise.

He didn't notice me seated at a table in the large entrance area until he'd greeted the receptionist and turned towards the Nespresso machine in the far corner.

'It's your shout,' I told him. 'Double espresso with a little milk.'

He stared at me, his mouth slightly open as if he was framing a retort, then thought better of it, turning his back on me as he stepped up to the coffee maker.

'There you are,' he said eventually, as he placed a cup on the small table before me. 'I'll even throw in a bit of shortbread,' he added, laying a sugary biscuit beside it. He settled himself beside me and sipped his own Americano. 'Are my brains so big,' he asked, 'that you think there might be more picking in them?'

'The opposite,' I replied quietly. 'They're so small that you think you can keep things from me and get away with it. Or is it your age?' I added cruelly. 'Is the memory loss starting to kick in?'

'Must be, Bob, for I don't know what the fuck you're on about.' He smiled, but not with his eyes.

'Austin Brass.'

I let the name hang there, watching him as he considered it, weighing me up.

'*Brass Rubbings*,' he acknowledged when he was ready. 'What of him?'

'You never thought to mention during that long chat we had on Friday that you had lunch with him in Haddington a couple of weeks ago.'

His gaze returned to his coffee. 'Why should I have? Brass and guys like him are always talking to retired police officers – and serving ones too,' he added.

'What did you talk about?'

'I don't need to tell you that,' he snapped.

'No, you don't. You don't need to because I fucking know. You talked about the Matthew Ampersand murder.' I paused, then held up a hand to forestall any retort. 'My interest in it is informal, Tommy, but before you deny anything, you should think very carefully about the wisdom of lying to me.'

He glowered at me. 'If you insist, yes, that's what we talked about. So?'

'Who instigated the meeting? You or Brass?'

'He did,' Partridge insisted. 'He called me and said he wanted to talk about an old case I'd been involved in. I know of Brass, and I don't like what he does. My first inclination was to tell him to fuck off, but he said there would be a lunch in it, so I decided I might as well eat it, then tell him to fuck off.' He nodded. 'Yes, you're right, he wanted to talk about Ampersand, but mostly it was about the investigation, and whether anyone else was involved apart from Alf and me. I told him up front that I had a high profile in the business only because of the situation between Alf and Greg Jay. I said that Alf wanted him out, wanted him back in uniform, but Hume, the chief constable of the time, he wouldn't hear of it. Jay was his boy, ye see; something to do with his father and the Old Pals' Act. You probably remember, Bob, the last thing that Hume did before he retired was promote him to DCI and give him a division to run.'

Yes indeed, I remembered. Alf had been incandescent; as soon as Hume had gone, he wanted to post him to Hawick, as far away as he could have sent him, but Jimmy, who had taken over as chief, talked him out of it by suggesting he would be better close to home where an eye could be kept on him.

'Was Brass interested in Jay?' I asked.

'He didn't seem to be. There's no mileage for him in Greg; the whole world knows he was dodgy, there's no news in it. No, he focused on Alf; he asked me about the interviews with Meads, how he behaved in those.'

'What did you tell him?'

'The truth, that he was impeccable. He could afford to be; we didn't have a witness sighting of Meads at the vicarage, but we had his car there and the forensic evidence we got from it was just overwhelming.'

'How did Brass take that?'

Partridge frowned. 'He brushed it off, more or less. It was obvious that I wasn't telling him what he wanted to hear. But then he asked me the most peculiar thing. He asked me at what point Alf's brother-in-law had been involved in the investigation. I had no idea what he was talking about. "Who would that have been?" I said to him. "Sir James Proud; ACC Proud he was then," he replied. I told him that was bollocks; he said no it wasn't. He said he'd looked up everything about Alf at Register House, and he'd discovered that his wife, his late wife, had been Proud's older sister. "Fucking news to me," I insisted. Did you know, Bob?'

'Not until a few days ago,' I confessed. 'Yes, you might think that's odd, but the truth is that Alf was so devastated by his wife's death that he could never bring himself to talk about her.'

'Maybe, but Brass was dead chuffed that he had dug it up.'

'And was Jimmy involved?' I asked casually.

Partridge stared at me. 'Of course not,' he laughed. 'You know, and I told Brass, that he never spent a single day on a criminal investigation in his entire career.'

'How did Brass react to that?'

'He snorted, then he said, "Trust me, he played a part in this one." I asked him what he meant by that, but he wouldn't go any further.'

'I may know what it was, Tommy,' I volunteered. 'When Barley Meads made his complaint, his first complaint to the police, about Ampersand having an improper relationship with his daughter, and it was dismissed, it was Jimmy that had to rubber-stamp that decision. That was his only involvement.'

Partridge scratched his chin, frowning. 'Maybe it was, Bob, but my impression was that Austin Brass was talking about more than that. Why don't you go and ask him?' he suggested.

'That was the general idea,' I replied, 'but suddenly Mr Brass has decided to become a recluse.'

Fourteen

The elusive blogger was still out of contact later that morning; he hadn't replied to Jimmy's voicemail, and when I lost patience and called him myself on the number that was published on *Brass Rubbings*, all I heard was a snappy message. 'This is Austin. I'm sorry but I'm busy righting more wrongs. Message me if you wish.'

I didn't bother. There was no exclusive on his site about the Ampersand murder, and his dodging the Waterside lunch date was, like as not, an indication he had decided that whatever tip he had wasn't worth following up. That was likely; of the three participants in the investigation, the accused, Alf and Tommy Partridge, only the last of them was still alive and I had his word that he had told Brass nothing that would have involved Jimmy. I knew in theory there was another who'd had knowledge of the affair. Greg Jay, for all that he had been marginalised by Alf, would still have had access to all the papers in a co-ordinator role. But any knowledge he had picked up had gone up the chimney with him at Warriston Crematorium after his death from lung cancer eighteen months before.

I could have walked away then. I could have sent the box of records back to Mario for him to consign to storage until someone in the Crown Office decided that it could be pulped. Indeed, I wish I had, but no, that isn't my style. My juices were flowing, and I knew they wouldn't stop until I was satisfied that everything about the Ampersand inquiry had been put on the table. I had no interest in exonerating Jimmy, because I didn't have to. However colourful Brass's threat had been, it was spurious, as his abandonment of the story had made clear.

My problem was that as a detective, I never liked or trusted easy answers. Alf Stein had taught me that; it was a lesson he had learned from an inquiry in which he had been involved as a young detective constable, the murder of a three-year-old child, by suffocation, in an upper-class house on the east of Edinburgh, not far from Mario and Paula's new home. The mother had been the obvious suspect. She had been alone in the house with the little girl, her husband having been away on a business trip to London; neighbours testified that they had heard her screaming at the child earlier in the evening. Her only defence was a claim that she had fallen asleep for an hour, during which time, the defence suggested, a third party could have entered the house. That strategy fell apart when the mother admitted under cross-examination that she had consumed over half a bottle of gin, losing whatever sympathy the jury might have had for her. She was convicted, and the judge passed the only sentence open to him at that time: death. Her appeal was rejected, her plea for a reprieve was turned down by the Secretary of State of the day, and she was executed by hanging.

Three months later, a man with a string of convictions for burglary was arrested when he tried to sell a diamond ring in Glasgow. Before buying it, the cautious jeweller checked its provenance with the insurance companies and discovered that it was listed in a household policy written by Scottish Antiquities Assurance, of which the executed woman's husband had been a director. Its loss had never been reported; after the trial, the husband had locked his dead wife's jewellery in his safe without ever checking it. When he looked again, he found that the ring was one of half a dozen valuable pieces missing.

'We had the thief brought back to Edinburgh,' Alf told me one night after work, when he'd had a drink or so too many. 'We did not treat him gently. It didn't take long before he admitted to having broken into the house. He took a look through the front window in the dark and saw the mother flaked out on the couch. The child was asleep in the mother's bed, and he never saw her, not till she woke up and started howling. So he shut her up. We had him by the balls, Bob, full confession, but the chief constable told us to let him have a lawyer before we had him sign it and charged him. Next thing we knew, the story had changed. He'd broken in the night before the child was killed; he had nothing to do with it. We wanted to charge him anyway, but the Lord Advocate said no, that without our old enemy corroboration, there was no chance of a conviction. Of course, the Secretary of State who'd turned down the reprieve was his pal, wasn't he?'

I can still remember Alf shuddering, and the glistening of his eyes. 'We killed that woman, Bob. We dropped her through that trapdoor and snapped her neck. If we'd done a proper, thorough job and discovered the theft, it would have given credence to her defence. At worst, the verdict would have been not proven, which is effectively the same as not guilty. But we didnae; we had an obvious solution and we took it. So, son, never be happy with an easy answer.'

I looked at the box on my table. 'And yet he was involved in the Ampersand investigation,' I told myself aloud. 'There can't have been anything else, or he would have found it.'

If Alf was still alive, and Jimmy had gone to him, as probably he would have, what would he have done? 'He'd have taken another look, Bob,' I told myself, 'because Meads also died in prison with a ligature round his neck, like the innocent victim who brought him to tears. He'd have done that, and so should you.'

But where to begin? What was missing from the box that might have been there if I'd been running the investigation all those years ago, with the experience I have now? Very little, but possibly one element. There was no biographical material about the victim. The body had been identified by his bishop, not by a family member. Nothing was known about him other than the fact that he was the rector of Apple Tree Episcopal Church. Why not? I could have called Tommy and asked him, but I thought I knew the answer. Meads had been identified so fast, and Alf – 'Scotland's top crime-fighter' – had been put under such pressure by his chief constable, and by the media, that he had seen no need. Against his own principles, he had accepted the easy answer.

My priority on my cautious way forward had to be to fill in the blank sheet of paper that was Matthew Ampersand's past. How easy would that be? Wikipedia is a precious tool and one that I support financially, but I couldn't expect to find it written there. I did try, but I came up empty-handed.

I scratched my head, thinking about it, and then came up with an avenue. Just as the case files had been in long-term storage, might his employer still hold historic personnel records? I could think of only one person to ask. I picked up the phone on my desk and buzzed my shared secretary. 'Sylvia,' I said, 'will you see if you can get me the name of the head of the Scottish Episcopal Church – that is, its chief administrative officer – and a contact number.'

While I was waiting, I sent a text to a guy I'd met when I was a serving police officer. He was then, and still is, a member of the Scottish Parliament, but now he's an opposition frontbench spokesman with responsibility for home affairs. *Jacko, can you do me a favour? Have one of your researchers look at your copy of the electoral roll for Midlothian and check on voters registered at Easterlee Farm, Midlothian. Bob Skinner.* I could have asked the same of one of my former colleagues, but I wasn't ready to set them wondering about my interest.

I had just received a brief *Will do* from my parliamentary pal when Sylvia buzzed me back. As usual, she gave me more information than I had asked for. 'The head of the Episcopalian Church,' she began, 'is called the primus; it's from the Latin, *primus inter pares*, first among equals. There are seven dioceses in Scotland, each with its own bishop, and the primus is chosen by them from among their number. I tried to find someone within the support staff for you to approach, but it wasn't that easy. When they heard I was calling from the *Saltire* office they put me through to the press officer, then when I explained it wasn't a media enquiry he said he only spoke to the press, and more or less hung up on me. Bob, it looks as if you're going to have to speak to the primus direct. Her name is Valerie Cornton and I managed to establish that she's based in the General Synod office. I've messaged the number to you.'

I thanked her and sure enough found the phone number among my WhatsApp chats. (I confess that I am a reluctant user of social media. I tried Facebook but closed my page very quickly when it became a pain in the arse. Likewise Twitter, although that seems to be a tool of governments these days. WhatsApp is okay because I can control those who have access to me.)

My call was answered by a man whose tone imbued both caution and suspicion into the two words, 'General Synod.'

'Good day,' I boomed, as briskly as I could manage. 'My name is Bob Skinner and I would like to speak to Bishop Cornton. May I?'

'What's your business with the primus, Mr Skinner?' Caution had disappeared, leaving only suspicion. 'Is it a spiritual matter? If so, you should contact your local priest or rector.'

'My interest is entirely secular, I assure you. I'm looking for information about a former minister of your church, one who died some time ago, in unfortunate circumstances. I'm happy to talk to you, Mr . . .'

I thought that he might have volunteered his name, but he didn't; instead, he subjected me to a staccato burst, 'No, no, no, no, no! I'm not authorised to provide information about anyone.'

'In that case, who is?'

'The primus, I suppose.'

'Which takes us back to my first question. May I speak with her?'

'The primus is very busy.'

'So am I. Is she in the building, or has she done an Elvis?' My wafer-thin patience had worn through.

'Who?' I should have known better.

'Never mind. Take a chance, chum; call her and ask her if she'd be prepared to speak to me about the late Reverend Matthew Ampersand.'

The intake of breath on the other end of the line was very soft, but audible. 'Very well,' he murmured. Caution was back.

Ten seconds became twenty, twenty became thirty, and so on up to a full minute. Believing that he'd disconnected me, I felt a snarl taking shape, until a cheery female voice sounded in my ear.

'This is Valerie Cornton, Mr Skinner. Am I speaking with our former chief constable, or are there two Bob Skinners in Edinburgh?'

'There probably are,' I told her, 'but I've never met the other one.'

'I believe you want to ask me about the long since departed Matthew Ampersand.'

'That's correct. A friend of mine has an interest in the circumstances of his death. I'm looking into it, but I find myself handicapped by knowing very little about the man himself. Do you have any accessible records that might help me?'

'Your friend,' she said, her voice noticeably less cheery. 'His name wouldn't be Austin Brass, would it?'

'No, it would not,' I told her firmly. 'He's on my call list as well, but I'm coming from a different angle. Has he tried to contact you?'

'Yes, he has, with a similar request to yours. I made enquiries about him and didn't like what I heard, so I've been rather slow in getting back to him.'

That was helpful, but I didn't admit it. 'Do you want to make enquiries about me too?' I asked her.

'I don't think that will be necessary,' she answered with a smile in her voice; one that turned out to be short-lived. 'However,' she continued heavily, 'there are some aspects of the Ampersand case that I don't want to see resurrected. Nothing personal, but I don't think I'm inclined to help you either. That was a very bad time for the Church.'

Work to do on this one, Skinner. 'Understood,' I said, 'and I promise you I have no interest in bringing it back. It's the investigation of his murder I'm interested in, and it would be useful to me in reappraising it if I could talk to someone who knew him. There's no mention in the police files of his having any close friends and I don't imagine there are too many of your clergy who'd be able to help me, even the older ones, so it's family members I'm interested in. Would there have been a personnel file on him in your office, if so does it still exist, and in that event does it include details of next of kin? Are you prepared to help me with that?'

She gave my question a few moments' thought. 'I'll look into it,' she conceded. 'There is an Ampersand file, I do know that, but it hasn't been opened since his death.'

'Not even after Brass called you?'

'No,' she confirmed. 'I didn't take to the man and decided I wasn't going to help him under any circumstances, so I didn't bother. Leave it with me, Mr Skinner. If there is anything there I feel I can pass on to you without prejudicing the Church, I will.'

'Thank you, er . . . How do I address you? Primus, Bishop, Your Grace?'

'Valerie will be just fine, thank you. I'll get back to you as soon as I can, one way or another; I can make no promises, mind. Give me your number.'

Without realising it, the primus had told me one thing already: there was material in the file that she regarded as sensitive, and it went beyond the detail of Ampersand's death. The fact that he had been bashed over the head and chucked into Traprain Law quarry was a matter of public record. If there was stuff that she didn't want opened up for public discussion, I suspected that it had to relate to his conduct in the cloth. Even though Barley Meads's complaint about him and Briony had been rejected, I wondered whether that was it.

I didn't have long to muse.

I had barely hung up on Bishop Cornton when I had a text from my MSP pal. There were no words, just an image: a scan of a page from the current electoral register for Midlothian.

I transferred it to my computer and enlarged it to the point of legibility. There were three voters registered at Easterlee Farm: Carmel Isobel Meads, Briony Lennon, and Michael John Winston Lennon. 'Somebody's folks were Beatles fans,' I murmured. 'So, Carmel kept the farm, Briony married, and she and her husband still live there. What does he do, I wonder?'

There was an easy way to find out. The more information you feed into a search engine, the more you are likely to get out. I entered all four of the Meads in-law's names into Google and scored an immediate hit. Michael John Winston Lennon was listed as a director of a limited company registered in Scotland, Easterlee Holdings Ltd. Out of little more than curiosity, I paid a small fee and downloaded the company's details, including its last published accounts, from Companies House. There were three directors: Carmel, who was chair of the board, Briony and Michael; a note to the accounts disclosed that he received a salary of eighty thousand pounds as general manager of the farm, and of a second business owned by Easterlee Holdings and identified as Meads Mushrooms. That contributed one hundred and twenty-five thousand pounds to an overall profit after corporation tax of three hundred and nineteen thousand. Carmel had taken dividend income of a hundred grand, with twenty-five grand each to Briony and Michael. The business was asset-rich, the farm being valued at five million and the mushroom operation at four hundred thousand. In addition, there were seven residential properties, which were tenanted and made small contributions to the profit figures. Cash in hand totalled six hundred and seven thousand and the firm operated a workplace pension scheme with ring-fenced assets of one and a half million.

Clearly the farming business was the gold mine that most people would assume it to be, but who actually owned it? I found that in the annual return that all companies are required to file. The share structure was very simple: one hundred Class A shares of one pound had been issued; of these, Carmel held seven, Briony two and Michael one. The other ninety were held by a trust, which I guessed Carmel controlled. I also guessed that the structure had been set up to minimise inheritance tax, since she had to be well over seventy.

I had been developing a line of thought that the family might have been behind Brass's aggressive reopening of the case, but those numbers stopped it in its tracks. The Meads-Lennon family were rolling in it. There was no reason for them to go raking up the past.

All the same, I needed to establish whether Brass had spoken to them, as I guessed he had. I added a visit to Easterlee Farm to an agenda that I had begun to draw up. The only judgement left was whether to make an appointment or to go in cold.

I decided on the latter, there and then. Indeed, I was heading for the door when my desk phone sounded, stopping me in my tracks. 'Bishop Cornton,' Sylvia told me. I sat down again behind my desk and took the call.

'Mr Skinner,' she began. 'I've had a look at the Ampersand file. It wasn't far away. Part of it is a personnel record of sorts, and there are details there that I can share with you. Matthew was a Cambridge man; in fact, his entire family were. Dad was an Anglican priest, pretty high church, and it was there that Matthew was ordained. Canon Ampersand went to his eternal reward a long time ago, before Matthew in fact, but there were three younger brothers. One was his twin, baptised Mark; he died in the week of his birth. The others were twins too, christened John and Luke; John is shown on the file as next of kin, from which I assume he was the elder. Mrs Ampersand, poor woman, passed away shortly after their birth. The coroner returned an open verdict, possibly because of her husband's calling, but it was understood in Cambridge, from what I gather, that she took her own life. That's all we have on record.

'However . . .' She hesitated. 'I've been doing a little of your speciality, detecting. I decided to call the vicar of Canon Ampersand's old church to see if he could be of any help, and he came up trumps. His name is Canon Merryweather, and he's getting near retirement; in fact, he's so old that he was Ampersand's curate. He told me he knew all three Ampersand boys – he called them the apostles. Luke joined the army, he said, and as far as he knows, never returned home. John was an academic; he read classics, got a first and became a don. Then he switched Cambridges; he went to the one in Massachusetts, to a chair at Harvard. That's where he was when Matthew died. He declined to come back for the funeral; it was left to my church to organise it, and to wind up the estate. He's back now, though, retired from Harvard. He attends his father's old church and Merryweather was kind enough to give me his phone number. Got a pen, Mr Skinner?'

I had, and I wrote down the number she gave me. 'Only one other thing to add,' she said as I finished. 'If you were wondering, Matthew never married. However, there was never any suggestion that he might be gay – and if one is, word gets around in the Anglican church. I hope all that helps,' she continued. 'Will our local rector be seeing you in church sometime soon?' she asked.

'Probably not,' I admitted, 'but thank you very much.'

The iron was hot, and so I struck, dialling the number on my notepad.

'Yes!' The voice was so loud that I held my phone an inch or so away from my ear. Clearly, its owner was also more than a little annoyed.

'Is that Mr John Ampersand?' I ventured.

'That would be Professor Ampersand,' he barked, 'and before you go any further, I lived abroad during the entire period when the PPI scam was happening, I have never been overcharged by a mortgage lender for the simple reason that I have never had a mortgage in the UK, and I have not been involved in a motor accident that was not my fault, unless you count having my foot run over by a mobility scooter.'

'I'm very pleased to hear all that, Professor Ampersand,' I replied, 'but I don't give a toss about any of it. My name is Bob Skinner, I'm a retired police officer from Edinburgh and I'm taking a look at the death of your brother Matthew, and at the conviction of a man named Barley Meads for his murder.'

The silence on the line made me believe that he had hung up on me before I'd even begun my response. I was about to do the same when he spoke again.

'Are you indeed?' he exclaimed; his voice had dropped to a

normal volume and his anger had vanished. 'I apologise for my outburst, Mr Skinner. I've had three calls from those ambulance-chasers within the last twenty-four hours. When I saw "number withheld" on the screen of my cell, I just assumed you were another.'

His accent was upper-class England, with something added by a prolonged spell in the United States. I'm no expert on its regional variants, but I thought I heard overtones of Sarah's East Coast twang in there.

'Your call takes me completely by surprise, sir. When Matthew met his end, many people tried to track me down, including your police force. I was able to keep them at bay by giving them a formal statement through my attorney, stating that I hadn't seen my brother in years, and at the time of his death I had been taking part in a midwinter classics symposium in Princeton, New Jersey. That seemed to satisfy them, but other approaches persisted for a little while: from insurers, but mostly from the media. I ignored them until they stopped coming. There was a brief resumption of press interest in me when Matthew's killer ended his own life in prison, but I took no satisfaction from that and so I did not respond.' I heard a sigh. 'Now here you are, when I thought I'd succeeded in forgetting the whole sorry business. Given my refusal to discuss it in the past, Mr Skinner, offer me one good reason why I should speak to you.'

'I can't,' I admitted. 'I'm not even sure myself why I'm interested.'

'Is it research for a book? Your memoirs, perhaps?'

I laughed. 'Your brother's death wouldn't figure in those, Professor, even if I was inclined to write them; I wasn't a police officer at that time. The case meant nothing to me until it was revived by a journalist with some peculiar ideas about the investigation.'

'Might this person contact me?'

'If he does a thorough job, that's possible,' I conceded. 'But it may well be,' I added, 'that he's given up the chase already.'

'Let's hope so,' he said. 'And you, Mr Skinner, if I decline to discuss the matter with you, will you give up the chase?'

'Not until I'm satisfied that Meads's conviction was safe. I've seen nothing so far to make me doubt that it was, but I will take it as far as I can.'

'But why? You still haven't answered that question.'

'For the peace of mind of an old friend, who is being targeted by the journalist I mentioned.'

'Does this reptile have a name?'

'Not one you'll have heard of: he's called Brass. Austin Brass.'

'There you are wrong, sir!' John Ampersand exclaimed. 'Not only have I heard *of* him, I've heard him; heard him speak, in the flesh. He took part in a Union debate here three or four months ago; the motion was "This House believes that every modern democracy needs a secret state within it." He spoke against, and very convincingly too, although I didn't care one little bit for the man or his politics. The motion was rejected by the substantial majority you'd expect in a student forum in the current climate.' He laughed. 'So, Mr Brass has an interest in Matthew's murder, yet he was in the same room as his brother for two hours and never knew it. That's a twist.'

'Is it a twist that will persuade you to speak to me?' I asked.

'You know, I think it might be. But not over the telephone. If I am finally to open my mind and heart to the tragedy of my brother's death, we must be face to face. Are you so committed that you would be prepared to come to Cambridge to meet me?'

I frowned; I hadn't anticipated his request. However, it took me little or no time to make up my mind. 'Yes, I'll come,' I promised him. 'Although God alone knows what my wife's going to say.'

Fifteen

'You're going where?' Sarah exclaimed, when I told her that evening.

'I'm going to Cambridge,' I repeated. 'Matthew Ampersand's brother has agreed to see me, after not a little persuasion, but it has to be on his terms. It's no big deal,' I assured her. 'I'll get a flight to Stansted, hire a car and scoot up the motorway; it's no distance at all. I'll be back for dinner with you and the kids, no problem.'

'Are you going to take Jimmy? After all, he started the ball rolling.'

'Hell, no!' I snorted. 'This man has never spoken to anyone about his brother's murder. It's a very big deal for him to be meeting me. If two of us turned up, he'd just walk straight out.'

She shrugged. 'You don't need to be doing this at all, Bob. You were no part of the investigation and you're not threatened by anything Brass might have. I think you're crazy to be taking it on.' She stopped and smiled. 'But I've always known that, haven't I? So go on, get it out of your system.'

I'd arranged to meet John Ampersand for coffee, but I could have made it breakfast, that's how early the flight was. Worse than that, there were no delays.

The professor had proposed that we meet outside Heffers bookshop, then proceed to a café close by. Even after a slow drive north on an almost deserted motorway, and time taken finding a place to park, I still had a couple of hours to kill. I spent them wandering around the city, absorbing its architecture and its age. At first, I was puzzled by its lack of familiarity, until I remembered that *Morse* and *Lewis* are actually set in Oxford.

Having spent the last twenty minutes of my wait browsing in Heffers, and even buying a real book rather than a download, I stepped outside at one minute after eleven to find a small, stocky man in a three-piece suit bobbing up and down on the balls of his feet, looking to his right, then his left, then his right again. The narrow street was one-way, cyclists only, and there were few of them around, so I reckoned that he was looking for someone rather than thinking of crossing.

'Professor Ampersand?'

He spun round at the sound of my voice, eyes wide below a high forehead and a grey widow's peak. He really was small; not Danny DeVito, but close to it, almost a foot shorter than me. 'My God!' he exclaimed. 'You are a true flatfoot, Mr Skinner, creeping up on a chap like that.'

'I'm sorry,' I said. I held up my purchase. 'There was a queue at the till or I'd have been here bang on time. Where shall we go?' I asked. 'This must be the last book store in Britain of any size that doesn't include a coffee shop.'

'Just as well,' he murmured. 'I'm a tea man myself. Follow me.' He turned on his heel and waddled off, penguin-like. He led me for a few yards, stopping abruptly in front of an establishment so discreet that I would probably have walked past it. I followed him inside to find him being greeted already by a slim middle-aged woman. She was clad in a tweed skirt that might have been forbidding on someone else, but she had an air of elegance about her that told me she could wear anything without seeming dowdy.

'Your usual, Professor,' she murmured, 'as requested.'

All of the tables that I could see were occupied, but the proprietrix, as I assumed her to be, escorted us to a smaller room at the back that was unoccupied.

'Thank you, Mrs Ingleby,' Ampersand said as he stepped past her. 'We'll have a pot of tea, please, your Earl Grey, I think, and possibly a plate of biscuits; your choice, but my guest is Scottish, if that helps. This is an unofficial common room,' he explained as she left. 'We emeritus academics like this place, but we also like a little privacy. This area is kept for us and not offered to the general public. At this time of day, I was fairly sure it would be private. Did you have a good flight?' he asked as we seated ourselves.

'Tolerable,' I replied. 'I fly because I have to, but I can't honestly say that I enjoy it.'

He pursed his lips and nodded. 'That's a frank admission from a modern man, but one that I understand. I spent the greater part of my career at Harvard when I could have shuttled between the two Cambridges, because having survived the journey, I had no wish to repeat it.'

I seized my chance to get to the point. 'Is that why you didn't come home after your brother's death?'

My question caught him off guard. He took some time to consider his answer, then, before he could offer it, Mrs Ingleby returned with a pot of tea, cups and saucers, and a plate of shortbread fingers. By the time she had poured, he was ready.

'That may have been one reason,' he admitted, 'but it wasn't the only one. I was devastated by Matthew's murder; it was such an awful thing to happen. When I heard about it, all I would think was "Why?" That was the first thing I said to the police officer who called me from Scotland. When he told me what he believed, that a father had killed him because he in turn believed that Matthew had abused his child, I was appalled.'

'Other than that,' I asked, sipping the Earl Grey (which I dislike, but I was on his turf), 'can you remember your first reaction?'

'What do you mean?'

'Did you believe it? Did it strike you as credible?'

He stared at me. 'Of course not. Not for a second.'

'There were no similar accusations made during his time in Cambridge?'

Professor Ampersand's face reddened, and his eyebrows rose. He shifted in his chair, and for a moment I thought that I'd blown it, that he was going to get up and walk out. 'Absolutely not!' he boomed, when he had recovered himself and decided to stay with me. 'I don't care what those twisted worshippers of his may have made up about him, Matthew was not that sort of person. He took after our father in every respect – and if you decide to ask people about him while you're here, you will find that Dad was absolutely revered in this community. His death was a terrible blow to us all.'

'I can imagine,' I said. 'My apologies if my question upset you, but if I'm going to form a complete picture of what happened to your brother, I need to know everything about him. I'm not making any assertions, I promise.'

He nodded, mollified, I hoped. 'Apology accepted,' he murmured. 'Mr Skinner, you may or may not know this, but I am a twin. My womb-mate, my brother Luke, he and I were not alike in any way, physically or temperamentally. Indeed, my father once told his congregation during a sermon that his sons John and Luke were the least identical twins he had ever known, and he had baptised a lot, believe me.'

'What happened to Luke?' I asked, although I knew some of his story.

'He joined the army,' John replied. 'Truth be told, he never fitted in here. He couldn't even punt properly.'

I laughed, but he looked down his nose at me, frowning.

'You think I jest,' he said solemnly, 'but I do not. In Cambridge when one punts, one stands on the flat surface at the stern. In the other place, they stand at the opposite end below the freeboard, in the mistaken belief that it makes them less likely to fall in.' He sighed. 'Luke was always falling in.'

I put the comical vision to one side. 'Is he still alive? If so, should I be talking to him?'

'Oh yes, he's still alive, but it would be pointless for you to talk to him, because he could tell you nothing of value. His military career was successful, even though he never fired a shot at a living target. He rose to the rank of major in the Parachute Regiment. A year or so before I went to America, in the mid seventies, he managed to get himself transferred to the Australian armed forces, where he became a lieutenant general, no less. He retired twenty-plus years ago and went into state politics. He's also a regular so-called expert analyst for Australian television whenever they need a military voice.'

This was news to me. 'When Matthew died – was murdered – did anyone get in touch with him? There's no mention of him in the investigation papers.'

'I did,' Ampersand told me. 'He was sorry to hear it, but he told me fairly bluntly that he didn't want to know any sordid details. His military career was on the up, and he didn't want it to be prejudiced by association with a vicar killed for allegedly spreading his seed among his flock. I quote him verbatim, Mr Skinner. To be fair to him, he was also worried that any public association might have an adverse effect on his young family. Luke is the only one of we three apostles who is carrying on the line. I have a nephew and two nieces,' he added. 'I had the pleasure of tutoring my younger niece, Amelia, at Harvard, but I've never met the others.'

'You're still in touch with Luke?' I asked.

'Christmas cards. Maybe a couple of phone calls in the course of a year. I send birthday gifts to his grandchildren, too. He has four of those. I'm sure that their parents have expectations of my will, but only Amelia will be satisfied.'

'Do you still see her?'

'Every day; she lives with me. She's the throwback, Mr Skinner. Niall and Victoria, her brother and sister, take after their father; they're both career soldiers. But Amelia, she favours the cloistered life that her uncles chose.' He paused; I waited. 'She's the reason I didn't want you coming to my home, Mr Skinner. She knows nothing of the true circumstances of her uncle Matthew's death. She pressed me once about it; she told me that Luke would not discuss it with any of them – in fact he'd forbidden any mention of Matthew's name. I didn't lie to her. I told her that he was a lonely man, unlucky in love, and that he had been found dead in a quarry, at the foot of a cliff. She assumed that I meant he had taken his own life, and I've allowed her to believe that ever since. If you had turned up there looking into it . . .'

I nodded my understanding. 'It would have brought the whole business up again, and you'd have had to tell her the truth.'

'Precisely, and that she doesn't need. I'd rather she lived with the image of a tragic lost soul than that of a sex pest who had his head bashed in for his trouble – even though he was entirely innocent,' he added hurriedly.

'Unlucky in love,' I repeated. 'Did you mean anything by that or was it just an embellishment?'

The little man drank some more tea and crunched a biscuit as he considered my question. 'A bit of both, I suppose. Matthew was interested in the ladies, no doubt of that. There was one in particular, very dear to his heart, but nothing came of it.'

'For any particular reason?'

The professor looked at me shrewdly. 'Are you thinking he might have pressed his suit too forcefully, Mr Skinner? That he might have been less than subtle in his courtship and that it might have had some bearing on his eventual death?'

The little bugger had read my mind, but I wasn't admitting it. 'I wouldn't go that far,' I replied. 'I sense a great closeness between you and your brother; I can understand your devastation when he died.'

'Your senses are acute; there was. I don't really know why, for there was a three-year age gap, a lot when one is a child. I remember him being kind when I was very small. Luke, on the other hand, was a nasty, aggressive little boy. He was much bigger than me, and he bullied me when he could. That was quite often; our father was a busy man with an important charge in the city, and our mother . . .' He paused, studying his tea once more. 'I don't remember my mother, Mr Skinner. She died when Luke and I were in our first year. The death certificate said organ failure, and the coroner recorded an open verdict, but both he and the physician who attended her were members of my father's congregation. He, Father, was insistent that if she had taken too many pills, she had done so accidentally, but I was never persuaded of that.'

'Was Matthew?'

'We didn't discuss it until I was fifteen years old and he was eighteen. I asked him what he thought the truth was, and he told me there had never been any doubt that she had killed herself, not in his mind. He found her, the poor little blighter. There was an empty bottle of some kind of sedative in her hand, he said. When the doctor arrived, Matthew watched from the door as he entered the room, and he noticed that the bottle had gone. We never dwelled on it, and it was never discussed again, but when Amelia asked me about her uncle's death, I told her about it to underscore the suicide suggestion.'

'You let her think it runs in the family?' I said.

He sighed. 'Yes, I suppose I did. Was that unkind?'

'Disingenuous,' I told him, 'but not necessarily unkind.'

'A white lie?'

'Not even that. What did the man say? "Economical with the truth." That covers it.' I waited as he refilled my cup, without being asked. 'Does it also cover any part of our discussion?' I continued.

'What do you mean?'

'Have you been steering me in any particular direction?'

He peered at me, buying himself some reaction time by biting on a chunk of shortbread. 'I'm sorry,' he murmured when he had consumed it. 'I don't follow.'

'I'm still struggling with your reason for not coming back from America when Matthew died,' I confessed. 'I'm not doubting that you have a fear of long-haul flying; that's entirely natural. But the more I listen to you and come to understand you, the harder I find it to accept that you couldn't overcome

106

that fear, especially when I hear you stress your closeness to your brother.'

I smiled. The journey on which I had engaged myself had taken me back in time, to the years of my youth. Since my encounter at the Waterside, I had been awash with nostalgia and thinking of Myra more than I had in many years. As I looked at the little academic and considered what he had told me, another memory threw itself at me.

'When my first wife and I had an argument,' I told him, 'and we had at least our fair share of those, her favourite tactic was to accuse me of "sidetracking". That was the word she used to describe my habit of focusing on a single fact and using it to obscure others. I wonder if you're doing that here, Professor. After all, you've got previous, allowing your niece to believe the fiction of her uncle's suicide. So I ask you, did you even consider coming back to Scotland to put your brother's affairs in order and organise his funeral, rather than relying on his church to take care of it?'

Little, round John Ampersand seemed to deflate a little. He laid down his cup as if it was the last of his defensive weapons and looked up at me. 'Yes, I did,' he replied quietly. 'For about two seconds.' Then he smiled. 'Are you treating me like a suspect, Mr Skinner? Is this the third degree?'

I laughed again, softly. 'No, I'm not, and we haven't moved beyond the first degree. I'm treating you like a witness, Professor; doing my best to make you less selective in your recollection of things that happened a long time ago. We've got to the point at which you've accepted that even if you could have driven back to Britain when Matthew was murdered, you wouldn't have. There must have been a reason for that. If you don't want to tell me, fine. It's none of my damn business and I doubt that it's relevant to the inquiry. However, you did hold it back from the investigating officers at the time, and as an ex-cop, that interests me.'

He laid his hands on his ample waist, fingers interlinked. 'My brother and I did not part friends, Mr Skinner,' he said. 'We had a furious argument, and as a consequence, I accepted a position at Harvard that I had just been offered. If what happened hadn't . . . happened, I would not have done that, for at that time I had no desire to leave this place.'

'Are you going to tell me what it was?' I asked him, bluntly.

'No,' he replied, with equal directness. 'I am not, because as you said, it's none of your damn business. All I will say is that Matthew and I never spoke again afterwards. When I had the call from the police in Edinburgh, I had no idea that he had moved to Scotland.'

'Do you have any idea why he did that? You and he; it's obvious from what you've told me that you two were Cambridge men to your bootstraps.'

'I suppose we were,' he agreed. He grunted. 'Maybe Matthew couldn't bear the place without me. If so, I wish he'd bloody well told me.'

'Would it have made any difference?'

'Probably not,' he conceded, 'but it might have given us the opportunity to clear the air. The fact that we didn't . . .' He paused. 'Well, it's something I'll regret for the rest of my life, now that I've been forced to think about it again. The issue over which we quarrelled: looking back, in the great scheme of things, what did it matter?'

'I can't comment on that,' I countered, 'since you're not going to tell me what it was. Can I ask you to think back,' I continued, when it was clear he wasn't going to respond, 'to the call you had from the police in Scotland after Matthew was killed? It's been a long time, but do you remember the name of the officer who spoke to you?'

He nodded with a small smile. 'Funnily enough, I do. It was Stein, pronounced with two "e"s. He had a great long police title; that I don't recall, but the name, yes, I do, because I asked him to spell it for me. When he did, I made a remark about German beer mugs, which he didn't find very funny.'

'During your conversation, did you volunteer anything about your quarrel with your brother?'

'No, I did not.'

'Did Alf say or ask anything that might have referred to it?'

'Alf?' he repeated. 'You know him?'

'Knew,' I corrected him. 'He passed away some years ago. He was my boss for several years. I succeeded him as head of CID in our force when he retired.'

'Did you indeed? As a matter of interest, how high did you rise in the police, Mr Skinner?'

'To the top: I was chief constable of two forces before I quit.'

'Looking at you, I assume that you took early retirement.'

'Your assumption is flattering, but wrong. My time was up and I knew it, so I walked away. I have a young family; it was an easy decision to make. But back to your interview with Alf.'

'It wasn't really an interview. He told me that my brother had been murdered. By that time I knew he was dead, of course.'

That took me by surprise. It must have showed on my face, for he continued.

'Oh yes, Mr Skinner. I had a call from his bishop on the day his body was discovered. A stuffy chap, tripping over himself in trying to be diplomatic. He went out of his way not to use the word "suicide", telling me only that he had been found dead, but I knew from his tone of voice that there was more to it than that. When I pressed him, he said that he appeared to have gone walking in the country and fallen off a cliff. "Or jumped," I replied, and he admitted that the police were proceeding on that assumption. He asked me when he could expect me in Edinburgh. I told him that he need not. Then I hung up. I didn't mean to be rude, but I was stunned. We may have been estranged, but we had a lot of shared history.'

'Had you no curiosity at all? Didn't you want to know what had driven him to that clifftop?'

'I did, but how could I have found out? I was still contemplating it when Mr Stein called and told me that Matthew's death was being treated as murder. He asked me if I knew of anyone from our past who might wish him harm. I told him I did not, then I advised him that as we hadn't spoken for almost twenty years, there was no point in asking me about the present. It was then that he volunteered the police theory that he had been killed by the father of a young woman with whom he had been accused of behaving inappropriately.'

'How did you react?' I asked.

'Much the same as I reacted to you earlier. I told him it was preposterous.'

I let his words hang in the air for a few seconds, before pushing my luck again. 'At the risk of offending you further, Professor, was there ever a moment, even a second or two, when your mind overcame loyalty and considered that possibility?'

He shook his head, sipped his tea, sighed and then looked back at me. 'I don't suppose I'd have been human if there wasn't,' he confessed. 'I did consider it, and realised there and then that if it was true, I didn't want to know and I didn't want any part of it. That was when I decided, irrevocably, that I would not be going back to Scotland. I told Mr Stein as much. He had no choice but to accept that, but he did ask me to provide him with a witnessed note, summarising our brief interview. I did so, rejecting any suggestion that my brother had a history of sexual deviancy, and had it dispatched to him by the US mail, registered.'

'This might seem like a daft question,' I said, 'but can you describe that document to me?'

'Describe it?'

'Yes, physically. What did it look like?'

'It was a single sheet of paper, that's how brief it was. On the letterhead of my attorneys, Horowitz and O'Reilly, signed by me, notarised and witnessed by Mr Horowitz.' For a second, his eyes twinkled. 'There never was an O'Reilly,' he murmured, 'but it was Boston, after all.' He held my gaze. 'I'm sure you never asked a daft question in your life, Mr Skinner, so why are you curious about that?'

'Because I've seen the case file on your brother's murder,' I replied, 'all of it, and your statement isn't there.'

Another silence developed, until Ampersand broke it. 'Is that significant?'

'I have no idea,' I said. 'However, I knew Alf Stein for a long time and worked with him for most of it. I have never met a more meticulous detective; he taught me never to leave anything out, however meaningless it might seem, and I spent the latter part of my career emphasising that to my people.'

It didn't take me long to dismiss my niggling concern about the absence of the affidavit from the case papers. It was an anomaly, no more than that. When I thought about it, I realised that the investigation had been wrapped up within a week.

When Alf had spoken to John, probably he would have been in possession of the forensic evidence that convicted Meads. If not, it would certainly have been in his hands before the document arrived from Boston. He had no need to wait for it before closing the file and sending it to the procurator fiscal for prosecution. The opinion of the victim's brother didn't strengthen his case one iota; it was irrelevant. Okay, technically it should have been disclosed to Meads's defence team, but what would they have done with it? The judge might not have allowed it to be introduced as evidence, for it wasn't relevant. The issue wasn't whether Matthew Ampersand had or had not been a predator upon young women. The fact, demonstrated on many occasions by the accused himself, was that Barley Meads believed that he was, and for that reason he had killed him.

I was about to say as much to his brother when the door opened and a woman stepped into the room. She was of medium height, with dark hair, in her late thirties; she was dressed in jeans and a sweatshirt, and she had an athletic bearing. There was something familiar about her but I couldn't nail it down. I decided that she reminded me of an Olympic gold medallist, one whose name I couldn't quite recall. She looked at the professor and smiled; then her eyes fell on me, sitting opposite him, and her expression became one of curiosity. 'Uncle John,' she exclaimed, 'I'm sorry; I'm interrupting. When Mrs Ingleby said you were in here, I assumed that you'd be with Billy. I didn't realise you were in a meeting.'

Her accent was mixed, but predominantly Australian, and incongruous to my ear. I don't know why, for I hear it wherever I go in Britain, even in my office building in Edinburgh on occasion, but in that room, in that city, she seemed as out of place as the first Roman to land on a south coast beach must have sounded as he addressed the bewildered tribesmen in vulgar Latin.

'Not at all, my dear,' her uncle replied, his composure undisturbed. 'I wouldn't call it a meeting, rather a conversation between new acquaintances. This is Mr Skinner, a friend of a friend in need of advice. His son has been offered a postgraduate slot at Harvard Business School. Someone told him of my long connection with the university and he asked if he could pick my brains about it.' He looked across at me. 'Mr Skinner, this is my niece, Amelia Ampersand. I'm happy to see you home, Amy, although I didn't think you'd be back until tomorrow. What brings you here? A domestic emergency? Is the damn cat stuck up that damn tree again?'

I nodded a hello, but said nothing; instead I sat and marvelled at the speed and fluency with which he had lied, working out how I was going to fall in line with his story if she pressed me for details. The only American college with which I am in any way familiar is the FBI training base in Quantico, Virginia, which I've visited a couple of times to lecture at its law enforcement executive development seminars. Happily, all she did was nod and say, 'Could do worse,' then turned back to her uncle.

'I'm locked out,' she confessed. 'I thought I'd taken my key with me, but when I looked in my travel bag it wasn't there. The damn cat's fine, though. She glowered at me through the kitchen window. I guess she expected me to come in and feed her.'

'You had better do that, then,' he said, smiling at her. I sensed that there were very few lights in his life, probably only one, and Amelia was it. He fished in a waistcoat pocket, produced a Yale key on a ring and handed it to her.

She took it from him. 'I hope your son likes Harvard,' she called to me from the doorway as she left.

'She makes me feel less old than I am,' John volunteered. 'Luke's daughter, no question of that; she rowed for the university in Boston and still does some over here. She inherited her father's physical attributes, but happily also her uncle Matthew's charm.'

'And your taste for academia,' I remarked. 'Has she always been single?'

'Yes,' he replied. 'She has a private life but she never brings it home. I think that's where she's been for the last week or so.'

'Who's Billy?' I asked, out of idle curiosity. I had no other questions left.

He coloured a little. 'Wilhelmina is her Sunday name; she's a friend of mine, but I never bring her home either.'

'I'm sorry,' I said. 'That was intrusive.'

He laughed. 'Not at all, my friend, not at all. I've never been married, but I've never been disinterested. You can take that disclosure as good news, that there is life after seventy.'

'My wife is twelve years younger than me,' I told him. 'I hope she'll be pleased to hear that.'

Sixteen

I kept my promise to Sarah with an hour to spare; in fact I made it home before she did. I had a light early lunch with the professor before driving back to Stansted. As we ate and conversed, I waited for him to drop a hint about the reason behind his estrangement from his brother, but he never did, and I didn't try to prompt him.

'Was it worth it?' she asked me as I handed her a glass of mineral water from the bottle I had just opened.

'It was interesting, and it was entertaining. The wee professor's a nice guy, once you break through the carapace, but the family? Talk about dysfunctional. You've got twin brothers who basically can't stand each other—'

'Maybe they had different fathers,' she said, interrupting.

I stared at her. 'Is that even possible?'

She beamed at me. 'God! You Presbyterians! There are so many things beyond your comprehension. Of course it is: two different men can fertilise two different eggs during the same ovulation period. I suspect it's more common than we realise.'

'Bloody hell!' I sighed. She was right about my Presbyterian roots: at heart, we're a colourless, unimaginative lot, us Scots. 'But let's assume that the canon's wife did not put it about,' I continued. 'You've got the antipathetic twins, and the saintly older brother, scarred by witnessing, more or less, his mother's suicide, who takes the wee one under his wing only for the two of them to fall out for life over some undisclosed issue . . .'

'Probably a woman,' Sarah observed.

'Probably,' I agreed, 'but it doesn't matter. The rift was so long ago that while I now know most of what there is to know about the terrible twins, I still know fuck all about Matthew Ampersand himself.'

'Do you really need to?'

'If I'm going to review the investigation properly, yes, I do.'

'Need I point out that Jimmy didn't ask you to do that? All he wanted was for you to meet the man Brass for him.'

'Which I have still to do, since the bugger stood me up on Sunday. But when I do meet him, it'll be good to be as fully briefed as possible, to give me a better chance of knocking down whatever story he thinks he has.'

'Have you managed to rearrange that meeting?' she asked.

'It's for Jimmy to do that, not me, but as far as I know, he hasn't. I tried to call the old bugger on the way back from the airport, but I got number unavailable.'

'Did you try his landline?'

'No, in case Chrissie answered. She knows nothing of this business.'

'Are you sure?'

'Yes. Why do you ask?'

'Because she phoned me at work this afternoon,' she said. 'I couldn't take her call, but she left a message. She said she'd tried to get in touch with you but you were unavailable, and asked if you could call her whenever you were free. Why didn't she use your mobile, I wonder?'

'I doubt that she has my number. Jimmy would never have had cause to give it to her.'

I laid my glass down on the kitchen work surface, and reached for the jacket that I had hung over a chair earlier. 'I'm going to see her,' I told Sarah. 'For her to do that now, something must be up.'

The Prouds' home is only a short distance from mine, one of no more than a dozen bungalows in a well maintained cul-de-sac that overlooks Gullane Bents. It was easier to walk than take the car. When I arrived Lady Proud must have been looking out of the window, for she opened the front door just as I reached it.

'Bob,' she exclaimed, and at once I could see her anxiety. For all my closeness to her husband, Chrissie Proud wasn't someone I knew well. We met on formal occasions, but Jimmy and I had never socialised during our working lives together, and after his retirement I had been too busy trying and failing to fill his shoes to see much of him. Even so, I was shocked by the change in his wife. I knew her as a cheerful woman, sturdily built and with a ready smile. The person who looked at me across her threshold was drawn, white of hair and of complexion. Her nose was sharp and her cheeks were almost concave.

'Sarah gave me your message,' I said, as she let me into the hall. 'I thought it would be easier to come and see you rather than call. Besides, there's something I need to talk to Jimmy about. Is he in?'

She clutched my arm and drew me into a small sitting room on the left of the hallway that Jimmy referred to as his study. The first thing I noticed was that an armchair had been placed in the bay window, turned away from its neighbour. She had indeed been watching the street. In another part of the house I could hear Bowser barking and scratching at a door.

'No, he's not, Bob,' she replied as she dropped into the seat that still faced the television. She was wringing her hands, and her face was contorted. 'That's the trouble. He's gone away. I think he's left me.'

I gasped, and couldn't stop the smile of sheer astonishment that spread across my face. 'Left you? Chrissie, don't be daft. Jimmy couldn't function without you. When he was still working and you had that heart scare, I remember what he was like; terrified sums it up.'

'I tell you, he has. I think he's gone off with someone. That oncologist of his in the clinic; he was fair smitten by her, I could tell. He's a changed man, Bob: that cancer he had, the treatment, it must have affected him in some way.'

'Chrissie, as I understand it, he had surgery to remove one testicle followed by three cycles of chemo. That is not going to turn him into a septuagenarian Don Juan; it'll do the opposite, if anything. The one thing I can promise you without having heard any of your story is that he has not run off with another woman – least of all his oncologist. Sarah knows her slightly, through the university; she's gay.' She stared at me blankly; in some ways Chrissie has never left the nineteen seventies. 'She's a lesbian,' I said.

'Oh!' She paused, brought face to face with a world she did not understand. 'But even so,' she countered, 'Jimmy's still a very attractive man.'

'It doesn't work that way,' I promised her. As I spoke, a chill ran through me. I feared that I was sitting with someone in the early stages of dementia. 'Now tell me, what's happened?'

'I just told you, he's gone. This morning he got up and took Bowser for a walk as usual. He came back with the paper like he always does, but he didn't read it. He put it down on the hall table and went into the kitchen for his breakfast. It was still there when I came back downstairs. I don't eat breakfast,' she explained. 'My appetite's disappeared. Jimmy does, though; I make it while he's walking the dog, then go and get dressed while he's having it. When I come down, I usually have a cup of tea with him, and we chat about this and that; often it's what's in that morning's *Saltire*. Not today, though. When I came down, he went upstairs, hardly looking at me on the way. "Who stole your scone?" I called after him, but he ignored me. He was up there for a while, but he can be if he decides to have a bath, so I thought nothing of it. But when he came down the stairs, he was carrying a suitcase. I looked at it and I said, "Jimmy, what's this?" He looked at me and . . . I don't know, Bob, it was like he was a stranger. He put his bag down, he kissed me on the forehead and said, "I'm sorry, love, I've got to go away for a bit." And then he picked his raincoat off its hook and he left, just like that. I didn't realise it, but there was a taxi waiting outside. I only saw it when it drove off.'

She seemed to collapse into herself, and tears ran down her cheeks. The effort of telling her story had exhausted her; before I set myself to thinking about it, I decided that looking after her was a higher priority. 'Have you eaten at all today?' I asked her.

She shook her head as she pressed a handkerchief to her eyes.

'Right,' I declared. 'We're going to do something about that. Come on.'

I knew where the kitchen was from previous visits; I held out a hand to raise her from her chair and led her through there. When I opened the door, an agitated Bowser jumped out at me, doing a dervish dance. I dealt with him by chucking him into the back garden, which is enclosed, then set about caring for his mistress. In the bread bin and the fridge I found the makings of two rounds of ham and tomato sandwiches. As she contemplated them, I brewed her a mug of coffee, instant, there being nothing else on view, which I fortified by adding a generous shot of brandy along with the milk, from a bottle that sat beside the toaster. Jimmy's evening tipple, I recalled.

I knew that Chrissie still wasn't hungry, but she was too polite not to set about the sandwiches. Once she started, she ploughed her way right through them, and I let her, not interrupting. She raised an eyebrow when she tasted the coffee, but finished that too.

As her energy level rose, her self-control returned, and my concern about her mental state eased a little. 'Why, Bob?' she asked me quietly. 'Do you know?'

'The only thing I know,' I assured her, 'is that he hasn't run off with a fancy woman.' I spoke the truth. As I put together Chrissie's snack, my mind had been working on the situation. I was more interested in why he had gone, rather than where. If I wanted to find him, I was pretty sure I could, but what had prompted his vanishing act? For all Brass's no-show, I had that situation under control; he knew from my review of the case papers that there was no smoking gun, and that between us, Alex and I would keep him safe from any threats or allegations by the bombastic blogger. My visit earlier in the day had reinforced that belief; if the guy had really wanted to research background on Matthew Ampersand, Cambridge was the first place he would have gone. Yes, he had visited the city and its university, but there was no indication that he had ever made a connection between them and the murder victim whose case he had disinterred.

'Chrissie,' I ventured, stepping forward as carefully as if I was looking out for landmines, 'has Jimmy mentioned anything to you recently that might have been on his mind?'

'The cancer, obviously,' she replied, 'but he got the all-clear on that a month ago. He told me his oncologist had signed him off after the chemo. Apart from that . . . Now I think about it, the last week or so, he might have been quieter than usual about the house, and his routine might have been different. A few nights ago, he insisted on taking Bowser out for an evening walk. That was unusual; the dog's getting on now, and one good walk in the morning's enough for him. The poor old fellow was confused . . . Bowser, I mean, not Jimmy.'

'Have there been any unusual phone calls? Any strangers asking for him?'

'None that I've answered. We've always been ex-directory, and with him being a former chief constable we've got an extra level of screening from nuisance calls. You'll know that, you'll have it as well.' Suddenly her eyebrows rose as a memory hit her. 'Wait a minute, there was one . . . oh, at least a week ago. I picked it up and a man asked if Sir James was at home. I said he was, and he took it in his study. He was in there for quite a long time. When he came out, I asked him what it had been about, but he was vague. "Old stuff," was all he told me. He said he hadn't been able to help the man.'

'When you picked up, did you ask the caller for his name?'

'I did,' she replied, 'but my memory's not what it was. Let me think now.'

I watched her as she concentrated, picturing myself at her age and not liking what I saw.

'Steel, was it?' she murmured. 'No, she's the chief constable now. It had a metallic ring to it, though. Brass!' she exclaimed in unexpected triumph. 'That was it, he said his name was Brass. Jimmy didn't know him, though. I'm sure of that, for he asked me to repeat it. Does the name mean anything to you, Bob?'

'Yes, it does,' I admitted. 'He's a blogger.'

'What in heaven's name's a bogger?'

'Blogger,' I corrected her. 'A blog is a personal record of thoughts, experiences and opinions that people post on the internet.'

'Why would they do that?'

'A good question, Chrissie,' I chuckled. 'For a range of reasons: loneliness, vanity, a desire to share, special interest campaigning, promotion of personal interests, or just to make money. Brass fits into a few of those categories. His blog's commercial, in that it has enough readers to attract advertisers. He calls himself a journalist. A lot of people agree with that description; mainstream journos don't.'

'Do you?' she asked.

'I don't, but I'm part of the mainstream media now through my part-time job, so I'm biased.'

'Why would he be calling Jimmy?'

I deflected her question. 'Brass's speciality is the police,' I told her. 'Jimmy is the most respected retired police officer in Scotland.'

That seemed to satisfy her, but it didn't affect her concern; or mine, for my old boss's behaviour was unusual and possibly irrational, and I was worried too.

'Before we go any further,' I said, 'let's just go back to basics.' I took my phone from my pocket and was about to call Jimmy when his wife interrupted me.

'That won't do any good. He left his mobile phone in his study.'

'Mmm,' I murmured, trying to appear unconcerned by the large spanner that she had thrown into the works. Very few men of Jimmy's age are masters of modern technology, and he wasn't one of those. However, he'd been around me long enough to know some of the basics. Among them, one of the first maxims is this: if you are going somewhere and you really do not want to be found, don't carry anything that is potentially traceable; for example, the SIM card in a mobile phone.

Seventeen

I left Chrissie clutching another brandy, without the coffee, in the hope that it might help her sleep eventually. I knew there was no chance that Jimmy would turn up that night with his tail between his legs; if he had even called her I'd have been astonished.

I took my worries back to Sarah and shared them with her, once we'd all had supper together and the children had begun to bed down for the night in their customary order. Something had made Jimmy run for it. My best guess had to be that Brass had contacted him again and had really spooked him second time around.

'I don't disagree with that,' my wife said, 'and we both know what that means.'

'We do,' I conceded. 'Jimmy wouldn't run away from nothing, so he must be seriously afraid that Brass can hurt him.'

'Which means, surely,' she continued, saying the thing that I didn't want to consider, 'that he did play some part in Matthew Ampersand's murder.'

'It suggests it,' I countered doggedly, 'but it doesn't prove anything. Brass may have offered him evidence, but it needn't be factual or even relevant.'

'But if it gave the appearance of truth, even if Jimmy knew it wasn't, and was going to draw him into a scandal, might he not run away from that?'

'I'd hope not; I think more of him than that. I prefer to believe he'd stay and face it, but that's not the way it's looking.'

Sarah sat beside me on the sofa, legs drawn up under her, holding a glass of orange squash in both hands; she's the top forensic pathologist in the east of Scotland, but she still has nights on call. 'Could anything like this ever happen to you?' she asked quietly. 'The modern world is full of people like Austin Brass.'

I had been contemplating that very question since my Yellowcraigs meeting with Jimmy Proud a few days before. I'd had a colourful career, during which I'd pulled a trigger on a few occasions. 'It's possible that someone might dig up a few matters,' I admitted, 'but I don't believe there's anything I couldn't see off. Nothing makes me wake up sweating in the middle of the night.'

'Nothing?'

I dug her gently in the ribs. 'Maybe you, on occasion, but nothing else.' I spoke the truth, most of it; I didn't mention the dreams, that's all.

'What will you do next?'

'What would you do?'

'Me?' she exclaimed. 'I'd never have got involved in the first place. Are you going to look for Jimmy?'

'No. I'm his friend, not his keeper. If he needs a couple of days on his own to get his head right, I have to respect that. If I'm going to find anyone it'll be Austin Brass. It's time I stopped lurking in the background; if he'd turned up on Sunday he'd have had no choice but to face me, so I might as well break cover and tackle him. Once I've spoken to him, and got to the bottom of this . . .'

'Will you send Mario's precious box back and let the Reverend Matthew rest in peace?'

'That's what I should do, but I have a problem. I'm looking at a near-perfect homicide investigation with an obvious and logical conclusion, and yet I'm starting to have doubts about Meads's conviction.'

'In the face of all the evidence?'

I nodded. 'It fits, no question, save for one thing: having reviewed the records, and even read the trial transcript on the flight down this morning, I am still asking myself, how come Alf Stein never broke Meads? He was completely one hundred per cent bang to rights. Even Archie Nelson, his defence counsel, believed he was guilty; that's obvious from the trial, in the way that he examined witnesses. His main hope was that he might shift it down to culpable homicide by planting the suggestion with the judge and jury that his client's obsession might have unbalanced his mind. But Meads maintained his innocence, through Alf's interrogation, through the trial and through the appeal. The story he told Alf was that when Ampersand was killed he was out on the farm, checking that his livestock were okay in the cold. His defence counsel never put him in the witness box, so that was never led at his trial, or the appeal, or even raised in his last, desperate, fruitless letter to the Secretary of State. When he took his own life in jail, did his guilt simply catch up with him, or had he finally run out of hope?'

'Could Brass have found evidence that he actually was on the farm?' Sarah asked.

'From thirty years ago? I don't see how, but even if he did,

Jimmy Proud had nothing to do with the investigation. His only involvement was in signing off the rejection of Meads's original complaint. And my only way of finding out what Brass thinks he has is by asking him.'

'When are you going to do that?'

I smiled and reached for my phone, which lay on the arm of the sofa. 'No time like the present.'

I found the *Brass Rubbings* number and hit it, putting the call on speaker for Sarah's benefit. All we heard was ten seconds of ringtone, then the same announcement I had heard a couple of days before; Austin Brass was still busy righting wrongs. The second time around, I did leave a message. 'Mr Brass, my name is Bob Skinner. I have information for you regarding Sir James Proud, and I would be grateful if you would call me back. This number will show as withheld, but you can reach me through my office at the *Saltire* newspaper.' I laid the mobile back where it had been. 'That should flush the fucker out,' I told Sarah.

'Information regarding Sir James Proud,' she repeated. 'Yes, I think it might, but what information do you have to give him?'

'The fact that Jimmy is an old and dear friend of mine, and that if he continues to harass him without cause, steps will be taken to make him cease and desist.'

She laughed. 'That sounds like put up or shut up, with menace. What if he shows you his smoking gun?'

'If it's justified, I'll pull the trigger,' I told her, 'regardless of the target.'

Eighteen

I went into the office mid morning, prepared for some form of response from Austin Brass, but there had been none. I called him again, through the *Saltire* switchboard, only to hear his smug voicemail message for the third time. I was doing my best to keep an open mind about the guy, but his crap about 'righting more wrongs' was making it difficult. His mind seemed as closed as mine can be, but on the other side of the argument.

I didn't repeat my message to him; instead I dealt with some correspondence from InterMedia's Scottish lawyers about an ongoing defamation claim against the *Saltire* – they thought it was spurious and recommended that we defend it, but they wanted a board-level decision and that was me – then turned my attention to my plan for the rest of the day.

I had left the house earlier than usual, but instead of heading straight into Edinburgh, I'd driven over the hill towards Haddington, under the busy carriageway that joins the capitals of Scotland and England, then headed east. I parked at the foot of Traprain Law, and climbed up towards its crest, carefully, because my pre-planning had not included bringing the correct type of footwear.

The path was bumpy, but most of it was wide enough for a vehicle, even one as big as a Dodge truck. The narrowing, where it occurred, was caused by vegetation, gorse bushes on either side. I assumed that thirty years ago, those had been a lot smaller, if they had been there at all. If I had been running the investigation, I would have filmed it to emphasise that the prosecution's scenario was possible, but yes, I'm a belt-and-braces man. Anyway, the tyre tracks at the top had proved that beyond much doubt.

At the top, a rigid six-foot-high fence had been erected to keep children and the unwary away from the edge of the quarry. There had been a fence at the time of the murder; I had noticed it in the crime-scene photographs. Even someone as large and strong as Barley Meads would have had a problem heaving a fourteen-stone dead weight over the modern version, but its predecessor had been flimsy, a chespale barrier no more than a metre high.

I demonstrated how difficult it would have been by climbing it myself, leaving my jacket and phone on the other side. I'm not great with heights, unless I'm in an aircraft, but I crept close enough to the edge to see over. The stagnant green pond that had formed in the quarry excavation was much smaller than I had expected, and the rock face that descended towards it wasn't sheer; it had a distinct slope. That set me wondering. Ampersand had been wearing a heavy overcoat when he went over the edge, but even so, I was surprised that the only marks on the body noted during the autopsy had been caused by the blow to the head that had killed him and the impact with the ice. *Bang*, then *splat!* If he had bounced down that sharp terrain, surely there would have been more, and his coat would have been torn. On the crime-scene photography that I had seen, his thick black clergyman's coat could have come straight off the hanger in Gieves & Hawkes. Okay, the quarry pond might have been drained since then and refilled over time, and the distance involved might have been different, but even so, I reasoned, Meads must have been a mighty powerful man to have cast the corpse over the side at a trajectory that missed the rock face altogether. Could I have done it, at my physical peak? In the gym, I can still bench-press more than my own weight . . . but I couldn't throw myself very far.

I was still pondering these imponderables as I drove out of the office car park and headed out of the city. As I do more and more these days, I relied on my satnav to find my destination. 'Easterlee Farm, Heatherston, Midlothian,' I told the system, and then followed its instructions as it led me south, through Penicuik and on for a couple of miles before turning off the main road.

There wasn't much to Heatherston, no more than a few dozen houses on either side of the narrow road that snaked through it, one pub with a garish sign advertising an all-day menu, and a general store that I imagined clung to its existence thanks to the post office services it provided. The turn-off for Easterlee Farm was a couple of hundred yards beyond the village's 'Thank you for driving carefully' sign. As I took the left turn, as ordered by my lady guide, I could see a big T-shaped building that I took to be the farmhouse on the crest of a hill about half a mile away. I've lived in the countryside for most of my life, and so I knew that the land on either side of the road was no use for crops. When the hedges on either side of the approach road allowed a clear view, it became very obvious that the main business of the farm was cattle.

The tarmac of the road surface gave way to gravel just as the dominatrix voice told me I had reached my destination. The front of the farmhouse faced south-west. It was built of red sandstone, two storeys, with a slate roof and a modern glass entrance porch that was spacious enough to accommodate a large cane armchair and matching furniture.

Its occupant rose as I stepped out of my car, and came towards the double doors as I approached. She was tall and upright; her hair had a bluish tinge, and as I drew closer I could see that her complexion was smooth, despite the age she must have been if I was correct in my assumption of who she was. Tommy had been right; I could still see a resemblance to Sophia Loren.

'Are you the man from Waitrose?' she asked in an imperious tone. Her accent was cultured Scottish. 'If so,' she checked a large black sports watch on her wrist, 'you're an hour early. Mr Lennon isn't here.'

'I'm not from Waitrose, Sainsbury or any other competitor,' I replied. 'My name is Bob Skinner, and I'm not here on a farming matter, Mrs Meads. It is Mrs Meads, isn't it?'

She appraised me from the doorway. 'It is; Carmel Meads. And you're the policeman, aren't you?' she added quietly, as if she was talking to herself. 'You're the man who used to be our chief constable.'

'That's right,' I confirmed, 'but I left the job a while back . . . or maybe it left me, I've never really worked that out.'

'What do you do now?' she asked.

'Among other things I'm a director of the company that owns the *Saltire* newspaper.' That was improvisation; I had realised as I was driving up the approach road that I had no sort of a cover story, nothing to justify my sudden interest in a thirty-year-old murder case, other than the truth, which I didn't feel like sharing with her.

'Does that bring you here?' she responded.

I kept on thinking on my feet. 'Yes, it does. Mostly I'm management, but I have a roving brief,' I replied, lying in my teeth. 'A couple of days ago, our editor, Mrs Crampsey, had a tip that one of our more determined rivals was looking into your husband's murder conviction. She asked me if I could find out if there's anything in it, if there's any reason why it should suddenly be of interest.'

She stared at me. 'If there is, it's bloody news to me. What would be the point? Barley's been dead for going on thirty years. His ashes are scattered on this land. I suppose you'd better come in, Mr Skinner,' she said grudgingly, moving to one side. 'Have a seat.' She pointed to a second chair, smaller than her throne. As I joined her, I saw that the porch commanded a spectacular view across the fields to the hills beyond.

'How much of that is yours?' I asked.

'A couple of thousand acres; it was in my late husband's family's ownership for generations. Two thirds of it is tenanted, mostly by arable farmers. They grow crops,' she explained, 'but some of them keep a few sheep also. We focus on dairy and beef; the latter on quite a big scale.'

'Who's Mr Lennon?' I asked, although I knew.

'He's our general manager; he runs the farm. He's also my son-in-law, married to my only daughter. The man I mistook you for, the man from Waitrose, is coming today to meet him. He wants to inspect our beef production before signing a long-term supply contract. There are very specific criteria we have to meet to be able to sell our beef as organic. But to hell with all that, Mr Skinner. What's this about Barley's case being reopened?'

'I wouldn't put it as strongly as that, Mrs Meads. A journalist sniffing around is what we've heard. You say that no one's approached you?'

'If he had, what would his name have been?'

'Brass. Austin Brass.'

'Never heard of him. Does that put your mind at rest?'

'Not necessarily,' I replied. I was playing it by ear. Or was I flying blind? I wasn't sure; as a police officer, my style of investigation never relied on subtlety. As a civilian, it had to. 'If he thought he was on to something he might not approach you until he had something concrete to put to you. Or he might have approached another member of the family.'

'That's a very narrow choice; there's only me, Michael and Briony, my daughter. There's Florence as well, of course, but she wasn't around when the murder happened.'

'Florence?'

'My granddaughter; Michael and Briony's child. The male line seems to have died out in the Meads family. However,' she went on, 'I have no doubt that if this man you're talking about had approached any of them, I'd have been told about it.'

'Might they not have wanted to keep it from you?'

'Hah!' she snorted. 'Because I'm an old lady, you mean? Mr Skinner, I'm only a couple of years older than the President of the United States, and I am still the chief executive of my family, probably with more control than he has. The only difference between us is that I don't have a Twitter account.'

I laughed at her comparison. 'Sorry,' I said. 'I wasn't being ageist. My thought was that the past must be painful for you, and your family might not have wanted to dig it up.'

'My past was cremated and scattered along with my husband,' she retorted. 'It might anger me, but it doesn't hurt me or scare me. I don't believe there is such a thing as time; as far as I'm concerned, we all live in the moment, and what happened thirty years ago might as well be a story in a book.'

'If your husband hadn't died, he'd still be part of your present,' I pointed out.

'But he did die, and of his own choosing. Matthew Ampersand didn't have that opportunity, or the opportunity of a long life. His was cut short.'

'That was why Mr Meads killed himself, wasn't it?'

'Guilt?' she said. 'I prefer to think of it as anger. He reached a point where absolutely nobody believed in his innocence apart from him, and it made him so frustrated that he simply exploded.'

'If he didn't kill Ampersand, who did?' I asked.

She frowned severely. 'Will this wind up in the *Saltire*?' she countered.

Her question took me by surprise, for I'd forgotten my cover story. I slipped back into character. 'Not if you don't want it to, at this stage; I'm an investigator, not a journalist. If there was anything in this I'd hand it over to someone else, but if we've been misinformed and Brass isn't interested, neither are we.'

'Very well.' The severity lessened. 'The jury found that my husband killed Ampersand; they did it in record time, too. They were persuaded that he bashed his head in and threw him into that quarry, thinking that his body would never be recovered. The point that nobody got was that he never believed himself guilty of murder. He thought the killing was entirely justified, to avenge the honour of his daughter. Frankly, Mr Skinner, Barley could be a beast of a man; latterly, he was insane. I was married to the man for twenty-one bloody years, so I should know. His counsel, Mr Nelson, wanted to offer that as a defence, but he wouldn't hear of it. He refused to see a psychiatrist; in fact, he became violent at the very suggestion. There's irony for you. Understandable, though, is it not? Do you have a daughter, Mr Skinner?' she asked suddenly.

'I have three. One of less than a year old, another's at primary school, and the third is in her thirties.'

'If anybody harmed one of them, what would you do?'

A long time ago, that had happened with Alex; it didn't end happily for the person who did it, but I wasn't about to tell her that. 'I'd report it to the police, not because I have a conventional view of justice, but because while killing the guy would satisfy me, it would have a catastrophic effect on the rest of my family.'

'Barley didn't have such an analytical mind, or a great deal of self-control. He did try the conventional methods – he complained to the police, he complained to Ampersand's bishop – but without Briony's co-operation, there was nothing that could be done. He never gave up his obsession. A few years later, it simply overwhelmed him. I believe that he took the law into his own hands because in his mind he had the right.'

'Do you believe he was right about Ampersand? That he had taken advantage of your daughter? I'm sorry,' I added, maintaining my apparent ignorance of the detail of the case. 'I don't mean to overstep the mark.'

'That's all right. Barley believed that Matthew Ampersand was a wicked man, and that he preyed on the young. But Briony never backed that up; she never would confirm his allegation. Maybe she was afraid of the consequences. Even now, I can't rule that out completely. But to be frank, I myself have no view.'

'Was Briony a witness at the trial?' Again I knew the answer but didn't want to appear too well informed.

'No, she was never called. The prosecution decided it didn't need to establish motive.'

'It doesn't have to,' I agreed. 'The court isn't interested primarily in why the accused did something. All it asks is that the Crown proves beyond a reasonable doubt that they did it. It doesn't even have to prove that he or she was mentally competent at the time; it's down to defence counsel to prove that they weren't. If Mr Meads refused to be interviewed by a psychiatrist, there was no chance of that. I doubt his QC could have made it stick anyway. From what you've told me, your husband might have been a psychopath, but in crude terms that would mean that he knew the difference between right and wrong, just didn't give a toss. As for not calling Briony, if the forensic and circumstantial evidence was strong enough, it would have been foolish to put her in the witness box.'

'Yes,' she agreed, 'that's what we were told at the time. I offered to give evidence, but I'd already told the police that Barley often went out at night to check on stock, and that on oath I couldn't say for certain that he hadn't done so that night. I wasn't going to say anything at all to the police, but the man who interviewed me, he was very tricky.'

'It's a long time ago, but do you remember the names of the detectives who questioned you?'

'As if it was yesterday. There were two of them. The older one was called Stein. I saw a lot of him, all through the trial. The younger one, the sergeant, he was a Partridge. I recall thinking that we shot those on the farm; that's why it stuck.'

'Do you know what you're telling me, Mrs Meads?' I didn't give her a chance to answer. 'You're saying that Barley had no defence, even though there were no eyewitnesses against him. Nobody saw him, anywhere, on the night that Ampersand was killed. Even the old lady who identified his truck, she didn't actually see him, only the vehicle, which was the only one of its type in Scotland at that time. All the physical evidence was forensic, backed up by the well-established grudge he had against the victim. But there was nothing to counter it. The verdict was nailed on. I tell you, if all my cases had been that simple, I'd have fewer grey hairs now.'

'You seem to know a lot about the trial, Mr Skinner,' she observed.

She had me there; I had slipped up and she'd seen through me. 'Okay,' I confessed, back-pedalling, 'I did some homework before I came here.'

'Then I wish you'd been around thirty years ago. Barley might have had a chance with an objective detective on the case; someone who was prepared to look for an alternative solution.'

'So you do believe he might have been innocent?'

'No, that's not what I'm saying.' She sighed. 'I don't believe there was such an alternative. Nobody tried to find one, that's my point. However reluctantly, I've always accepted that Barley was guilty, because I knew him better than anyone else. I wouldn't have minded if there had been sufficient doubt for him to have been acquitted. That's all I'm saying.'

As she spoke, there was a loud crunching of gravel. I looked round and saw a Volkswagen Touareg pull to the side of the house. 'Briony and Michael,' Carmel Meads said as a couple emerged, the woman descending from the driver's seat. 'He's lost his licence, silly bugger,' she volunteered. 'Fortunately he can still drive our vehicles on the farm, or I might have had to come out of retirement and do it myself.'

'You were a working farmer yourself?'

'Oh yes,' she said. 'And with a degree to back it up.'

The couple looked across at the porch, and at us. Briony began unloading supermarket bags from the back of the vehicle, but her husband came towards us, glancing at my car as he did so. He was of medium height, with fair hair, dressed out of season in a Hibernian FC T-shirt and shorts, which displayed the thickness of his brown, weather-beaten arms and legs.

'Who's this, Carmel?' he asked as he arrived, with only the briefest of glances in my direction. 'Not the Waitrose man, that's for sure; supermarket buyers don't drive cars like that.'

'Manners, Michael,' she chided him. 'This is Mr Skinner. He used to be our chief constable. Now he's something in the media.'

'I don't care if he used to be a field fucking marshal,' Michael retorted, unfazed by the correction. 'What's he doing here unannounced?'

His mother-in-law tutted disapproval. 'He has his media hat on,' she replied. 'It seems that a journalist has developed an interest in Briony's dad's case, and he came . . . to alert us, I suppose. Isn't that right, Mr Skinner?'

'I suppose it is,' I said; my pretext for being there felt flimsier than before. 'Obviously, Mr Lennon, if the matter is reopened we'll have an interest in it, but I don't want our journalists wasting time chasing something that isn't there.'

'Well there isn't anything,' he snapped, 'so your journalists and anyone else can fuck right off.' I had stood as he joined us; now he stepped up to me, putting himself in my face, or as close as he could get to it, being five or six inches shorter than me. 'You hear that?' he hissed, staring up at me, eyes wide open.

'You're making yourself clear,' I murmured. 'Now step back just a little, please.'

'Not me, pal. You can fuck off as well!' He grabbed my forearm and pulled, digging his thick fingers viciously into my jacket and the flesh below.

'Michael!' Carmel Meads cried out. 'Stop it!'

I'll never know whether he would have obeyed, for as she spoke, I took half a step back and jerked myself free from his grasp. Released, I reached across while he was still unbalanced and seized his right wrist, twisting it quickly, spinning him round and forcing his arm upwards and behind him, crooking my left elbow under his chin at the same time, raising him up on his toes, rendering him helpless.

'This will end one of two ways,' I whispered into his ear as he strained, hopelessly, against me. 'Either you will regain your self-control and your manners, or I will dislocate your shoulder. It's your choice, but I know which I would enjoy more.'

'Okay, okay, okay,' he cried out. 'You win.'

I gave his arm one last jerk, to make sure he believed me, then let him go. 'It was hardly a contest,' I told him, 'but never lay hands on me again. I hate to break this to you, but I've dealt with many tough guys in my time, and you are not one of those, Mr Lennon, not even close.'

I pushed him away, then turned to his mother-in-law. 'I'm sorry about that, Mrs Meads.' I flipped a card from my breast pocket and handed it to her. 'If the man Brass, or anyone else, does contact you, please do the *Saltire* a favour and give me a call.'

As she took it from me, I was sure I saw a smile in her eyes.

Nineteen

I dwelled on my confrontation with the unpleasant Michael Lennon all the way back into Edinburgh. Even in my office, as I brewed myself some fine Colombian coffee from Steampunk in North Berwick, I still hadn't forgotten the aggressive little bastard.

His mother-in-law's barely hidden pleasure at seeing him put in his place stayed with me too. I wondered about Briony, and about the nature of that relationship. It occurred to me that life had handed her the shitty end of the stick when it came to men.

However, the exchange had been no more than a postscript to my visit to Easterlee Farm, and my conversation with the formidable Carmel Meads. Having spoken to her, and heard her account of the murder and its aftermath, I could see no way forward in my review. Alf's investigation had been perfunctory, but it had produced all the evidence needed to convict Barley. I'd have wanted more, I told myself, but if I'd been under the sort of pressure he'd been under, from his boss, Chief Constable Sir George Hume, and through him from the media, I'd probably have cut and run too, without digging any deeper. As Carmel had admitted, even though she'd have liked to see him better represented, she had been as convinced of her husband's guilt as everyone else.

If that was as far as I could get, with the co-operation of the police and the parties involved, then I was sure that Brass's threat to Jimmy had been ill-informed and possibly even malicious. His only connection with the business had been in approving the rejection of Barley's original complaint against Ampersand. If the blogger was suggesting that act had led ultimately to the venal vicar's murder, he was stretching the point to the edge of imagination and beyond. I was keen to tell him as much, so I called his mobile again, only to hear the same snippy message, which by that time was getting seriously on my tits. I snarled into his voicemail and hung up.

Finally, I did what I hate to do: I accepted my own shortcomings, if such they were, and moved to pack up the case records – after one last look through all the witness statements, and a final check that John Ampersand's affidavit from America hadn't been there all the time, clipped to another document by mistake. It hadn't.

Carmel Meads's statement was there, though, the one that had pretty much nailed Barley, the one in which she had admitted that she couldn't alibi him for the night of the killing; it was neat and complete, signed by Alf Stein, and with the initials 'TP' below.

I was filling the box when my mobile sounded on my desk. I picked it up and saw a number that I recognised but couldn't place, not until I was sliding the symbol to accept the call. It was my one-time HQ, the hub of what had been my domain but which had become just another outstation of the unloved national police service.

'Yes,' I said, expecting to hear Sammy Pye or Sauce Haddock

in return, but when the caller's voice sounded, it was female.

'Mr Skinner?'

'Yes, you've got me.'

'This is Noele McClair, detective sergeant. Remember me? We met at your daughter's birthday party.'

'Of course I remember you, Noele,' I replied. 'What can I do for you?'

'Nothing,' she said. 'It's just that something's come up that I thought you might be interested to hear, informally.'

'Try me.'

'Remember the man we talked about at Seonaid's party? Austin Brass, the man Terry and I love to hate?'

'You and a few others,' I muttered. 'But go on.'

'He's just been reported missing, by his father. The report was made through the one zero one number, but it was flagged up to CID offices because of who he is.'

'When was he last seen?' I asked.

'He visited his dad on Saturday. That's the last the old man heard of him.'

'Where does he live?'

'Mid Calder. He keeps a small office unit in the Almondvale Centre in Livingston. Uniform checked both locations. He hasn't been seen at either since the weekend.'

'What are you doing about it?'

'Us? As in this office? Nothing; it's not our shout.'

'Mmm,' I murmured as I thought about the situation. 'Do you know if uniform tried his phone?'

'There's nothing about that on the report. Where would they get the number?'

'Off his website,' I told her. 'Is Sammy there? DCI Pye?'

'No, but the DI is. Do you want to speak to him?'

'Yes please, Noele,' I said, 'but you'd better tell him why you called me, before he asks.'

'Yes, I will do. Hold on, sir.'

I've been gone for a couple of years, but I still find it difficult to shake the 'sir', even from officers who never worked with me. I waited for more than a minute, until a familiar voice came on the line.

'Sir!' Detective Inspector Harold 'Sauce' Haddock exclaimed.

'Fuck's sake, Sauce,' I moaned. 'It's Bob, okay.'

'No, sir, it can't be,' he replied, 'and it never will unless we're facing each other with a beer in our hand. Noele said you wanted a word.'

'A quick one,' I confirmed. 'This Austin Brass shout she told me about; you know who he is?'

'*What* he is,' Sauce said. 'I'd heard the name, but to be honest I'm not a big reader of stuff like that. Noele filled me in, though. Nasty bastard, she says.'

'By all accounts,' I agreed. 'But that doesn't mean that he's a mere troublemaker. If you look at his blog, you'll see it carries plenty of advertising; it takes a decent readership to generate that. If you dig a little deeper, you'll also find that he's never been successfully sued, or even interdicted by someone seeking to stop publication. If he's on a story, it would be foolish not to take it seriously.'

In the silence that followed, I could picture Sauce thinking, and was ready for what came next. 'Are you suggesting, sir, that we should treat this as more than just a missing person?'

'I'm suggesting that you might want to go a bit further than uniform did. For a start, call his mobile and see what you get. Who knows, he might even answer and that'll be an end of it.

If not, and it goes to voicemail, you'll be able to pin down its location.'

'Thanks, sir,' he said. 'We'll do that. If we get anything out of it,' he added, 'I might come back and ask you to answer the question I'm putting off for now. How come you brought up Brass's name, out of the blue, with DS McClair? I wouldn't normally expect the likes of him to be under discussion at a child's birthday party.'

Twenty

In his relatively young career, Sauce Haddock had worked with quite a few top detectives, among them Maggie Rose Steele, who takes credit for being the first to spot his talent; Sammy Pye, known to his colleagues behind his back as Luke Skywalker; and the late great Stevie Steele, who died in action. Sauce had never been under my direct command, but I like to think that principles and techniques filter down. Of all the cops I know, he is the one who reminds me most of me, although Neil McIlhenney runs him a close second.

I hadn't been trying to play him when we spoke; just as well, for his throwaway remark at the end was a clear reminder that he wasn't to be taken for granted, not even by me, 'sir' or no 'sir'.

I was still thinking about him, wondering what he would find when he pinged Brass's phone, as I knew he would, while I finished packing away the Matthew Ampersand case papers. At the same time I was considering anew what I had said to him. No successful legal action had ever been taken against Brass; his stories had always been sound. I thought I had worked out his mistake in coming after Jimmy, but on reflection, I wasn't as sure as I had been.

The lid was on the archive box and I was sealing it with thick brown tape when my phone rang. I looked at the caller identification, but it showed 'unknown'. I took the call with a sharpish 'Yes?' for I'd been interrupted enough for one day, but my attitude and my tone changed when I heard Bishop Valerie Cornton's soothing voice. There was something mesmeric about the woman; if she'd been in my local pulpit every week, I might have been compelled to attend.

'Mr Skinner. Are you well?'

'I hope so,' I replied.

'Are you in Edinburgh?' she asked. 'If so, there's something I would like to show you. I don't want to discuss it over the phone, or even draw attention by meeting you in the General Synod office, so would you be free to call on me in my residence? It's in Inverleith Place, opposite the park. There's a sign on the gate.'

'I can do that,' I told her. 'Give me twenty minutes. You going to drop me a hint as to what it's about?'

'I'd rather not. You'll know soon enough.'

'That's okay; mystery is my business,' I chuckled, as I ended the call.

Postponing the return of Mario's box, I took my jacket from its hanger and headed for the lift, letting Sylvia know that I was leaving, probably for the day. The mid-afternoon traffic wasn't too bad, and I was crossing the main flow rather than joining it, so I made good time; my twenty minutes had shrunk to fifteen as I turned into Inverleith Place and cruised along, looking for the sign that Bishop Cornton had mentioned.

I had just spotted it and pulled up in front of the residence when my phone sounded yet again, its tone magnified by the car's hands-free system. 'Incoming call: Sauce', the display advised me. I pressed the 'accept' button on the steering wheel and leaned back in my seat, unfastening my seat belt with my left thumb. 'Detective Inspector Haddock,' I said loudly. 'Congrats on the promotion, by the way. I forgot to say earlier.'

'Thanks very much, sir,' he replied. 'I've got to live up to it now. This thing could be the first step to doing that; I just don't know. I called Brass's mobile, as you suggested, and it did indeed go to voicemail. Ever obedient to my master's voice, I got the techies in and called it again so they could track it down. It's in Bruges, in fucking Belgium, would you believe.'

'Belgium?' I echoed. 'What the hell's he doing in Belgium?'

'My question exactly. I don't have an answer. Do you?'

'As my youngest son would say, not a Scooby.'

'Could it be that Scotland's dried up for him,' Sauce suggested, 'and he's chasing scandal abroad? Europol, possibly?'

I considered that idea, then dismissed it, gently. 'I doubt that Scotland will ever dry up for him, son. As a general rule, the bigger a police service gets, the harder it is to ensure its integrity. Our old force was bad enough; I had a few very rotten apples there. In my brief spell in Strathclyde, I saw a couple of officers go to jail, and I dealt with a few others summarily. As for Europol, if Brass was sticking his nose in there, he'd be asking for it to be broken. However,' I said, heavily, 'keep this in mind. All that your clever techies have proved is that his phone's in Belgium. They haven't proved that it's in his pocket. Nor will anyone until he answers it or until you find it, physically.'

'How are we going to do that? He's not wanted for any offence. We can't ask the Belgians to pick him up.'

'No, you can't. All you can do is keep an eye on what you assume to be him. Keep pinging him and see if he moves again. If he does, try to pin him down to a precise location.'

'I'll do that, sir,' young Haddock agreed. 'Now, about that question I didn't push you on earlier. Your interest in Brass: what's it about?'

Fortunately I'd had time to consider my answer. 'At the moment,' I told him, 'it's private and personal. If and when it becomes a matter for you, Detective Inspector Haddock, you will be among the first to know.'

'Not the very first?'

I laughed. 'You're not the head of CID yet, lad.'

Twenty-One

Valerie Cornton looked less like a bishop than anyone I'd ever seen as she opened the door of her residence. I'm tempted to say that the primus was hot stuff; that would be an exaggeration, but not by much. She was fresh-faced, pretty, with thick red hair that hung down to her shoulders, five to ten years older than Sarah but certainly still in her forties, and she wore a black T-shirt with Satan's face emblazoned above a caption that read 'God is busy. Can I help?'

I looked at her for a few seconds, then realised I'd been reading her chest. 'Valerie?' I ventured.

'No, I'm Gladys, the chalet maid,' she replied. 'It's the bishop's day off.' She stayed in deadpan mode for a couple of seconds, then laughed. 'Yes, it's me. I'm sorry, Mr Skinner. I should have warned you I'd be in civvies. Come in.'

I was certain that I'd seen her before. It took me a few seconds to pin it down to an interview on STV news following her installation six months earlier. She'd looked very different then; not in full regalia, but wearing a dog collar and with her hair severely restrained.

'It must help you to avoid being recognised in the news-agent's,' I observed as she walked me through an oak-panelled hall to a room at the back that I took to be her study.

'I don't go there very often,' she replied. 'I have someone who does it for me.'

'A curate?' I suggested.

'A husband, name of Justin, although sometimes he delegates to George, our older son.'

'Is your husband in the Church too?'

'Hell, no!' Her chuckle was deep and throaty. 'He's an agnostic at best, but he isn't usually so open-minded. He's a heart surgeon; he doesn't believe in anything beyond the corporeal state. I've given up hope of trying to persuade him.'

'You shouldn't,' I insisted. 'My wife's a pathologist and she does believe there's more.'

'And you?'

'The afterlife troubles me,' I admitted, 'when I contemplate it. Whatever else, I don't believe in the concept of hell, which means that every bad bastard I've ever put away might be waiting for me on the other side.'

She winced, theatrically. 'Don't say that. You might put me off.'

'I wonder how Barley Meads and Matthew Ampersand are hitting it off,' I said as she offered me a chair close to her desk and took the black swivel beside it. The furniture was IKEA; it looked completely out of place in its traditional surroundings. 'If there was a hell, would Meads be in it?'

'I'm not sure,' she confessed. 'My Roman brethren would probably say so, but I might be able to make a case for him: I might plead extenuating circumstances on his behalf. What do you think?'

'Your plea might succeed, if it focused on his mental health. My research makes me suspect that the guy was bat-shit crazy, but he wouldn't even consider that as a defence.'

'And the Reverend Ampersand? What about him, if Mr Meads's claim had been justified?'

'What would guarantee a ticket to the underworld? If I believed in it, I know many people who are there for sure, and others who will be, but it's not cut and dried. Years ago, I put a man away for murder. His name is Lenny Plenderleith, and there was no doubt about his guilt in all but one of the killings he was jailed for; that one he denies, and if Lenny says he didn't do it, I'll believe him without question. He found himself in jail, and he's worked ever since to redeem himself; as for the people he killed, they belong on Beelzebub's bus more than he does.'

'But he denied them the chance to redeem themselves,' Valerie pointed out.

'True,' I conceded. 'As for Ampersand, if he abused his position? If a relationship had developed that wasn't forbidden by law, would that have been a form of abuse?'

'In a vicar's case, the Church would probably say so, if, as Meads insisted, the relationship developed on its premises.'

'If the relationship matured, would the Church be that unforgiving?'

'On a one-off basis, I might be inclined to forgive, as primus. In the face of denials by both parties,' she added, 'as was the case with Ampersand and the Meads girl, I wouldn't have a choice. I might have a word with the vicar involved about the need to avoid exposing himself to such a charge, but that would be that. Like you, I've reviewed the Meads complaint and I find that's all I could have done, initially.' She paused. 'However, in looking at Matthew's career file, I came upon something else.'

She took a folder from her desk and handed it to me. Two markers, the top one red, the lower yellow, protruded from the top; I opened it at the first page and read. It was a summary on General Synod headed paper of the complaint by Barley Meads against Matthew Ampersand, with summarised versions of the statements by everyone involved. It ended with a note of the findings of the inquiry, which had been conducted by the bishop of the day and two other clerics. Their unanimous view was that the complaint had no substance and was rejected, that decision to be conveyed to the complainer by the Church's legal adviser. It told me nothing I didn't know already.

I turned to the pages marked in yellow – and stepped on to entirely new ground. They were headed, 'Complaint of misconduct against the Rev. Matthew Ampersand, by Mrs G. Meikle, on behalf of her daughter Miss J. Meikle.'

That got my attention. I was aware that the primus was watching me, and I nodded to her as I focused on the report. It told me that in the winter of the year in which Ampersand died – only a couple of weeks before, in fact – he had been accused of 'fondling', specifically, touching the inner thigh of an eighteen-year-old chorister in his church, Joanna Meikle. Again, an investigation had been carried out by a three-person panel, chaired by the bishop as before, but with two different vicars involved. The mother had not been a witness to the incident, but the young woman had mentioned it to her, she told the trio, in the light of the earlier complaint by Barley Meads. The girl had not felt threatened by Ampersand, and no inappropriate language had been used, but her mother had insisted that it should be reported.

Again the vicar had been interviewed; he had admitted that there may have been contact in the way that Joanna had described, but insisted that it had been accidental and very brief. Once again the complaint had been rejected; the same letter by the same solicitor, framed in uncompromising legal language: 'The Synod's learned panel finds no evidence to support your claim and rejects it entirely. Any repetition, or any attempt to question the character of the Reverend Ampersand, will be viewed most seriously and action may be taken.'

I read that paragraph aloud. 'That's a bit over the top, isn't it?' I suggested.

'I'd say so,' Valerie agreed. 'The first sentence would have been enough, without the threat. If you read to the very end of the report, it does note that Matthew was ordered never to be alone again with any of his younger flock, of either gender. The suggestion was that mud sticks, and that if another complaint was received, it would not be defended.'

'How did the mother take it?'

'Take another look at the folder,' she said.

I did. A single item followed the report; it was a letter from Joanna's mother to the bishop, short and to the point.

Dear Sir,

I have received notice of your disposal of my complaint from your solicitors, with an undisguised threat which I take as an attempt to frighten me into silence. I have to tell you that this will not work. I have other means of putting a stop to this man's unpleasant activities, and I intend to use them.

Yours truly,

G. Meikle, Mrs

Again I felt a niggle; something I was missing. Again I

couldn't nail it down, so I let it pass. 'Is that it?' I asked the primus. I held up the folder. 'Is there any hint in here of what those other means might have been?'

'No, there isn't, but look at the dates on the two letters. December the tenth, and December the twelfth. A week or so later, Matthew Ampersand was dead.' Her eyes lit up with excitement. 'Maybe the other means she spoke about was a hit man.'

Her enthusiasm was fetching and I didn't want to curb it, but I had to. 'This is a middle-aged churchgoing woman,' I reminded her. 'In my experience, which is pretty extensive, people like her don't have easy access to contract killers. It's very interesting, though,' I added, 'and thanks for sharing. I don't know what I can do, but I'll think about it.'

'You could start by talking to Joanna Meikle,' Valerie said. 'She's a worshipper at my church these days. I recognised the name at once; before I got in touch with you, I called her to ask if she was the person at the centre of the complaint. She said she was – then she added that she's spent thirty years trying to forget it.'

'What a shame,' I said. 'Too bad you don't always get what you want.'

Twenty-Two

I left the residence with Joanna Meikle's address and phone number tucked away in my pocket, courtesy of Bishop Cornton. In fact, I took more than that with me; having met the primus informally, I had decided that I'd like to see her at work, and planned to sneak into her congregation at the first opportunity. There was a refreshing practicality about her that I hadn't encountered before in a cleric; it led me to surmise that whatever her relationship with God might be, it wasn't servant and master.

The afternoon was wearing out; rather than fight my way back to Fountainbridge, I decided that Mario's box could stay where it was and be returned next time I was in the office. I was home before Sarah; Seonaid and the boys were amusing themselves, and Trish, our long-serving carer, was taking care of Dawn, who was still teething and fractious. In the lull, I went into the small office near the front door that my wife and I both use when we need some privacy, picked up my landline phone and called the number that Valerie had given me. It was still early evening and so I expected to hit an answering machine at best, but Joanna Meikle surprised me by being home.

'Miss Meikle,' I began as she took the call.

'Ms,' she corrected me. I sensed a chill in her voice. 'Would that be Mr Skinner?' she asked, and my sense became a certainty.

'It would. You were expecting my call?'

'Not only that, I was fearing it,' the angry woman countered. 'Bishop Cornton phoned me, in what she described as a fit of remorse, after giving you my contact details. She said that you're digging into a period of my life that I'd prefer stayed undisturbed.'

'It wasn't me who put the spade in the ground first, Ms Meikle. A friend asked me to get involved.'

'And you couldn't resist?' she challenged.

'I could have, but I chose not to. Look, I have no wish to upset you; if you don't want to talk about the Ampersand incident, I'll respect that and hang up right now.'

She sighed, a little less frostily. 'I'll talk to you,' she said. 'I know who you are, Mr Skinner; in fact I've heard lots about you. I'm sure you'll keep on digging, with or without my co-operation. I won't speak over the phone, though; I like to look my subjects in the eye. I can see you at ten tomorrow morning, but you'll need to be gone by eleven.'

She hung up, leaving me wondering what the hell she had meant by 'subjects'.

I stepped out of the office just as Sarah was coming in; we almost collided in the hall. I kissed her. She looked more than a little frazzled; she was full of tension and she was shaking. 'Tough day?' I asked.

'The worst,' she replied grimly, her eyes glistening. 'Three teenagers, two boys and a girl, in Daddy's car on the bypass. They were late for school; they're late for everything now. The driver was seventeen and passed his test yesterday. His father celebrated by letting him drive his souped-up sports saloon to school; all legal and allowed by the insurance. Haven't you heard about it? It was top of the midday news cycle.'

'Sorry, I hadn't,' I said. 'It passed me by.'

'Something needs to be done, Bob. We need to extend accountability.'

'What do you mean?' I eased her out of her coat and hung it on a hook by the door.

'I mean the Crown should be able to prosecute Daddy,' she exclaimed angrily. 'The boy lost control doing around ninety according to witnesses, hit three other vehicles, rolled over the central fence and wound up under a sixteen-wheel truck going in the other direction. I attended the scene, and I had a team of six junior pathologists working on the bodies; they were in bits, literally. Something needs to be done,' she repeated. 'People should know about it.'

I held her to me. 'So tell them,' I said.

'How can I do that?'

I tapped her head lightly with my knuckles. 'Earth to Sarah. You're married to a director of a media group. I can get you access.'

'I wish I could, but my contract has a confidentiality clause in it.'

'In that case, I'll do it,' I declared, to my own surprise as much as hers. 'I've still got a name, and there are absolutely no contractual handcuffs on me. Are you up for that?'

Her eyes narrowed. 'Too damn right; no specific autopsy details, but otherwise go for it.'

I went back into the office and called June Crampsey. 'How's the world?' I asked her.

'Quiet,' she replied.

'What have we done with the bypass fatality?'

'We ran it big online, but so did everyone. I'm looking at something else for a print edition lead; possibly more Brexit shit.'

'Okay,' I said. 'Put me on speaker, switch on your recorder and try this for size.' I waited until she had done so, then began. 'Tonight in Edinburgh there's a grieving father. He knows what he did, and his conscience will carry the burden for the rest of his life. But is that enough? In my career, my officers attended the aftermath of countless tragedies like today's on the bypass; countless, yet one is one too many when it's preventable. Ask the cops, ask the pathologists, ask the undertakers, ask everyone involved in the clean-up. Don't bother asking the doctors; they're not needed when the victim's head is on one carriageway and the body is on another.'

I paused, considering what I would say next. When I knew, I continued. 'This evening my wife came home from work in tears. I'm sure that several of her colleagues did the same. It's never happened before, and I never want it to happen again.' I stopped short of blaming the father directly for Sarah's tears, but not by much. Instead I laid the blame on the system and demanded a change in the law to extend liability to the owners of vehicles. I spoke for ten minutes. When I was done, the line was silent; for a moment I thought it had all been in vain, that I had been cut off or June had hung up. It wasn't until she spoke that I realised she had been composing herself.

'You realise I'll have to run that past the lawyers?' she asked gently.

'Christ, I hope you do,' I chuckled, breaking the tension. 'I wasn't exactly in control there.'

'It'll be cleared, I'm sure. I'll run it under my own byline, to put my authority behind it. Also, can I use your knighthood in your quote?'

'What knighthood?' I muttered.

'The one you don't talk about. I'm the editor; I know everything, remember? I'm also very close to your daughter,' she added, although I had worked out her source by that time. 'It'll help. "Sir Robert" carries more gravitas than plain "Bob". You can't stay Mr Skinner for ever.'

'Okay,' I agreed grudgingly, 'but you can tell Sarah you've outed her as a lady.'

Lady Skinner was in the garden room when I emerged, sipping something that looked suspiciously like a mojito. 'I take it you're not on call tonight,' I said.

'Neither are you,' she replied, pointing towards another of the same that stood on a side table. 'Now tell me about your day,' she ordered. 'I hope it was less traumatic than mine.'

I picked up the minty concoction and sat beside her. 'Varied and eventful,' I told her. 'Met with a murderer's widow, had a confrontation with her surly son-in-law, tracked Austin Brass down to Bruges—'

'Bruges?'

'It's in fucking Belgium. Then I had a private meeting with a very atypical lady bishop.'

'Valerie Cornton?'

'That's the one. You know her?'

She shook her head. 'No, but I heard her speak at a leading ladies lunch that one of the big accountancy firms put together. She's very impressive. You saying she invited you into her boudoir?'

'No, just her palace. She has some new information on Matthew Ampersand that she decided to share.'

'For or against?'

'Somewhere in the middle, from what I read, but I'll know better tomorrow. I'm meeting the party involved.'

'Lady or gentleman?'

'The former. There's no suggestion that Matthew was a switch-hitter.'

She laughed; that pleased me, but I knew it would take more than that to get her over her day.

I was about to offer to make supper for the family when my bloody mobile sounded again. At New Year I made a resolution to switch it off at five o'clock every evening. That lasted three days.

I checked the screen, ready to reject the call, but it was from Sauce, so I relented.

'Yes, Inspector?'

'I thought you'd like to know, sir. Brass is on the move; they pinged him again ten minutes ago. He's on the motorway; seems to be heading for Holland.'

Twenty-Three

I was five minutes early for my meeting with Joanna Meikle; my concern was that if I was at all late, she might revert to angry mode and use it as an excuse to cancel. I needn't have worried; when I pressed the button on the video entry system to her Palmerston Crescent building, she answered at once.

'Come up,' she said briskly. 'Top floor; you're better walking. It's a bit of a hike up the stairs, but it's quicker than the Victorian lift.' I took her advice and was beginning to regret it when I reached the fourth storey. The stair was carpeted, which made it even tougher on the legs. As I climbed, I wondered how often Ms Meikle took her own advice.

When she opened the front door, I realised that she did. She was a lanky woman who wore her late forties well; slim in a blue denim shirt, tucked into tight-fitting plum-coloured trousers that emphasised the strength in her legs. The shirt was smeared with paint and half of a brush protruded at an angle from a pocket just above her left breast.

She read my surprise, and smiled. 'Obviously the bishop didn't tell you. I'm an artist – a portrait painter mostly. We'll talk in my studio; it's in the attic.'

The apartment was a duplex. As I followed her on to the

upper level, I saw that it was mostly open-plan, with only two doors in the far wall. It was bright, illuminated by four modern skylight windows, two on either side of the high roof. Looking around, I counted three easels, each supporting a board. At least one was a work in progress; I peered at the face that was taking shape on it, wondering if it would become someone I recognised.

There was something familiar about Joanna Meikle too. I was sure I had never met her before, but another of those annoying bells rang in my head. 'Stand there,' she ordered, pointing at a spot beneath one of the windows, through which strong sunlight shone. 'You've got a face that I must paint. If I'm going to talk to you, this is the price. Look at the wall behind me and don't move.'

'I didn't realise I'd commissioned you,' I said.

'You haven't, not yet, but if you like what I've done by the time you leave, you never know. I doubt that you've met many artists in your line of work.'

'You'd be surprised,' I chuckled. 'Quite recently I encountered one; name of Augusta.'

Her eyebrows rose. '*The* Augusta? The one who does crowd scenes and makes a fortune from print sales?'

'That's the one.'

'Well now,' she exclaimed as she took up her position behind one of the easels and picked up her palette. 'She is big-time; far bigger than me, I'm afraid.'

'Don't be afraid,' I countered. 'Be ambitious. I imagine that's how she got where she is.'

She smiled again, relaxed as she went to work. I took advantage of her mood to get straight to the point. 'What happened with Matthew Ampersand?' I asked.

She glanced across at me from the board that would soon display my image. 'With the benefit of hindsight,' she replied, 'not very much. Not as much as my mother made of it; that I realise now.'

'At the time?'

'At the time, I was swept along with it by my mother. She kicked up the fuss, not me. Even at eighteen, I'd have put it down to experience and kept a few feet between me and him from then on, but with the whole Briony thing having happened, she went wild. I should never have told her, but once she had made the complaint, I felt, I'm afraid, that I had no choice but to back her up.'

'Was there a Briony thing?' I asked.

'Her father said there was and that was an end of it; you didn't argue with Mr Meads. He was a very scary person. Even now, I shudder at the mention of him. There was only one person in the world who had his measure, and that was Mrs Meads. She had him by the nuts.'

'What did Briony say about it?'

'Nothing, ever. She didn't talk to me about it at the time, even though we were best friends, and she never has since then.'

'You're still close?'

'Not as much as we used to be, but yes, we're still pals. I'm godmother to her daughter, Florence, and I take that seriously. Florence is the heir apparent, you know, not her mother. Briony doesn't know the difference between a bull and a cockerel, but Florence does. She's doing a farming degree in Ayr, then she plans to do a business management course. When old Carmel finally hands over the reins, it'll be to her, and not to her mother or her father.'

'So tell me about it, what did happen? If it wasn't very much, why were you so defensive when I called you yesterday?'

Joanna leaned away from the easel and looked at me directly. 'Because I've felt guilty about it ever since. When it happened, my mother went running to the Church. After they set up their lightning tribunal and exonerated him, she was incandescent; it all just exploded. Days later, Matthew was dead and Barley was in jail for killing him.'

'How did Briony react?'

'I didn't see her. She was at university in Dundee, in the first year of her social sciences degree. I had started at Edinburgh College of Art. Accidentally or otherwise, we just didn't see each other while it was all happening. Afterwards, it was a subject to be avoided. Briony never said she was relieved her father was in jail, but I think she was. He never forgave her for not backing up his allegation against Matthew. He refused to support her at university, until her mother put her foot down. Horrible creature, especially when he was drunk, which was pretty much every night.'

She went back to work. 'Keep looking at the wall,' she instructed. I did, realising that it helped her avoid making eye contact. 'Matthew and me,' she continued quietly. 'He was a charming man, and he certainly liked the ladies. He was a good-looking guy too, no kidding; we girls thought he was a dead ringer for Tom Wopat. He was the older guy in *The Dukes of Hazzard*, remember. He was a touchy-feely bloke, I must admit, hands round shoulders, patting arms, that sort of thing, but honestly I never felt threatened by him, not even after the Briony accusation. The man was thirty years older than me, but he was still Bo Duke's older brother in my eyes. I do remember thinking he'd be more likely to fancy my mother than me.'

'Was he a nice man?' I asked, keeping my gaze straight ahead.

'Yes, but distant. I remember his smile; it was strange, as if he was looking at a picture nobody else could see.'

'What do you believe? Was he a predator?'

She frowned at me over her easel. 'Honestly, I can't be sure. What happened was I'd been in church practising my solo for the performance of Handel's *Messiah* we were doing at Christmas. The choir stalls were tiered; I was on the top one, he was at floor level. He'd been saying how well I'd sung, that I could do it professionally, and that if I wanted to he knew some people who might engage me. As I started down the steps, he reached out and touched my arm. I was startled; I tripped and fell, awkwardly. He went to catch me and somehow his hand wound up grabbing the inside of my thigh, close enough for me to feel it very close to my pubes. He didn't grope me, you understand; I had no thought of penetration or even attempted penetration, but I was shocked and I did scream.' Out of the corner of my eye, I realised that her cheeks were flushed. 'Thing is, I wasn't wearing any knickers, only tights. I was living the college life and I'd run out.'

'How did he react?'

'He released me at once, and apologised profusely. He said that he hadn't meant to frighten or alarm me, that he had been afraid I was going to fall and hit my head on one of the stalls.'

'Did you believe him?'

She stopped painting once again. 'I didn't know whether to believe him then and I don't know now; that's a fact. It's what I told the Church inquiry. He could have been telling the truth, he could have been lying, or he could even have been in complete denial about what he had done.'

'How long did the investigation take to convene?'

'Two days. The incident happened on Sunday, I saw the panel on the following Wednesday, and on the Friday my mother received a letter saying he was exonerated. He was back in the pulpit the very next weekend, although the congregation was noticeably smaller than usual, my mother having put the word about. A couple of days after that, he was dead. So I never saw him again to ask him whether he had meant it or not.' She looked at me. 'Eyes front,' she said sharply.

'During the police investigation, Meads maintained that the Briony complaint had been justified.' I recalled something from the case file. 'It was even said that their relationship had developed and that he had visited her in Dundee. Did she ever give you any hint of that?'

'Never, and I think she would have. We were fairly frank with each other about our sex lives. We still are when we see each other,' she chuckled. 'From what she says, hers is pretty boring – which doesn't surprise me at all, knowing Michael. That man thinks foreplay's a card game. Now, will you tell me something?' she asked, without breaking her concentration on the easel. 'Why is all of this being brought up now?'

'Because somebody is suggesting that Barley didn't do it.'

'He bloody did!' she retorted. 'There was never any doubt. Carmel told my mum and my mum told me. Carmel never told the police, but she saw him leave in the truck.'

'Did your mum tell you that too?'

'She did.'

'Could I speak to your mother about it?'

'Not without a medium,' Joanna replied. 'She died seven years ago, from a massive stroke.'

She had told me all she could and I had used up all my

questions, so we fell silent as she worked on my likeness. At five minutes to eleven, she stopped.

'Okay,' she called out. 'Come and have a look at how I see you.'

It was graphic, it was older than the guy who lives inside this body thought he looked, but it was savagely impressive. I knew at once that it couldn't hang anywhere but in my house. We reached a financial agreement, without haggling on either part.

I turned to leave. As I did so, I noticed a framed certificate on the wall. I took a closer look. It bore the crest of the Royal Scottish Society of Painters in Watercolours. 'You do water-colours too?' I asked idly.

'No,' she replied. 'That's my mother's. She was a painter too, of a different sort.'

I read the name, Grayling Meikle, and the vague hint of a resemblance I had felt earlier solidified, and as it did, part of my life began to fall apart. Grayling: my friend Jimmy, whose cause I was fighting, had two sisters, the ill-fated younger one, Peggy, who had married Alf Stein, and one older. The latter had been widowed in nineteen eighty, when her husband had died in an accident on board an oil production platform on the North Sea. I knew this because his brother-in-law had told me.

'You're Jimmy Proud's niece?' I exclaimed.

'Of course,' Joanna Meikle replied. 'Didn't you know?'

Twenty-Four

Rather than face the inevitable time-consuming search for a non-resident parking space, I had walked from my office to Joanna Meikle's studio. From start to finish it was no more than a mile, as the fly crows (as James Andrew is fond of saying) and it had taken me a brisk fifteen minutes. The journey back took much longer, partly because I was walking more slowly, as the implications of the artist's revelation took shape in my head.

I had decided that I wasn't going to search for Jimmy. Whatever the reason for his vanishing act, I had intended to respect it. I was very close to reversing that decision as I walked along Grosvenor Street. 'Bugger it,' I muttered in my frustration, stopping in my tracks and walking into the Hilton Hotel in search of coffee to head off the pangs of withdrawal.

The waiter was an old-timer, so he brought me a large cafetière. He recognised me from the days when the Hilton, or whatever it had been at the time, had been the unofficial local for the Torphichen Place nick and the officers who were stationed there. The very thought of that place brought back memories; it was where Stevie Steele, God bless and keep him, had been stationed, and where Sauce Haddock, all ears and enthusiasm, had caught the attention of Maggie

Rose, triggering his rapid and inexorable rise to the top.

As I savoured the coffee, which was more than acceptable, I ran through an imaginary conversation with Jimmy, when I had run him to ground.

Me, Mr Angry: 'What the fuck were you playing at?'

Jimmy, wide-eyed and innocent: 'What do you mean, Bob?'

Me: 'You know what I mean. Why didn't you tell me you had a grudge against Matthew Ampersand yourself?'

Jimmy, still acting the daft laddie: 'What grudge? I don't know what you're talking about.'

Me, going for the jugular: 'Yes you fucking do! A week before he was murdered, Ampersand was accused of assaulting your niece Joanna.'

Jimmy, defensive: 'That? I'd forgotten about that.'

Me, seizing on his slip: 'So you did know about it?'

Jimmy, caught out: 'Yes, my sister Grayling told me. But Bob, it isn't relevant.'

Me, stoked up: 'Of course it's fucking relevant! It gives you an interest in the investigation. That's what Brass's story is about and that's why he's after you.'

Jimmy, out of wiggle room: 'That's far-fetched. How would he even have known about it? The accusation never made the papers.'

Me, relentless: 'It didn't have to. As soon as he started digging it was always likely to come out.'

Jimmy, worried: 'Has he approached Joanna?'

Me, slightly thrown but recovering: 'No, he hasn't, not yet. But that's not the point, is it? You've been playing me, Jimmy, like a fucking banjo. You've been using me to find out what Brass's story is about and if he knows about your connection with the Ampersand murder.'

And that's where my imaginary conversation stopped. I wasn't angry any more, just sad. My urge to track down my old boss, my old friend, had evaporated. Playing out the confrontation in my head had been enough. There was no need to do it for real.

That said, the Joanna connection had changed everything and it had to be followed up. I found myself in a quandary. I had new information that might be relevant to a cold case. If Mario McGuire's role and mine were reversed, if I was still on the inside and he was a civvy, would I be irked if he didn't bring a fresh discovery straight to me? Too right I would. But alongside that, would I trust him enough, as an investigator, to let him carry the ball a little further? Yes, probably I would.

My decision on my next step had been reached by the time I had emptied the cafetière. One quick phone call and I was ready to take it.

I left the Hilton and carried on walking, across the Haymarket multi-junction and into Morrison Street, turning almost immediately into Torphichen Place, where the West End police office is sited. I strode into the public area of the old, familiar building. The officer behind the counter was a young woman, one of the new generation, the kind who don't have a clue who I am or what I was.

'Yes, sir?' she said, greeting me with the questioning smile that cops are taught these days to offer the public. Chief Constable Maggie Rose Steele would be proud of her, I thought.

'Inspector Montell, please. Tell him it's Mr Skinner; he's expecting me.'

I caught a flicker of recognition; on a desk behind her I saw a copy of the print edition of the *Saltire*, with me as the front-page lead, and surmised that she had been reading it in a quiet moment. 'Of course, sir,' she replied. 'One moment.' She turned, picked up a phone on the desk, hit a button and then spoke. She was still smiling as she faced me again. 'He says you're to go on up, sir. He says you'll know where he is. I'll buzz you through.'

I thanked her and walked through the double door that she had unlocked for me, into the secure area of the building, jogging up the stairs that faced me.

Inspector Griffin Montell, to give him his full name, is a South African who joined the old Edinburgh force after several years in his home nation's police service, which is as good a training ground as I know. He'd caught my attention professionally, and also because he'd lived next door to my daughter Alex. They'd been close for a while – how close, I never asked – and were still good friends. He'd made it to detective sergeant under my regime and the one that had followed, but I'd heard from Mario that when Maggie Steele became chief she had decided that he was too volatile for CID, and had returned him to uniform, on promotion, as station commander in Torphichen Place. I wouldn't have made that call, but who the hell am I any more?

He stood as I walked into his small office. 'Sir Robert,' he began, extending his hand. 'Congratulations, I didn't know.' Already I was beginning to regret the credit that I'd been hustled by June into letting her use.

'Neither did too many other people until today. It didn't happen in the usual honours list way and I asked that it wasn't announced. To tell you the truth, it embarrasses me.'

'Why?' Montell laughed. 'You earned it.'

'Did I?' I asked. 'Can such things be earned? The fact is, Griff, I turned it down twice before, because it was one of those things that came automatically with the job. When it came up again, I was going to decline again, but I didn't, for two reasons. The first one was Julius Caesar: he turned down a high honour three times, and look what happened to him. The second was the person who offered it, and the reason; it would have been churlish to refuse him, so I let him talk me into it.'

'Quite right. I know cops who've been calling you Sir Robert for years. Plus, it should get you into the directors' box at Tynecastle.'

'Fuck that for a game of soldiers,' I retorted. 'Fir Park maybe, but not if I've got something better to do; cutting my toenails, for example.'

He smiled. 'You're looking good on it anyway. How's Alex, by the way?' he asked casually.

'Busy,' I told him. 'Her career change paid off. The money isn't so good, but she has a hell of a lot more job satisfaction, especially when she gets a result: same as us, but on the other side. She's happy.'

'That's good. Is she—'

I answered before he finished. 'She's single as far as I know; if there was anyone serious, I'd hear about it before too long. She sees the chancers coming a mile off, I know that.'

'Your presence must discourage those.'

'It didn't discourage you,' I pointed out. 'But don't dwell on that,' I added quickly. 'I appreciated you looking out for her. Now,' I continued, 'you're wondering why I'm here. Short answer, I'm looking for a favour. I need someone traced. I could do it through another agency, but it would take time and someone might ask why. You, on the other hand, having had a brief acquaintance with the thing we used to call Special

Branch, know how to go about it and probably won't have to look too far.'

'I owe you plenty, sir,' he said. 'Who is it?'

'When I became head of CID,' I replied, 'I succeeded my old mentor, Alf Stein, on his retirement. Alf didn't last too long after he quit; I know exactly where to find him, in the cemetery at Seafield. However, he had a spinster sister, name of Magnolia. She was a few years older than him, which would put her into her eighties now. We met a couple of times, but the last time I saw her was at Alf's funeral, nearly ten years ago. She was going strong then. Maybe she's dead too, but I have a feeling that if she was, I'd have heard about it. She lived in a third-floor flat in Abbeyhill, but I'm guessing she might not be there any more, with all those stairs. If she is still around, though, she'll be voting somewhere and her name will be on an electoral roll. She was staunch SNP, even in the old days.'

'Magnolia?'

'As in the tree.'

He scribbled the name on a notepad. 'Can I have your mobile number?'

'Of course.' I flipped him a card.

'I'll be back to you soonest.'

'Thanks,' I said. 'You enjoying uniform?'

'More than I thought I would,' he admitted. 'I'd been long enough at the sharp end.'

'In all my years,' I told him as I left, 'I never found a blunt one.'

Twenty-Five

Montell called me back just as I was entering the *Saltire* building. 'I found her,' he announced. 'No problem at all. You were right, she's still on the electoral roll. She lives in a sheltered complex out in Corstorphine, but she must still be fairly active, for she has a car and a valid driving licence, renewed last year, on her eighty-third birthday. I'll text you her address.'

'Thanks, Griff,' I said. 'And thanks also for not asking why I needed it. If you ever feel like a move back to CID, let me know and I'll have a word in the chief constable's ear.'

'I'll bear that in mind,' he replied, 'but I doubt it would do much good. She seems to have made her mind up about me.'

'Maybe she has for now, but things can change. Chief Constable Rose is a small "c" conservative; she's risk averse. There I differ from her. I believe you need a mix in criminal investigation: solid, clear-thinking citizens like her and Sammy Pye to keep everyone focused, with a sprinkling of risk-takers like you for the flash of inspiration when it's needed. Ninety per cent of the job is routine; evidence-gathering and analysis. It's the other ten that makes the difference.'

'Were you one of those?'

'I like to think I still am, son.'

I would have gone straight into my office, but Sylvia called to me as I walked past her open door. 'You're a wanted man, Sir Robert. I've had BBC and ITV wanting to interview you about this morning's story. What do you want me to tell them?'

'Decline as politely as you can. Tell them I don't want this to turn into a personal campaign. You could say that my hope is that there will be a serious public debate about driving standards and the motor vehicle as a lethal weapon, but that it's up to the politicians to do something about it. And by the way, it's still Bob, and always will be.'

'Will do,' she said. 'What if they insist?'

'They're not in a position to insist. If anyone pushes it, tell them I'm unavailable. You won't be lying. I'm off out again in a minute and I don't expect to be back for the rest of the day.'

In my room, I checked my phone and found, as he had promised, a text from Montell with Magnolia Stein's address and a landline number. I thought about phoning to make an appointment, but decided instead to surprise her. I waved to Sylvia as I left, but she didn't see me; she was too busy on a call, to one of the TV stations, I guessed.

The housing complex was just off St John's Road, to the south, and consisted of a series of small terraced and semi-detached bungalows, fifteen by my quick count, set around an older building that seemed to have given its name, Carnoustie House, to the community. It might have been a small hotel at one time in its existence, or even a private residence. A single access road led to two blocks of four garages each and to a dozen parking spaces, of which eight were filled. I made it nine, and stepped out. As I looked around, I noted that three of the properties had 'For Sale' boards outside; by the nature of the place I guessed that they changed hands frequently.

Alf's sister's bungalow was number seven, in the furthest corner of the complex. As I reached the path that led to it, I saw her half crouching over one of two wooden tubs filled with daffodils that stood on either side of her front door. She didn't seem to hear me approach; to avoid startling her, I called out from a few yards away.

'Miss Stein. Magnolia.'

She straightened slowly, stretching her spine and tilting her head back slightly, and gazed at me through large spectacles. It didn't take long for recognition to dawn.

'Bob Skinner!' she exclaimed, breaking into a smile. 'As I live and breathe. What brings you here?'

'Nostalgia?' I ventured.

She stared at me. 'Nostalgia? Nostalgia my arse! You might have left the force, Bob, but you're still a polis in your heart. And like most successful polis, my late brother among them, you never do a bloody thing without a motive.' She looked at a pink wristwatch with a large face. 'I'm just about to have lunch. You'll join me.'

It wasn't an invitation, it was an instruction, one I could not disobey, so I followed her indoors. The house was small, but adequate for a singleton. There was very little in it that marked it out as an elderly person's home, other than a red wall button beside the gas fire that I took to be an alarm . The furniture was modern and a wall-mounted television was linked to a Sky box and a Blu-ray player. Only the photographs on the sideboard hinted at the past. I scanned them, but only recognised the people in two of them: Alf and a younger version of Magnolia herself, looking formidable in a nurse's uniform. I recalled him telling me that she had been matron in a city hospital before ending her career in nursing management with the regional health authority.

The living room led into the kitchen, and an appetising smell drifted through. 'Vegetable broth and ham rolls,' she said. 'Will that do you?'

'Perfectly, but do you have enough?'

'Always. Everything's home-made, even the rolls. All right, the ham's no', but I haven't killed a pig since I turned seventy-five.' I watched her silently from the doorway as she spread butter on to four rolls. 'If you want to make yourself useful,' she said, 'you can set the table. You'll find place mats and cutlery in the sideboard.'

I did as she asked, raising a wing of the gateleg table below the window, and setting it so that we faced each other. When I was ready, so was she; I offered to carry our lunch from the kitchen on a tray, but she shooed me away. When we were seated, I waited. Years ago, Alf had mentioned that she was 'old-fashioned religious' and I wanted to give her a chance to say grace. She didn't; instead she looked at me and said, 'Tuck in. There's more in the pot.'

The broth was excellent, thick with barley and vegetables. I guessed that she had made the stock from the ham in the rolls. It wasn't too hot, either; it held my attention until I was finished, and beyond, as I accepted her offer of a top-up. If I hadn't known she was eighty-three, I'd have taken her for mid seventies at most. She had the patience of a torturer as well; I could tell she was bursting to ask me what my visit was all about, but politeness demanded that we get the hospitality over with before she did.

I played by the rules to the very end; in fact I let her take the lead, and even then she played her cards well. 'Are you missing it?' she asked, as she filled two mugs with tea that would have satisfied the most seasoned builder.

'That's a two-part answer, Magnolia,' I replied. 'Am I missing being a chief constable? No, I never have and I never will, not for a single day. Am I missing being a detective and the satisfaction of achieving justice for victims of crime? Yes, and I always will.'

'You're keeping yourself busy, though?'

'Annoyingly so, at times.'

'That's good. Our Alf didnae do that after he retired. His days were full of nothing but bitterness and booze. I tried to get him out of it, Bob, I really did, but when he had to give up the job, his life was empty. All he did was brood over the past, and grieve for Peggy. He never stopped doing that. The only thing that raised his spirits was when he saw your name in the papers after you'd solved a crime. When you caught those terrorists that attacked the Festival, he was fair full of that. He really was very fond of you, son. He admired you. He even told me that he learned from you.'

'I learned a hell of a lot more from him,' I assured her. 'Too bad he never learned how to get over losing his wife.'

'You had a child, Bob, he didn't. He had nothing but a barren old spinster sister who spent more time at the kirk and at the bridge club than she did with him.'

'What about Jimmy Proud?' I ventured. 'Did he see much of him? They were brothers-in-law, after all.'

'No, he did not. I don't remember Jimmy ever visiting Alf after he retired, and I don't recall Alf ever saying anything about visiting him. Come to think of it, I don't recall Alf ever mentioning him at all.' She frowned; I sensed an anger in her. 'He was full of sorrow at the funeral, of course. So were you,

I mind, but yours seemed to me to be more genuine. You had the presence of mind not to come in uniform, making it clear you were there as a friend, no' as a colleague. Jimmy, though, he wore the full silver braid, and stood beside the chair of the Police Committee. That's why you got a cord at the graveside and he didnae.'

Her revelation, and her obvious bitterness, took me by surprise. Even though I hadn't known of their personal relationship until very recently, I had always assumed there was a continuing friendship between them. And yet, when I thought about it, I realised that there had never been anything from Jimmy's side to support that. As I sat there facing her, I was racked by my own guilt. Yes, I'd called Alf from time to time after his retirement, but I'd rarely visited him, nor had I asked him about himself, or shown the concern that a true friend might have. Yes, I had a new wife and a young family, but I should still have made time to include him in my life.

Magnolia seemed to have a gift for mind-reading. 'Don't take it on yourself, Bob,' she said. 'There was nothing you could have done to help Alf. He was devoted to Peggy; at the end he was lookin' forward to seein' her again.' Her gaze sharpened. It seemed to pierce me. 'Now that's dealt with,' she murmured, 'are you goin' to tell me why you're here? My vegetable broth is famous all over Corstorphine, but I doubt the legend's spread as far as you. It wouldn't have to do wi' a long-dead vicar, would it?'

My astonishment was undisguisable. She grinned. 'Never mind how I ken. It is, isn't it?'

I nodded. 'I'm reviewing the case,' I admitted.

'Why?' she asked. 'It was before your time, wasn't it?'

'By a couple of years,' I admitted. 'I've got an interest in it, that's all.'

'Your interest bein' Jimmy Proud?'

I'd stopped being surprised by Magnolia Stein. 'Yes. He got me involved, and once I picked it up, I couldn't put it down.'

'What are you trying to prove?'

'Nothing,' I replied. 'If there's anything new to find, I will find it, but that's it.'

'Why are you talking to me about it?'

I sensed coyness in her question. 'You knew that was why I'm here,' I said. 'Why do you think?'

She picked up the teapot, assessing how much was left in it, then topped up both mugs. 'I'm thinkin' you've found out about Joanna, Alf's niece.' I blinked, realising that until then I'd been thinking only of Jimmy as her uncle, but of course, Alf had a claim to her also, as his younger sister's husband.

'Not only that,' I replied. 'I saw her this morning. Until then, I had no idea there was a relationship between her and Jimmy or Alf. In fact I'd never heard of her at all before yesterday afternoon. I certainly never knew about her mother's complaint against Matthew Ampersand until I started making enquiries in the right quarter. It was never referred to during the trial of Barley Meads, or in the investigation file. Did you know about it; at the time or subsequently?'

'At the time. Alf told me about it; he was furious. He said Grayling had told him that the man, Ampersand, had . . .' She paused. 'He'd tried for a feel, not to put too fine a point on it. Grayling wanted him to investigate, but Alf was cautious about that, with them being related. He told her to make a complaint to the Piscie Church first, so she did. They rejected her in double-quick time and even threatened action if she said any

180

more about it. I remember how angry Alf was. "It's being swept under the carpet, just like the last one. We'll bloody see about that!" he shouted. I knew nothing about the other complaint, but a few days later the vicar was found dead and Meads was arrested; I found out all about it then.'

'Did it strike you as odd that the Joanna incident wasn't mentioned?'

'No,' she declared with vigour. 'Alf had two reasons for that, he told me. He wanted to spare his niece the embarrassment, but also he was worried that if it came out that he had a personal grudge against Ampersand, Hume, the chief constable, might be forced to take him off the case. He wasnae having that, Bob.'

'Yes, I can understand that. Can you remember, Magnolia, was Jimmy Proud involved at all?'

'No, his name was never mentioned. He was assistant chief by then. If he'd known, he might have had to do the same as Hume.'

'Didn't Grayling tell him?'

'Not that I ever heard. Alf might even have told her not to.'

'I see.' I drank some cooled tea and pondered her story; it all fitted, and did nothing to cast doubt on Meads's justice. I had only one question left. 'How did you know?'

'You're no' the first visitor I've had in a while. A man named Austin Brass called on me, one day last week, Wednesday, I think. He claimed to be a journalist, but he had no credentials other than a scruffy business card wi' his name on. He said he wanted to talk to me about the involvement of Sir James Proud in the death of Matthew Ampersand. I told him that I had no acquaintanceship with James Proud, current or historic, and to get his foot off my doorstep.'

'How did he take that?'

'Badly. I thought I was going to have to slam the door on it, hard, but the lassie who was with him told him not to make a fuss, and more or less hauled him off.'

'Did you catch her name?'

'It was never thrown at me. Not young, not old, not Scottish by her accent. That's all I can tell you, Bob.' She sighed, and for the first time her age showed, just a little. 'This isnae going to be a bother to me is it, son?'

'Not if I can help it, Magnolia,' I promised, but with no feeling of certainty that I could.

Twenty-Six

Magnolia had a Dundee cake, home-made, that she insisted I sample before I left. I realised that she enjoyed company, and hung around for longer than I had intended, talking about old times, hers and mine. I recalled a few stories, some of them slightly edited, about her brother and a few other CID veterans I thought she might have known. Tommy Partridge wasn't one of them, but to my surprise, she asked me about him.

'Tommy's still around,' I told her. 'His daughter's a colleague of mine at the *Saltire*, so I see him fairly often. It didn't occur to me until I started looking into the Ampersand business, but he and Alf couldn't have been that far apart in age.'

'They weren't,' she confirmed. 'Alf was sorry for Tommy, because he never made it as far up the ranks as he should have. He was a contemporary of that man Greg Jay; Alf told me that his father had the ear of the chief constable, and he put the poison down about Tommy; he let slip that he was a Catholic, and that was enough in those days. He was stuck in uniform, and he'd have been there for life if Alf hadn't got Jimmy Proud to authorise his transfer to CID when Hume was off having haemorrhoid surgery. Is Jay still in the land of the living?' she asked. When I told her that he wasn't, she expressed the opinion that the world was a better place for his absence.

Magnolia's career had been almost a mirror of her brother's, she suggested, each having reached the top of their professional tree. They had differed only in his refusal to leave operational policing for top-tier management. 'Alf never wanted to be anything more than he was. Jimmy would have got him an assistant chief promotion if he'd wanted it, but he never did.' She glanced across at me. 'I remember, when you made ACC, he said you'd regret it.'

'He was almost right,' I conceded. 'ACC was okay; I could keep the reins in my hands then, but not as chief. Truth be told, I never really enjoyed a day behind that desk.'

Eventually, I left Magnolia to get on with her gardening, promising to keep in touch. It's a vow I intend to keep. She assured me that I had no need to reproach myself for drifting away from Alf, but I do and I will. I left her with my phone number and with her mobile in mine's memory.

Back in my car, I stayed in the park for a while, weighing up what she had told me. I found myself disturbed and in something of a quandary. 'We'll bloody see about that!' Alf had shouted. Had that been a threat? I didn't look back at my old boss through rose-coloured specs. He had been old school, and although he never encouraged it among his juniors, or even tolerated it on my time, I'm sure that on his way through the ranks he hadn't been above giving someone a good kicking if he thought it was warranted. I doubted though if he'd ever bashed somebody's head in.

However, that wasn't the real issue. Mario McGuire had given me access to the Ampersand case file under the general heading of Old Pals Act; I'd done similar things myself on

occasion on a smaller scale, but always with an implicit understanding that if anything emerged that changed the game, it
would be reported back. Had I done that by uncovering the
Joanna Meikle complaint? There was an obvious irony in Alf's
carpet outburst. It had been made in anger, when Matthew
Ampersand was still alive. After his death, Alf had done the
same thing himself; he had swept the incident under another
carpet, to protect his niece and to ensure that he would not be
deflected from securing a conviction in an investigation that
would be the making of him, by justifying Chief Constable
Hume's grandiose label as Scotland's top crime-fighter. It might
not have been corruption, but it was unprofessional behaviour
for sure, dereliction of duty at worst, because there was no
doubt in my mind that the incident should have been disclosed
to Barley Meads's defence team.

I'm not a lawyer, but I know a good one. Still seated in the
Carnoustie House car park, I turned my phone back on, called
Alex and found her in the office. I told her the whole story,
beginning with my call from Valerie Cornton and ending with
Magnolia Stein's Dundee cake, home-made. When I was
finished, I sat in silence for a couple of minutes. I expected her
to tell me she'd need to think about it for a while. It's a rare
occurrence for me to underestimate my daughter, but that was
one of them.

'If I was acting for the heirs of Barley Meads,' she declared,
'I would be taking that straight to the Scottish Criminal Cases
Review Commission. I have no doubt that if Meads was alive,
the conviction would be set aside and at the very least a retrial
would be ordered. But he isn't, so he'd be declared innocent.
Pops, you say you're in a quandary; so am I because of what
you've told me. And yet I'm not. It's quite clear in my mind.

I'm an officer of the court; I have an obligation to report this to the Crown Office. You have to get me off the hook here; you have to go to Mario yourself.'

'You've made my mind up for me,' I told her. 'I'll go and see him right now. Thanks, love.'

I was about to call him there and then, to wedge myself into his busy day with a view to ruining it, when my phone sang its song. It was Sarah, calling from her office in the university.

'Bob,' she exclaimed, 'where the hell have you been?'

'Lunching with an old lady-friend,' I replied. 'Don't worry, she's really old. What's up?'

'Sauce Haddock's been trying to contact you. Eventually he gave up and asked me to track you down. He wants you to meet him at the Aubigny Sports Centre in Haddington, right away. Thing is, he wants me to go there as well.'

Twenty-Seven

I put my visit to Mario on hold and headed for Haddington. I was close to the city bypass, which would be less busy than usual in the early part of the afternoon; I reckoned I could make it in no more than half an hour. I knew what was waiting there. Sauce had asked for Sarah, and that had to mean a body. If he was there himself, that meant a crime scene – or it would have in normal circumstances. The wild card was the disappearance of Sir James Proud. I had a vision of him sitting in a quiet place, with two empty bottles by his side, one pills, the other whisky. Yes, my thoughts were that dark.

I didn't need help to find the Aubigny Sports Centre; I've swum in its pool often enough with my kids, even Alex in her childhood, and my five-a-side football crew, the Thursday Legends, have used the sports hall on occasion when North Berwick, our usual home, has been closed. Sauce was waiting in the car park when I arrived, with a parka-clad figure I recognised after a couple of seconds as Noele McClair. Neither of them was wearing a scene-of-crime tunic, and the area wasn't taped off in any way. That struck me as odd.

'Sir,' the brand-new detective inspector called out as

I approached. 'Thanks for coming. If I'm right about this, I thought you'd want to be here.'

'Right about what?'

'Come and see; it's a wee walk from here, but this is the easiest place for cars.' He turned to his sergeant, junior in rank but senior in age by two or three years, I guessed. 'Noele, will you wait here for Professor Grace, please. She shouldn't be long. You'll recognise her, won't you? She'll be carrying a black bag as usual.'

She nodded. 'Our kids are at primary together,' she said.

'No problem, then.'

He led the way out of the car park and along Mill Wynd, away from the centre. In recent decades, new houses have been built close to the Tyne. I wondered if the crime scene was in one of those, but we carried on past them, until we reached a wooded area, quiet enough for me to hear the running river. We continued until we stood on its banks; it was narrower at that point than in the Nungate, but still fairly wide. Beside the far embankment, I could see two divers; a third person was directing them. He – or she, for I couldn't tell – wore the type of blue crime-scene tunic that I had expected to see on Sauce and DS McClair. They were working, carefully, on something that seemed to be trapped under a thick fallen tree trunk. I didn't need to be told what it was.

'I get it, Sauce,' I said. 'Now are you going to tell me? Why am I here?'

'Because of this,' he replied. 'We haven't got an absolute identification yet, but from the first description from the divers, added to the fact that we've found his car parked up the road there, we're pretty sure it's Austin Brass.'

I should have been shocked, but I wasn't. The phone

making its way across the Low Countries had thrown me for a little, but there and then it made absolute sense. I wondered if Sauce had worked it out too; part of me hoped that he hadn't, for nobody should be that precocious. 'What about the mobile?' I asked.

'It's stopped again in Holland, so the Dutch police told me this morning. I'm going to tell them to pinpoint it and pick it up.'

'No rush,' I grunted. 'You'll find that it's been planked on a lorry. The thing could have gone anywhere. When you find the vehicle, check the Haddington CCTV tapes for Sunday and you'll see it heading out of town.'

'Why Sunday?' he asked.

'We'll get there,' I replied, 'but you need to bring the big boys in on this. Where's Sammy Pye?'

'Police College, on a course.'

'Then you have to call DCC McGuire. Tell him I'm here and I believe it relates to the thing I've been looking at. He'll understand. When he gets here, you'll hear the whole story.'

'Can't you tell me now?'

'No, Sauce, I can't,' I assured him, 'because to keep you on the side of the angels, you have to treat me as a suspect.' He gasped; before he could say anything, I held up a hand to stop him. 'Also, you have to detain DS McClair, or at the very least take her phone and forbid her to communicate with her husband.'

'If you say so, sir,' he murmured, 'but fuck's sake, why?'

'Because they're suspects too.'

Twenty-Eight

By the time Mario arrived, the body under the tree had been recovered and landed on the northern bank of the Tyne where we stood. Sarah had beaten him to it, and was close to completing her initial examination, with Sauce, suited up, watching her. Fighting all my instincts, I had stayed in the background, too far away for a clear view, but even if I had been standing over him, I doubt I could have identified the remains as those of Austin Brass. I had only seen images of the guy, in the press and on his website; after being immersed in a fast-moving river for several days, the corpse was hardly going to be a perfect match.

The area had been fenced off and all the pathways leading to it had been secured by 'Police – do not cross' tape. I heard a twig being crushed behind me and looked over my shoulder in time to see DCC McGuire easing his considerable bulk under the makeshift barrier.

'Who's going to be the first to say it?' I asked as he approached.

'Just like old times?' He smiled, but I thought there was a touch of weariness in it. If high office in the police service doesn't age the holder, he isn't doing the job properly.

'I was thinking we must stop meeting like this, but that'll do just as well.'

'Austin Brass, DI Haddock told me.'

'Not confirmed yet, but that's the suspicion. His car's—'

'Parked up the road,' he said. 'Sauce told me that too. I saw the tape around it as I passed. Bob, why . . .'

He paused his question as Sarah approached, with Haddock beside her. 'I've done as much as I can here, Mario,' she told him. 'I can't give you a positive identification. He's been in there for several days and he's been battered about facially, possibly by the tree trunk he was wedged under. There's nothing in his pockets, no wallet, no phone—'

'No car keys?' I blurted out, then closed my mouth tight, remembering that I wasn't a player any longer.

'No car keys,' she repeated, without a glance in my direction.

'Can we rule out accidental death?' the DCC asked.

'Not before the autopsy.'

I couldn't contain a chuckle. McGuire looked at me, eyebrow raised. 'Go on,' he murmured.

I accepted the terse invitation. 'My London friends told me a story,' I began, 'about a Russian oligarch who was found dead in a snowdrift on the outskirts of Moscow. The police declared it a tragic accident, a hit-and-run. If that was right, it was a small miracle, for the car that hit him managed in the process to relieve him of every form of identification he had on him: wallet, cards, the lot. It took two days to work out who he was, and by that time, all his bank accounts had been emptied and his investment portfolio liquidated. A river will do things to a body, but it's unlikely to pick its pockets.'

'Suicide?' Sauce ventured. 'Covering all possibilities.'

Mario shook his head. 'I never heard of one where the deceased tried to hinder identification.'

'Maybe his stuff's in his car.'

'It's not locked, sir.' Noele McClair's voice came from behind us. 'I've just checked.'

'Sergeant,' Sauce said, with an icy tone in his voice that I had never heard before, 'I thought I told you to stand down from this investigation.'

'I was just trying to help, sir,' she replied.

McGuire frowned at the DI, then at me, as if for a clue.

'Did you touch the vehicle, DS McClair?' I asked.

'Only to check whether it was locked. I only had a quick look inside.'

'Were you wearing gloves?'

She flushed, and bit her lip. Fucking lovely, I thought. If she or her husband were involved, she'd just given an excuse for her prints being inside the car, if there had been something in it she needed to retrieve.

I nodded to Mario, gesturing that he follow me as I walked a few yards away from the group and stood with my back to them. 'Listen,' I whispered, 'you need to have this woman isolated and searched, intimately if necessary, by a female officer, before she leaves the scene. Her husband is ex-job and his career was ruined by Austin Brass. She told me this herself.'

'When? How?' he murmured.

'Sunday afternoon, at Seonaid's birthday party. Her kid's a classmate.' As I spoke, a realisation came to me. 'I believe that is Brass over there, and that he's been there since Sunday. If that's so, I can probably alibi her myself, but I can't vouch for him. I told Sauce he should relieve her, and he did, but it was too public for him to ask for her phone. You need to do that, and all the rest. I know before you say it, there's a line of angry ex-cops would like to do Brass in, but she's here and so is what's left of him.'

192

'Understood,' Mario said. 'I'll do what you suggest, but first, do I have to ask Haddock what the fuck you're doing here, or will you volunteer it?'

'If this hadn't happened,' I told him, 'you and I would be talking in your office right now. We need to go somewhere quiet and let the crime-scene team get to work properly, then I'll tell you the whole story.'

'You'd better,' he growled. 'You seem to know a hell of a lot about this, and that makes me very uncomfortable.'

Twenty-Nine

Ds McClair was a chastened cop as she was taken away to be searched by two women officers in uniform, one of them an inspector summoned from the Haddington police office. At first she had refused to co-operate, or to hand over her mobile; her heels were dug in, figuratively, and she demanded, as was her right, that her Police Federation representative be brought to the scene.

I did not want to be involved. My first instinct was to get the hell out of there, but when Mario, who wanted to contain the situation, asked me to return the favour he had done me in sending the Ampersand case file, by having a word with her, I couldn't refuse.

Sarah offered to join me as I spoke to her, but I declined. What I was doing was unofficial, but I wanted to make it as formal as I could. I wasn't sure how to begin: it was clear that she blamed me for shopping her to her bosses; her body language shouted resentment. 'Tell me something, Noele,' I said, when I had her full attention. 'If I had known nothing about your husband's history with Austin Brass, would you have volunteered it?'

'We don't know that it is Brass yet,' she countered.

'I know it, and so do you. Unless he used his own car to dump somebody else's body in the river then buggered off leaving both to be found, that is the man who ended your Terry's CID career. So I repeat, would you have put DI Haddock in the picture if I hadn't?'

Her stance became more defensive. 'That might have depended on Terry,' she replied.

'Gimme your phone, please,' I asked, quietly.

She handed it over. I checked through her recent activity; she had made no calls, but forty minutes earlier she had sent a text to her husband: *Austin Brass body found. At scene now.*

'Jesus,' I muttered. 'Even if you are wholly innocent, Noele, that was goddamned stupid. Sending that text from an active crime scene, that's a disciplinary landmine you've just stood on. Understand this: you're in a job-threatening situation right now. You withheld information that should have been out there as soon as Brass's name was mentioned, you exposed yourself to accusations of crime-scene tampering when you touched that car, and now you've given information about a potential homicide investigation to someone that you must know, as an experienced CID officer, will be on the list of persons of interest, until he's eliminated . . . or until he moves on to the shortlist. I don't care who he is, you shouldn't have done it.'

'Terry wouldn't—' she began.

'That's not your call. It's for DI Haddock to determine, along with other lines of investigation. Noele, please, for the sake of your career, and your life in general, do the right thing here. All those mums in our kids' class: you don't want them whispering about you, do you?'

'No,' she whispered.

'In that case, go to Sauce as your line manager, cap in hand if you've got one, apologise for your misjudgement, give him your phone, own up to the text, and tell him that you'll submit to a search to eliminate you, and to allow the inquiry to go ahead without unnecessary distractions.'

'Will he let me stay on the team?' she asked.

'The only person with that choice is DCC McGuire, but trust me again, you don't want to ask him that question right now. I tell you, if you'd done this in my time, you'd have been back in a PC's uniform the day after, practising your traffic control. Mario's a kinder boss than I was, but don't poke him with a stick. Stay quiet and see what happens.'

'What about Terry? What do I say to him?'

'Not a fucking word, Detective Sergeant, if you have any hope of holding on to the rank.'

'Thanks for that,' Mario said, a few minutes later, as she and her escorts headed for the women's changing room at the Aubigny sports centre. 'I'd have arrested her if she had stuck to her guns.'

'What are you going to do with her?' I asked.

He winced. 'I don't know,' he admitted. 'If she hadn't sent that bloody text, I'd just have told Sauce to keep her in the office until her husband was eliminated as a possibility. As it is, there'll have to be a reprimand at best.'

'And if he isn't eliminated?'

He shuddered. 'She'll have to prove she had no knowledge . . . unless she did. What do you think?'

'I don't know Terry Coats, from the job or my local community but I do know this. His beef wasn't simply against Austin Brass, although he may have seen it that way. The story Brass ran was true, on the face of it, but there were factors that he chose to leave out, as the complaints people acknowledged. Coats might have blamed Brass, okay, but his source was just as much a villain, and so to an extent was Toni Field, his chief constable, for shoving him under the bus when she should have backed him.'

'Field's dead, and beyond anyone's reach now,' Mario observed, 'but what about the source?'

'I don't know about him. Noele told me that he was a colleague, one Charlie Ruiz, a detective sergeant through in Glasgow, where it all happened. Seems he was jealous of Coats's promotion. Ring any bells?'

'No, but I'll ask HR to check him out.'

'You'd be better asking Dan Provan; he'd get back to you quicker and tell you a lot more.'

'Dan's gone, remember. Retired.'

I smiled. 'So am I. Ask him.'

'Indeed,' Mario growled, 'but it's never felt that way. Okay, I'll do that. Now, finally, what have you got to tell me?'

'Much,' I assured him, 'but not here, for it'll take some time.'

'Where then? The sports centre?'

'Too busy, but I know the very place. Come on, I'll drive.'

We walked back to the car park, briskly and in silence. I drove off, took a right at the junction and found a back road that led to the Waterside Bistro. The sun was heading westwards, but there was still a little warmth in it, allowing us to take one of the unoccupied outside tables. I went inside and bought two double tomato juices, with Tabasco and a slice of lemon; of all the guys in Haddington at that moment, we were the last two who needed to be seen sitting outside a pub packing away pints, then getting into our cars.

'Sir Bob,' he grunted as I laid the tall glasses on the table. I'd wondered when that would come. 'You kept shtum about that when I asked you what you'd got from the London business. "Ten per cent of bugger all" indeed. Why were you so coy about it? That's not you.'

'I'm a bit embarrassed about it, to tell you the truth. Okay, it was offered and I was persuaded to accept.'

'Who did the persuading? Sarah?'

'No way; she wouldn't have tried. Actually it was Amanda Dennis, of MI5; she said it would have been churlish to turn it down, given who proposed it.'

'Who did?'

'I'm keeping that to myself, but it might not be who you think. But enough of that, commoner: to business. This is a good place to start,' I told Mario, glancing around at our surroundings. 'I was due to meet Austin Brass here for lunch last Sunday, but he never showed up. Sarah may or may not be able to confirm this, given the time that's elapsed, but I reckon he was too busy getting murdered and chucked in the river.'

My friend smiled wickedly and raised an eyebrow. 'But not by you, before you turned up here? Sauce told me what you said, about him needing to treat you as a suspect.'

'No, not by me. Mario, you know me well enough to realise that if I was going to kill Austin Brass or anyone else, they'd never be fucking found. That said, to give you comfort, and for the record, my car's navigation system will have recorded my journey from Gullane to here, door to door. On top of that, the proprietors' dad will vouch for the fact that I didn't leave from the moment I got here until after I'd eaten and paid the bill. By that time, Brass was dead; if he wasn't, he'd have shown up here, because he was chasing what he reckoned was a hot story for his blog, one that could have doubled his readership and his revenue. If you need belt and braces, my car will have been picked up by Haddington's comprehensive street cameras from the moment I passed the Aldi supermarket until I drove out of town. The same system will have picked up Brass from his arrival until he turned into Knox Place. As I said, I believe that happened on Sunday, somewhere between twelve and one o'clock. You'll need to check all this out, I know, and have an officer look at my satnav. In fact I insist that you do, for everybody's sake.'

McGuire is shrewd. 'Bob,' he said, 'your insistence tells me you might have had a motive right enough.'

'Someone with a fertile imagination and career ambitions might think so,' I conceded. 'But it would be stretching a point. Brass never went for me, so I had nothing against him.'

'Okay, you didn't do it. That was taken as read anyway, but it will be confirmed for the record. Are you going to tell me who did?'

'I hope not,' I replied, 'either way, for I can see two candidates, but when I've told you the whole story, we may both need to reflect on it for a while.' I had done some reflecting as I was speaking. 'But before I do that,' I said, 'I'd like Sauce here. He'll be the SIO on this inquiry, unless you say otherwise, so he needs to hear this as well. At the very least it's background, and besides, I owe the lad.'

'I think he owes you more,' Mario observed, 'but if that's what you want, I'll summon him.' He took out his phone, keyed in a text and fired it off. 'I've told him to drop everything and be here inside ten.' He drained his tomato juice. 'Want another?' he asked. 'Maybe a bit heavier on the Tabasco this time?'

'Why the hell not?'

He returned in three minutes, with three drinks, the spare for Haddock, I assumed. 'Bob,' he said, as he placed the tray on the table, 'if you don't know Brass, and your paths have never crossed, why was he meeting you for a nice Sunday lunch by the riverside?'

'That's the thing, my large friend. He didn't know he was. It was meant to be a big surprise for him. Clearly it wasn't nearly as big as the one he actually got.'

Thirty

'What's in it?' Sauce quizzed the DCC, eyeing the double tomato juice suspiciously.

'Double vodka, what else?' McGuire barked. 'You want to be a player in CID, son, you need to learn to play with the big boys.'

Haddock frowned at him, then at the drink. 'You are kidding me, sir, right?'

'Suck it and see. You can always get someone to drive you back to Edinburgh.'

He reached out, picked up the glass and took a large mouthful: too large. 'Jesus!' he gasped as it hit his taste buds.

'Like he said, Sauce,' I laughed, 'welcome to senior rank. When it comes to loading up the Tabasco, McGuire is completely Italian.'

'Thanks for the belated warning, sir. Is that why I'm here, so that you guys can strip the lining off my throat?'

I shook my head. 'No, that was his idea. I need to make something official, a business I got drawn into a week ago and have been working on ever since.'

'Who drew you in?' McGuire asked.

201

'Sir James Proud,' I told him, letting the name hang in the air, studying each of them as they took it in. Mario was inscrutable, Sauce bewildered.

'The old chief constable?' he asked.

'I don't know another one.'

'The Matthew Ampersand murder,' Mario said. 'The case file you asked for; you were looking into it at Jimmy's request. Did he tell you why?'

I nodded. 'Yes. Brass has been threatening him. It began with a cry for help, last week.' I launched into my story, from Jimmy's call as I was leaving the Balmoral and our furtive meeting in Yellowcraigs, taking it step by step, discovery by discovery, to the conclusion and my visits to Joanna Meikle and Magnolia Stein.

'You are telling us, sir,' Sauce whispered, when he had processed it all, 'that the head of CID of the day investigated the murder of a man who'd just been accused of sexually assaulting his niece, who was also Assistant Chief Constable Proud's niece, and didn't make that part of the investigation?'

'He wasn't head of CID at that point, but other than that, exactly.'

'Are you saying that one or both of them killed Matthew Ampersand?'

'No, of course he's not,' McGuire intervened. 'The case against Meads was unshakeable. He was the prime suspect from the start and very strong forensic evidence convicted him.'

'You remember a lot from that training course case study,' I observed.

'I've read up on it since you asked for the papers,' he confessed. 'Meads did it; you believe that, Bob, don't you?'

'On the basis of the evidence I've reviewed, yes; that's me thinking as a detective, and I'm still firmly of that view. However, when I asked my Alex to look from a defence counsel perspective at the conclusion Alf reported to the Crown Office, and then told her about the Joanna Meikle incident, which was still fresh in everyone's mind at the time of the killing, she said straight away that any unreasonable doubt there may have been had suddenly become very reasonable indeed. The exclusion of that second complaint from the case compromised the Crown. It's clear to me that Austin Brass found out about Joanna, and made a quantum leap that led to his threat to Jimmy.'

'Did Meads know about Joanna?' Sauce asked.

'She was left out of the investigation, so we can't know for sure, but she was his daughter's best friend, so it's a fair assumption. It may well have tipped him over the edge. It's clear to me that Barley's QC believed he was unstable, because he wanted to look at a temporary insanity plea.'

'Didn't the prosecution look at his mental health?'

'Why should they?' I countered. 'I never met a prosecutor who'd go out of his way to undermine their own case. That's the defence's job, but in this case the client wouldn't allow it.'

'He's right, Sauce,' McGuire said. 'He's right about Brass too. On the face of it, it appears to me that Alf suppressed the Joanna incident as it would only have muddied the waters and threatened the quick result that the chief constable had pressed him to deliver. Sir James must have known about it, and gone along with it.'

'How does that place him legally, sir,' Haddock persisted, 'if we take this to the Crown Office now?'

'That would depend on how hard the Lord Advocate – for it would go right to the top – wanted to go at it. What do you think, Sir Bob?'

From the way Sauce stared at me, I could tell he wasn't a *Saltire* reader. 'Cut that out, DCC McGuire,' I growled. 'As Alex said,' I continued, 'the verdict would be overturned. Alf would be vilified, and if Jimmy's knowledge could be proved, he'd face charges of withholding evidence, perverting the course of justice, or however the Crown wanted to frame it. However, I have to correct myself, because it isn't hypothetical. "Would" no longer applies. I've reported this to you guys, here and now, at this table, instead of in the DCC's office, where I was headed when I got your message, Detective Inspector Haddock. You don't have a choice: you're serving police officers and I've given you clear evidence of a serious crime that may have led to the wrongful conviction of a man for murder. Whether Meads was guilty or he wasn't, that doesn't matter, gentlemen. He was tried on an indictment that was fatally flawed, a fact that was known to the senior investigating officer but withheld from the procurator fiscal. You have to report this; it's your duty. If you don't, you'll be complicit in the original crime.'

McGuire finished his ferocious red concoction in a single gulp, then went off without a word, returning shortly afterwards with three more. 'I wish that this was a proper drink,' he grumbled. 'Sauce,' he continued, 'he's right. This has to go to the Crown Office. But I'm not going to lay it on you; I'll take it to the chief constable tomorrow morning, and we will report it together. Your job is Austin Brass, assuming that does turn out to be him and the autopsy does produce clear evidence of foul play; you're the SIO. That's the pressure on you; we'll carry the flak for the other thing.' He turned to me. 'Okay with that, Bob?'

'It has to be,' I replied, 'but there's another aspect that's worrying me – more than one, but I'll get to the other later. This happened just before I joined the police. Later I worked with both Alf Stein and James Proud for many years, and yet they never disclosed their relationship to me. I knew nothing about it until last week, when Jimmy confessed it, only, I believe, because he had to. My suspicion is that their reticence about it had nothing to do with any reluctance to appear to be playing favourites within the force, but that it was tied to the Ampersand affair. That emphasises the conspiracy.'

'I can see that,' Mario agreed. 'What's the other?'

'Brass. Only three people knew about our lunch date on Sunday: him, me and Jimmy. He's dead, I didn't kill him and Jimmy's disappeared.'

The DCC buried his face in his hands and murmured something that was barely audible.

'Sorry, sir?' Sauce ventured.

His boss laid those hands on the table, palms down, and glared at him. 'Is there any part of "Fuck me!" that you don't understand?'

The young man took a risk by grinning. 'No, I get the picture, boss.' He turned to me. 'Sir Robert—'

'Don't you start!'

'Sorry, just plain sir. When you say that Sir James has disappeared, what do you mean?'

'Basically, Sauce, I mean that he's done a runner.' I explained that he had left home without telling Lady Proud or anyone else where he was going or when he'd be back.

'Do you think it's connected with Brass's threat and your review of the case?'

'I don't know and I'm not going to speculate.'

'Do you have any idea where he might have gone?'

'If I did, I would drive you there myself.'

'In that case, I'd better interview Lady Proud.'

'Over your dead body!' I snapped, then instantly reined back my reaction. 'Sorry, Sauce, of course that's your call, but I've already spoken to Chrissie and I can tell you all she would. She has no idea where he is; mentally she's fragile. She's imagining all sorts, including him having run off with a fancy woman, an idea that would win the Festival Fringe funniest joke award in other circumstances. If Jimmy had been in touch, she'd have let me know, I'm sure. If you visit her, what's she going to think? She answered a call from Brass and handed it to her husband; he didn't discuss it with her afterwards. She knows who and what he is now, because I told her, but she doesn't know anything about his interest in Jimmy. If you don't mind, and if DCC McGuire agrees, I'd prefer that you didn't visit her, not at this stage.'

'Yeah,' Mario drawled. 'I don't want to put handcuffs on you, but I agree with Bob. There's no point in alarming her any more than she is already, given that her old man's absent without leave.'

'Very good, sir.' Sauce's tone was neutral; a sure sign that he was slightly miffed. 'Do you have any advice on how I should proceed?'

'I'd pitch it stronger than advice,' he said. 'Your focus is on the death of the man we believe is Austin Brass, and your first task is to identify him, even before confirming that he was a murder victim. For all we know for certain right now, that thing in the river could have been some tramp juiced up on meths who just fell in, plain and simple. Does anyone know who Brass's next of kin is?'

'His father reported him missing, so I'm guessing it's him.'

'Magnolia Stein said there was a woman with him when he visited her,' I volunteered. 'She didn't describe her in detail, beyond being sure she isn't Scottish, but I didn't press her on it. She may be able to tell you more. If – when – you visit her,' I added, with a grin, 'make sure you go at lunchtime.'

'Bring the father in,' Mario continued, ' as soon as you can, and ask him if he can identify the body. You saw it close up, I didn't; is he badly disfigured?'

'Not pretty,' Sauce admitted. 'I've seen his picture on his blog, and I couldn't swear it's him, but he should be recognisable to a close relative once he's been tidied up. Worst case, I'll take a DNA sample from the father. If that's a match, we'll be in business.' He stopped for a couple of seconds. 'Sir, what about DS McClair?'

'How did the body search go?' Mario retorted.

'Negative. I had a call on my way here.'

'Thank the good Lord for that. As far as I'm concerned, she's just on the side of the angels, by a couple of centimetres, apart from that text, but her husband must be a person of interest until we've proved otherwise.' He glanced in my direction. 'Bob, you said that you saw the file on Terry Coats when you were in Strathclyde. Was anyone else mentioned in it, apart from the informant who was murdered after Brass went public on the case?'

'No, but he'll have had friends and associates himself, and any one of them could have had a mind to get even with Brass. Find the file,' I suggested. 'I didn't destroy it. I left it in the private safe in my office in Pitt Street. Andy Martin inherited it when he took over as head of the new force; maybe Maggie got it when she succeeded him.'

'If not, do you know where Andy is now? I don't.'

'I'm the last guy you should be asking.' My successor, one-time sidekick and former friend had been involved with my daughter for ten years, on and off, before and after his failed marriage. Their relationship hadn't ended well either. 'And Alex would be the last woman. If Maggie doesn't have the file, Brian Mackie might; sensitive material goes to him, doesn't it?'

McGuire grunted again. 'Is there anything about the inner working of my office that you don't know?'

'Maybe.' I winked. 'I don't know.'

He turned back to Haddock. 'Leave that to me, Sauce. With DS McClair being grounded, you will need a replacement.'

'She's there already, sir; Jackie Wright. Good at everything but her promotion exams.'

'I know her; she's fine by me. Set her to work on Brass's blog, and have her compile a list of people you should be looking at, as well as Coats and his wife. They'll nearly all be cops, because of the stories he went after.'

'Very good, sir, but . . . I focus on Brass, understood, but what about Mr Skinner, Sir Robert's, original investigation? Can we just put it to one side? What if there is a connection?'

'No, we can't,' Mario agreed. 'Fortunately there's a man at this table who's dead keen to be involved, even if it's strictly unofficial. Bob, there is no police investigation into the Ampersand case, at least not yet. Would you be prepared to carry on what you've been doing, and be available to advise DI Haddock whenever there's an overlap or he feels the need to consult you?'

I did my best to keep my smile within bounds, but I doubt that I succeeded. 'Try and stop me,' I replied.

'Good; but remember, everything gets reported back to me, by both of you. Understood?'

'Understood,' I repeated, crossing my fingers behind my back.

Thirty-One

I drove us back to the sports centre, where I parked once again. In our absence, a mobile HQ van had arrived and was taking up a third of the available space. 'The punters will be delighted,' Mario observed, 'but at least it'll give our PR people somewhere to drink their coffee.'

We were about to walk back to the putative crime scene when a female voice called out, 'Sir?'

All three of us turned simultaneously, but it was on McGuire that Noele McClair was focused as she approached. She was still angry. 'Those two did a good job,' she hissed. 'They made me strip completely. I thought they were going to ask me to spread my bum cheeks. They found nothing, of course. Couldn't they have taken my word for it?'

To my surprise, I saw that Mario was embarrassed; that was a first in my experience. I tried to let him off the hook. 'If you were in their position, Noele,' I asked, 'what would you have done? They were doing their job as you'd have done yours. Whether it was inadvertent or not, you put yourself in that situation. Okay, you're a police officer. Does that get you special treatment?'

'I'll bear that in mind,' she shot back, 'when I'm back in

uniform and one of your kids steps out of line in the village.'

'That's enough, DS McClair,' Sauce Haddock warned her. 'You're standing in a hole that you made yourself. Stop digging and put down your shovel before you find you can't climb out.'

She looked at her gaffer as if she had never seen him before; I doubt that she had, in that mode. She took a deep breath and held it for a few seconds; the pose of someone who knew meditation and was trying to calm herself. She released it, and was back in control. 'Sorry, boss. And sorry, Mr Skinner.' She tried a smile. 'I won't nick Seonaid, I promise.' I wasn't ready to return it, or reply. Instead I waited for Mario.

'You are stressed, Detective Sergeant,' he said. 'That's understandable. Now please realise that we are trying to do our best for you. That's why I'm not going to suspend you for sending that text. I'll have to deal with it, but meantime I want you in the office tomorrow handling all the everyday shit. For now, have a patrol car take you home, but when you get there, you must not – this is a direct order – say anything to your husband about any aspect of this situation. If he asks you, tell him flat out you can't talk to him and that it comes from me. He was a DI: he'll understand. You clear about that?'

She nodded. 'Yessir.'

'On you go then.'

He watched her as she left to find transport. I could have told her to stick around and taken her back to Gullane myself, but I didn't fancy the inevitable silence in the car.

Situation resolved, if only on a temporary basis, we walked along Mill Wynd and back into the woods. As we came close to the scene, a figure came towards us; red hair laced with grey poked out of the hood of his tunic. I tried to recall the last time I'd seen Arthur Dorward dressed in any other way, but I couldn't. He stopped short as he saw me. 'You again?' the head of the crime-scene unit exclaimed. 'Are you stalking me?'

'Heaven forfend, Arthur,' I laughed. 'I have a feeling I'd hate to know what you get up to after hours.'

'So would Mrs Dorward,' he said, peering up at me; I couldn't tell whether he'd been joking. 'Has MI5 got an interest in this?' A small circle of people are aware of my occasional connection with the Security Service, and he is one of them.

'Not that I know of,' I replied.

'Then why the . . . Nah. Forget it, I won't bother to ask. Which of you three bears is the SIO here?'

'That would be me,' Haddock told him.

'Baby Bear?' he gasped in mock astonishment. 'God, the world's running away from me, fast. In that case, you should have this.' He handed over the large flat object he had been holding. It was wrapped in a large evidence bag, but I thought I could guess what it was. 'We found this in the car, under the front passenger seat, as if it had been hidden out of sight. I'm not surprised. It's a laptop, a MacBook Pro, an expensive piece of kit. There was nothing else, though.'

'Not even a service manual for the car?' I asked. 'Credit card slips for fuel?'

'Clever bastard,' Dorward growled. 'Okay, the service book was there, and the owner's name was on it, Austin Brass, but you'll have that from DVLA already. Other than that, entirely fuck all; not another document, credit card slip, water bottle, sweetie paper, nada. That neatness, by the way, is at odds with the appearance of the car itself. It was badly in need of a clean both inside and out: not that we're complaining, for it makes it easy to get prints and DNA off it. Muck has an adhesive quality.'

'Are you doing that now?' Haddock asked.

'Nah, we'll take it back to the campus at Gartcosh, where there's more room to work.'

'Soon as you can, please. I'd like a name put on everyone who's been in that car.'

'That won't happen, Sauce – the database isn't that good – but we'll get you as many as we can. Are you thinking he drove his killer out here?'

'I'm thinking nothing yet, Mr Dorward, but given what this man did for a living, it'd be interesting to know everyone he's been talking to.'

'From what I've heard, and read on his blog – I'll admit that just in case you decided to check on who's been logging into it – a fair few people will be glad he's been silenced. Not that I'm one of them, you understand.'

He waved us a quick goodbye and returned to the river, where his team were conducting a yard-by-yard search of the northern bank, trying to establish the spot where the dead man had gone into the water.

Haddock looked at the laptop in its bag. 'I'd better get this back to the HQ van,' he said.

'And we might as well tag along,' I added. Sauce looked at me; he was still unsure what to make of my presence, and probably how to handle it. 'Think of me as a resource base,' I told him with a smile. McGuire said nothing.

'Don't you have to get home, sir?' the DI ventured. 'For the kids?'

'No hurry. Sarah won't be doing the autopsy tonight; she might even be home herself by now. Even if she isn't, the children have a nanny – although we're not allowed to call her that; James Andrew insists that she's their carer.'

It was a few years since I'd been in a mobile HQ. I was never a great fan of the things, to be truthful, but our PR people liked them because they showed a sense of drama to the public and also because they got them out of the rain while the cops were out there slogging. They were useful in the immediate aftermath of a serious crime, but their facilities were limited, and after the first couple of days they could be seen as physical evidence of a lack of progress. However, I had to admit that the new generation was impressive. The sound of its generator, which had been loud on the outside, was barely more than a whisper indoors. It had been adapted to the digital age, everything seemed much smaller but twice as functional, and it could accommodate more people. I recognised two members of the communications staff; in my day there would have been one, and he would have been outside, like it or not, dealing with the press as they arrived, not leaving a PC to marshal them.

There was a small desk at the far wall, with a sign labelling it as the SIO's workspace. Haddock occupied it automatically, checking the drawers and noting where everything was, including power sockets and USB points. The first thing he did was put his phone on charge; then he had another rummage in the drawers. Failing to find what he was after, he called out to the unit's controller. 'Kofe, do we have a charger for a MacBook Pro?'

'Should have,' the man replied, exploring his own desk. 'Yeah,' he called out, then tossed a chunky white object across to us. The DCC caught it and handed it on. Wearing disposable gloves, Sauce withdrew the laptop from the bag and powered it up. I saw that it was covered in white residue: Dorward had taken prints from it before sealing it and handing it over.

'Problem one,' he muttered as the screen lit up. 'Bastard wants a user password. Any ideas?'

'Rumpelstiltskin?' I suggested; that's Seonaid's favourite fairy tale. She demanded it most nights until she was five, when she decided that fairy tales were no longer cool. Thing is, it's my favourite too; I'm looking forward to introducing it to Dawn in a couple of years.

'Very funny,' Haddock growled, but he tried it nonetheless: unsuccessfully. 'Any more bright ideas? I could ask the Passport Office for the information they hold, but they'd probably want a warrant from the court.'

I looked at McGuire. 'I know that Strathclyde Special Branch had a file on Brass,' I said, 'full of personal details. There was a reference to it in the folder I inherited from Toni Field. I ordered it destroyed because SB wasn't supposed to keep tabs on journalists, but I never checked that they had done it. Gimme a minute.'

I walked across to the other side of the van and called in a number from my contacts book, filed under 'H'.

'Mr Skinner,' a quiet voice answered at once. 'How can I help you?'

'That's what I like to hear, Clyde,' I chuckled.

Clyde Houseman and I have a personal history that goes back twenty years. We first met when I was a detective super and he was a gangbanger in one of the rougher parts of Edinburgh. I gave him some advice about straightening himself out while he had time, then I forgot about him. I didn't know he'd taken it until he walked back into my life as a field officer in the Security Service, which he had joined from a Special Forces unit with the dust of Afghanistan still clinging to his boots. Today he runs the Millbank outstation in Glasgow. He's free to call on my experience when necessary, and that cuts both ways.

'I'm with the police at the moment,' I continued, 'observing, let's say, a newly opened investigation. We have a dead man we're fairly sure is one Austin Brass, a journalist slash blogger and general nuisance to authority, but we have eff all information about him. I'm fairly sure that the Service will have, since all the sensitive material the old Scottish forces generated was copied to you. I need as many of his personal details as you can get me, emailed, and I need it yesterday rather than tomorrow.'

'Thy will be done,' he murmured, and cut me off.

I watched for ten minutes as Sauce and Mario made repeated attempts to get lucky, starting with 'ABRASS' then continuing the metallic theme and running through most of the periodic table. My phone vibrated, telling me that I had incoming. There was no message, just a file; the sender's identity was blocked. I opened it. Clyde had come very good indeed. MI5 had been keeping all of Brass's personal information on file, right back to his birth and his first primary school. I was astonished to see that I had gone there also, eighteen years before him.

'Try Knowetop,' I said, spelling it out letter by letter for Sauce to key in. He clicked and the screen lit up.

'Fuuuuck,' he whispered, glancing at me sideways. 'How the fuuuuck did you do that?' Even McGuire looked impressed.

I beamed at both of them. 'I may have taught you guys all you know, but I didn't have time to teach you all I know.' A shade boastful, I agree, but in the circumstances, I forgave myself.

With the door to Brass's world open to him, Haddock

stepped inside. Mario and I left him to it. 'Where will you go with the Ampersand thing?' he asked me quietly.

'There's one survivor from the days of the murder that I haven't spoken to yet: Briony, the daughter. You could say she's the key to the whole thing. I need to get her on her own, with that husband of hers nowhere around. I didn't say earlier, but the little bastard had a pop at me when he found me talking to Carmel.'

McGuire's eyes gleamed. 'That was unfortunate.'

'He thought so, although his mother-in-law seemed quite amused. I don't think he'll do it again, but I'd rather not give him the opportunity.'

'Can I help?'

'How?'

'He's a farmer; I could arrange for all his road-licensed vehicles to be called in for inspection to get him out of the way.'

'He can't drive off the farm. He's disqualified.'

'I can ask for him to be present.'

'That would work,' I agreed, 'but at the moment, I don't believe it's top priority.'

'What is then?'

'Terry Coats,' I said. 'He needs to be checked out immediately, if only to get Noele McClair off the hook.'

'Have you got a personal interest in her?' Mario asked bluntly.

'I have,' I admitted. 'We live in the same community. She's the mother of one of my daughter's classmates. Whether she realises it or not, I'm her alibi for last Sunday. However, I can't vouch for him. I've never met him, but I know he wasn't at Seonaid's party. We – sorry, you – need to find out where he was.'

'Not least since he's had that text.'

'Correct.'

'Okay, I'll prioritise that; the sooner he's cleared, the sooner I can get McClair back to full duties. I don't want a newly promoted DI to be running half a sergeant short of a load.'

'What about that improper message to her husband?'

'Slap on the wrist,' he retorted. 'A reprimand and a note on her record.'

'Sir!' Sauce called from his desk.

'Yes?' McGuire responded. I managed not to react.

'I'm into Brass's diary,' he announced. 'Bugger's cute; it tells me where he went but not what he was doing. All the listings are venues; the subject of the meetings is always omitted.'

'What have we got for last Sunday?' I asked as we rejoined him.

'Two entries: there's Waterside Bistro, Haddington, thirteen hundred hours; but before that, at twelve thirty, there's another. Mill Wynd, that's all it says. The system tells me when the entry was made, though; your lunch went in last Friday, but the Mill Wynd meeting wasn't entered until nine twenty-eight on Sunday morning.'

It was Mario who asked the heavy question, the one that had been weighing me down. 'Apart from you and Sir James, Bob, did anyone know about the lunch in Haddington?'

'Not to my knowledge,' I admitted.

'Do you know where Sir James was while you were heading for the Waterside?'

I sighed. 'Not for sure. My assumption is that he was at home.'

'But you don't know, so it's possible that he brought the

time forward, changed the venue and met Brass himself beside the river. It's possible,' he repeated, 'do you agree?'

'Come on, Mario,' I protested. 'Martians could land tomorrow. There could be one in the White House as we stand here.'

'There is, and that makes my point. Until we prove otherwise, my suggestion is possible.'

I raised both hands in surrender. 'Okay, I give in; it is possible.'

'And now he's gone missing,' he added.

'Yes,' I agreed quietly.

'Then we'd better find the old sod, for his own sake.'

'But Terry Coats first, Mario, please.'

He nodded. 'I'll give you that; but not tonight. Noele will be home by now, and even though we've told her not to discuss it, she may well tell her husband that he's got to turn himself in and eliminate himself as a potential suspect.' He looked at Haddock directly, frowning. 'Let's give him a chance to do that. Sauce, it's your show, but I suggest that you spend tomorrow morning going through that laptop and getting as much as you can out of it, including a list of all the people who'd enjoy pissing into Brass's open grave. Give Terry Coats that leeway, but if he hasn't been in touch by midday . . . myself, I'd be going after him. You're the SIO, though. It's your shout.'

Aye, sure, I thought, but I kept it, and my inner smile, to myself.

Thirty-Two

'Y ou don't really think that, do you?' Sarah asked.

'That Jimmy set Brass up and chucked him in the Tyne? No, I can't imagine it, but until a couple of days ago, I couldn't have imagined that he and Alf Stein could have kept a relationship secret from me for all those years, or that he didn't cough it up when he told me about this damn business.'

'That's if it is Brass,' she cautioned me. Earlier, but after we had eaten, she had shown me some images she had captured on her phone that afternoon, close-up shots. The cadaver had been pretty badly smashed up facially. It had been trapped by submerged branches on the tree trunk; an eye had been ripped from its socket and the forehead gashed to the bone. I found myself agreeing with Sauce Haddock; I too had seen shots of Brass on his site and elsewhere, but no way could I confirm that was him.

'Who's doing the ID?'

'His father, I believe. He's a retired dentist and lives down in Kelso; Sauce is having him brought up for nine tomorrow. That means I'll have to be off early. I'll need to stick his eye back in and make him as presentable as possible. I can't ask the old guy to look at him the way he is.'

I shrugged. 'Fine. You can whip the eye out again afterwards.'

'Bob!'

'Or not as the case may be. I'll have to be off sharp myself tomorrow,' I added quickly. 'I have InterMedia papers to process, and a video conference with Xavi and a couple of guys about the company's post-Brexit expansion in Britain. I want to get all that done by twelve so I can pay a call on Sauce to see whether Terry Coats has handed himself in.' I sighed. 'You realise that the simple approach would have been for me to nip along to Chez Coats and McClair in West Fenton this evening and front the guy up, but I didn't like to suggest that. Yes, Mario asked me to stick around the investigation and to carry on with my own, but I had the distinct impression he wished he didn't have to.'

'I doubt that. How long has he worked with you? Twenty years?'

'The best part of,' I conceded.

'Could be it's you who needs to cut the umbilical, not him. But you don't want to, do you? That's why you let yourself be seduced by Amanda Dennis and her Service. You need the adrenaline, you need the action.'

'I need a quiet life more,' I insisted, but I couldn't deny it outright.

Thirty-Three

Sarah left for work at seven thirty; I wasn't under her deadline pressures, so I took Seonaid to school as I do whenever I can. James Andrew hitched a ride, but he made it clear that I wasn't actually taking him, you understand, Dad.

The InterMedia papers didn't take long. Recently I've asked that the routine stuff be sent in Catalan, to help me with learning my employer's working language, but the morning's batch related to policy and financial decisions being taken at full board level, and had been translated for me because of their importance.

The Xavi meeting began on time, as his always do, at eleven sharp, midday in Girona; it was conducted in English, with Sylvia taking the minutes. June Crampsey sat in with me, and the boss was flanked by Hector Sureda Roca, the group's digital genius, and his mother, the venerable Pilar, the oldest member of the board since Xavi's half-brother Joe passed away last year. June was there because of what was proposed: the creation of a wholly owned subsidiary company registered in Scotland and managed from the building in which we sat, which would be renamed Saltire House. Its directors would be June, Hector and a financial controller, to be appointed, and I would be its chair. It would double my official commitment to InterMedia from one day a week to two, but that would still be less than the time I'd been contributing in practice since my appointment. Its brief would be to develop the *Saltire*, and create a range of specific interest websites for commercial development.

We talked it around for almost an hour; I wanted June to get used to the environment and the others to get used to her, as she had been a chalk-face operator until then, but I was starting to fidget by the time Xavi brought the meeting to a close. I had somewhere else to be.

Once everything was squared away, I signed myself off for the day and headed for the car park, en route to Fettes Avenue and my old office, where the Serious Crimes CID unit was based. I expected to be asked to wait by security until I could be collected, but to my surprise, I was waved through.

There were two coffees on Sauce's desk as I walked into his office suite. 'You know me so well,' I laughed. 'Is it drinkable?'

'It's the usual shite; judge for yourself.'

I tried it. The beans had come from more countries than the border queue at Heathrow Airport, but there had been nothing but sparkling water at the board meeting, so I was entering withdrawal. 'I thought I'd take you to lunch,' I said as I sat. 'But first, how's the investigation?'

'The body's been identified,' Sauce began. 'It was confirmed as Austin Brass by his father. The bad news is that I can still only call it a suspicious death. I've just had the headline post-mortem findings from Sarah. The cause of death was drowning, and her estimate of the time would fit with the appointment time in the laptop. There were significant injuries to the head, front and back, and to the neck, but she can't say for certain that any of them were sustained before he went into the water.'

'Who says you can only call it a suspicious death?' I asked.

'The PR people; they say that's all it justifies. I'm briefing the media in half an hour.'

'Have you ever done that before?'

He shook his head. 'Not alone and not like this.'

'Are you in any doubt that Brass was put in the water, rather than jumping or falling in?'

'No, but I can't prove it.'

'You don't have to prove it. You've got a full-scale serious crime squad working on this; you're treating it as a homicide. The investigation will determine whether it is or not. When we were there yesterday,' I asked, 'did you notice a couple of birds?'

He frowned. 'Those ducks? Yes.'

'How do you know they were ducks?'

'Because they quacked?' he ventured.

'Exactly. This is a fucking homicide because everything about it says it's a homicide. You are the SIO on this case, not the communications director or any of his people. You decide what you can and should tell the public, not them. Usually you tell them the truth, or as much of it as you can without compromising your investigation. Your old tutor as a PC, Charlie Johnston, he was just a plod all his career, but he knew and understood; that's why he was put in the press office after he retired, until the new regime got rid of him because he didn't fit the image.'

Haddock winced. 'I don't know, sir,' he murmured. 'That man Allsop, the PR director, he's a crusty bastard. What if he goes over my head?'

'With Sammy Pye away,' I pointed out, 'there is nobody over your head.'

'I meant the DCC.'

'He won't do that, because he knows Mario McGuire would cut him off at the knees. If he argues with your decision, tell him his presence isn't required. That's a polite way of saying you-know-what.'

'Sammy shut Allsop's deputy out of a media briefing once,' he recalled. 'Closed the door in her face.'

'Then don't be afraid to do the same to him.' I grinned. 'You're not afraid of anything, kid, are you?'

'Not much,' he agreed. 'Okay, that's the line I'll take.'

'Good, now that's sorted, what about Terry Coats?' I glanced across the room. Noele McClair was seated at a desk that was as far away from her DI as possible. I wondered if it was her choice, or his preference. 'Has he been in touch?'

He frowned. 'No, he hasn't. I've had Jackie Wright go through Brass's website and make that list the DCC suggested. There are five other names on it, folk he made trouble for, but four of them are still on the force, two in Glasgow, one in Paisley and one in Aberdeen, and the other's retired and living in Lanzarote. Terry Coats is the only serious possibility left, but . . .' He paused; I waited. 'Wouldn't he have needed to know that Brass was going to be in Haddington on Sunday, to set up the meeting?'

'Who says he did? Brass could have suggested the venue if Coats approached him.'

'Either way, time for a look at him, beginning with his whereabouts on Sunday.'

'I can give you a steer on that. When I asked if he was at the party, Noele told me he was at work, at Edinburgh Airport security. A quick call to verify that and he's off the hook.'

'I'll get Jackie Wright to make it while I'm at the media

briefing.' He glanced up at the office wall clock. 'I've got to go now, in fact. Do you want to come?'

'There's nothing I'd rather do less,' I assured him. 'I'll make that call if you like.' He frowned as he considered my offer. 'Nobody will ever know,' I said.

'Okay, if you're sure. Go ahead, but—'

'Don't worry, I'll be discreet.'

And I was: as discreet as a well-thrown brick. I called the airport's chief executive, told him I was MI5 and on the trail of a cell that we thought might have entered the country through Edinburgh the previous Sunday. I asked if his security chief had been on duty that day, as we wanted to contact him privately, not on general view in his office. He bought it, without question.

'Let me check that out for you,' he said, 'and call you back.'

'I don't share my number,' I told him curtly. 'I'll hold for as long as it takes.'

I waited for longer than I had expected; the wall clock had ticked off four and a half minutes when he came back on the line. 'I don't think Mr Coats is going to be of any use to you. He was supposed to be on duty on Sunday, but he called in sick. I tried to locate him, but his deputy tells me that he's off site at the moment for a short-notice appointment. How do you want to proceed?'

'I don't,' I replied. 'Do I need to tell you that this call never happened?'

'Of course not, Mr . . . er, Mr . . .'

By the time he had worked out that I hadn't volunteered my name, I had ended the call.

Thirty-Four

Sauce looked pleased with himself when he returned from the media briefing; I guessed that the death of Austin Brass, which would have been a story in itself, was now officially listed as a potential homicide. The headline writers would have a field day, but for the reporters it would be less so, there being precious little for them to report.

I was more than a little pleased with myself too, but I tried not to let it show as I told him that Terry Coats's alibi had vanished, and so for the moment had he.

'Bloody hell!' he exclaimed. He sneaked a quick look across at Noele McClair, but she was oblivious to it, her attention focused on her computer screen. 'Should I—' he began, but I held up a hand to stop him.

'You know what you should do, Sauce. You're a DI and this isn't a training exercise; consider your options and decide on a course of action.'

He nodded and dropped into his chair, brow furrowed in thought. 'His wife stays out of this,' he murmured eventually. 'I'm not going to question her, not until I know all the answers.' He looked at me, for a reaction I guessed, but I offered him nothing. After a second or two, he nodded, picked up his desk telephone and dialled a number.

'DCC, please,' he said as it was answered. 'DI Haddock.' Pause. 'Haddock.' Pause. 'Just tell him it's Sauce.' The message got through to whoever was on the other end, and after a few seconds the connection was made. 'Sir, I've got a situation with Terry Coats.'

I stayed silent as he explained. There was no need for Mario to know that I was in the room. 'No, sir,' he went on after a pause. 'I don't plan to involve DS McClair at this stage. She told the . . . Sir Robert . . . Mr Skinner that he was at work on Sunday. You can see why that worries me. My intention is to keep her in the office for the rest of the day and under surveillance after that if necessary. Meantime, I'd like your help. You can get information faster than I can. I need to know from HR where DS McClair's salary goes. Then I need to find out whether Coats has an account at the same branch. If he does, I want it checked for recent activity. As I say, you can push those buttons; if I ask for that stuff, it'll be referred upwards anyway . . . Yes, sir, thank you.'

He hung up and looked at me across the desk. 'How did I do?'

'You did bloody well. If it had been a training exercise, you'd have passed. Now,' I said, pushing myself upright, 'I wasn't kidding about lunch. Come on.'

There's a gastropub, a gourmet boozer, in Comely Bank Road that's become very fashionable of late. I'm sure it's very good, but I've been going to the place opposite for as long as it's been there, and that's where I took Sauce. If he was disappointed, he didn't let it show. Hell, it could have been the Pizza Hut next door.

'Am I ready for this, sir?' he asked suddenly, halfway through the main course. 'The jump up to DI? I was no time at all at

DS before I got bumped up. I heard Noele saying to one of the DCs that the Glasgow guys call me the teacher's pet.'

I looked him in the eye. 'If that's true, Sauce, those guys better pray that the teacher never hears them, because if he does, their balls will be in his trophy cabinet. You should ask McClair for a note of their names. When you're the teacher yourself, you might like to bring it up with them. DI rank isn't reached by seniority but by ability. The people who authorised your promotion didn't do it because they like you, but because they rate you. Suppose they had asked me what I thought about it – not that they would – I'd have asked them what they were waiting for. If you're worried about self-confidence, be aware that everyone else has complete confidence in you.'

The truth of it was, that's why I'd wanted to have lunch with him, in a quiet place away from the office. His insecurity had been clear to me the day before, and I had felt that he needed a pep talk from someone with authority but who was a step away from the game.

He had barely finished his dessert when his phone sounded, a banal off-the-shelf ringtone that needed improvement. I had been lecturing him about the woes of Scottish football, but fell silent.

'Sir . . . Yes. One minute, please.' He produced a notebook and pen. 'Ready now.' I watched him as he took notes. 'Thank you, sir, got all that.'

He pocketed the phone and looked at me. His boyish excitement was undisguised, and I admit, I understood why those disgruntled Glasgow guys had said what Noele McClair had claimed.

'That was the DCC,' he said, as if I hadn't known. 'He tracked down Terry Coats's bank. He has a joint account with

Noele, a current account in his own name, and a credit card. That's been active within the last ninety minutes, in a Premier Inn at Edinburgh Park. I need to get there fast, but I don't want to go back to the office and possibly alert McClair that something's up. Do you fancy it, sir?'

'I'll take that as a rhetorical question,' I replied. 'Let's leg it back to Fettes Avenue, and I'll drive. One more suggestion,' I added as I left enough cash on the table to cover the bill. 'Get back on to Mario and ask him if HR has a photograph of Coats. If they don't, suggest that he gets one from the airport. He should ask the chief executive, but shouldn't say why it's needed. If he's asked, he should say, "In connection with the earlier matter." That'll do it. When he has it, he should send it to your phone.'

The sun hit us as we stepped into Comely Bank Road. Haddock's eyes were screwed up as he looked at me. 'What have you been up to, sir?' he asked.

I winked at him. 'You don't have the security clearance to ask that question, DI Haddock.'

I know most of the city like the back of my hand, but still I have problems with Edinburgh Park; the place has grown so fast. It's the same with hotels; just when I've got them pinned down in my mental map, the damn things go and change their names. Happily, I spotted the Premier Inn without too much trouble. It's a big bugger, a bit of a landmark in daylight. We had reached it within half an hour of leaving the restaurant; the image of Terry Coats had hit Sauce's phone within twenty-five minutes.

I parked outside on a yellow and let Sauce lead the way inside. The receptionist was a lady, not the young kind with pancake make-up, but in her prime, with sensible hair and a sensible attitude. Her label bore the name Esther Ransome, which must have been a burden to her, I surmised. Show her some boyish charm, Sauce, I thought as we approached, but I didn't have to worry. 'Afternoon, madam,' he began. 'I'm a police officer.' He made a show of presenting his warrant card, and she took equal care to study it.

'Yes, Detective Inspector,' she said when she was satisfied. 'How can I be of assistance?' She cast a quick glance in my direction. I smiled at her, but she stayed glued to Sauce.

'We're trying to locate someone,' he told her, then showed her the image on his phone. 'We know that he was here within the last two hours and we wonder whether he still is. His name is Coats.'

She nodded. 'It is indeed. That was the name on his credit card, I'm sure. Yes, he's still here, in room five eleven, but the reservation isn't in his name.'

'Whose is it? Can you tell me?'

'I shouldn't,' she sighed, then smiled again, 'but you are the police. The customer is Miss Aisha Karman. She's one of our regulars, aircrew with a budget airline. We get a lot of those. Her schedule is very unpredictable, so she tends to turn up with only a couple of days' warning. The booking is made by the airline, but the crew have to cover their own bills. These budget outfits can be such cheapskates. Would you like me to call Mr Coats for you?'

'Thank you, no,' Sauce said quickly. 'We wouldn't want to disturb Miss Karman, would we?'

Esther gave him a knowing smile; I suspected she would have been happy to break into cabin crew slumbers. 'Perhaps not,' she murmured.

'Were you on duty last Sunday?' he asked.

'No,' she replied regretfully, 'I'm afraid not.'

'Is it possible for you to check and see whether Miss Karman was here on that day?'

'Easy. Give me a second.' She crossed the reception area, activated a computer terminal and scrolled down a few pages. 'Yes, she was. Early check-in nine thirty a.m., left at seven for her next flight. They do that sometimes; take a room for the day. I see that Mr Coats paid on Sunday also. For all the glamour of the job, most of the cabin crew on these cheap flights are on pretty low wages.'

'So it seems,' Sauce murmured. I willed him to ask one more thing, and he did.

'One more thing, Ms Ransome. Do you have a photocopy of her passport?'

'Yes, and Mr Coats's driving licence. We need to identify everyone in the hotel. Would you like copies?'

'Absolutely. The credit card slips too, if you can.'

I had stayed silent all the way through, and I kept it up until we were back in the car. 'Bloody hell,' I exploded as soon as the door closed on Haddock. 'Was that a result or was it not? But poor Noele: I hardly know the woman, and here I am playing a major part in wrecking her life. We got her out of one crisis, and land her with one that's even worse, because it's real.'

'Do we have to tell her?'

'I don't,' I retorted, 'because I was never here, but you do. She's a cop. She knows Terry has to be cleared, and when he is, she's going to want to know how. She's been ordered not to speak to him about the investigation, so she's going to ask you. Are you going to tell her less than the truth? Are you going to lie to her, flat out?'

He sat there for a while, staring at the photocopies he held in his hand. Even in an unsmiling passport photograph, Aisha Karman was a very attractive woman. Terry Coats? His eyes were shifty. He didn't look very trustworthy to me, but my judgement was coloured because I knew he wasn't.

'So?'

'Neither,' he replied. 'Even at my new exalted rank, that decision is above my pay grade. Will you come with me to see Mr McGuire?'

'As in hold your hand? I don't think so, Sauce. Once again you're doing the right thing, but you have to do it on your own.'

Thirty-Five

I don't change my mind very often, but I did on that occasion, principally because I decided that I wanted to see for myself how Mario would handle the situation. Rather than take Sauce back to his office, I drove straight to the senior command base, which was located in Stirling, for no logical reason that I could detect. I had the young DI call ahead not only to make an appointment with the DCC but also to warn him of my presence, and give him the chance to veto it if he felt I was too close to an investigation in which I had no official role.

There was no negative feedback, and so I strode into the building with Haddock when we arrived, and straight up to the chief officers' floor. I led the way; I'd been there before, he hadn't.

'What have you got, Detective Inspector?' McGuire asked brusquely as soon as we entered his office. 'And why have you brought your minder with you?'

Sauce had his answer off pat. 'In view of the delicacy of the situation, sir,' he replied, 'with DS McClair's involvement, I didn't want to involve another member of the unit, and Mr Skinner . . . Sir Robert . . . was there.'

'And you couldn't have kept him away if you'd tried.'

'Almost certainly not,' I agreed. 'It was a pragmatic decision, and a wise one given the way things worked out.'

Mario grinned. 'You don't need to defend him, Bob. I did tell him to take advantage of your experience, and I didn't set a limit. If there's fault, it's mine, not his.' He turned back to Sauce. 'So what's happened that you have to bring it to my door? Did you find Coats at the Premier Inn?'

'We did, sir, and as a result he's no longer a suspect, and by extension, neither is DS McClair. However, we also found this.' He handed over the photocopies that Esther Ransome had provided.

McGuire's eyes widened as he studied them and understood their meaning, then narrowed again. 'I get it,' he muttered. 'Coats is shagging an air hostess on the side, and you want to know whether you should tell his wife, your colleague.'

'That's it, boss. What do you think?'

'I think . . . I'm going to do exactly what you did, namely, take the problem up the chain of command for a decision. Hold on.' He picked up his desk phone and pressed a button. 'Maggie,' he said after a few seconds, 'I've got a couple of suspects with me who are giving me a problem. I need you to solve it. Do you have a minute?'

Sauce gulped. I smiled. Half a minute later, the door opened and Chief Constable Margaret Rose Steele stepped into the spacious office. She nodded towards me without the slightest show of surprise. 'Hello again, Bob. Good to see you. I knew it was you,' she explained. 'I saw your car in the park; its personalised plate is a giveaway. CC54RMS indeed!'

'Blame my daughter,' I told her. 'Birthday present; not my idea.'

'But you love it, admit it.' She nodded at Sauce. 'DI Haddock. Congratulations and welcome to the bunker. I see it hasn't taken you long to start making waves. What have you been up to?'

'This,' Mario growled, handing her the documents.

She read through them, then handed them back, as puzzled as when she had begun. 'Who is Terry Coats, and why are you monitoring his love life?'

Sauce glanced at me; I told him with the briefest of nods that it was down to him to reply.

'Austin Brass ruined his police career, ma'am. That made him a suspect in the homicide investigation, but he isn't any more.'

'Oh yes,' she murmured, 'the homicide investigation. I had Perry Allsop bending my ear about that an hour or so back.'

Out of the corner of my eye, I saw Mario's nostrils flare; I knew that he was not a fan of Mr Allsop, a holdover from the Andy Martin era.

'Don't worry,' Maggie continued. 'I told him I'm a firm believer in giving youth its head. Back to Mr Coats; if he isn't a suspect any longer, what is he?'

'He's still the husband of Detective Sergeant Noele McClair, my new sidekick.'

She gasped, then laughed. 'You guys! You want me to decide whether you should tell her or not.'

'Come on, Chief,' Mario exclaimed. 'There could be legal implications here. If we show her those papers and the marriage blows up, Coats might sue us for invasion of privacy. Knowing our lawyers, they might tell us to settle out of court.'

'I doubt that,' she countered. 'You were making legitimate enquiries about a suspect in a homicide. His wife happens to be a member of the team. Can she be denied access to information gained during the investigation? That's the issue.'

'There is another one. She sent him a text from the crime scene saying that Brass's body had been found.'

'She probably thought it would make his day, Mario, but I don't believe for a second she thought he might have killed Brass. Is she excluded from the inquiry at the moment?'

'Yes, ma'am,' Sauce confirmed.

'Then I reckon you should bring her back in. She's a valuable resource.'

'Let me be clear,' Mario said. 'You're saying that she should be told what we've discovered.'

'Yes, and I'm saying specifically that DI Haddock should tell her, and to hell with any legal consequences. If Coats makes a fuss, I will tell him, personally, to fuck off, and I will not authorise one penny in compensation. Guys, this isn't really a professional issue, it's a matter of morality, pure and simple. Sauce, if Coats was married to your sister not your sergeant, what would you do?'

'Knock ten bells out of him and tell her,' he replied instantly.

'Let's forget about the first part of that, but the second, yes. You're a family in CID. You look after each other at all times. Tell McClair and bring her back on to your team. Mario, give her a written reprimand for the text, but leave it at that.'

I hadn't planned to say a word, but I felt compelled. 'The man's a member of an airport security staff,' I pointed out, 'who's been neglecting his duties to service his girlfriend. Potentially that makes him a security risk.'

'Can you plug that hole without us being involved?' Maggie asked.

'No problem; I'll have a word with my friend Mr Houseman and he will call on the airport CEO.'

'Do you need copies of these documents?'

'No, but it wouldn't do any harm.'

She smiled. 'Crisis sorted. Sauce, get it done today. Bob, I imagine you'll be having your spook friend check out Miss Karman also, just in case.'

I nodded to hide my reaction. That precaution hadn't occurred to me. Sloppy, Skinner, I chided myself.

The meeting broke up; Maggie went back to her room and Mario shooed us out of his. I drove Sauce back to Edinburgh and his meeting with DS McClair. We were halfway there when he spoke up.

'You realise, sir, this means we're down to one suspect for Brass?'

'I do, and we know who it is.'

'How should I proceed?'

'Side by side with me,' I replied, 'and very carefully indeed.'

Thirty-Six

I didn't want to be around when Sauce broke the news to Noele McClair; rather than come into his office, or even be seen in the driveway, I dropped him at the corner of Fettes Avenue and Comely Bank Road.

Before we parted, we agreed a plan of action. I would make a few calls in the evening to see if I could come up with a lead to Jimmy. I would report anything I found back to Sauce, for action if necessary, but without involving others. Discretion was important to me; if Sir James Proud came under scrutiny in the context of a murder inquiry, there was every chance that it would leak. Even in my time that would have been a possibility, despite my looming presence within the building. Under the new regime, there were simply too many people that I didn't know.

I called Clyde Houseman from the car, before I'd gone beyond Stockbridge. I told him what I had discovered, and asked him to brief the airport chief executive. 'If he wants documentary evidence, I'll get it to you, but I doubt that he will. Once you've done that, I'd like you to call Millbank and put a background check in place on Aisha Karman. I've got no reason to believe she is a risk, but given her boyfriend's

239

job, it has to be done. If he flagged her through security and she blew up the aircraft she was on . . .' I didn't need to say any more.

That done, I switched on my in-car music. Lately I've become a fan of Mark O'Connor, an American fiddler who is a unique blend of country, bluegrass, Cajun and classical, with echoes of the great Aly Bain thrown in. He was halfway through 'Jole Blon' when an incoming call silenced him.

'Bad timing, Sauce,' I grumbled.

'Sorry, sir,' he said, without sounding it, 'but I thought you'd want to know. I took Noele into my office and showed her what we had on her husband.'

'How did she take it?' I asked, my interest sparked suddenly.

'Put it this way. SpaceX are looking for people to send to Mars in a few years; if Terry has any sense, he'll be volunteering. I sense this isn't the first time he's pointed his dick in the wrong direction, but I doubt that it'll be getting anywhere near her again. She started with shock and a few tears, then she went to mortified, followed by angry, then into full-blown vengeful.'

That prompted an undesirable scenario. 'Sauce, he could still be at the Premier Inn for all we know.'

'That occurred to me too; I'm keeping her in the office, but I've let her call the hotel. She's in my office now. If he is still there, when he picks up the phone I'll put him right off his stroke.'

I laughed. 'There's a streak of evil in you, Haddock, that I had no idea was there. Was my name mentioned at all in this context?'

'No, but she must have noticed you in the office, so she may figure it out.'

'I'll look out for incoming fire. Cheers.'

I ended the call and went back to Mark O'Connor. He saw me home, where I discovered that we had a visitor.

'Daddy, this is Harry,' Seonaid announced as a small fair-haired boy looked out from behind her. 'His mummy called Mummy and asked if he could stay with us until she can pick him up tonight. His mummy's in the police. I told Harry you used to be in the police too.'

'I'm pleased to meet you, Harry,' I said. 'Is Seonaid looking after you?'

He nodded. 'Yes, Mr Skinner.'

'That's good. Seonaid, you two go and play while I say hello to Mummy.' I left them in the hall and headed for the kitchen, where I found Sarah preparing something that looked suspiciously like macaroni cheese.

'Don't worry,' she assured me. 'This is for the kids. We're having steak pie. I heard you being introduced to Harry. There's some kind of crisis in the Coats–McClair household. I had a panic call from Noele this afternoon. Luckily I was able to leave early; we only got here ten minutes ago.'

'Have you ever met the husband?' I asked.

'Yes, briefly, at a parents' night when you were away.'

'What did you think of him?'

'I think he's an oily creep who fancies himself for no reason that was obvious to me. Why?'

'Your assessment may be pretty accurate. I have knowledge of the crisis.'

'Oh dear.' She sighed. 'Are you going to share?'

'No, I don't think so. I'll let her tell you as much as she wants to.'

'Is she still in trouble with Sauce and Mario?'

'No. Maggie gave her a free pass on that one.' I grabbed a Corona from the fridge and uncapped it. 'I need to make some calls,' I told her, and disappeared to the sanctuary of our small office.

Because of the nature of my job, I've never had much need for a taxi service. I've heard of Uber and I don't like it, having a natural antipathy to anything that sets out to achieve global domination. However, I was absolutely certain that it had never crossed Jimmy Proud's radar. The taxi that Chrissie had seen at their door when he had left would have been a local.

I had only ever used one of the East Lothian private hire firms, a crew from North Berwick, but I knew most of them by name, having seen them driving in and around our village. To back that up, I found a copy of one of the *Local Life* magazines that keep popping through my letter box. I never read them, but I know that they're heavy with advertising for goods, shops, restaurants and services. I made my way through it, and fifteen minutes later I had a list of targets, with contact numbers. I took a slug of my Mexican happy juice and picked up my phone.

My pitch was simple, and unashamedly untruthful. I was looking for the driver of a vehicle that had picked up a friend on the previous Monday. He had contacted me to say that he had lost a personal item and asked me to find out if he had left it in the taxi. Every one of them bought my lie without question, but one by one they all denied having had Jimmy as a passenger. I was thinking of how I could broaden my search even as I dialled the last number on my list.

The Law of Sod has many forms, one of them being that if you have a list to work through in search of a single response, success will elude you until the very last number you call. 'AJ Private Hire,' a calm voice announced. I launched into my pitch, with little expectation and less enthusiasm.

'Yes,' he said, 'I picked up a hire from that address. An elderly gentleman; I took him into Edinburgh and dropped him at the Market Street entrance to Waverley station. But I found nothing in my vehicle afterwards, and I'm pretty sure I would have, for I clean it every night. What's he lost?'

I wasn't prepared for that one. 'A lower set of dentures,' I replied, and hung up quickly.

I guessed that Sauce would be home, enjoying some hard-earned down time, and probably regaling the beautiful Cheeky . . . it amuses me when I reflect that my son Ignacio is now her step-uncle, his mother having married her grandpa . . . with details of his exciting day. I felt a twinge of guilt about interrupting, but it didn't stop me.

'Sir,' he sighed as he took my call.

'I need you,' I began without pleasantries, 'and no one else to check with the booking office at Waverley station to see if Sir James Proud bought a rail ticket on Monday, and if so, where he was going.'

'Wouldn't it be better to check his bank for the first part of that?' he suggested.

I knocked that down quickly. 'Waste of time, Sauce. Jimmy's not daft. He left his phone behind so we couldn't trace him; if he got on a train, he'll have paid cash.'

'Suppose he didn't. Couldn't he have got on a bus?'

'Yes,' I growled, 'he could. If he did that, we're fucked, because he's got a bus pass.'

'I'll check it out tomorrow morning,' he said. 'I'll print an image off the internet and show it to the counter staff. But don't hold your breath.' I expected him to hang up, but he didn't. 'You know what I'm thinking, sir?' he asked.

I reckoned that I did, but I needed to hear it. 'Go on.'

'We're agreed that we're down to one realistic suspect—'

'Sauce, please,' I interrupted. 'Call him a person of interest, not a suspect.'

'Call him what you like, sir, but it doesn't change anything. My supposition is that Sir James contacted Brass and persuaded him to meet him earlier in a private place, to avoid any risk of them being overheard. Maybe he made it a condition of telling him the whole truth.'

'Whatever that is.'

'That he was involved in rigging the case against Meads, what else? I believe that Sir James lured him down to the riverbank, hit him on the head with an object, knocked him unconscious and tossed him into the river, leaving you short of a lunch companion and us with a murder on our hands. Do you have any alternative suggestions?'

He was challenging me; I was pleased by that, even though I didn't like his conclusion. I didn't like it, but I couldn't demolish it either. 'No, I don't,' I admitted. 'But how are you going to prove it?'

'By placing him at the location,' he replied, with an unsettling degree of confidence.

'That will be difficult if he wasn't there,' I pointed out.

'Agreed. The first step has to be to interview Lady Proud about his whereabouts on Sunday afternoon.'

'If she says he was sitting alongside her reading the *Sunday Times*, are you going to believe her?'

'I don't know,' he admitted. 'I'd probably have to proceed on the assumption that she was lying.'

'Then fucking proceed,' I snapped, 'but please, don't go near Chrissie. She's an elderly lady, and I don't want her frightened. I'll talk to her myself, if you're happy with that; while I'm doing so, you can put other checks in place, the first of them being the street cameras, I would suggest.'

'Wouldn't he know how to avoid them?'

'Don't be daft; I doubt that he knows they exist. Start with those, then look at his phone records; they should tell you if he called Brass. So will Brass's phone. What's the latest on that?'

'The Dutch police have recovered it from a flower truck in a place called Leiden. It's on its way back to us.' He paused. 'Sir, if you go to see Lady Proud, maybe you could collect Sir James's phone. You did say that he left that at home.'

'Not a problem. I'll pick it up. Can't you speed things up by asking Brass's phone provider for access to his records?'

'I don't know who that is,' Sauce admitted. 'He bought SIM cards, put credit on them and changed them every time it ran out. Jackie Wright's doing a very thorough job on his laptop; she's painting a picture of the guy. He was very security-conscious and protected his privacy very thoroughly. There's no contact list on it. She has a theory that when we get his phone back, we'll find that he made most of his calls through WhatsApp or something like it, so that he can delete the records.'

'Is any of his work on it? Specifically, the Matthew Ampersand case?'

'Not a sign, and I asked her to look for it.'

'Have you been into his office in Livingston yet?'

'Not yet, sir,' he said. 'I've been running one woman short today, but now that DS McClair's back in the fold, I can put her on that. I'm calling her in tomorrow, as soon as I can get a hold of her.'

'Don't count on it,' I warned. 'Her wee boy's with us right now, while Mummy castrates Daddy, I imagine. If she asks for compassionate time, it'll be tough to turn her down, in the circumstances.'

'If that happens, I'll ask the DCC for a replacement. I hear Talvin Singh's waiting for a slot.'

'You could do worse; he's a safe pair of hands, and he's the size of a house.' I paused. 'Whoever goes into Brass's office, I'll be interested in what they find there, if you can share.'

'If Noele does ask for leave, that will probably be me. If it is, I can always leave Cheeky at the Almondvale shops while I do it. You wouldn't happen to be passing by there tomorrow?' he asked casually.

'Not a chance.'

'Nah, I didn't think so. When will you see Lady Proud?'

'I'll take a stroll along there now,' I replied. 'My boys have been walking Jimmy's dog. I'll probably need to round them up for supper, so that'll give me an excuse for being there.'

As it transpired, I met Mark and Jazz as I turned into the Prouds' cul-de-sac, heading in the opposite direction. I hurried them home and carried on.

I was even more shocked than before when Chrissie came to her front door; she seemed to have aged by several years in a few days. I knew that Jimmy had just turned seventy-four, but his wife looked ten years older than that. 'Come in, Bob, come in,' she said. Her voice was quiet and quavering. 'It's nice of you to call. Your lovely boys have just gone; they're very good, walking Bowser for me.'

'They enjoy it,' I assured her. 'I thought I'd call in to see how you were doing.'

'I'm fine,' she replied. 'I'm sure Jimmy'll not be long. He's probably just gone for the papers.'

I drew a quick breath. 'Like as not, Chrissie,' I murmured. 'Have you heard from him?'

'Not since he went out, son. That's why I'm sure he'll be back soon.'

'I'm sure he will.' I took a closer look at her. Her face was more lined than I remembered it, and there was a yellowish tinge to her skin that I didn't like at all. I was fairly sure that she was wearing the clothes that she'd had on the last time I'd seen her. 'Chrissie,' I ventured, 'can I make you a cup of tea?'

She smiled, but her eyes were a little vacant. 'That would be very nice of you, son. You'll have one yourself, of course.'

'Yes, I will.' I went through to the kitchen; Bowser was in there, scratching the door. His food and water bowls were full; I assumed that the boys had done that. I filled the kettle and switched it on, took three tea bags from a caddy that was placed beside it and chucked them into a pot. As the water boiled, I glanced around. There was a toaster on the work surface, with a pack of butter and a few crumbs beside it. There was one plate, smeared with butter, a knife and a mug in the sink, but nothing else on view. I checked the fridge. The milk was three days past its best-before date, the bacon in a pack that had been opened was curling at the edges and the few vegetables in their compartment looked sorry for themselves. In East Lothian we have a system for recycling food waste. I checked the small grey box that sat by the back door; apart from a couple of crusts and a tea bag, it was empty.

The kettle's thermostat clicked off and it fell silent. I filled the teapot, found two mugs, sugar, put some of the milk, which was just about usable, into a jug and carried it all back to the sitting room on a tray, followed by the dog. As I filled the old lady's mug and handed it to her, I couldn't help noticing that she smelled a bit.

'Chrissie,' I asked her, 'have you been eating properly?'

'Me? Yes, fine, I don't need much, son. Tea and toast do me fine.'

'You've got no bread left, and the milk's about done for. What are you going to have for supper tonight?'

'Oh, I'll find something, don't you worry.'

'Please,' I said. 'Allow me to worry. You have to take care of yourself.'

'Yes, yes, yes,' she whispered.

I hated getting down to business, but I had to. 'Have you heard from Jimmy since he left? Has he been in touch?'

She looked at her watch. 'No. But I'm sure he won't be long now.'

'Do you remember last Sunday?' I continued.

'I'm not sure,' she replied. 'Is that the day all those cooking programmes are on TV in the morning? And that man with the glasses?'

'That's it. Can I ask you, was Jimmy in all day or did he go out at all?'

She frowned and closed her eyes as if she was trying to feel her way through the mists in her mind. 'Yes, he did, after the cooking programmes. He switched the golf on so I could watch it and said he was going out in the car for a while.' She sniffed, and I could sense annoyance. 'He didn't take Bowser with him either. He just left him; he hardly ever does that and yet he's done it twice in a few days.'

'How long was he gone?'

'Oh, I couldn't tell you that, Bob. It was still light when he got back, though, because I made him take Bowser for a walk.'

'Did he tell you where he'd been?'

'No, but I know he must have been in Haddington.' She straightened a little in her chair as a flash of clarity came to her. 'I remember. He brought back cakes from that German baker who used to be in Gullane.'

Fuck, I thought.

'How did he seem?'

'He was quiet. He hardly spoke for the rest of the day. The cakes were nice, though.' She smiled, then checked her watch again. 'He can't be long now. I hope he brings some more back with him; maybe a loaf, too. We like his bread, the German's.'

She picked up her mug, blew into it to cool its contents, and sipped some tea. 'Mmm. Not enough sugar, Bob,' she chided me. I apologised and added two more spoonfuls. 'That's better. Jimmy always gets it right. I'll be pleased when he's back. Remind me, son, what day is this again?'

'It's Friday, Chrissie.'

The more I studied her, the more serious my problem became. In all conscience, I could not leave the old lady in that condition. Her mind had lost track of time. I was concerned, and I was angry too with Jimmy for deserting her, whatever the cause.

'Do you hear much from your daughter, Chrissie?' I asked. The Prouds had one child, but effectively she was lost to them. Yvonne was a banker in Hong Kong, where she had lived for twenty years, since just after the handover to China. She was married to a Chinese guy, and seemed to have been assimilated into his culture entirely, for she never came home. They had two sons, grandchildren that Jimmy and Chrissie had never seen other than on video.

For a few seconds she was puzzled. 'Who? Oh, our Yvonne? We had a Christmas card, I think, with a picture of the boys.'

'Do you have a phone number for her, or an email address?'

'No, I don't. Jimmy will have. You can ask him when he gets back.'

I could have found her without too much difficulty, but I realised that at best she would be a long-term solution to what was an immediate problem. 'What about Jimmy's niece, Joanna?'

'The painter lass? She visits us from time to time. She's fond of her uncle Jimmy. Is her mother still alive? His sister with the funny name.'

'No, not for a few years now.' As she spoke, I'd been making decisions. 'Chrissie, I don't believe that Jimmy will be home tonight, and I'm not happy with you being here on your own. I'm going to arrange for someone to stay with you, tonight at least.'

She tutted. 'Son, you don't need to do that.'

'I know I don't, but I want to. Her name's Trish, she's from Barbados and she looks after our children. I'm going to go now and make arrangements, but I'll be back.'

I left her there, but I didn't go straight home; instead I headed for our village Co-op. On the way, I called Trish and checked that the offer I'd made was all right with her. I had no doubt that it would be; she's a good person with a heart the size of a bucket. I carried on my way and did a mini shop for the old lady, all the basics I reckoned she needed, for a couple of days at least, until an extended arrangement could be made. Next, bags in hand, I went next door to Gullane Superfry and bought battered haddock and chips, deep fried, no salt, vinegar or brown sauce. It was still hot when I returned to the Proud bungalow. I plated it and served it to Chrissie on the tray I'd used earlier. 'There,' I said, 'that'll save you having to cook something yourself.'

I hadn't been sure how she'd react, but she looked up at me with the surprised delight of a young girl. 'Oh Bob, I love a fish supper. I keep telling Jimmy to get me one, but he never does.'

While she ate, I phoned Joanna Meikle, hoping that she hadn't gone out on the razzle, and even more, that she would want to hear what I had to tell her. To my relief she picked up on the third ring. 'It's Bob Skinner here,' I began. 'It's about your aunt, Chrissie. I'm calling from her house. Jimmy's had to go away for a while on private business, but I don't think he realised that she's not as capable as she once was. She's alone, she's confused, and she definitely needs a carer. I've made arrangements for tonight, but I'm hoping that you can come down tomorrow and look after her until a more permanent arrangement can be made.'

'Oh,' she exclaimed, her distress evident. 'Poor Auntie Chrissie. I must admit, the last time I visited, I thought I saw signs of deterioration, but I put it down to Uncle Jimmy's illness. Of course I'll come. I was going to work on your portrait tomorrow, but that can wait. It's too bad, with him having done so well to beat the cancer. I'll stay until he comes back. Do you know how long he'll be away?'

'I wish I did, Joanna, I wish I did.'

Thirty-Seven

Chrissie had just finished her fish supper and was turning her attention to a white chocolate Magnum when Trish arrived. The old lady had been starving, literally. I thought I saw an improvement in her awareness of her surroundings, but she was still frail and uncertain.

'Call me if you need to,' I told her temporary carer. 'Any time.'

'We'll be fine,' Trish assured me. 'I'll suggest that she takes a bath before bed and give her some cocoa later. More than anything, I reckon she needs sleep. You go back to Sarah now.'

I did as I was ordered, but before I left, I looked for Jimmy's phone as I'd promised Sauce I would. I found it quickly, tucked away in a drawer of the hall table, but when I switched it on, I saw that he really had been thorough. The screen showed me a message: 'No SIM card'.

By the time I arrived home, junior supper was over, Noele McClair – grim-faced, I was told – had picked up her son, and my wife was preparing saltimbocca, with thin veal slices, accompanied by baby potatoes, roasted, and steamed asparagus.

'How was Chrissie?'

'Sad,' was my considered reply. 'Jimmy's fucked off and left her without a thought for her mental state. He must have noticed that she has memory problems.'

'She probably doesn't when he's there to fill in the gaps. Would it help if I go along to see her tomorrow? I am a doctor, remember; I may specialise in the dead now, but I'm pretty good with the living too. When I practised in the US I had quite a few elderly patients, so I am familiar.'

'It would do no harm,' I admitted. 'Yes, why don't you.'

'And Jimmy,' she continued. 'What's the situation with him?'

'He's in the wind. He's a fugitive; sounds crazy, I know, but that's the best way of describing it. He's the prime suspect in a homicide investigation and he's disappeared.'

'But? I hear one there.'

'But I'm struggling to imagine how a seventy-four-year-old man who's just undergone surgery and chemotherapy for cancer could have killed Austin Brass in the way that Sauce described.'

'So am I,' Sarah agreed, 'and I did the post-mortem. Brass wasn't a huge man, but he was five feet ten and weighed a hundred and seventy pounds – twelve stone two. He was in good general health, and I'd say from his musculature that he spent some time in the gym. While I can't prove yet that most of the injuries to his head and neck were sustained before he went into the water, that's what I believe. He was either overcome by a stronger attacker or he was rendered incapable of resistance by a single severe blow. Unless I'm underestimating Jimmy's strength, I have difficulty envisaging him doing either.'

'Until you can prove it,' I said, 'accidental death remains an option. Will you ever?'

'Possibly. I recovered several wood fragments from the

injuries. They've gone to the lab for identification. If that shows the presence of a substance that wasn't in the river, I'll be there.'

'Could he have been hit by something like a wooden baton, for example?'

'Like an old police truncheon?'

'That's what I have in mind. There are plenty of those in the possession of retired cops.'

'It's possible,' she conceded. 'I found no evidence of that type of weapon having been used, but the body had been in the water for days before it got to me. There could have been marks that had deteriorated, or been covered by subsequent injuries.'

'How about a fist?' I suggested. 'Could he have been knocked out, then heaved in the river?'

'Come on, who are we talking about here? Jimmy Proud or George Foreman? It takes a very hard punch to knock someone completely unconscious for more than a few seconds. That happens very rarely, even in boxing. No, Bob, as you said, it's crazy to imagine Jimmy doing that.'

'Agreed, but Sauce's theory of him setting up an earlier meeting with Brass does make sense, because only he and I knew of the first one. Also I can place him in Haddington at the time of the attack. Sarah, the question needs to be put to him. But it can't be, because he's run away, and taken pains to ensure that he can't be followed. I hate to say it, but that's not the act of an innocent man.'

Thirty-Eight

The night went by without a call from Trish. Next day I waited until ten and then went back to the Prouds' place. When I arrived, I saw an elderly Ford parked in the driveway: Joanna's, I guessed, correctly, as I saw when she opened the front door. There was an unusual silence about the house; it took me a few seconds to identify it as an absence of Bowser.

'No dog?'

'Trish has taken him for a run on the beach, God bless her. I'm not good with dogs, and that one is . . .'

'Quirky?' I suggested.

'That's being kind. He's too much for Auntie Chrissie, that's for sure.'

'How is she?'

'Still in bed. Trish said that she woke twice through the night. The first time she couldn't find the bathroom, even though they've an en suite; the second she opened the front door and went out into the street in her nightdress, because she thought she heard Uncle Jimmy's car arriving. Where is he? Do you know?'

'If I did,' I said, 'he'd be back here by now. All I can tell you

255

is that he has a private situation and he feels that he needs space to deal with it.'

'He has a situation in his own house,' she retorted, 'and he needs to deal with that.'

'Don't be too hard on him, Joanna. A marriage can be a confined space, especially when you're retired and together twenty-four seven. It's possible not to be aware of changes that are obvious to people who only see you on occasion.'

'This situation?' she ventured. 'Does it have to do with Matthew Ampersand and the questions you asked me?'

'What makes you think that?'

'It's a bit of a coincidence. You come to see me asking about something that happened in the last century, and at the same time, one of the very few people who knew about it decides to vanish. Am I right?'

I nodded. 'Yes, I think you are.'

'Could he be in trouble?'

'Not in the way he feared. The man who might have made that trouble is dead.'

'Does he know that?' she asked.

'He does if he's read a paper this morning.'

'Let's hope he has, and that it brings him home.'

'Yes, let's hope,' I agreed, without a shred of expectation that it would. 'One thing, though,' I continued. 'My interest in this goes beyond Jimmy now. I'd like to talk to Briony about what happened, if possible on neutral ground. I met her husband at the farm when I was talking to Carmel, and let's just say that he and I didn't get on too well. Can you help me with that?'

'I don't see why not,' she replied. 'How about here? I can invite her out to visit my temporary home.' She grinned. 'I can see why you and Michael might be a bad mix; he's very territorial and bound to resent another alpha male on his patch.'

I returned home by way of Gullane Bents. I was halfway there when I stopped, and called Sauce. 'Progress?' I asked him.

'Only another box ticked,' he said. 'I'm in Brass's office now. It's neat and tidy, obsessively so; the pens on the desk are in straight lines, and the magazines on his coffee table are arranged perfectly, one on top of the other. There are no paper files at all, none. I am hoping that they're all in his desktop computer, but that wants a fucking password. I've tried the one you came up with for the laptop, but it doesn't work.'

'Try Dalziel,' I suggested, 'as in the fat fictional detective.' I spelled it out for him, in case he wasn't familiar with the work of the late great Reginald Hill.

'What the hell?' he exclaimed. 'I'm in. How did you do that?'

'It stood to reason,' I replied. 'He had his primary school as his password for the laptop, so it was a fair guess that he'd use his secondary for the other one. Local knowledge, son, local knowledge; you can't beat it. What about his home?' I asked.

'Jackie Wright and Talvin Singh are there right now. You were spot on about McClair. She asked HR last night for compassionate leave, "to make domestic arrangements". They consulted me about it and I did a deal, with Sammy Pye's approval. She's got a week if she needs it, and we've got DS Singh full-time.'

'Congratulations. I hope you get as good a result out of that computer. I'm still looking at the Ampersand affair, as you know, so anything you find there could be of interest to me. While you're doing that, I thought I'd talk to Brass's father. Is that okay with you?'

'Be my guest, but please report back anything that might be useful to my investigation. We know little or nothing about Austin Brass's life outside of his work. It may be that his death isn't related to his threat to Sir James. We could be heading in the wrong direction.' He paused. 'By the way, I haven't been able to do the traffic camera check yet. Did you speak to Lady Proud last night?'

A question I'd been hoping he wouldn't ask, but even if he hadn't, I couldn't have withheld what I knew. 'Yes. From what she told me, Jimmy was in Haddington last Sunday.'

'Not what you wanted to hear, eh?' He knew me so well.

'No, but it doesn't prove a damn thing. I warn you, Sauce, even if you gather enough evidence to let you charge him, you're not going to convince me.'

I could almost see his frown. 'Consider me warned, sir, but I have to go with what I can see before me. The direction it's heading just now, the best way you can protect Sir James is by finding the person who killed Brass, if it wasn't him.'

'If I can, I will,' I promised. 'Now, can you give me an address for Brass senior?'

'Of course; I'll text it to you as soon as I can.'

'Thanks.'

'Did you pick up the phone, by the way?' he asked.

'That's another story.' I told him about the missing SIM card.

'That doesn't look good, sir, him doing that.'

'Tell me about it,' I sighed, sadly.

I ended the call and carried on my way across Gullane Bents and up the gentle incline towards my garden gate. The morning was pleasant; I'd expected to find Seonaid playing outside, but there was no sign of her or of either of her younger brothers.

As I reached the house, I heard a noise: a shout, a man's voice, angry, then another, Sarah's, shrill, warning. I took the most direct route to the source, through the garden room into the hall. As I reached it, I saw Seonaid in the doorway; two of her brothers were beside her, and Mark was restraining James Andrew, with some difficulty even though he's older and bigger. Beyond I could see Sarah, with Dawn in her arms, and past her, my oldest son, Ignacio. He was holding a stranger, a man almost as tall as his six feet three, a hand wrapped round each of his biceps, gripping tight: but not tightly enough, for as I approached the aggressor tore free and hit him, a quick, vicious blow, full in the face.

Before Ignacio could react, I was between them, at pace, pushing the attacker, slamming the heels of both my hands into his chest and sending him backwards, off balance but not quite off his feet. I've been in some tough situations through the job, things I've had to handle; this was different because I was angry and my blood was up. So was the invader's; he came back at me. He had almost twenty years on me, but he'd hit my son and scared my family; that made it a mismatch. I stopped him with one punch with my right fist; it nailed him exactly where I was aiming, in the middle of the forehead. I felt the impact all the way up to my shoulder. He froze in mid-air for a split second as he absorbed the power, then went down on his back on the driveway.

'Get the kids inside, Ignacio,' I said, forcing myself to breathe slowly and deeply to recover my self-control. 'Sarah, phone the police.'

'Who is he?' she asked. I glanced to my left as she handed Dawn to Ignacio; his face was reddened and his nose was bleeding.

To my inner relief, the man on the ground, who had been completely unconscious for more than a couple of seconds, began to show signs of life; his eyes were glazed but he seemed to be trying to focus. He tried to roll on to his side, but I put a foot on his chest, pinning him down. Having looked at him closely, I knew who he was, even if he didn't at that moment in time. I'd seen his face on a file in the safe in my old office in Glasgow. 'You stay there for a bit, Mr Coats,' I said. 'Maybe hold off on the cops for a while, love,' I called to Sarah. 'Noele McClair's probably had enough grief for one weekend.'

'That's the husband?' she exclaimed.

'The very same; no longer of West Fenton, from what I hear. How do you treat a concussion?' A lump was growing on his forehead; it had begun as a quail's egg, but was moving up to hen size.

'An ice pack is a good way to start; I'll go make one up. Do you want Ignacio back here, in case he needs to be restrained?'

'I think I can manage that on my own, thanks. I do want you to photograph the boy's injuries, though.' I could hear tears from indoors: Seonaid. Coats made another feeble effort to rise, but I put a little more weight on his chest. 'You need to stay there, mate,' I told him. 'Until I'm feeling a wee bit calmer, you won't be safe on your feet.'

Finally, he was able to meet my gaze. 'Bastard,' he hissed.

'Spare me the righteous anger, Coats.'

'What happened to me?' His speech was slurred.

'I did,' I replied, 'and if my boy has any more than superficial damage, I might not be finished.' If so, I suspected I might have to use the other hand; my right one was starting to throb.

'Maybe I don't care,' Coats sighed. 'You and your fucking mate, that baby DI, you've ruined my life.'

I gasped at his audacity. 'Oh yes? Which one of us shagged your girlfriend? Which one of us used your bank card to pay for the hotel room? Terry, you ruined your own fucking life.' I took my foot off his chest. 'If you're looking for someone to blame, start your investigation by looking in the mirror.'

'It's not as simple as that,' he groaned as he raised himself, propped up by his elbows.

'What?' I laughed. 'You were being coerced into banging her?'

'No,' he protested, with a vehemence that surprised me, for nine times out of ten, it's a reaction of the innocent. 'Look, I can't tell you any more; it could put lives at risk.'

'Did you try that line on DS McClair?'

'It's not a line! Yes, I tried to explain, but she wasn't having any of it. Thing is, I've got previous with Noele; after the last time, she warned me, never again. I should have told her what was happening, I know that now.'

'You should have asked her for a pink ticket?'

'Something like that, but I couldn't; with her being still in the job, I was afraid she'd want to get involved.'

'A threesome? She doesn't strike me as that sort of girl.'

'That's right, take the piss.'

'Hey,' I exclaimed. 'You're the guy who came to my house, frightened my wee girl – your son's friend – and attacked my grown-up son. Me taking the piss is the least of your worries. What are you trying to say? Is it something sensible, or did I hit you even harder than I thought?'

As I spoke, Sarah appeared by my side, carrying a recycling bag filled with ice, and her medical kit. She gave Coats the ice pack but told him to wait for a moment before applying it. Kneeling beside him, she took his pulse, shone a torch in his eyes to check his pupil reaction, then looked into them with another instrument. 'Follow my finger,' she instructed, holding up a single digit, moving it from right to left and then back. 'You seem to be okay,' she told him when she was finished, but her voice was as cold as the bag Coats pressed to his lumpen forehead.

'You were saying,' I murmured as she left. 'It had better be good, because I'm still thinking about calling our former colleagues and having you lifted.'

He tried to stand, but his legs were unsteady. I took his elbow to support him, then walked him to a circular stone table with benches in the centre of the front lawn. It's decorative more than anything else, but it served my purpose. 'Spill,' I ordered, as he sat.

'Aisha's a potential informant,' he began. 'I've been grooming her, trying to get inside a smuggling operation.'

'Smuggling what?'

'Krugerrands and other gold coins. I had a tip from somebody on the staff that they're being accepted as payment in one of the groundside stores, at half value. The way it works, a flight crew member makes a small purchase, tenders the krugerrand and gets the change in US dollars or euros. The coins are trousered, and when there are enough, they're melted down and sold as gold bars.'

'Why dollars and euros?' I asked.

'Because at this moment in time, the principals in the operation would rather not have sterling. That's what my informant thinks. The store has a stock of both; it accepts them from returning travellers who just want to get rid of the stuff, any way, anyhow.'

'Couldn't the smugglers sell them on the bullion market themselves?'

'If they did, there would be a record of the transaction. But there might be another reason. I did some checking with a mate of mine, a South African who works over here now; obviously he knows a hell of a lot more about krugerrands than I do. He told me there was a bullion robbery in Pretoria about twelve years back, when he still worked there. It was huge; the value of the heist was understated by the South African treasury. They said it was five million, US, but the police believed, from the size of the truck and the number of vehicles used in the robbery, that it might have been six or seven times that: thirty, thirty-five million. The thieves were never traced and the haul was never recovered. My mate believes it's been sat on for all that time, until the people involved reckoned it was safe to start moving it.'

'Are you telling me that these masterminds are selling on the coins for a fraction of their value and letting some fucking shopkeeper make most of the profit?'

'No, I'm not. The store in question is one of a chain; it has outlets all over Europe and it's owned by a Russian investment trust.'

'Okay,' I said. 'But how does this tie in with your bird on the side?'

'My staff contact reckons that all the store transactions are made by flight crew on her airline. It's called WisterAir, and guess who owns it?'

'The same Russian investment trust that owns the shops?'

'You got it.'

'Okay, let me work all this out. Russians pull off the robbery and sit on the takings for ten years. Launder them through their airline and their stores. Why not just melt them down themselves?'

'They'd still have to get the gold out of South Africa. It's no fucking use to them there. They reckon this route is fool-proof.'

I laughed. 'Obviously not, if you got on to it.' He scowled at me. 'Your story, the one you're trying to sell to Noele and me, is that you're trying to infiltrate the smuggling ring through Aisha; that getting into her knickers is part of a subtle plan. Has it worked so far?'

'I was on the verge,' he said, 'almost there. She'd started to talk about this thing that she was part of, she and her crewmates; how simple it was and how they were fooling everybody.'

'Hold on,' I exclaimed. 'You're airport security and she's telling you this?'

'She thinks I'm a stockbroker.'

'How did you hook up?'

'I hit on her in the airport hotel bar. She and her pals sometimes drop in there for a drink.'

'Mmm. How long?'

'What do you mean?'

'Fuck's sake!' I snapped, exasperated.

'It's been going on for two months,' he admitted.

'I'm humbled by your self-sacrifice,' I told him. 'But what I don't get is why you did it. You had this information. Why not do the obvious and hand it over to Noele? You're not a cop any more, Terry.'

'No, but I'd like to be. I hate it on the outside. When I quit it was because I couldn't see any future under that woman Toni Field. I'd only just handed in my warrant card, then she was gone. My idea was to develop my investigation until I had something solid, then take it to Noele's boss, gift-wrapped, and ask him to put in a word with the top guns so I could get my job back. And I was that fucking close,' he hissed, 'when young Haddock and you turned up at the Premier Inn.'

'Haddock showed his warrant card,' I said, 'but I never identified myself. How did you know I was there?'

'The receptionist told me. You're famous, man; a woman that age, there's a better than even chance she'll recognise you. You could have left it at that, but no, Haddock had to go and tell Noele, no doubt with your approval.'

'With the chief constable's approval,' I corrected him. 'Noele was hopelessly compromised, man; we were after you for Austin Brass, whose death her unit is investigating.' His eyes widened. That hadn't dawned on him. 'Whatever,' I continued, 'coming up here, trying to take it out on me: that was unbelievably stupid. How did you ever make DI?'

'I was good in the force,' he murmured. 'And I could be again.'

'You will never get back into the police, Terry, for I won't allow that to happen. You lack the self-control and the judgement.'

'You think you can stop me?'

'I know I can. One more thing,' I added, 'before I tell you to get the hell out of here. This mate of yours, with experience in South Africa: how much did you tell him?'

'About the operation? Nothing, I just asked him how secure krugerrands are. I couldn't tell him any more; he's on the job over here. That's how I know him; our paths crossed on a joint operation.'

'What's his name?'

'I can't tell you that.'

'Fucking better,' I warned him.

'Montell. Griff Montell.'

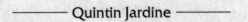

'I thought so; not too many have that background. This is what you do: you go and see Griff in Torphichen Place, officially, and you tell him the story you've just told me. He'll take it upstairs. You're fucked, but if it stands up, you might just be doing him a favour.'

Thirty-Nine

Coats's car was parked in Hill Road, but Sarah refused to allow him to drive for at least an hour, to ensure that he had recovered properly from being flattened. There was no way he was coming into the house; instead I took him down to the village café and left him there nursing a mug of tea and an aching head.

I was walking back home when Sauce called me. As I answered, I noticed that I'd missed a text: Brass Senior's address, I surmised.

'The computer's no help either,' he grumbled. 'There's nothing on it other than what's already published on the blog, and duplicates of some of the stuff I found on the laptop. No new material, no work in progress, nothing that relates to the Matthew Ampersand case, or to Barley Meads, or to Sir James. It's the same in his house, Jackie and Talvin tell me; the place is spotless, and obsessively tidy, just like the office. We're missing something here, sir, and I can't think where else to look.'

'Me neither,' I admitted. 'I plan to visit Kelso this afternoon. Sarah and the kids need a break; they've had a dramatic morning. I thought she might take them to Floors Castle while I call on Austin Brass's dad.'

I told him about my visit from Terry Coats and the alter-cation. 'Do you want him arrested?' he asked. 'Say the word and I'll have him picked up and charged.'

'He's been dealt with,' I replied. 'I'm only telling you in case he decides to pay a call on you and Cheeky, but I don't think that's likely, not after the chat he and I had.' I decided against sharing the story of Coats's undercover operation; Sauce had enough on his plate. If there was any mileage in the smuggling story, it was better that Montell handled it. I knew that he would see it as a potential way back into CID.

'Were there any signs of a female presence in Brass's place?' I asked, thinking of the woman who had been with him when he had visited Magnolia.

'Not that Wright and Singh mentioned. Jackie says the place was so neat there was hardly any sign of human occu-pancy.' He paused. 'I don't suppose Sir James has been in touch, sir, has he?'

'No, but if he does make contact, I'll hear about it. His niece has moved in with Lady Proud for a few days.'

'The same niece that Ampersand was alleged to have molested?'

'That's her; I have to say she survived the experience very well.'

'More than he did,' Sauce retorted. 'Sir,' he continued, 'I've been thinking. Should I be treating Sir James as a missing person? Should I make a public appeal for sightings? Issue a photo?'

'Sorry, did you say you've been thinking?' I exclaimed. 'You could have fooled me. You're suggesting that we trigger a full-scale manhunt for a respected former chief constable? Try that on the chief constable and the DCC and see how they react.'

'Mmm. Maybe not,' he murmured.

'Look, Sauce,' I told him, 'you're playing by the book as you must, and the book says that Jimmy's a suspect given the evidence you have, but I'm telling you he didn't bloody do it. More significantly, so is Sarah, who doubts that he'd be physically capable.'

'In that case, I'm stuffed. There are no other leads.'

'Then be patient. You've done all you can. Take some time off and share it with your partner.'

'Just like you're doing?'

'Exactly. I'm going to Floors Castle, am I not?'

Even Sarah's Renault struggles to accommodate the full family, and Trish had more than earned her time off, so we couldn't leave the baby behind. Happily the day was made more comfortable by my two oldest sons. Ignacio had come home for a weekend of distraction-free study, and Mark expressed less than no interest in spending a day touring a stately pile, so we were able to leave them together. Our slimmed-down party fitted easily into the hybrid, with Jazz in the front seat and his mother between her daughters in the back.

I had no great interest in touring the stately pile either, even if it is the largest inhabited castle in Scotland. 'Inhabited' is the word that put me off. Even if I was skint, no way will there ever be tours of Skinner Towers. Once I had the family ticketed and installed, I bade them a temporary farewell, and headed into Kelso. It's a nice country town, and small enough for Sarah's satnav to guide me to my destination in a couple of minutes. I had established from Sauce's text that Brass Senior's forename was David, and from a phone call made before we left Gullane that he would be home and prepared to see me. He opened his front door to greet me as I reached it, a

269

stocky man with rounded shoulders and a grave expression.

His grip made me wince as we shook hands. I had driven down with a residual ache from thumping Terry Coats. It must have shown on my face, for he apologised. 'It comes with my former profession,' he explained. 'It doesn't help my golf swing, though.'

'You play?'

'I'm a member at the Roxburghe course. It's part of the great estate; there's still a feudal feel to this community, Sir Robert. Come in, come in, please.'

Shit, another *Saltire* reader.

'Please, Mr Brass, just Bob; it's easier.'

'As you wish. I'm David, but I expect you know that. You strike me as a man who'll have done his homework.'

He led me through a dining hall and into a sitting room beyond. Its focal point was a double glass door opening on to a small balcony that offered a spectacular view of the fast-flowing River Tweed and the fields on the opposite bank. I could see two anglers, in waders, in the water, rods deployed.

'That's one of the most famous salmon stretches in the country,' David Brass advised me. 'I wish I owned it.'

Two chairs were positioned to enjoy the view. I wondered how often the one he offered me was used. 'Do you live alone, David?' I asked.

'At the moment,' he replied. 'Austin's mother and I divorced eighteen years back; I've had a couple of relationships since then, but realistically I suppose that these days I'm in the market for a nurse rather than a partner.'

I smiled at his candour. 'Is Austin's mother still alive?'

He frowned. 'No, Marcia took her own life nine years ago. It was most unfortunate; a real tragedy. She was accused, falsely she insisted, of shoplifting from a supermarket in Kilmarnock. They prosecuted, said it was a rule they never broke. She was a local councillor, and the papers went to town on her. She couldn't deal with it, and took an overdose.'

'Let me guess,' I ventured. 'That's when Austin started his blog.'

'Not quite,' his father replied. 'He spent a couple of years pursuing a theory that his mother had been framed at the behest of one of her sworn enemies on the council, and that Strathclyde Police had colluded in it. Ranks closed, he said, and he got nowhere. *Brass Rubbings* was started after that.'

'Do you believe there might have been a conspiracy?'

'My son was convinced, and I wouldn't rule it out,' he said. 'Marcia could be a difficult woman; there were several of those sworn enemies. She was accused of stealing clothing, hidden in a bag she had attached to her trolley, a matching dress and jacket, but Austin managed to establish that they were size ten, while she was a size fourteen.'

'Didn't she plead not guilty?'

'The proceedings never reached the plea stage; she was dead by then. Austin pounded away at it; he wrote letters to the press at first, then articles, for anyone who would publish them. After months of digging, he established that a few days before the incident, Marcia had had a major row with one particular lady opponent. Furthermore, he discovered, she had a daughter who worked in the supermarket in question, and who was engaged to a police constable. That was the basis of Austin's conspiracy theory,' Brass sighed, 'but he got nowhere with it. He tried his best, but he had to give up when the supermarket's lawyers threatened him with a defamation action that would have crippled him.'

'Before this happened, what was Austin's job?'

'He was a child psychologist, quite a successful one too; he had many referrals from education authorities. His obsession with his mother's death caused his practice to wither away, but he didn't care. In fact I think he was pleased, because it gave him time to build up his blog.'

'I've read that blog,' I said, 'but I can't recall any mention of his mother. I'd have thought it would have been his first story.'

'He was biding his time on that front. He recognised that he couldn't take on the supermarket's lawyers. Instead he focused his attention on the detective sergeant who had handled the case. Austin suspected him of leaking the details to the media.'

'Can you recall his name, David?' I asked.

'Yes, it was Coats, Terry Coats. Austin pursued him until eventually he got something on him; he was more or less drummed out of the force by the chief constable of the day. She was an interesting woman,' he murmured. 'Austin told me that she fed him stories; she gave him names that he might like to investigate. I think she used him as an informal internal affairs investigator. Of course that all came to a stop when she was—'

'Yes,' I exclaimed, cutting him off. 'She was a piece of work, was Toni Field.'

'For the last day or so,' he murmured, 'since they told me about Austin, I've been thinking about that man Coats. I wonder what he's doing now. I wonder if he could have had anything to do with my son's death. He was furious with Austin after the story ran.'

'As were a lot of people, David. A man was killed as a result of that story.'

He stared at me. 'Are you sure? Austin never said anything about that.'

'That doesn't surprise me. I don't suppose he was proud of it. As for Terry Coats,' I continued quickly, 'he didn't kill your son. That I can tell you for sure.'

'Do you have any idea who did, Bob?' he asked. 'I'm not usually a violent man, but if I had that person strapped in a chair, and a drill in my hand, I'd introduce him to pain the like of which he'd never imagined.'

A quick vision of the movie *Marathon Man* passed before my mind's eye. 'I'm sorry, David,' I said. 'I only know who didn't do it. Can you tell me when Austin last visited you?'

'A week ago,' he replied. 'The day before he died, so the pathologist believes.' His lips tightened; I knew that I was intruding into grief, and tried to step lightly.

'When he was here, did he mention any story he was working on, or any names?'

'No, but he rarely did. He had a fear of compromising me if something went wrong. On Saturday he was more concerned with introducing his new lady. Austin was always an introspective boy, and after he qualified as a psychologist he became even more insular. When he arrived with a woman last weekend, unannounced, I was mildly astonished. I could see what he saw in her, though; she's dark-haired, very attractive, and she struck me as highly intelligent. He told me they met when he spoke in a debate at Cambridge University. She was in the audience and at the reception afterwards. She's Australian, but she said that she never goes back there any more. I'm ashamed to say I can't recall her surname, but her Christian name was Amelia, although she insisted that I call her Amy.'

Forty

I had no option; I had to go back to Cambridge. It took me a while to explain the situation to Sarah, over afternoon tea in the Floors Castle Terrace Café, but once she understood the situation, she agreed with me.

No, that's not quite the case. Of course I had an option; I could have, should have, reported my discovery to Sauce Haddock, and left the follow-up to him. But I persuaded myself – and Sarah, eventually – that he had enough on his plate, he was still growing into his rank, and by developing a line of enquiry that I had opened up myself, I was doing him a favour.

The one concession I made to my wife was that I would devote the rest of the weekend to her and the kids. That's what I did, beginning by watching James Andrew and Seonaid navigate and negotiate the adventure playground, then driving us home through Duns and over the spectacular Lammermuirs. (That was a big step for me: when Jazz was a baby and Seonaid was the merest twinkle, I saw the aftermath of an air disaster there and hadn't returned since that horror.) Sarah and I ended the day over dinner in the Main Course restaurant while Ignacio child-minded, then next morning I took the school-age children to Edinburgh by train and walked them up to the

Royal Scottish Museum in Chambers Street; that's one place Mark is always keen to visit.

I was in a good place when I boarded the aircraft on Monday. Although it was still unfeasibly early, I had developed a strategy for confronting Amelia, thanks to some internet research. I had located her as a fellow in Clare College, and established that it was in session. I hoped that I would find her at work, and that there would be no need for me to kill time.

The college wasn't difficult to find; I had spotted it on Google Earth and knew that it was close to the bookshop where I had met John Ampersand. I parked in the same place I had used on my first visit and walked the short distance. The little city was shrouded in a fine drizzle; I was glad that I had studied the weather forecast and brought a raincoat. The university buildings are old and they are beautiful; as I made my way to Clare, I took time to admire them yet again.

I have to admit that my means of locating my quarry was lifted straight out of *Endeavour*, the telly series. When I reached my destination, the college quadrangle, I stopped a porter and asked him where I might find Miss Ampersand.

He turned out to be no mere tourist guide; not a pushover. 'Your business with her, sir?' he asked solemnly. I hadn't expected that. Stuck for a reply, I said nothing; instead, I took out the piece of plastic I carry that defines my loose and occasional relationship with the Security Service. He peered at it; his right eyebrow rose slightly in what may have been a sign of distaste, but otherwise he remained impassive. 'You'll find her rooms on that stairway,' he said. I followed his precisely pointed finger. 'First floor. If there is a supervision in progress, there will be a sign on the door. Please wait outside until it is finished.'

I thought about tipping him a fiver, but that would have been pushing my luck. I followed the path to the stairway and jogged up to the first floor. I'd been hoping not to find a sign on the door, but there was. My university days are well over thirty years behind me, but as I far as I could remember, none of my tutorials lasted any longer than half an hour, that being the attention span of the average student. I perched myself on a windowsill that was just wide enough to accommodate me, and waited. Eighteen minutes later, the door opened and young people began to emerge, one by one. Amelia Ampersand followed the last of them and stopped, framed in the doorway. Before she could retreat and close it I stepped forward; she looked at me, with a moment of confusion as she tried to place me. When she did, it gave way to surprise. 'Mr Skinner, isn't it? Uncle John's friend from London with the Harvard-bound son?'

I was impressed by the precision of her memory. 'That's me,' I replied, 'other than being displaced by four hundred miles. I'm from Edinburgh.'

Her manner struck me as odd. There was something missing, and it didn't take me long to identify it: grief. 'What brings you here?' she asked, in her multi-layered accent that remained predominantly Australian.

'Can we be private?' I countered.

'Of course, come in.' I followed her into a large study, where a dozen wooden chairs were arranged haphazardly, facing another with soft black leather upholstery. She offered me its twin.

'I need to talk to you, Amelia, about Austin Brass.'

'People call me Amy,' she replied, with a smile that made me realise how little of the life of everyday Scotland penetrates south of the border. 'What's Austin been up to? Has he upset you too? He's narked me, I can tell you; he hasn't returned any of my calls in a week.'

'He hasn't upset me personally. A friend of mine, yes, he has. But Amy, I'm afraid I have some bad news for you. Austin is dead. His body was found in a river in Haddington last week.'

Instantly she collapsed into the softness of her armchair; she seemed to shrivel into herself as if she had been punctured and was deflating fast, her hands covering her face as if she was trying to hold her remnants together. I'm a cynical bastard; I've given many people, too many, the death message, and now when I do it I watch them closely, trying to assess whether their reaction is spontaneous and genuine. Amy Ampersand passed on both counts, with flying colours. She came close to fainting; for a few seconds her expression reminded me of Terry Coats as he tried to remember who and where he was.

'I'm sorry,' I said, when I reckoned she could hear me. 'There's no easy way.'

'And you came all this way to tell me?'

I spotted a box of tissues on her desk, by the window; I fetched it and handed it to her, then waited as she composed herself.

'I came to talk to you, Amy. It didn't occur to me that you wouldn't know. I'm a director of a newspaper group and I have the naïve assumption that our coverage gets everywhere. I'm also a former policeman doing a favour for a friend who may have been implicated in a story Austin was working on, about the death of your uncle Matthew.'

'How did he wind up in the river?' she asked. Her sobbing had subsided, but there was still a catch in her voice.

'The police are trying to find that out, but they're treating it as homicide. At the moment the prime suspect is my friend, and I'm trying to establish his innocence.'

'Are you absolutely sure he didn't do it?'

'I'm as certain as I can be. His name is Sir James Proud. Did Austin ever mention him to you?'

'No, he didn't; and that's not a name I would forget.'

'When did you see him last?'

'Eight days ago,' she replied. 'Sunday of last week; I'd been with him since the previous Tuesday. He drove me to Edinburgh Airport from his place; it's not very far. I flew to London, spent a day or so at the Royal Over-Seas club, and got back here at the same time you were meeting with Uncle John.'

'When he dropped you off, did he tell you where he was going next?'

'He said he had a lunch date, but that was all.'

'That would have been with me,' I told her, 'but he didn't show up. It fact he wasn't seen again until his body was recovered last Thursday. Amy, did he mention another meeting, just before the lunch date? There was one noted in his diary on his laptop, but it doesn't say who he was meeting.'

'No,' she murmured, 'he didn't. I'm sure of that, because he told me very little about the thing he was working on; he wanted me to wait until he was ready to tell me everything, and to publish it.'

'The police have a problem with that,' I said. 'They have his laptop, and the desktop in his office, but there's nothing on either that gives them a clue to what he was working on. I happen to know, and so do they, that he was looking into the circumstances of your uncle's murder, Matthew Ampersand, and the conviction of a man named Barley Meads. He was in a position to make a vague allegation against Sir James Proud, but there is nothing anyone can find that shows how he got there.'

'Don't they have his iPad?' she exclaimed, taking me by surprise. 'He did all his development work on a tablet. He wrote his posts there and only put them on the blog when he was satisfied with them. He took it everywhere, in a satchel that he carried over his shoulder. It was on the bedside table when he slept.' The faintest smile appeared. 'In fact, one night after we had sex, he got up to go to the toilet, and I asked him why he wasn't taking it with him. He laughed, and said, "Because you don't know the password." I'm pretty sure he meant it too.'

'What university did he go to?'

'Exeter. He did an honours degree in psychology.'

'Chances are that was the password, given the others that we found, but the iPad wasn't recovered, Amy, so we'll probably never know. Tell me, though, how much did you know about the story he was working on?'

'I knew the same as you,' she replied, 'that he was looking into my uncle Matthew's death.'

'Is that how you met? Did he seek you out in Cambridge?'

'No, not at all. We met by sheer chance, at a reception after a Union debate, when he spoke against the Secret State. I thought he was very eloquent, and I told him so. I said he'd made me change my view of the issue, and not many people ever do that. That's how our thing began. Austin had never heard of Uncle Matthew or his murder, not then. I was the one who raised the subject, by accident. We were talking about Scotland, after we'd . . . connected. He was trying to persuade me to visit him there. He asked if I had any Scottish connections; I told him that I'd had an uncle up there, a vicar, but that he'd taken his own life. He asked me why, had he broken up with God? That made me realise that I knew nothing about Uncle Matthew. I had been tempted to ask Uncle John about him, but I sensed that it might hurt him, so I never did. Instead, I said to Austin, "If you're an investigative journalist, why don't you investigate Matthew's death?"

'He did, there and then, sitting up in bed in his hotel room; he reached for his iPad and he googled the name. What came on screen wasn't a suicide at all, it was a murder, and in its day it had been high-profile. When he saw it, Austin became another person. He switched into investigator mode. He read all the accounts he could find on the net, and when he was done, he said, "Amy, this was all too easy for the police. I hate simple cases; I need to look into this." I told him to go ahead, but not to say anything to Uncle John, because he'd let me believe the suicide story and my guess was that he didn't want the truth to hurt me like it had hurt him.'

'You said you weren't involved in his investigation, but weren't you with him when he visited an old lady in Edinburgh?'

She nodded. 'Yes, I was, but I stayed in the car most of the time. She didn't look that old to me. She practically filled her doorway when I saw her. I couldn't hear what they were saying, but I could see that she wasn't about to invite him in for coffee. In fact, it looked pretty heated. I thought she was going to clock him, so I got out of the car and hauled him out of there.'

'Did he say anything afterwards?'

'Not much; he was quite shaken. He just muttered something about her being a good match for her brother. Austin wasn't really a confrontational guy. He was passionate about his work, but that didn't mean that he was fearless. If he was really worried about something, he told me, he'd go talk it through with his dad, to get himself a shot of courage.' She paused. 'How is David?' she asked. 'He must be devastated; he and Austin were so close. There was nothing they didn't share.'

'Are you saying that Austin discussed his work with his father?'

'Absolutely. The day he took me to meet him, I was persuaded to go for a walk by the river while they talked through his investigation.'

Forty-One

I had an open ticket to Stansted and so I was able to catch a return flight that got me back to Edinburgh before two thirty. I could have gone home, but I didn't; instead I headed south, over Soutra Hill towards Kelso. David Brass had lied to me and I wanted to know why. The Cambridge weather seemed to have followed me northwards. The clouds were low and rain-laden and the roads were wet and treacherous. Nevertheless, I made it to my destination in good time.

The bell went unanswered when I rang it, although the elderly Rover saloon that I had noticed on my previous visit was still sheltering in a covered carport. I walked a few yards along the pavement to a walkway that led down towards the Tweed, offering a limited view. David Brass was standing by the waterside, shoulders slumped in a Barbour jacket, his feet encased in half-length wellies. I keep a pair of those in my car, always; it's a holdover from my police career when one never knew what sort of shit you could find yourself plodding through at any unpredictable moment. I dug them out, donned my coat and trudged down the path to join him.

I called out as I drew close. He turned and stared at me, eyes wide. 'Bob Skinner,' he exclaimed. 'You're the last person I expected to see today. I thought you were in Cambridge.'

'You've heard from Amy.' It was a deduction, not a question.

'She called me this morning, after your visit. She was quite distraught, poor thing. I didn't realise she and Austin were so close.'

'I don't believe she did either,' I told him. 'The relationship was brand new; I don't think she'd realised how much Austin meant to her.'

'I don't have her phone number,' he said, 'so I couldn't have called her, but I confess that such a thought didn't occur to me. I feel guilty about that.'

'Come on, there's no reason for that, David. You barely know the woman; she visited your house once.'

'On the day before he died,' he countered. 'It was obvious to me that they liked each other. I'd like to see her again; I feel the need to talk to her about Austin, and to share memories, to tell her things about him that she never had time to find out. That's what I'm doing down here,' he explained. 'I'm remembering my son, and thinking of the awful irony in my living by a river and him dying in one. I'll have to sell up and move,' he declared. 'I will never be able to look at this stretch of water without thinking of him, but not in a way I want to remember.' He shuddered. 'But enough of that: it's cold and it's wet and you haven't come here to listen to the ramblings of a sad old man. Let's go up to the house and you can tell me why you have come.'

That seemed like a plan to me. We turned and squelched back up the slope towards the pathway and the street above. When we got there, I swapped my wellies for my shoes and followed him indoors.

'Will you have coffee?' he asked.

'I rarely say no,' I confessed.

'Then go sit yourself down while I brew.'

In the sitting room, the chairs were turned away from the view; I found that dreadfully sad, but I understood why David Brass would never again be able to live happily in what had been a beloved home. Not for the first time, I was an intruder into grief. For a moment I considered apologising and leaving, then thought better of it. Perhaps company was what he needed.

He rejoined me bearing a huge tray with two mugs, a coffee pot, milk, sugar, and a bottle of Famous Grouse whisky. A tea towel hung over one end. 'I like a tot in mine,' he explained, catching my glance. 'You're welcome too.' I declined and waited for him to pour. 'So, Bob,' he said as he finished. 'Welcome as you are, what's behind the return visit?'

'Nothing, if you don't want there to be, but . . .' I paused, gathering my thoughts. 'David,' I continued, when they were all together, 'you may well be wondering what my role is in all this. To tell you the truth, I'm not quite sure myself. The one thing I do know is that Austin and I were chasing the same fox, even if we were coming at it from different angles. So I'd like you to think of me, if you can, as an investigative journalist, a colleague of your son, rather than an adversary. I want what he wanted, to establish the truth about the death of Matthew Ampersand, Amy's uncle, and the conviction of Farmer Meads for killing him. The truth: that's my objective, and if it's inconvenient for friends and colleagues, so be it. My problem is that Austin had more information than me. I know you told me yesterday that he didn't share what he had with you, but in the light of something that Amy said, I'd like to ask you again . . .'

The old dentist held up a hand, stopping me in mid sentence. 'It's all right, Bob,' he said, 'you can stop being delicate; it doesn't become you. I confess, I admit it: I didn't answer your question honestly. Austin invariably discussed his stories with me before he went public on them. Before he committed to publication, he needed affirmation that his reasoning was in line with the facts he had uncovered. He needed reassurance and for that he came to me. I was a silent partner in *Brass Rubbings*, Bob. I gave him the money he needed to set it up, and I encouraged him every step of the way. His mother and I might have been divorced, but that was my fault, not hers. I had a drink problem that I've never entirely solved, and I played the odd away game. Eventually she'd had enough and left me, but I never left her, not in my heart. I was as convinced as Austin that the theft accusation was a stitch-up; I still am, but we were bullied out of proving it.'

'Is that why you took revenge on Terry Coats through the site?'

'Yes, it was. I admit we did that, but on reflection we might have wronged him. He might not have been responsible, not personally. He was the detective in charge of the case against Marcia, but he wasn't the arresting officer. We never found out who that was, nor did we discover who the witnesses were from the supermarket. Their lawyers shut Austin down before he got that far. We would have gone back to it, you know, once *Brass Rubbings* had established itself as a real force and built up an audience that couldn't have been ignored, given us power of our own. That'll never happen now; the blog died with my son.'

Bitterness and frustration came off him in waves. 'Do you still want to pursue your wife's death?' I asked.

'More than ever now, for Austin's sake, but what can I do?'

I carry a stock of Alex's business cards, just in case. I produced one and handed it to him. 'You could do what you should have done in the first place: consult a lawyer. That's my daughter. She'll tell you if anything can be done.'

He accepted it, studying its details. 'Thank you. I'll give it some thought.' He pocketed it, then looked back at me. 'But you didn't come here for that, Bob. You want to talk about Amy's uncle. Yes, my son and I did discuss his investigation, in broad terms. He didn't go into detail; he said it was safer for me not to know too much. I could see that he was nervous, even scared. When I told him so, he said that he had uncovered a name, someone very senior, a man with a couple of friends who could make bad things happen. "Heavy-duty, Dad. These people are heavy-duty. If I cross them, I'm not sure how they'll react." I asked him who they were, and he gave me two names; yours was one of them. The other was the deputy chief constable, a man named McGuire. Now here you are, asking me about my dead son.' He pulled the towel from the tray, picked up a pistol that it had been covering and pointed it at me. It was a large weapon, a clumsy old-fashioned revolver. 'That's fortuitous in a way,' he said, 'for I have a question for you, Sir Robert. Austin feared you. Was he right about that? Did you have a hand in his death?'

I stared at him; I confess that I was astonished. 'David,' I replied, 'I've had guns pointed at me before by people who meant it. I've even been shot. I've fired back too. It takes a certain type of man to point a firearm at someone else and discharge it. You're not one of those.' Quickly I reached across the space between us and took the gun from him; he offered no resistance. I pocketed it, then picked up the Famous Grouse and poured another shot into his mug.

He sat there for a couple of minutes cupping it in his hands. 'How could you be so sure I wouldn't shoot you?' he murmured. 'Am I so obviously a weak man?'

'I wasn't sure,' I admitted; then I smiled. 'But the fact that the safety catch was on gave me a degree of confidence. David, I never even met your son, and I certainly didn't kill him. However, I have a real interest in finding out who did, and I will. I promise you that.'

'What happens now?' he asked dolefully. 'Do you call the police?'

'Bloody hell, no! What happens is that you tell me what little you do know about Austin's Ampersand investigation. When we've done that, we go back out in the rain, back down to the river, and you chuck that thing in there, as far as you can throw it. Okay,' I continued, 'what did Austin tell you about his story?'

'He said that he had approached a woman named Briony Lennon; he said she was at the heart of the business according to the reports of the Meads trial that he had read. They met in a café in the Straiton shopping park. It didn't go well. She became agitated, he said; she insisted that the verdict had been correct, and told him that Miss Ampersand should let her uncle rest in peace, because she might not like what she dug up. Then she walked out on him.'

I pictured that meeting in my mind, wondering what Briony had meant by her dramatic exit line. 'How did he react to that?'

'To Meads's daughter insisting that her father was guilty?' he retorted. 'How do you think? He believed her. He was ready to call a halt, to walk away. And he would have done too, if he hadn't received a phone call a couple of days later. It was from a young woman, asking to see him. He didn't tell me much about her; only that her name was Florrie. He met her, he said, but he kept their discussion to himself – "For your own good," he said to me. Hell's teeth, the boy should have worried more about himself.'

I let David finish his loaded coffee; while he was doing that, I wrapped the pistol in a supermarket bag that I found in the kitchen. It was a Webley Mark VI, which meant that it was at least ninety-five years old, that model having gone out of production shortly after the First World War. It hadn't been cleaned in decades, and was more of a danger to the shooter than the target – or would have been had it been loaded. It was an heirloom, he confessed, handed down by his grandfather; there never had been any ammunition. We walked together down to the Tweed, where I did the chucking, tossing the package into the middle of the fast-flowing river.

'Call my daughter,' I urged him as I left. 'I'm not trying to drum up business for her, but it's clear to me that neither you nor Austin ever came to terms with your wife's death. If there was a conspiracy, she'll get to the bottom of it, and she won't be scared off by any supermarket lawyers.'

As I drove away from the pretty town, heading back towards Soutra Hill, it took me almost half an hour to get the sad old dentist and his ill-fated son out of my mind. I had gone into my investigation with a typical cop's view of Austin Brass, without knowing anything about him or his motivation. Now that I did, I felt desperately sorry for him, and for his father, who would never be happy again, even if he did consult Alex – not that I imagined he would – and even if she proved his conspiracy theory correct.

I had cleared Soutra and was on the minor road that led to Haddington when finally I was able to focus on Florrie, the young woman David had named as his son's source. I didn't know any Florries, but I did know of a Florence, and thanks to her godmother, Joanna Meikle, I knew exactly where to find her.

Forty-Two

The contrast between Cambridge University and Scotland's Rural College could not be greater, but their degrees have equal validity. A quick call to Joanna helped me establish that Florence Lennon was studying agricultural bioscience, and that yes, I should be able to find her there on a Tuesday morning.

I had done some semi-official business in Ayr not long before and was familiar with the road. The Riverside Campus wasn't too difficult to find, me being a detective and the name being a major clue. Florrie wasn't too hard to find either; she didn't have a lecture, but I tracked her down in the cafeteria, with a couple of friends, one male, one female. She was blonde, possibly genuinely so given her father's appearance; even if she hadn't been pointed out to me by the lady on the till, I'd have picked her out as his daughter.

I approached her table. 'Miss Lennon,' I began, 'may I have a word?' I had dressed for comfort, not for show, in chinos, T-shirt and a blue suede jerkin. In that environment, in a suit, I'd have looked like a collector from the Student Loans Company and the place would have emptied.

Her expression as she stared up at me gave further evidence

of her paternity. Her instant reaction was suspicion, rather than curiosity. 'That depends,' she replied evenly, in a city accent that struck me as affected, 'on who the fuck you are.'

'I'm a friend of Joanna Meikle,' I told her, smiling in the face of her hostility when what I really wanted was to clip her round the ear.

She eyed me up and down. 'Aye,' she said, 'you look like her type. You're the new bit of rough, are you? I wonder how long you'll last. The average seems to be about a year an' a half.' She smirked at her mates. 'Is she a good shag, my godmother?'

I'd done my best to be polite, but it hadn't worked. I grabbed a chair from another table and pulled it up to hers. 'You two,' I snapped in the direction of her pals, 'you can piss off now. Florrie and I are going to have a chat, whether she likes it or not.'

The boy made a show of defiance but thought better of it; he picked up his Diet Coke. The other girl had already moved across to a table in the corner. 'We'll be over there if you need us, F-Star,' he declared as he left.

'She won't, sonny,' I promised.

'Have you got a name, Auntie Jo's friend?' Florrie asked once we were alone, clutching her bottle. Her preference was for Dr Pepper.

'My name is Skinner.'

Her little eyes narrowed. 'Are you the guy that came to the farm last week? My dad said he saw you off.'

'What did your granny say?'

'She laughed at him when he said it; I don't know why.'

I had a small chuckle myself. 'I do, but it's not important. Yes, I paid a call on Mrs Meads. I wanted to ask her about your grandfather's trial and imprisonment.'

'For doing in the guy that played about with my mother and groped my auntie Jo? Why the sudden interest in that? It all happened long before I was born.' I sensed a change in her manner. Her cockiness had gone, replaced by a nervous caution.

'There's been a suggestion that your grandpa might not have done it,' I told her. 'A man called Austin Brass was investigating that theory. He thought he was making progress, but all of a sudden he wound up dead. The police are fairly convinced that he was murdered. I even had to prove to them that I didn't do it. They have a prime suspect they're trying to trace, but I don't think he did it either. That's why I need to talk to you.'

'What's it got to do with me? It's ancient fucking history as far as I'm concerned. Who cares about it now anyway?'

'I do,' I said. 'From everything I've learned about your grandpa, he'd have been on the podium in the Arsehole Olympics, but if he was convicted of a murder that he didn't commit, that's a wrong that should be put right, regardless of how long ago it was. Do you not agree with that?'

'Why should I? I never knew my grandpa, but what you said about him, that seems to be the universal verdict.'

'If that's how you feel, why did you call Austin Brass and give him the story?'

If I'd thrown a bucket of water over her, it would have had the same effect as my challenge. She recoiled from me. 'I never!' she squealed.

'You did, lass,' I retorted, 'and you know it. Your mother told Austin that Barley was guilty as charged. He'd have accepted that, and walked away from the story, had he not had a phone call from you. And now he's dead. I could argue that whoever killed him, you're responsible. You can't lie your way out of that, kid.'

She gripped the table. Those little eyes seemed much bigger as she stared at me. 'I'm saying nothing,' she hissed. 'You really can fuck off now, or I'll call campus security. You ever come near me again, you can look forward to another meeting with my dad.'

I smiled as I stood. 'I might enjoy that, Florrie,' I chuckled as I turned to leave. 'But I doubt that he would.'

Forty-Three

I had exceeded my brief by a few miles and I knew it, but I wasn't ready to go back to Sauce. There was one small part of Alf's neatly truncated investigation that was out of shape. The problem was, I couldn't pin it down and that was niggling away at me. It was still at the forefront of my mind as I drove into the *Saltire* car park. As I reached Sylvia's open door, I stuck my head round and asked if there had been any calls.

'Detective Inspector Haddock,' she replied, 'but he said to tell you "no progress" and only to get back to him if you had something new. What is this, Bob; are you going back to your old job?'

'No danger,' I grunted.

As I moved on, she called after me, 'Hey, when you dress like that, you look ten years younger.'

'This is how most people go to work at head office in Girona,' I laughed. 'Maybe we should have a new dress code here.'

'We'd need to consult the unions about that,' June Crampsey warned. She had appeared in the doorway that led into her sanctum. As I looked at her, an unbidden thought of her father came into my mind, and that last annoying niggle clicked, and began to resolve itself. I couldn't see everything, but I knew where the fault line lay.

'You know if your old man's at home, June?' I asked.

'Yes, he is. I've just spoken to him. He's planting potatoes.' I turned on my heel and went back to the lift.

I called Tommy Partridge from the road. He took longer than usual to pick up the call. 'Sorry, Bob,' he said when he did. 'I had garden gloves on.'

'Have you had lunch yet?'

'No, not yet.'

'Me neither; I'll bring something. I had an early start and I'm fucking starving.'

'Something' evolved into four hot Forfar bridies, accompanied by two coffees to go, from a branch of Greggs that I spotted on the way to Tommy's place. When I arrived, he had shed his wellies and gardening gear and was waiting for me in the kitchen, looking ruddily healthy.

'Spot on,' he said as he accepted my gift. 'I'll plate them and microwave some beans.'

I wasn't sure about the beans, but they were Heinz and therefore okay. You have to understand that Tommy and I were both career cops. Fast-food tastes come with the job, and as long as they don't become the norm, they're okay.

'I used to eat in a café along Nicolson Street that did brilliant bridies,' he reminisced as we faced each other across his kitchen table. 'Is Forfar famous for anything else?'

'Its football team?' I suggested. 'Although there's a very fine line between fame and notoriety.'

We concentrated on lunch until it was over; I had picked up a couple of iced cakes as well and they served as dessert. 'Brilliant,' Tommy exclaimed as he leaned back and drank the last of the coffee from its insulated container. 'You could have brought a Fortnum and Mason hamper and it wouldn't have beaten that. How can I repay you? There is no such thing as a free bridie.' He smiled at my momentary hesitancy. 'Come on, Bob, you don't pay social calls; you're too fucking busy.'

'Okay,' I admitted. 'I need to pick your brain again, and I thought I should fuel it up first. I'm still digging up the Matthew Ampersand case.'

'Aye,' he exclaimed, 'and what about the guy Brass being fished out of the Tyne? Is there a connection there?'

'That's for CID to determine, but it's where my money would go. Me, I'm still looking at the original investigation.'

'You mean you're trying to prove that Alf and I got it wrong?'

'Not necessarily, and certainly not you. You and I both know that Alf drove that thing from start to early finish; your main function was legal corroboration at the trial. Think back to then and tell me, does the name Joanna Meikle mean anything to you?'

'Joanna Meikle?' he repeated. 'No, not straight away.' He took some time to trawl his memory banks before standing, suddenly, saying, 'Wait a minute,' and rushing from the room.

I was left alone, wondering whether the bridies or the beans might have caused his sudden departure, but he returned brandishing two small objects that I recognised immediately as police notebooks. 'I still have every book I ever used,' he explained. 'They're up in the loft, all of them, waiting for a day like this, when an old investigation comes to life again. I never really thought one would, but what do I know? These are the two that cover the Ampersand murder. Make yourself another coffee if you like while I go through them.'

I accepted the invitation and left him to it. It was instant, Millicano, not as good as the Greggs I'd brought, but better than nothing. I made two, laying the other before Tommy as he scanned his notebooks. When he was finished, he looked at me across the table. 'No,' he declared firmly. 'No mention of a Joanna Meikle in there. Who was she?'

'She was, and she still is, Jimmy Proud's niece. She was, and she still is, Briony Meads's best friend. She was at the centre of another allegation of sexual indiscretion made against Matthew Ampersand a week before he was murdered but rejected very quickly, probably with undue haste.'

He took a deep breath; his face showed concern. 'Honest to God, Bob, I never knew about that. Did Alf?'

'Of course he did.'

'Then why did he keep quiet about it?'

'My best explanation is this. If you have a very simple case against a suspect, one with almost a certainty of conviction, why make it complicated by introducing another line of enquiry – especially if your chief constable has put you on the spot to get a result?'

'I can see that,' he conceded, 'but wouldn't it have to be disclosed to the defence?'

'Yes, it would; that's what I'm advised.'

He shook his head. 'I never knew, Bob, I swear. What are you going to do about it?'

'I've told you, I believe you. It should be reported to the Crown Office, sooner rather than later. The question is, by whom?' I paused for a shift of focus. 'That's not the main reason why I'm here, though. I want to take another look at the placing of Meads's truck at the scene. There was something fortuitous about that, door-to-door just turning Mrs Royce up, and her being able to identify it.'

'Maybe so,' he agreed, 'but she did. It was me that showed her the picture.'

'Can you remember the interview?'

'Just about. She was getting on, the lady, and very frail, but she had her wits about her. I asked her how old she was and she said she was born the year Hibs won the Scottish Cup. I had to look that up; it was nineteen-oh-two.'

'There's no chance she was mistaken?'

'No. It's hard to believe, but they really did.'

'Tommy!' I barked.

He grinned in return. 'No, there was no chance. I asked her several times if she was sure, and she never wavered.'

'How did she stand up under cross-examination?'

Tommy laughed. 'She didn't; she sat in the witness box. She walked on a Zimmer or on two sticks. Her grandson looked after her. He was there at the interview and in the court. She was a good witness. She identified the truck again, firmly. Archie Nelson, the defence counsel, tried to suggest that her memory might not be what it was. She asked him if he could name the Famous Five, the Hibs forward line from the late forties. When he said he couldn't, she recited them, first names included: Gordon Smith, Bobby Johnstone, Lawrie Reilly, Eddie Turnbull and Willie Ormond. Even the judge laughed at that, and he was a Hearts supporter.'

'The grandson. Can you remember his name? Is it in your book?'

'No, I can't, and no it isn't. I had no cause to note it, for he wasn't involved. If you're barking up a tree here, Bob, it's the wrong one. Mrs Royce was the best witness we had.'

I allowed Tommy to return to his garden, and was heading back to the office, fighting off a touch of acid reflux from the unnecessary second bridie, when I had a call from Joanna Meikle. 'Can you drop by this evening? Around six thirty? Briony's coming out for a visit.'

'I can make that,' I told her.

'I'm not guaranteeing that she'll talk to you, mind,' she warned me. 'I've told her you've been looking at her dad's murder conviction because somebody asked you to; she seemed okay with that.'

'She might have changed her mind if she's spoken to your goddaughter since then.'

'She's unlikely to have done that. Florrie's a daddy's girl in every way, temperament, looks, attitude. '

'Yes,' I agreed. 'You and God might have a bit more work to do there.'

I did some more work myself for what was left of the afternoon, all of it gainfully on behalf of my employer, rather than gratis on behalf of my old friend, even though he no longer seemed interested in my findings. I stayed at my desk until five thirty, by which time I judged the commuter traffic would have eased. It hadn't, not by much, a result of the boom in house-building that East Lothian residents have witnessed since the turn of the decade. Rather than be late for my meeting with Briony Lennon, I drove straight to the Prouds'. As I pulled up behind a Volkswagen Touareg that I recognised from my visit to Easterlee Farm, I saw Chrissie, on sentry duty at the study window, looking out in the increasingly vain hope of seeing her husband heading home. As I stepped out of my car, her face brightened and she waved. I could see she hoped that

I was bringing her good news. Walking up the path, I shook my head; her optimism vanished in an instant. I felt terrible.

Joanna opened the door. 'You're prompt,' she remarked, then she saw my car, parked behind Briony's.

'I came straight here,' I explained. 'My day's been hectic. I've been to Ayr and back.'

'You went to see Florrie?' she exclaimed. 'I didn't realise that was what you meant when you mentioned her earlier.'

'Yeah, it was a real pleasure.'

'Tell me about it.' Her mouth was set in a firm line. 'She treats her mother like shit. Unfortunately, Briony's always been too meek for her own good. The last time Florence and I talked, I told her she needed to learn respect. She told me to . . .' Her eyes blazed but her voice tailed off; she didn't need to complete the sentence.

I grinned. 'She told me much the same; she threatened to set her father on me.'

Her eyes hardened. 'When that happens, can you let me know?'

'You don't like Michael?' I ventured.

'He's a C-word. Unfortunately the only people on the planet who don't recognise that truth are his wife and his daughter.'

'When did he appear in Briony's life?' I asked.

'He's always been around Heatherston. He was a local boy; it's not a huge place, us kids all knew each other.'

'You were schoolmates?'

'Hardly. Briony and I both went to Watson's; he was at the local secondary.' She led me towards the sitting room. 'Come on through. We're a bit rushed for time. I'd hoped that Briony would stay over, but she's under orders to be home tonight. Michael needs driving somewhere tomorrow morning, he says.

And I believe that? Not. I'll bet it's another piece of control-freakery. Do you know,' her voice dropped to a whisper as we neared the open doorway, 'the son of a bitch won't even let her have a mobile.'

We stepped into the room. Briony Lennon stood with her back to the fireplace, a small, diffident smile on her face. 'Hello,' she said, without any offer of a handshake. 'So you're the great Mr Skinner.'

'Sir Robert,' Joanna corrected her. 'Don't you read the *Saltire*?'

'I don't answer to that, though,' I retorted, 'only to Bob. Nice to meet you, Mrs Lennon.'

Until that moment, my only sighting of Briony had been at a distance. Up close and personal, she was taller than I had realised, and looked like a younger version of her mother.

'Mum tells me you're interested in my father's case.' She was holding a tall glass of what I hoped, given the car outside, was orange juice, that she twisted in her hands as she spoke.

'I'm curious about it.'

'So was that poor man Brass, but it didn't do him much good. Do the police know what happened to him?'

'They think they might,' I replied. 'I'm waiting to see them prove it, but I don't think they will.'

'Your curiosity isn't going to get you anywhere either,' she said firmly. 'Dad killed Matthew. He thought he had found out that we were having a relationship and that he had been right all along. He went after him and he killed him.'

'He thought he'd found out? What do you mean?'

'When I was at college in Dundee, Matthew came to see me. He phoned me when I was at home, and we arranged to meet, in the flat I shared with another girl. Dad must have overheard us, because he followed him.'

She had my full attention, and Joanna's.

'How the hell do you know that?' I asked.

'Because he told me the next time I was home. He accused me all over again. I told him, "What do you think?" He went ballistic; he hit me, and shouted that he was going to fucking kill Matthew. Then he did just that. It's what happened.'

'I've read the police report, Briony. There's no mention of your father attacking you.'

'I was never asked about it, so I didn't mention it.'

'But you did admit to him that you were having a relationship with Matthew? As he insisted all through his trial and appeal?'

'Not in so many words, but I wasn't in a position to deny it,' she said.

I have a very straightforward belief system: if I can hold it in my hands, it's real. That extends into the quality of answers to questions: if it's a matter of an unequivocal 'yes' or 'no', I won't settle for anything else. 'You can only build a case on certainty, son.' Alf Stein taught me that, yet his against Barley Meads had fallen short of that mark. It was that anomaly that had troubled me all along.

I pressed her; the informal chat was over. 'What do you mean by that? Why couldn't you?'

'Because I didn't want to tell him the truth!' Joanna had been watching us, fascinated. Briony's shout made her jump. I admit that it made me twitch a bit too. 'Matthew didn't come to see me for sex,' she continued. 'I liked him, and I knew that he was very fond of me, but there was never anything physical between us, whatever Dad thought, whatever he thought he saw through a slit of a window that was always filthy. Matthew came up to Dundee to ask for a sample of my DNA. I didn't know what he was talking about. I'd never heard of DNA. He explained that it was a genetic profile, and he said that he needed samples from different people for a research project a friend of his was involved in. So I gave him what he wanted. I let him pull a couple of hairs out at the roots, and I licked a cotton swab he'd brought with him. It wasn't until after he left that I began to wonder. I went to the college library and I looked up some scientific journals. They told me what it was really for.'

There have been many things in my life that I did not see coming. Some were major, some minor, but that was right up there with the big ones. I did a quick calculation. Sir Alec Jeffreys invented DNA profiling in nineteen eighty-four; by the time of Briony's encounter with Matthew Ampersand, the technique was well established.

She glared at me. 'You see?' she challenged. 'I couldn't tell Dad the truth, because I was afraid for Mum. After he did what he did, after he killed Matthew, it didn't matter. The police never asked about Matthew visiting me, but if they had, I wouldn't have told them either. Why should I? It wouldn't have changed anything. My father killed Matthew Ampersand, and for all he denied it, there was never another suspect, and that's all there ever was to it.'

My head was spinning as I drove the short distance back home. With the family I tried to behave as if everything was normal, but I was no use to any of them, not even to Sarah, until I'd made a couple of telephone calls.

The first was to Mario McGuire. 'I'm speaking to you,' I said, 'because you have the clout to get this done; Sauce hasn't. I suggest, strongly mind you, that you get a warrant to monitor calls made by three people: Carmel Meads, Briony Lennon and Florence Lennon; mother, daughter and grandmother.'

'Okay,' he replied. 'Are you going to tell me what we might hear?'

'I don't know,' I admitted, 'but I'm waiting for a shoe to drop.'

The second was to Amelia Ampersand. She was surprised to hear from me; her instant fear was that I was calling to give her bad news about David. 'He's okay,' I assured her, 'apart from the fact that he finds himself living in a haunted house. There's something I need you to get for me, Amy. It's pretty delicate and I can't explain why I need it, but you're the person best placed to secure it for me.'

Forty-Four

It's funny, the way that people can drop out of your life for no reason other than laziness on your part, then pop up again out of the blue, of their own volition, at the most opportune moment.

I had a pressing problem next morning. If all the bits of the Brass and Ampersand investigations that were kicking around in my brain were given form and laid on my desk, they would have been a disassembled jigsaw puzzle so large that I'd have had to move them to my conference table. My immediate attention was focused on just one of them; it had been added to my to-do list after my impromptu lunch with Tommy Partridge, but my difficulty was finding the time to bloody do it. I had thought about asking June if I could borrow her half of Sylvia and delegate it to her, but realised that if she had made the same request, probably I'd have said no, for it didn't come close to fitting within her job description. I was resigned to a few hours of tedium, and doing it myself, when my desk phone rang.

For quite a few years I had dealings with a friend called Jim Glossop; he worked in the Registrar General's office, in Edinburgh, and he was a great help to me and my troops in tracking down individuals, their antecedents and their progeny. Then he retired, and those contacts stopped. A rumour of his death reached me a couple of years ago, but I should have known better than believe it.

'Eh, Bob,' his voice sounded in my ear as I took the call, 'you've changed your ways. I never took you for a newspaper man.' His ironic laughter brightened a dull morning.

'Jim,' I exclaimed. 'Great to hear from you. What are you doing with yourself?'

'Keeping busy, as usual. I help out with things, day centres and such. That's why I'm on. Remember Jacob Such-a-body, worked as a printer at the *Saltire* until he retired a year or so back?'

'Jacob Reynolds? Sure.' The Such-a-body clan was a general term to which Jim had always resorted when he was stuck for a name; this happened often.

'Well, he and I are involved with this charity auction, in aid of the Riding for the Disabled Association, and we've been given this big piece of antique furniture as a donation. Thing is, though, the donor doesn't have any way of getting it to where it needs to be, and neither have we. Jacob, he remembers that you've got vans, wondered if you could help us. We're in Linlithgow and the thing's in Uphall,' he added.

'Sure, Jim,' I said, 'I can arrange that. Our vans lie for hours doing sod all, so I can arrange a special lift. Give me a note of the addresses.'

'Brilliant.'

I scribbled the collection and delivery points on my pad as he dictated. 'Leave me your number and someone will call you, tell you when to expect them.'

'Great, Bob, thanks. I owe you one.'

'I know,' I chuckled, 'and I'm going to cash it in. Your old trade: do you still do bits of freelance genealogy research?'

'Not lately, but I could do. Who are you wanting found?'

'There was a lady, name of Mrs Esme Royce; she lived in Heatherston, late eighties. That's all I know about her, but she's not my main interest. I'd like birth details for all her grand-children, deaths too, if they've been unlucky.'

'That doesn't sound too difficult. Are you sure this Mrs Royce is dead herself?'

'She'll be well over a hundred if she isn't,' I told him. 'But if you find that she's alive, yes, let me know. I'll pay you, by the way.'

'You paid me forward,' he retorted, 'with that van.'

We spent the next ten minutes catching up, before Jim went off to continue with his busy day, having given me a lot more free time in mine. I put it to use right away, returning yet again to the Matthew Ampersand investigation file, and the box that I had unpacked for the second time. Tommy Partridge had told me that the lead to Mrs Royce had come from routine door-to-door enquiries; that niggle I'd had the day before had been my failure to recall having seen the feedback report anywhere in the file.

Believing that I must have overlooked it, I spent two more hours going through the papers in detail, checking each page individually in case the one I was after had been misfiled, but with no success. I did a quicker recheck before finally giving up.

Frustrated, I called Tommy. Once again he was in his garden and took a while to answer. 'Again?' he grumbled.

'Yes, and no bridies this time. Tommy, the door-to-door feedback that led you to Mrs Royce: I can't find it. I was hoping

I'd find a PC's name on it and that they might have been a local and able to tell me a bit more about the old lady. Do you have any thoughts?'

'Only one, now that you force me to think about it. I don't remember ever seeing a report or any other paperwork. All that happened was I was given the old dear's address, told to go and see her and show her a pic of a Dodge truck. That was all.'

I didn't need to ask, but I did. 'Who was it told you?'

'Alf Stein. Who else?'

Forty-Five

I was in the middle of a working lunch with June Crampsey in her office when I was interrupted by Mario McGuire. I had switched off my mobile, but he had come though on the landline. Sylvia had been told we weren't to be disturbed, but the deputy chief constable can be pretty forceful.

We hadn't been discussing my recent conversations with her father; he had agreed that those would be kept from her. Instead we had been setting out our hopes and visions for the new InterMedia UK subsidiary, ready for a report to the main board that Xavi had requested. I was keeping a close eye on June, looking for signs of her stepping out of her comfort zone. In truth, I wasn't sure how far mine extended or whether or not I had bitten off too big a mouthful.

I took Mario's call in my own room, having had a premonition that voices might be raised. I wasn't far off the mark. 'I want you to listen to something, Bob,' he began. 'That shoe you were waiting for; it may have dropped. If you're alone, you might want to put it on speaker.'

'Okay,' I said, although I had done so already. 'Fire away.'

'This was picked up late last night, not long after we started monitoring the landlines at Easterlee Farm. There are two.

309

One seems to be for Carmel Meads and the other for the Lennons. This came through on the Lennons' line.'

I waited, then heard a ringtone, followed by a click, and a voice, Briony Lennon's, saying, 'Hello, Easterlee.'

'Mum!' It was Florrie, loud and strident. I suspected she might have imbibed something stronger than Dr Pepper. 'I had a visit from that guy Skinner this afternoon, the cop that Dad threw off the farm when he caught him talking to Grandma. What the fuck has she been saying to him? Or you, for that matter? Why's everyone so fucking worried about Grandpa all of a sudden? Why did you send him to me?'

'I didn't,' I heard Briony protest. 'It wasn't me, but I know who might have. It could have been your auntie Jo. She's painting his picture just now; she told me tonight, even showed me it in progress. She might have said something to him while she was working.'

'Well, fuck her! Wait till the next time I see her, she'll be in for it, I tell you.'

'No she won't!' The sudden ferocity of her mother's retort surprised me. 'You'll say nothing to Auntie Jo, or to your grandma either. What did you tell Skinner anyway?'

'SFA, 'cos I know SFA, don't I. I told him to get lost. Has he spoken to you?'

'No, why would he?' And why would Briony lie? I wondered

'I dunno.' Her tone changed; she became an anxious kid. 'Mum, can you tell Dad, get him to sort this guy out?'

Briony snorted. 'Not a chance. Last time he tried that, he wound up with his arm in a sling, stinking the bedroom out with Voltarol. We need him to work on the farm. Look, love, forget about this thing. It's sorted. Skinner won't bother you any more.'

There was a click as the recording ended, then something resembling a growl as Mario came back on speaker. 'Much the same question as hers, Bob. What the fuck is going on?'

'I've been busy, Mario,' I replied, 'covering a lot of ground.'

'Without involving Sauce?' he exclaimed. 'Come on, man, he's the SIO in the Brass case.'

'I haven't been pursuing the Brass case,' I countered. 'I've been concentrating on the Ampersand murder. I've been able to do things that Sauce couldn't do, that even you couldn't do without going through all the protocol shite when you go on to another force's territory. This thing didn't start and finish in Heatherston, Mario, it goes a lot further than that.'

'The phone taps? What were they about?'

'You've just heard what they were about, man. I've been shaking the trees and something very significant just fell out.'

'Did it?' he said. 'I never heard it. All I heard was complaints about you harassing a teenage girl and beating up her father.'

'That's because you didn't know what you were listening to. I did, and what I heard was both mother and daughter lying to each other. I know that Florrie was Austin Brass's source, and as for Briony speaking to me, not only did she, but there's a witness to the conversation.'

My friend's silence told me that he was mollified. 'Where do you go from here?' he asked. 'Do you want me to maintain the telephone monitoring?'

'Absolutely. There's more to fall out of that tree. As for me, now I'm ready to go to Sauce, because I sense that my investigation is beginning to overlap with his. Where is he?'

'Knackered and getting nowhere,' Mario replied. 'I've told him to go home, forget everything else and reflect on his investigation to date, to assess what he knows, what he needs to establish and how he can go about it. I'm also considering that we need to support him by making a public appeal for sightings of Jimmy – not in the context of this case, you understand, as a missing person.'

'Please don't do that,' I begged him. 'It's unnecessary, and it can only do harm, to him and to Chrissie. You tell Sauce to expect me in his office by ten tomorrow morning. I'll give him all the support he needs.'

Forty-Six

'Good morning, sir,' the fledgling detective inspector greeted me as I stepped into the private room that he had appropriated in DCI Sammy Pye's absence. His smile turned to surprise as I dumped a box on his desk. 'What's in there?' he asked.

'The head of Alfredo Garcia,' I shot back, only to realise from his bewilderment that the generation gap was even wider than I'd imagined. Sauce had never heard of Sam Peckinpah. 'It's the sum total of the original investigation into Matthew Ampersand's murder. The DCC loaned it to me, and now I'm passing it on to you.'

'Have you learned anything from it?'

'From its contents, nothing that I hadn't picked up from the *Saltire* coverage of the trial. Subsequently, I've learned that it's half the size it should be. Alf Stein, my old boss, mentor and sometime hero, secured Barley Meads's conviction by suppressing a line of enquiry that didn't suit him, and reporting to the Crown, and to the defence, only the findings that made it certain. The prosecution was flawed, the conviction was unsafe, and even now it deserves to be overturned.' I grinned at him. 'The only remaining question, Sauce, is who gets the glory?

313

Who reports a potential miscarriage of justice to the Crown Office?'

He spread his arms wide, in a questioning gesture. 'So? Who does?'

'You'll have to sort that out with big Mario, but as far as I'm concerned you do. My involvement in this is strictly off the books.'

He frowned. 'Thanks, sir, I suppose,' he said. 'What do I have to do?'

'I don't know,' I admitted. 'It's not something I've ever had to deal with. You should report it to the procurator fiscal, I suppose, as you do with any CID inquiry – once I've given you the full story. And here it is . . .'

I took the seat facing him, and talked him through my findings, beginning with my amazement when I discovered that Alf Stein and Jimmy Proud were brothers-in-law and had hidden that relationship from me for as long as I'd known them both. I took him on to my meetings with the primus – 'The what?' Sauce asked. 'The bishop, that'll do' – and her sharing the suppressed story of the complaint against Ampersand by Joanna Meikle's mother, Sir James Proud's sister. 'Alf knew about that,' I said. 'He had to, yet he kept it to himself, even kept it from Tommy Partridge, his DS. Actually Tommy was just his cipher; his main function was to fetch and carry, and rubber-stamp everything when Alf was ready.'

'Sir,' Sauce murmured. 'This is more than just tinkering, isn't it? It's perverting the course of justice.'

'In your shoes,' I replied, 'that's something I would be happy to let the Crown Office decide, but I would say yes, it is.'

'If it is, was Sir James involved?'

'Just knowing about the incident and keeping it from Alf would make him liable to prosecution. Sharing it and then going along with hushing it up, that would make it a slam-dunk conviction against the pair of them.'

'Can you prove that he knew?'

'I wish I couldn't, but the fact is, he did.'

'Is that what Brass had on him?'

'No. I haven't got to the bottom of what he knew, but it's clear he had never heard of Joanna or of the second complaint. Austin came to the story from a completely different angle.' I paused and pointed at the office coffee supply; he took the hint.

When we were both supplied, I took him through the story of my visit to John Ampersand, looking for background on his brother, my casual encounter with his niece, and my subsequent discovery, thanks to David Brass, that she and Austin had hooked up during his trip to Cambridge for the student debate.

'This wasn't a big crusade on Austin's part. It began with him doing his girlfriend a favour. He'd have walked away from it too, after just one meeting with Briony, had he not had a call from Florence, her daughter, which she refuses to talk about.' I drank some coffee; it had an aftertaste that wasn't too nice, appropriate in the context of our discussion.

'I take no pleasure from any of this, Sauce,' I said. 'Ampersand's dead and gone and largely unmourned; the same is true of the man who was convicted of killing him. I wouldn't have touched this with a bargepole if Jimmy Proud hadn't come to me and asked me to get him off whatever hook Austin Brass thought he had him on. And where are we now? Austin, who was as much a victim as any of the people whose cases he fought through his blog, he's dead, poor bugger. Jimmy Proud has disappeared, and when – if – he returns from wherever he is, his reputation and his life will be in ruins. Yet none of it would have happened if Austin had missed his train to Cambridge, or if Amy Ampersand had gone straight home rather than to a reception after the debate. If they'd never met we wouldn't be here and that fucking box on your desk would still be gathering dust in a store.'

'But they did,' Sauce countered quietly, after what I took to be a respectful pause, unless he was simply humouring a maudlin has-been. 'Austin Brass is very dead, and it's my job to find out who killed him.'

'It wasn't Jimmy Proud,' I snapped.

'He had motive and he was in the area. You helped me establish that.'

I laughed. 'And having bumped him off, he then stopped off at Falko's to buy cake for Chrissie. I don't think so somehow. Look, Sauce, I agree that Jimmy has to be eliminated as a suspect, but it wasn't him. Now we've got inside the Ampersand investigation, I suggest that you focus on that; the two are linked, no question in my mind.'

'Even that's stalled, going by what you've just told me.'

By that time I had shared almost everything with him, all but the single thread of Briony's revelation, and that I was keeping to myself until I saw whether it wove into anything significant. If not, it didn't matter; enough lives had been disturbed, I reckoned. 'I'd have agreed with that,' I replied, 'were it not for a call I had just before I got here from a pal who's been doing some family research for me. The key witness in the conviction of Meads was the old lady I told you about, Mrs Royce, who saw Barley's truck outside the vicarage on the night Ampersand died. Agreed?'

He nodded. 'Yes. If I'm getting it right, without her there would have been no link to him.'

'Exactly. So how did she get involved? Tommy Partridge said that a door-to-door sweep turned her up. That's what Alf Stein told him, but there's no paper to support that in that box; believe me, there isn't, I've been through it often enough. I don't believe it ever existed. Tommy was simply sent to show her a photograph. Afterwards she identified the actual truck herself. The old lady wasn't at all mobile, so she was helped on each occasion by her grandson. His name was never noted, because he was a carer, not a witness. Well, my pal Jim has been doing what he does best, and this is what he found: Mrs Royce, a widow, died in nineteen ninety-three, leaving two daughters, two granddaughters and a grandson. The younger of the daughters married a man named Gerald Lennon, and their only son, Esme Royce's helpful grandson, was christened Michael. The same Michael was born and brought up in Heatherston; he went on to marry Briony Meads in nineteen ninety-five, and is now general manager of Easterlee Farm. Was that pure happenstance, Sauce? Was Mrs Royce actually found by a careless plod, who told Detective Superintendent Stein, who then forgot to type up his notes? Was Michael Lennon's connection innocent? Anything's possible, I admit. Coincidences do happen,' I said. 'I concede that too. But when they pop up in the middle of a murder investigation, I flat out don't believe in them.'

Forty-Seven

I couldn't stand any more of Sauce's crap CID coffee. In search of an upgrade, I took him out to a café in Stockbridge that Alex and I had frequented when she lived there. I discovered that it had changed hands since then. The brew wasn't quite as good as I remembered, Kenyan rather than Colombian, which is my preference, but on the plus side, the home-baked scones were excellent. Sauce and I polished off four between us. I had gone for a thinking run before a breakfast that had consisted of cereal and orange juice, and I was hungry again. So was my young companion; I didn't speculate upon what he might have been doing.

'Where do I go?' he asked.

'What do you know?' I replied, as I accepted a top-up from our friendly waitress. 'What facts do you have that lead you to a definite conclusion?'

He removed a jammy crumb from a corner of his mouth as he considered my challenge. 'On the basis of what you've told me – assuming that you can prove it – I know that the conviction of Barley Meads needs to be overturned.'

'Agreed, and I can. That's where you should focus for now.'

318

He frowned. 'Hold on, sir. My investigation is into the death of Austin Brass.'

'Sure, and that's ongoing. As part of it, you've been looking at the Ampersand murder, given that was Brass's particular interest at the time of his death. That's thrown up new information indicating a potential crime. It's your duty to investigate it and act as necessary.'

'I suppose,' he conceded. 'So I take formal statements from witnesses: Bishop Cornton, Joanna Meikle . . .' he hesitated for a second, 'Sir James Proud, if we can find him.'

'You don't need Jimmy,' I said. 'Magnolia Stein will testify to Alf's knowledge of the Joanna incident – although she won't like it when she realises it will destroy her brother's reputation. Tommy Partridge will testify to his own lack of knowledge. He'd never heard of Joanna until I told him. That's your case made; you can take that straight to the Crown Office. If you want to . . .'

'What else would I do?' Sauce asked. 'As you say, with those statements, it would be clear.'

'You could interview Carmel and Briony also, to check whether Alf mentioned it to them. That would be a pretext, of course; once they were in there, you could broaden the scope of the interview and ask them about what happened thirty years ago. They might still get up and walk out, but it would give you a chance to look them in the eye.'

'Why do I need to do that? My remit is Austin Brass.'

I tapped the side of my head. 'Use this,' I advised him. 'You're going to prove that Barley Meads's conviction was unsafe. When you do that, citing an act of omission by the senior investigating officer, the entire case is reopened. As the new SIO, you can go back to scratch.'

'Gotcha.'

'What's your first move?' I was enjoying myself; also I was beginning to understand something that had never been stated.

He gazed at me with a faint smile. 'Take a look at Michael Lennon? If we can establish a link between him and Alf Stein, or even Sir James, the whole thing takes on a new dimension.'

'There is a link,' I told him. 'Briony knew Michael when they were kids; Joanna told me. How well did she know him? Did her family know him? That's what you need to determine.'

'I need to talk to Joanna?'

'Yup.'

'Do you want to come with me?' he asked.

'Yes, but not alone: I don't want to be your corroborating witness in any trial. That needs to be a cop. Talvin? Jackie?'

He was mulling over that choice when my phone sounded. It was McGuire; I took the call.

'I've had some more feedback from the monitoring we have in place,' he said.

'Not for me,' I retorted. 'For DI Haddock. I'm with him now and he's fully up to speed with what I've been doing. He reckons he has enough evidence to have the Meads conviction thrown out.'

My friend laughed. 'You're loving this.'

'Yes,' I agreed, 'and so are you. I've just figured out why you've been letting me run so far with this.'

'It's about time you did,' he said. 'You need to stay involved, Bob, you know it and Maggie and I have known it from the day Andy Martin chucked it and she took over as chief. She's made suggestions before and you haven't fancied them, so this time we saw a chance to ease you into something that would be perfect for you. If you really have figured it out, you'll see that you've been mentoring Sauce. With Sammy away, it was needed, too. It wouldn't have been fair to toss him into a murder investigation without closer support than I could give him. You're doing that now. Would you do it again when necessary, if we feel that officers need a bit of extra support?'

'Can I have a second to think that over?' I retorted. 'Of course I would, if I'm available and if it doesn't impact too badly on the rest of my life. However, there's a practical side to consider. A couple of times in the last few days I've felt naked. Do you understand what I mean?'

'Without a warrant card? Yes, I get it. We can overcome that by making you a special constable, a sworn officer under the Crown. We think of specials as back-up plods, but in fact they can do whatever the chief constable says. You up for it?'

'On one condition,' I replied. 'You tell Sarah.'

'Christ,' he sighed, 'you're asking a lot.'

'Non-negotiable, pal. Now, what do you have for Sauce? Here he is.'

I passed my phone across the table to Haddock, who had been watching me all through the exchange. He put it to his ear, listening, then produced his book and scrawled notes on a blank page. When he was finished, he killed the call, returned the phone and examined what he had written.

'*Digame*,' I said.

'What?'

'I'm practising my Catalan: tell me.'

'The monitoring of the Meads and Lennon phones that you never got round to telling me about has thrown something up. Carmel's sent Lennon a text.' He went back to his notebook. 'She said, "Briony called me, wetting herself, sure that Skinner knows. Told her no way he can." His reply: "I'll sort her. No worry." What do you reckon to that, sir?'

I beamed at him. 'I reckon the tree is shaking. It tells us there is something to know, something they fear. As it happens, I don't know what it is. But I never interrogated Briony about the murder, so why the damp knickers? This changes the batting order, Sauce. I recommend that you and I, plus the detective sergeant of your choice, get across to Ayr and make Florrie Lennon even more nervous.'

Forty-Eight

Sauce's chosen back-up was Noele McClair; she had decided she needed work more than compassion. That suited me, because I was driving and Talvin Singh would have put a lot of pressure on the rear suspension. If she was puzzled by my presence, she kept it to herself. However, she did whisper to me, as we were heading for the car, 'I hear you had a visit from Terry. I'm sorry about that.'

'Don't be,' I murmured back. 'Somebody had to straighten him out.'

'Yes. You did a good job. I saw the lump on his forehead when he came by to pick up some more of his stuff. Did you believe his fairy story?'

'I'm neutral. If there's anything in it, the guy he's talking to will find it out. But while that's happening, my advice would be to keep him at a distance.'

I didn't want to be talking all the way to Ayr, so I put some music on and turned it up; my car, my choice. I didn't ask if my companions liked Hugh Masekela; I find him good for the soul, and I always feel better after listening to him. Remarkably, nobody had a single phone call on the journey. That too was a welcome relief.

When we got there, we discovered that 'F-Star' was in a class. We hadn't come to fit in with her timetable, so Sauce and Noele pulled her out of there. I could see that she was frightened, however much she tried to cover it with truculence.

'What the fuck is this?' she demanded as we took her into the empty lecture room that had been made available to us. 'And what the fuck's he doing here?'

'Mr Skinner is helping us with our enquiries,' Sauce told her solemnly, 'just like you're going to.' He gave her a formal caution; it alarmed her even more, as I had anticipated when I suggested that they do it that way even though it wasn't strictly necessary. 'It's for your own good, Miss Lennon,' he said when she protested.

She pointed at McClair, throwing her what was meant to be a scorn-filled glance, as she set up the recording device we had brought with us. 'What's she here for? The strip search?'

'No, Miss Lennon,' the DS replied, meeting her eye, 'not unless it becomes necessary. But don't worry if it does; I brought surgical gloves and I will be gentle.'

'I want a lawyer.' (How many times had I heard that one?)

'You don't need one,' Sauce said, 'because you're not suspected of an offence.'

'Then what am I suspected of?'

'Knowing more than you let on to Mr Skinner when he visited you before. To formalise this,' he continued, 'I am Detective Inspector Harold Haddock accompanied by DS Noele McClair. We're here to interview Miss Florence Lennon, who is present. Miss Lennon, I'm not here to debate with you or listen to denials that I know are lies. You called Austin Brass and you gave him information about the investigation that led to your grandfather's imprisonment. That started a chain of events. Austin Brass is dead, almost certainly murdered, and another man has disappeared. The way things stand just now, that all comes back to you.'

'No comment.'

'I'm not asking you to comment, Miss Lennon. I'm asking you to disclose the content of the conversation you had with the late Austin Brass.'

'And I'm telling you to fuck off.' She glanced at the recorder. 'For the tape,' she added.

Sauce glanced at Noele. 'Have you got those rubber gloves handy, DS McClair, or are they in the car?'

'They're here,' she replied, patting her pocket.

'That's good, because this interview's heading in a direction where they might be needed.' I sat silently in a corner of the room, admiring the boy at work. 'Miss Lennon, let me make something very clear to you; let me spell it out. I'm the senior investigating officer looking into Austin Brass's violent and unpleasant death, almost certainly at the hands of another person. You gave him certain information that we believe led him to approach a third party and make specific threats against him related to the murder, thirty years ago, of a man named Matthew Ampersand, a crime for which your grandfather was convicted and jailed for life. If you wilfully withhold that information from me, be in no doubt that I will arrest you and you will be charged with the obstruction of justice. That's not a slap-on-the-wrist misdemeanour, it's a crime. Trust me, the judges really don't like to be obstructed, and they come down on it heavily. You will go to prison.

'Now, I'm not going to tell you that our women's prisons are like Cell Block Eleven. They're not; they're humanely run places. But this much is true: every day you are locked in a functional but unattractive building, without a sight of greenery; every night you get locked up in a small cell; there is no supply of your favourite beverages on tap; there is no constant stream of admiring young men to tell you how cool you are; every so often, one of your fellow inmates gets so depressed by the experience that despite the best efforts of the staff, she manages to top herself, just as your grandfather did, and winds up blue-faced on a mortuary slab. You play games with me, Miss Lennon, you obstruct my investigation, and that's what you'll be looking at, a couple of years of it at best. So,' he said, in conclusion, 'are you still telling me to fuck off, for the tape?'

I'd been watching Sauce, but I'd been watching Florrie Lennon also, watching her change from 'F-Star' into a pale-faced, frightened young woman.

'Would you like some water?' Noele asked her.

'Yes please.' Her voice was a croak.

There was a drinks fountain in the corner, beside me. The DS made to rise, but I waved her back down, filled a plastic beaker, then another for luck, and took them across to the table at which Florence was sitting. She drained the first of them. As I walked back to my chosen seat, I heard her murmur, 'Okay, but I'm sure it doesn't mean anything.'

'We'll see about that,' Sauce replied. 'Go on.'

'I was home from college, two or three weeks back,' she began. 'I was bored out of my skull. There is fuck all to do there, on the farm or in the village, and my dad wouldn't lend me the car. It's always the same: he says I'm home to visit them, not to bugger off to the Bongo Club. I did my daughterly duty for a while; I listened to their banal chat, or rather to his, for my mum was even quieter that she usually is, until I'd had enough and told them I was off to bed.

'I went upstairs, then realised that the beer fridge in my room was empty. I went down to the kitchen to nick a few of Dad's, and I was on my way back when I heard them talking – or rather, my mum. She'd said next to nothing all night, but now she was almost shouting at him. "The man phoned me," she said, as near as I can remember. "He promised it would just be a wee chat, so I met him. It was only when I got there that he said he wanted to talk about my father's conviction for murder. I told him there was nothing to talk about, that the whole family knew he was guilty. He accepted it, Michael." Then my dad said, "Are you sure?" and she said she was certain. Then he said, and I'm sure about this, "Even so, Austin Brass, for heaven's sake! He's the last guy we need nosing around. Look, Briony, you know as well as I do that your father was an evil bastard and it suited everyone to have him put away for murder, whether or not he did it. We know . . ." Then there was a big round of applause off the telly and I missed a few words. The next thing I heard was him mentioning a name I never caught, and then "and James Proud".

'I'd never heard of James Proud,' she continued, 'but I sure as hell knew about Austin Brass. We all read his blog at college; the guy was a student hero for the way he went after you bastards. Next day I googled James Proud and found out he'd been the chief fucking constable, no less. Jesus! So I looked up Austin's number, I told him who I was and that what my mum had told him wasn't right. He came down to Ayr the next Monday, and I told him what I had heard.'

Sauce held up a hand, interrupting her. 'The information

you gave him,' he began. 'Can you remember how he noted it down?'

'On an iPad,' she replied. 'He pulled it out of this man bag thing he carried.' She gulped some more water. 'Look,' she exclaimed, 'you need to understand that I never knew my grandfather. The way he was portrayed to me, he was this dark, evil man who'd murdered a church minister because he was convinced he was having it off with my mother. That might have made him dark and evil to them, but to me it made him fascinating. Do you know, there isn't a single photograph of him in the house, either in Grandma's wing or in ours? I wouldn't even have known what he looked like if I hadn't found a picture on the internet. It was obviously one that was taken when he was arrested, and that was all there was. I looked at it, and I didn't see anyone who was dark and evil. I saw a poor man who looked scared and confused and very, very sad. That's why I went to Austin Brass.' She buried her face in her hands; I was relieved for her as a person when she gave in to her weakness and started to cry. 'But I never, ever thought,' she said, her voice muffled by her sobbing, 'that it would get him killed.'

Forty-Nine

I invited Noele to choose the music for the return journey; she was in the back seat, so I thought it only fair. She amazed me by asking for Amanda Marshall, a Canadian singer who hasn't recorded anything for ten years. I may have amazed her also by having her catalogue in my library. My companions – my mentees, as I was beginning to think of them – were chuffed by the outcome of the interview with Florence Lennon, and I was chuffed for them. Sauce had handled it perfectly, better than I would have at his age and stage. My only part in the proceedings had come at the end, once the interview was over and Florence had signed a statement summarising what she had told us. I gave her a solemn warning not to contact any member of her family, and if they should contact her, to say nothing at all about our visit.

The volume wasn't quite as high on the way back to Edinburgh; Sauce and I were able to discuss the state of the investigation, and the questions that Florence's story, which all three of us believed absolutely, had raised.

'If Barley was framed,' I ventured, 'there is only one reason why: to protect someone else. The one thing we know for sure is that as far as the rest of his family was concerned, he was expendable.'

'Agreed,' Sauce said, 'but, if Ampersand was killed by the name that Florrie never heard—'

I interrupted. 'You may assume that was Alf Stein.'

'Accepted; and by Sir James, that kicks up more dust. Why would the Meads family go along with fitting up Barley to protect a couple of cops?'

'Excellent point,' I agreed. 'Look at another possibility: that Florence did indeed hear her father mention Jimmy Proud, but in another context, not as a killer; the Joanna incident, for example. If they didn't do it, who was Barley sacrificed to protect? Who was at the heart of the matter? Who was it who inspired Barley's fury so much that it made him the obvious prime suspect?'

'Briony.'

'Indeed. However, she was nineteen at the time of the killing. I've been up Traprain Law, and I'm here to tell you that even if she did bash his head in, there was no fucking way she could have dumped him in that quarry on her own, in high summer, far less in the depths of winter.'

'Do you think it's feasible that Barley could have helped her and then taken the consequences to save her?' he asked.

'No,' I told him, 'for two reasons: one, he was vehement in his denial from the moment of his arrest until the day of his suicide; and two, he refused to allow his defence team to go for diminished responsibility, when there was a pretty good chance that would have led to an acquittal and a referral to hospital, with the possibility of release after treatment, instead of a life sentence.'

He shifted in the comfortable passenger seat, 'What do we do now, sir? What are you thinking?'

330

'No, what are you thinking, SIO?'

'I'm thinking that we need to find out whether Michael Lennon was a part of Briony's life when this happened. Joanna Meikle might be our best bet there. Then I reckon we should bring the two of them in for questioning, her first, him second. Agreed?'

'I don't disagree,' I conceded.

'Then there's Sir James,' he added tentatively. 'He needs to be interviewed as well. Are you certain, sir, that Lady Proud has no idea where he is?'

'The way Chrissie is,' I retorted, 'I doubt she's fully aware of where she is. Don't piss about, Sauce, come out with the real question.'

He shrugged. 'If you insist, sir. Are you sure you have no idea where he is?'

'I don't, I promise you. Anyway, you don't need him yet. Wait and see what you get from your interviews with Briony and Michael. If it helps you, I can talk to Joanna about him.'

'Without telling her about her uncle's involvement?' I threw him a withering look, sideways. 'Sorry, sir. Yes, please do that. I'll hold off on bringing in Briony until I've heard from you.'

My Amanda Marshall playlist was exhausted by the time we reached the outskirts of Edinburgh; Andrea Bocelli kept us company for the rest of the journey, and me for part of the way back to Gullane after I had dropped off Sauce and Noele at Fettes. I was approaching Longniddry when I had an incoming call, cutting him off. 'Yes?' I said as I pushed the 'accept' button on the steering wheel.

'Mr Skinner?' a plummy voice replied; it was distorted by the Bluetooth link, but I recognised it.

'What can I do for you, Professor Ampersand?'

'I sense that you are on the road,' he said. 'Are you alone? Can you speak?'

'Yes to both,' I replied. I took a left turn off the main road, pulled over and parked. 'Go ahead.'

'Since we met,' he began, 'I've been thinking about what I told you, and also about what I didn't. I understand that since then you've been speaking to Amy, and that she is now aware of the truth that I had been keeping from her, the truth of her other uncle's death.'

'That had nothing to do with me,' I told him sharply, to forestall any attack that might be on the way.

'I'm aware of that,' he reassured me. 'She told me how she came to find out, and about the unfortunate death of her man friend. She's rather upset; she blames herself.'

'You should tell her not to; Austin was always at risk, doing what he did. There's no certainty that his death was linked to your brother's case.'

'I'm trying,' he said, 'but she's badly hurt. She would like to visit his father, but she isn't sure that she'd be welcome. She's afraid he'll blame her too.'

'He won't, I promise. You should encourage her. It would be good for them both.'

'I will. Guilt is corrosive, Mr Skinner. It eats into you if you don't wash it away. That's the main reason for this call. I've been feeling guilty myself about withholding from you the truth about the rift between my brother and me. It may have had nothing to do with his death, but that wasn't a sufficient reason for my silence. The truth is, I was embarrassed, and still am, by my own pettiness and lack of magnanimity both at the time of our quarrel and of his death.'

'I'm not pressing you,' I said, 'but if it helps you to get it off your chest, go ahead.'

'Thank you. Sordid as it may be,' he continued, 'Matthew and I fell out over a woman. She was a postgraduate doing a master's in another college; she was twenty-four, around my own age, and a real beauty. She and I met socially, and became involved, quite seriously involved. I was very committed to her, perhaps more than she was to me. I knew from the start that there had been someone back at home, a relationship from which she was happy to be taking a break. That didn't deter me, but inwardly I was jealous of him and of his very existence. Even at that, things were going well, I thought, and probably I was right, until I made a very serious mistake.'

'What was that?' I asked.

'I took her to church. I told her it was time she saw my older brother at work in what was really the family business. Matthew was in superb form that day; he was a most charismatic preacher and, with his congregation, a most charming man. Unfortunately, my lady friend thought that too; they met after the service and then again at a college function to which I invited him. They met for a third time and a fourth, but I wasn't told about that. I didn't find out about it until one morning when I made a surprise early visit to the rectory, walked into the kitchen unannounced and found them having breakfast.

'There and then a huge argument ensued. I have to confess, Mr Skinner, that I was a volatile young man. I was also a keen sculler and fairly sturdy. I punched my brother, as hard as I could, and walked out. When I had cooled down, I went to see my lady and confronted her. I found her packing her bags. She told me that after I had left, Matthew had been so full of guilt and remorse that he had turned on her and accused her of leading him astray. I told her it didn't matter, that I could forgive her. She called me something very rude, then said that she wanted no part of either of us. She meant it too. She gave up her studies and went back home to Edinburgh.'

Another shoe dropped; that week they seemed to be raining down.

'That's quite a story, Professor,' I murmured. 'There's only one thing missing.'

'Her name? Do you really need that?'

'No, but I'd like to hear you say it.'

'It was Milligan: Carmel Milligan.'

Fifty

Once again, I went straight to the Prouds' place when I reached Gullane. Once again, Chrissie was at her pathetic perch by the small study window, looking out in vain. I sat in the car for a couple of minutes. I knew that she was watching me, but there was a call I had to make.

'Sauce,' I exclaimed as soon as he picked up. 'Everything is changed. The tactics we discussed on the way back, forget them. Tomorrow morning, we go to Easterlee Farm, but not to see Briony and Michael, not immediately anyway. Top priority is Carmel, the mother. I'll explain why when I see you, but between now and then, I'd like you to go into the box I left with you and check some dates for me. Got your notebook handy? Right.'

When Joanna opened the door, she was wearing a paint-smeared shirt, buttoned at the cuffs. 'I've been working on your portrait,' she told me. 'I'm pleased with it. I hope you will be too.'

'Can I see it?'

'No, not until it's finished.'

I shrugged. 'That's not why I came anyway, Joanna. I need a couple of things from you. The first is clarification about

Michael Lennon. You told me that he was one of the kids in the village when you were young. Right?'

'Yes. We did all go to the same school for a couple of years, the local primary, but Briony and I left when we were seven, to go to Watson's.'

'Okay, now move on. When did Michael move on from being just a village kid to being part of Briony's life?'

'As soon as he left school; he went to work on the farm, until he got the sack. Look, Bob, shouldn't you be asking Briony about this?'

'Maybe, but I'd rather ask you, because I trust you to tell me the truth.'

She sighed. 'Okay. Michael worked on Easterlee Farm as an apprentice, until Mr Meads fired him after he caught him and Briony together in one of the outbuildings. They were just fooling around really, she told me, but when Barley walked in, he had his hand inside her drawers and she wasn't minding it at all. He went daft, even dafter than usual, screamed at them and threw Michael right across the room. He might have killed him if Mrs Meads hadn't been close by and come in to see what the noise was about.'

'How long was that before the Ampersand murder?'

'I'd guess about six months.'

'The thing between Michael and Briony, did that put an end to it?'

She laughed. 'Hell, no! They used to meet at mine, every Tuesday night when my mother was at bridge club. They nearly got caught once, when one of Michael's johnnies didn't flush away properly. Fortunately I spotted it before my mother did.'

'You and Briony were best pals, but how about Carmel and Grayling, your mother?'

'No, not specially. They were different types completely. Not enemies, but not friends either. Uncle Jimmy was more of a chum. He knew Barley, and he was wary of him, especially after his complaint against Matthew Ampersand was thrown out. He used to look in occasionally, just to say hello, according to him, but I'm sure it was to check that Carmel was all right.'

'Did Jimmy know about Briony and Michael?'

'Yes, he did,' she said, 'because I told him. Michael knew he was taking a risk, but he was reckless. I warned Uncle Jimmy in the hope that he'd tell him to be more careful. I think he did too.'

'How about your uncle Alf? Was he ever at the farm?'

She nodded, firmly. 'He went up there once that I know of. Something happened in the Heatherston Saloon one night: I know, because I was there, although I wasn't eighteen at the time. It was the local then, although it closed years ago. There was a young policewoman in for a drink with her boyfriend, in civvies; Barley was being obnoxious, and he asked him to mind his language. Barley hit the boy, she got her police ID out, he threw a pint over her and stomped out. The boyfriend wouldn't let her call the cavalry, because he was embarrassed at being knocked over, but the girl was CID and she told Uncle Alf. He went up to the farm and he saw Barley. As you know, the man was a brute, but Briony told me he was very quiet after that chat.'

I whistled. If nothing else, that private conversation would have ended Meads's trial if the judge had known about it.

'Does that help you?' Joanna asked.

'Honestly, I don't know. But the other thing I came for might, if you have it. Tell me, when was the last time you ran the dishwasher?'

Fifty-One

Sauce needn't have invited me to the Easterlee Farm party, but he did. He even delayed it for half an hour to allow me to fit in a meeting with Arthur Dorward, to hand him two packages and ask him for a shedload of favours in one go.

We travelled from Fettes in a highly visible police vehicle, blue lights, the lot. That was Sauce's idea, not mine, but I approved one hundred per cent. I briefed him, and Noele, on the way; it took them no time at all to understand the significance of what John Ampersand had told me. In turn, he briefed me on the dates I'd asked him to retrieve from the original investigation record. All three of us understood their potential significance.

As we approached the farm, Sauce ordered the driver to switch on the lights; we wanted to make as much impact as possible.

'Sirens?' Noele suggested.

'That would be overkill,' he replied. 'We don't want to frighten any livestock. Scare the crap out of the family by all means, but not the cattle.'

As I had done on my first visit, we made a satisfactory scrunching noise on the gravel, pulling up in front of the massive farmhouse. Carmel was in her customary lookout position in the glass porch. I had a momentary flash of Chrissie Proud at her window, and felt a pang of sympathy for the woman. Her life, as she had known it, was about to end.

She rose from her chair, and I could see her concern as the three of us moved towards her. I placed myself at the rear of the trio. 'Mrs Meads,' Sauce began as we stepped into her sanctum, 'I'm Detective Inspector Haddock and this is my colleague, Detective Sergeant McClair; I believe you know Mr Skinner. He's here in an advisory capacity.'

'If this is about the man Brass,' Carmel exclaimed, 'I know nothing about his death. I never even met him.'

'No,' he replied. 'We need to talk to you about other matters. It might be better if we could do so indoors rather than here where we can be seen by—'

'Mum!' Briony's shout came from the doorway of the farmhouse. 'What's going on here?' I turned half towards her, and she saw me. 'Mr Skinner, what is this?'

'As DI Haddock was saying,' I replied, 'the police need to talk to Mrs Meads. We have information about Matthew Ampersand's death that we need to review, first with your mother and then with you and your husband. Where is Michael?'

She paled; even with her olive complexion, it was noticeable. 'He's on the farm, checking the herd, but he's probably on the way here.' She glanced back at the police car; its blue lights were still flashing. 'You couldn't miss seeing that thing.' The driver, a uniformed PC, had left his seat and was standing beside his vehicle; I signalled to him to turn them off.

'Mrs Lennon, we need you and your husband to wait with the constable until we're ready for you,' Sauce told her. 'We will want to interview you separately. Please don't try to leave the farm, or Constable Whiting will have to detain you.' He waved the PC across and gave him quiet instructions, then turned back to Carmel. 'Mrs Meads, can we go inside, please?'

She sighed, then looked past him at me. As she met my gaze, I could see resignation in hers. 'We'll go to the kitchen. It's the heart of every farmhouse.'

We followed her inside, leaving Briony in the porch with the PC. As we left, I heard the sound of something large on the gravel, but I didn't turn back. The cop was a seasoned officer and he could handle Michael Lennon, no matter how unreasonable he chose to be.

The kitchen had a rustic look, but I could see that it was modern; there's a designer in Gullane and it reminded me of the display I see through his window every time I walk past. We were led past the island that enclosed a large gas hob, to a solid round table surrounded by four chairs: Carmel, Briony, Michael and Florence, I assumed. We seated ourselves, Sauce facing Carmel, Noele on his right and me on his left.

'Mrs Meads,' he began, as McClair set up the video recorder and switched it on.

That was as far as I allowed him to go. There was something that needed saying and I had to make sure that it was. 'Carmel,' I said. He glanced at me sharply, but I wasn't about to be halted. Matthew Ampersand had waited thirty years for justice and I would not see it frustrated by a clever defence lawyer. 'This interview will be conducted under caution,' I advised her. 'It relates to a crime in which you may be a suspect. That means you are entitled to legal advice before being questioned, if you wish. Do you?' I sensed Sauce's body language change beside me; maybe he'd been about to give her the same warning, or maybe I'd helped him dodge a bullet. Only he knew, and I wouldn't ask him.

She frowned. 'Mr Skinner, I gave up listening to those buggers many years ago, just like Barley. It's okay.'

With a brief nod in my direction, that might have meant either 'Thanks', or 'Thanks, pal!', depending on the tone, Sauce resumed. For the tape, he identified the four participants, read the statutory caution and then asked Carmel to confirm that she had declined legal advice. After she had done so, he surprised me. 'Mr Skinner,' he continued, 'you've done much of the investigation in this case; would you like to begin?'

'Thank you, Detective Inspector.' He'd pitched me in at the deep end. His way of getting his own back? I doubted it, but I didn't care. I had been imagining the interview for much of the night. 'Mrs Meads, why is it that at no time, before or after his murder and during your late husband's trial, did you disclose that many years before, in Cambridge, you and Matthew Ampersand had a relationship?'

She nodded; her purple-tinged white hair rippled. 'So you got there,' she murmured. 'I had a feeling you would. I didn't tell anyone because I didn't want anyone to know, least of all my husband and his defence team.'

'Why was that?'

'You know why it was, Mr Skinner. It was because I killed him.'

Sauce straightened in his chair. 'Stop there, Mrs Meads. I'm bound to ask you again. Do you want legal advice? Think carefully about it, please.'

'I could think all day,' she retorted, 'but I won't change my mind. I don't want a lawyer, I just want to get this over with. I repeat, Mr Skinner, DI Haddock, DS McClair, that I killed Matthew Ampersand, in his kitchen – that's why I suggested this place for my confession – in his vicarage. I bashed his head in with a big stone rolling pin that I doubt had been used for any other purpose in fifty years.'

'What prompted you to attack him?'

'I didn't go there with that in mind,' she replied. 'I went there to remonstrate with him for his attack on Joanna Meikle, my daughter's friend. I meant to be calm, but I lost it. He denied it, as loudly as I had accused him; then he said, "To hell with it, I've had enough. I wasn't guilty when Barley accused me of assaulting Briony, and I'm not guilty now. I had no intention of harming Joanna, but when he hears about it, this will drive your husband even crazier than he usually is. I've been silent for too long. I'm going to see him, and I'm going to tell him the truth!" I screamed at him, "No you are not. I won't allow it," but he replied, "Just watch me!" and made for the door.'

She stopped, licking her lips, which had gone quite dry. I could see a Pyrex jug beside the kitchen sink; I rose, filled it and brought it to the table, with four glasses. Noele filled all of them and passed them round. I watched Carmel as she drank; as she gathered her resolve and her strength.

'The only clear memory I have of hitting him is the noise it made. It was a crunching sound and I knew it was bone-shattering. He fell at my feet. There was a tremor in his right leg for a few seconds, but then it stopped, and I knew he was finished. There was blood, of course, a pool of it, but that stopped too; I was sure he was dead then.'

'Did you touch him? Did you try to help him?'

'No. I knew he was beyond that. I work with animals,' she

said calmly. 'People die in the same way; it takes a little longer, that's all.'

'How did you feel?' I asked her quietly.

'Numb. For a minute or so I just felt numb. Then the enormity of what I had done came home to me and I knew what had to happen next.'

I had a vision of what she had done next, and I didn't want to be involved in the telling of it. 'Sauce?' I whispered, passing the ball back to him.

'What was that, Mrs Meads?' he asked, moving on seamlessly.

'He was dead at my feet. I called the police.'

'When you say "the police", are you saying that you called 999?'

'No, I called James Proud.'

'Why him?'

'Because it was he who had told me about the attack on Joanna. I knew he was her uncle; we had met once or twice at social things his sister Grayling was involved in. He had called round to the farm earlier that day, wanting to apologise to Barley for not believing his original complaint. He was furious, quite convinced of Matthew's guilt. "The man's a sexual predator right enough," he shouted.'

'What did he say when you called him?'

'Not what I expected. I thought he'd tell me to stay where I was while he sent officers to the scene, but he didn't. Instead, he told me to get the hell out of there and back to the farm. I did as I was told; I still expected to be arrested and charged, but I wasn't. Instead James came to the house himself, this house, with another man. He introduced him as Alf, his brother-in-law. He had been to the farm once before to talk to Barley; they'd had a bit of an argument.'

'Where was your husband at this time, Mrs Meads?' Noele McClair asked.

'In bed, out of it as usual. Barley had a very simple pattern, all year round. He would rise early, work all day, come home for dinner and drink himself to sleep.'

'Was there anyone else in the house?'

'No. Briony, my daughter, had gone back to college.'

Sauce frowned. 'James Proud and Alf Stein: what did they do?'

'First thing,' she replied, 'they gave me a large whisky; I was a wreck by that time. I asked them what would happen to me. I remember Alf saying, "Nothing, hen. You're not going down for that creature." I was bewildered; I didn't know what was going on, but I began to think that it might be all right after all. They talked together for a while, then James asked me where Barley kept the keys to his truck; I showed them. Before they left, one of them told me to have another whisky then go to bed, so that when Barley woke he would see me there and assume I'd been beside him all night. I did. When I woke next morning, he was up and gone and it was as if nothing had ever happened. I thought for a while that I had dreamed it, but not for long; it all came back to me pretty soon. I realised what I had done.'

'Later, after the body was found, what happened?'

'Alf came back. He was worried, but he said that there was a way out of it. If we could find someone to identify Barley's truck and place it at the vicarage on the night of the murder, there was so much forensic evidence in it tying Barley to the crime that he'd be stuffed. It was the only way to save myself, and him, and James Proud. He promised that he could make it work, and he did.'

'Who came up with Michael Lennon?' Sauce asked.

'I did. I knew quite well that Briony was still seeing him. I also knew that he had an ancient grandmother who lived within sight of the vicarage. I told him that the police had a problem; they were sure that Barley had killed Matthew, but they were one witness short of proving it. He understood what I wanted him to do without me even asking. He was only too willing. He wanted revenge on Barley . . .'

'And you wanted the farm, and to be shot of a drunken boor of a husband,' Haddock added.

'Exactly,' she shot back at him, 'and we both got what we wanted – until Austin bloody Brass showed up.'

'Did Briony know any of this?'

'Not until after she'd met Brass. What she told him, she thought it was the truth, but he made an impression on her. She pressed Michael about it afterwards and the bloody fool told her the whole damn story – or as much of it as he knew.'

'Did you kill Brass?' Noele asked bluntly.

'No.'

'Do you know who did?'

'No, but if I did, I wouldn't be telling you; Michael and me, you've got us, but no more.'

'Briony too, I'm afraid,' I murmured. She stared at me. 'As soon as Michael told her, and she did nothing about it, she became a party to the cover-up. The Crown might even argue that it extends to the murder too.'

'No!' she cried out.

'I'm afraid so. The longer it went, the more people it sucked in.' I gazed at her. 'Are you ready to tell us the whole truth now, Carmel? All of it?'

'I have done!' she protested.

'Ah, but you haven't. You've given us a graphic account of the crime and the cover-up, but you've left out the heart of the matter, the key to everything. My colleagues here, unlike me, they haven't met Briony. If they had, and seen how alike the two of you are, they'd get it too.'

The light of defiance left her eyes. 'You've guessed?'

'No, not a guess. I think I started to understand as soon as I met Briony.' I rose from my seat and stepped across to something that looked like an old-fashioned dresser, but which was actually a piece of modern furniture integrated with the rest. Several family photos stood upon it, but I focused on one: mother and daughter, one in her forties and one in her mid teens, but both tall, dark-haired, with olive skin, and remarkably alike. I picked it up and showed it to the two detectives. 'Barley got it wrong, didn't he? He did see two people entwined through that window, and one was Ampersand, but the other, it wasn't Briony, it was you.'

She inhaled deeply. 'It was,' she admitted. 'Briony was twelve when the charge in the Episcopal Church became vacant, and Matthew was appointed. It was a great surprise. He was a rising star in the Church of England, an archdeacon, on the way to becoming a bishop and after that who knows what. Nobody could understand it when he turned it all in and moved to Scotland, but I did; he'd come after me.'

'Looking to renew the fling that you and he had in Cambridge when you were a student there? We know about that,' I added. 'John told me.'

'John? Matthew's brother?'

I nodded. 'Nice man, if a little pompous; never married, dotes on his niece now. How long did it take for you and

Matthew to become involved again once he came to Heatherston?' I asked.

'A couple of months. I knew Barley for the monster he was by that time; Matthew was like a gift from God.' She paused, and smiled, 'Well, from the General Synod, if not Him personally. We carried on quietly for three years, he and I, until the Briony incident. Realising what had happened, realising Barley's mistake, we thought it best to cool it for a while. To be frank, Barley was drinking so much by then, I was hoping he would get himself out of the way by dying.'

'But he didn't, until it was too late.'

'No, he didn't; the man never did a thing to make me happy, not even something as simple as that.' Her voice cracked, and she sipped some more water. 'Our relationship in Cambridge, Matthew's and mine, when I studied there, was intense, but it was brief, and it ended badly. People were hurt, me included. I left there and then, gave up my course and came back to Edinburgh, where I'd been seeing Barley in vacations. In those days, he wasn't the man he became after the drink got to him. He was energetic, and he wasn't unattractive; he was also rich, the heir of a landed family. He had a farm, he had security, and that was what I wanted, before and after my Cambridge upset. He had asked me to marry him a couple of times. I'd put him off, but when I returned I said yes, and we did the deed as soon as possible in the registry office.'

'And seven and a half months later,' I said, 'Briony was born. The birth records don't tell you everything, but I'm pretty sure she wasn't premature. Was she?'

'She was full-term,' Carmel murmured.

'Did Barley never ask you about that?'

'No, because he didn't have to. I'd been home for a weekend

around the time of Briony's conception, and he and I had . . . spent some time together.'

'In that case,' Sauce asked, 'who was Briony's father? Barley Meads or Matthew Ampersand?'

She drew him a long look, then smiled. 'To tell you the honest truth, Detective Inspector,' she replied, 'I don't know.'

In that moment, I almost felt sorry for her: almost. 'You know what, Carmel?' I said. 'That truth you spoke of, the truth that you killed Matthew to stop him from revealing to Barley. What did you think he'd have done if he'd learned? Killed Matthew? Probably not, because he was all wind and piss, as you'd seen when Alf Stein paid him a visit before. Killed you? Even less likely. Chucked you out? Much more likely. And that, instinctively, was what you were trying to prevent when you picked up that rolling pin and smashed your lover's head in. You did it to protect all this.' I glanced around the expensive kitchen. 'The wealth, your lifestyle. You know what, if that body had never been found, chances are you and poor old Barley – the monster, as you described him, something I don't believe he ever was – you and he would still be sat at this table, you the lady of the manor, him quietly drunk every night or shouting the odds in the pub, trying to pretend that he was the master of his own household, when in fact he was under your thumb from the day he set eyes on you.'

Fifty-Two

I hadn't planned to sit in on the interviews with Lennon or Briony, even if they'd taken place. If I'd been present at his, my physical confrontation with him might have become a factor at any future trial. As for her, I wouldn't have been comfortable being there, with certain matters unresolved. In the event, neither happened, as Michael insisted on taking legal advice, and when she heard that, his wife followed suit. All three were arrested and taken to the custody centre in Edinburgh, in separate vehicles, where the two younger prisoners would see the lawyer of their choice, and where Carmel would wait until Sauce was ready to charge her.

My two companions were pumped up as we drove back to Fettes. Even PC Whiting had a faint smile on his face, and he was a man who gave the impression that those were infrequent visitors. I wasn't as high as they were; I was on the way back down from the high of securing Carmel's confession.

Noele McClair read my mood. 'Why so glum?' I realised that she didn't know how to address me; I'd been Bob at the children's party, but there we were seated side by side in the back of a police car, and I wasn't in handcuffs.

'Bob is still okay,' I murmured. I nodded towards Haddock.

'It is for him too, but he has this thing about it. I'm not glum, Noele; I'm back in the real world, and thinking about what happens next.'

'We charge her,' Sauce said, twisting round awkwardly in the front seat.

'Say that again?' I challenged.

He frowned for a few seconds, then continued, 'Okay, technically we report to the fiscal, and then we charge her.'

'It's not technical, Sauce; the police report to the Crown in criminal investigations. You don't draw up the indictment; Her Majesty's Advocate does, and prosecutes the case. To do that, he's going to need more than Carmel's confession; the law requires corroboration, supporting evidence to confirm an admission of guilt. Where are you going to get that? You have no forensic evidence. You don't have a body; Matthew Ampersand was cremated after the trial and his ashes scattered in the River Cam, as per his will. But even if you did, there's no weapon to match with the skull fracture. There never was; look at the files, there's no mention of a stone rolling pin, because Alf and Jimmy will have got rid of it. You need a corroborating witness? Where are you going to find one?'

My young friend and protégé looked at me; I hadn't just nicked his last Rolo, I'd taken the whole fucking tube. Then his eyes lit up. 'Ah,' he exclaimed. 'Michael Lennon. We can let him plead guilty to aiding his granny's perjury, to get out of the murder charge.'

'I doubt that the Crown could charge him with murder, Sauce,' I countered. 'His defence will be that he didn't know about Carmel's guilt at the time. He wasn't a witness to the killing, only the frame-up, so you've got him for perverting justice at most – only you haven't, because at the moment you have no corroboration of that either.' I paused, and smiled; I've lectured a few times at police colleges in Scotland and around the world, and I felt like I was back in the classroom. 'There is only one man alive who can testify that Carmel killed Ampersand, but if he did, he'd be confessing his own guilt of the murder, art and part, as our wonderfully quirky Scots criminal law system has it.'

'Sir James Proud,' Noele murmured.

'That's the man,' I agreed. 'But he has the right to remain silent. He can't be compelled to give evidence against himself. And there's this: the Crown might decide that technically his evidence was hearsay, as it also relied on Carmel's confession – he didn't see her do it. The more I think about this, Carmel is not going to court.'

'Aw, shit!' Sauce cried out.

'Sod it,' his DS murmured.

The muscles in PC Whiting's neck tensed, and his face grew even more dour than normal.

'So what have you got?' I asked the detectives.

'We've got Sir James's part in disposing of the body,' Haddock suggested.

'That needs both Carmel and Michael to incriminate themselves. She might, but with her being untouchable for the murder itself, that's not likely. Go back to basics, Sauce. Why are you really here?'

'I'm the SIO in the Austin Brass investigation. And Sir James is my prime suspect.'

'But you and I and Noele know bloody well he didn't do it. People, it's pretty obvious who did it. The trick is proving it. Bugger it,' I growled, 'I'd been planning to steer clear of Michael Lennon's interview, but I've changed my mind. This is what you do – I suggest.' I checked my watch; it showed ten minutes after midday. 'In four hours, have him brought to Fettes from custody for interview, but not on the Ampersand murder, and not as a suspect, so he doesn't have a right to legal advice. Between now and then, there are two other things you need to do . . .'

Fifty-Three

Michael Lennon glared at me as I stepped into the small room. It had seen better days. The Scottish national police service has spending priorities, and refurbishment of the former Edinburgh headquarters building does not feature high on the list. I expect that pretty soon it will be closed and sold; it's too big a piece of property to house its remaining functions.

'What's he doing here?' he asked Noele McClair, as she checked that all of the recording equipment was functioning properly. 'He's not a police officer, is he?'

I glared back. 'Ah, but I am,' I replied, brandishing the brand-new special constable credentials that Mario McGuire had given me after he had sworn me in earlier that afternoon. Yet another piece of plastic; I'm going to need a bigger wallet.

Lennon had been brought to Fettes free of restraints, in line with the assurance given to his solicitor that he was required for interview on a separate matter not directly related to the Ampersand case. He was still in his working clothing, a one-piece overall not dissimilar to the garment that had helped send his late, and still unlamented, father-in-law to jail. He was leaning forward, hands clasped, forearms on the table. He looked alone and vulnerable, and that was exactly how I wanted him to feel.

Sauce followed me in. If I looked a little menacing in my casual clothing, jerkin carried over my shoulder and a close fitting Under Armour T-shirt, he looked more like a social worker in the well-cut suit that I always suggested that my plain-clothes officers, male and female, should wear.

'Thank you for joining us, Mr Lennon,' he began. 'We haven't met, but for the benefit of the tape, I'm DI Haddock, and this is DS McClair. I believe you have met Mr Skinner.'

'Fine,' he retorted, 'but why am I here?'

'I'm leading the investigation into the death of Mr Austin Brass,' Sauce said. Lennon leaned back, arms off the table, but his expression didn't alter. 'I have to make it clear that you are not a suspect but I believe you may be able to assist us.'

'I don't see how.'

'It's like this. We know that Brass contacted your wife a few days before he died. He wanted to ask her, on behalf of a friend of his, about the death of the Reverend Matthew Ampersand thirty years ago, and her father's conviction for her murder. We know that Mrs Lennon satisfied him there was nothing to it, no story there. However, we also know of a further contact with Brass, one that rekindled his interest in the case in a big way. That was made by your daughter, Florence. She remains our only link to Brass, and she's our chief suspect. I want you to look at this.' He paused while McClair switched on a disc player that sat below a monitor. The screen came to life, displaying a vehicle, a Volkswagen off-roader, driving along a stretch of road that was recognisable as the east-bound side of the Edinburgh bypass.

It was my turn. 'That's yours, Michael. Statement, not question; we both know it is. And here's the thing, we can follow it all the way to Haddington, where Brass was killed. So, who was driving? You're disqualified. Mrs Lennon, we know, was with her mother that day. We've asked them both, independently, and that's what they told us. So, who else has access to that vehicle? Only your Florence, that's all, and this is my thinking. She spilled her guts to Brass, in a fit of outrage over what you helped her granny do to Barley Meads. It felt great at the time, but pretty soon she realised the implications of what she had done. Ruin for her grandmother, ruin for her parents, but more than that, the ruin and disintegration of the family business that one day she was going to inherit. She wondered how to put it right, and the only way she could see was to get rid of Brass. She called him again, she made another meeting, at a place of his choice, and there she killed him and heaved him into the river. You won't like this, but all we need is for you to confirm that she has access to your car, and used it that day.'

'Stop!' he shouted. 'This is where I do need to speak to my lawyer again.'

Arrogant bastard that I am, I winked at him. 'I thought you might say that.' I rose, stepped to the door and opened it. 'Susannah,' I called out. 'Your client needs you now, Ms Himes. The room's all yours.'

I held it wide, and a few seconds later, an elegant middle-aged woman, with very sharp eyes, stepped into the room. She was even better dressed than Sauce, as befitting one of the nation's top criminal lawyers; maybe the very top, although my kid is coming up fast. The three of us left her and her client alone.

'Susannah Himes? Who's she?' McClair asked as we stood in the corridor.

'You're new to these parts or you'd know; her nickname is the Barracuda, and her main diet is prosecution witnesses. Sauce knows her, don't you, Detective Inspector?' He did indeed; once upon a time in the past, she'd kept his girlfriend out of jail.

Her face fell. 'So we can all go home?'

'I don't think so; wait and see.'

Sauce looked at me. 'Are we all right here, legally?'

'As long as she never finds out we knew that enhanced CCTV can identify Lennon as the driver of the car. If she did, she might argue that she should have had access sooner, but that isn't going to happen.'

'What about the other thing?'

'That's where our fingers are still crossed.'

I had barely spoken before the door reopened. Himes looked at me, then Sauce. She was about to speak when Haddock's mobile sounded. He excused himself and took the call, with his back to the rest of us. 'Sorry about that,' he murmured when it was over. 'Ms Himes, please carry on.'

'Thank you.' She made eye contact with all three of us, then continued. 'I was about to say that my client would like to make a statement.'

'I thought he might,' I murmured. 'I could even make a stab at what he's going to tell us.'

I leaned over and whispered in the lawyer's ear for a few seconds. She smiled, and replied, 'No comment.' We followed her back into the room.

Once we were all seated at the table, and the recorders had been reactivated, she took the lead. 'My client has asked me to put the following on the record. In relation to the CCTV you have shown him, he wishes to say that it was not his daughter who was driving the car, but himself. He realises this lays him open to a charge of driving while disqualified, and is willing to accept the consequences. He was going to Haddington for a prearranged meeting with Mr Austin Brass, near the Aubigny Sports Centre. Its purpose was so that Mr Lennon could persuade Mr Brass to abandon his investigation of the case of Mr Lennon's late father-in-law, on the grounds that it was futile, and could only cause the family distress. Mr Brass agreed to this and Mr Lennon left the scene. At that time, Mr Brass was alive and well.' She stopped and looked directly at Haddock. 'I don't believe you have any sort of a case, Detective Inspector. Can we go now?'

Sauce nodded. 'You'd probably be right too, Ms Himes, but for one new development. That call I took just now, it was from the officer in charge of a search, under warrant from the sheriff, of Easterlee Farm and all of its vehicles. His team have just recovered from the spare-wheel compartment in a Volkswagen Touareg a man's shoulder bag containing an Apple iPad. Various witnesses have spoken of Austin Brass carrying such a bag and such a tablet with him at all times, yet none was found at the scene of his death.' He inhaled slowly, then continued. 'Obviously, Ms Himes, these items have still to be examined forensically. That said,' he paused again and smiled, 'I may be new at this rank, but I'm learning fast from my mentor alongside me here, and I know just as well as he does that the only prints we're going to find on them are those of Austin Brass and your client. I'm afraid the only place he's going is back to the custody suite, until we can charge him with Brass's murder.'

Fifty-Four

It should have been all over with Michael Lennon's arrest, and as far as the police were concerned it was. The Brass homicide was solved, and that was the only open case under investigation. I might have proved to my own satisfaction that Barley Meads didn't kill Matthew Ampersand; I might have proved that Jimmy Proud didn't do it either, not personally at least; but the plain truth was that nobody gave a toss. Worse than that, to the people in the power seats, the Lord Advocate, the Justice Minister and even Chief Constable Margaret Rose Steele, my findings were an inconvenience.

Carmel Meads wasn't going to jail; that had been clear to me almost from the moment of her confession. She was back at Easterlee Farm before the sun went down on the day of her arrest, and so was her daughter. Her husband's case wasn't going anywhere near the Scottish Criminal Cases Review Commission, because nobody had any desire to take it there, least of all the trio named above, whose sleep was disturbed for sure by the prospect of two senior police officers being fingered as art-and-part murderers and perverters of the course of justice. The fact that one of them was still alive, possibly, made it even worse. My box from the archives went back to Mario, and in all likelihood, although I've never asked, from him to the incinerator, and finding the vanished Sir James Proud fell right off the police to-do list.

It didn't fall off mine, but I had a solemn task to fulfil before then, one that was no relevant part of any investigation – although if Barley Meads had known of it when he was alive, his future might have been different, but probably not.

The day after Carmel's release, I had an email from Arthur Dorward, well off the books and sent from his private account to mine. Its findings took me by surprise, but they didn't affect what I knew to be my duty.

She was in her accustomed place when I drove up to the farm. One day, she'll probably be found dead there. I looked at her, trying in vain to categorise her in my personal gallery of the wicked. There were some adversaries during my career for whom I developed a grudging respect; others earned my undying hatred. For Carmel, I felt nothing.

'Hello,' she greeted me as I approached. 'I didn't expect to see you again. Have you come to tell me you're disappointed I got away with it?'

I shrugged. 'Do not confuse me with a man who gives one about that,' I replied. 'I'm sorry for Matthew, and for your alcoholic lummox of a husband, but banging you up for your last few years will be of no use to either of them, and frankly, it's better that you're feeding, clothing and heating yourself than having the public purse do it. That's not why I'm here, Carmel. I need to give you this, that's all, and leave you with one last decision, one that I hope you'll take more calmly than you did thirty years ago.' I handed her an envelope that I'd been holding.

'What's this?' she asked.

'Test results,' I replied. 'The answer to a question you've been avoiding for half a century. When I learned from your daughter that Matthew Ampersand had asked her for a DNA sample . . .' I paused to watch her reaction; she gasped and her eyes widened, and from that I knew that Briony had said nothing to her. 'I knew then what might be on the cards. When I checked the dates, it was obvious. So I got hold of Briony's DNA, without her knowledge, and also of a sample of John Ampersand's.'

'John?' she whispered.

'Yes. Didn't you know? He's still alive, and back home where he began. His contact details are in that envelope, along with other stuff. I can see that he might have been a bit full of himself as a young man, but he's aged well. You might like him better now.'

'I liked him a lot then,' she retorted. 'I got myself in a pickle, that's all. Pickle, fickle; they rhyme and they're both apposite to how it was.'

'You're bloody right there. The other stuff in that envelope is the result of a paternity test. When I commissioned it, I expected it to tell me that Briony is either Barley's daughter or Matthew's. Tell me, you said she was full-term, but was she possibly a week or so early in arriving?'

'She was, around ten days.'

'That, I suspect, will fit, if you really test your memory. Carmel, Briony's father is still alive. She isn't John's niece, as I expected she would prove to be; she's his daughter. Whether either of them ever gets to know that is up to you, for I'm leaving all the evidence with you. That's the decision you have to make; I hope you get it right.'

Fifty-Five

She did.

A phone call I took from John Ampersand the very next day confirmed that, as did Joanna Meikle when she delivered my portrait and told me of her amazement that Briony and her mother were heading south in a couple of days to meet her new dad.

I was cut in two: full of the glow of a happy ending for John, and Briony if she saw it that way, but saddened by the continuing presence of Chrissie Proud at that little window every time I called round to see how she was, or to walk Bowser.

As I've said, Jimmy had gone from being a wanted man to a very unwanted man indeed, save by his family and me – and his bloody dog, I suppose.

Michael Lennon had appeared in court by then, charged with the murder of Austin Brass. It was a big story, not one that a prolific newspaper-reader like Jimmy would miss. It didn't offer the relief of saying that his name didn't figure anywhere on Brass's iPad, but he didn't know about that so it wasn't a consideration.

I thought about it for days, and all the time the question I was asking myself was, 'Why is he doing this to Chrissie, even now that it's safe for him to come home?'

I thought about it at night as well, in the dark, until at two o'clock in the seventh morning after the Lennon story had hit the press, I snapped wide awake and said aloud, to a snoozing Sarah, 'He isn't doing this to Chrissie; he's doing it for her.'

'Whzzz,' she muttered as I crept out of bed.

I had kept in touch with Jimmy during his cancer treatment, but there had been things going on in my own life and I hadn't been there for him as much as I'd have liked. I knew what he been treated for and I knew where, but although Sarah had said she knew his oncologist, she hadn't volunteered her name and I hadn't asked.

When she came downstairs that morning, showered, half dressed and carrying Dawn, who had given us a quiet night for once, I was waiting for her with orange juice, China tea, and croissants straight from the oven. I watched her eat, then spent the brownie point that I hoped to have earned.

'I need you to do me a favour, if you can. I want you to talk to the consultant who was in charge of Jimmy Proud's cancer care, and ask if I can speak to her informally. Can do?'

She licked the last fragments of croissant and ginger preserve from her lips. 'The first, no problem,' she replied. 'The second . . . that'll depend on her attitude and on how busy she is. Some of these people are so much in demand that they have to build walls around themselves. Access to them can be very difficult; even God would have to be referred by a GP. I'll see what I can do, though. Is there any point in asking why you need this?'

'Because I don't have anything else,' I admitted.

She went to work and so did I; already my expanded role in

InterMedia was cutting into my family and leisure time. My informal arrangements with the police and with the Security Service were both dormant, but I could be called on at any moment. If that happened, there was a danger that my golf handicap, which was at its lowest ever, an achievement for a man in his fifties, might start to rise.

I was in a video meeting with Hector Sureda when Sarah rang me, just after eleven; I put his call on hold and took hers. 'Jimmy's consultant. Her name is Ms Shakira Crowe; she's based at the Western General, and if you can get yourself along there for midday, she will see you. Ask for her at reception in the oncology centre. You know where that is? First entrance road as you go up from Comely Bank, first building on the right.'

'Thanks, love,' I said.

'Don't mention it. Will you make the reservation at Osteria or will I? I hope you don't imagine this is only worth a couple of croissants.'

'You do it.' I laughed. 'You can even choose the wine.'

I finished the business with Hector as quickly as I could, then headed up to the Western General. I knew better than to try parking in the hospital itself, and so I slipped into the first free bay I could find in Carrington Road and walked the rest of the way, arriving at two minutes to twelve.

Shakira Crowe was as prompt as me; I walked into her small office on the first floor at midday on the dot. She rose to greet me, but not very far. She wouldn't have been more than five feet tall.

'How can I help you, Mr Skinner?' she began. 'Your wife, whom I know and respect, told me the minimum necessary to get you through that door, but not enough to risk refusal.'

'I'm a friend of Sir James Proud,' I blurted out, 'but . . .' I held up a hand. 'I'm not here to ask about his condition. He's given me his official bulletin, but I've drawn a conclusion of my own: that he's been lying to me, to his wife and to everyone who knows him. He told us all that he's in remission, but I don't believe that. Thing is, Jimmy was in some trouble arising from his old life that he asked me to investigate. I have done, and I have some news for him, but I can't tell him, because he's disappeared. He told his wife he was going away for a while, got into a taxi and that's the last anyone's seen of him. My initial assumption was that he was running away from his professional difficulties. That was unfair of me, for whatever else he may have been, he's no coward. Jimmy is a compassionate man. Lady Proud, whom he loves dearly, is quite clearly in early-stage dementia, maybe even beyond that. My new belief is that he's gone away to spare her from things he knows she will be unable to handle. Bluntly, I'm afraid he's gone away to die. Am I right? That's what I'm here to ask.'

Ms Crowe shuffled a couple of folders on her desk before looking across and up at me. 'And I can't tell you, as I'm sure you knew before you came here. I can't discuss my patient's condition.' She stopped, as if she was drawing the meeting to a close, but then she continued. 'What I can tell you is that my last consultation with Sir James was around three weeks ago, on a Sunday, at Roodlands Hospital in Haddington, where occasionally I will see patients who live in East Lothian, to save them the stress of travelling to this place. I mean "last con-sultation" literally, Mr Skinner, for I don't expect to see him again. At that meeting I did give him my clinical findings, but we went a little further. He asked me for advice and I gave that to him also. There's nothing in my code of ethics that prevents me from sharing it with you. I don't know where he is either, but if you really need to find Sir James, if you feel you have to, as colleague or as friend, I suggest that you look in the Stirling area, where there are several establishments offering end-of-life care. But,' she added, 'don't put it off too long.'

Fifty-Six

I found him just outside Bridge of Allan, in a place called The Hermitage. It had been a mansion once, owned by a shipping magnate in the great days of the River Clyde yards, who had spent his last days in its quiet peaceful grounds and had decided that a similar privilege was the best gift he could bequeath to the society that had served him rather well. He had created a management trust, endowed with several million pounds and a remit to care for the dying regardless of social status. In other words, you couldn't buy your way into it, but wealth and status need not keep you out. There was no indication of its purpose on the sign at its entrance; it might have been a hotel. In a way it was: you could check in any time you liked, but you could never leave.

It was the third place I checked, on a list of four. The first two were on the periphery of Stirling itself, run by charities. They were secure units but altogether too visible for a man on the run, so I had no doubt that when the receptionist in each told me, 'No, we have no patient of that name,' they were telling the truth.

There was no receptionist in The Hermitage. Instead I was faced by a manager, who told me the same thing. I had no doubt that he was lying. He flared up at me when I told him so, but I didn't buy his denials. 'Unless you want me to take this place apart room by room,' I warned him, 'you go and tell Sir James that Bob Skinner's here, with his fucking dog!'

Whether the addition of Bowser to the visitor list made any difference I will never know, but when the man returned, he was conciliatory. I told him not to worry, that I understood he had only been obeying orders, and he led me up to the first floor, to a small room equipped with all the gear that care of the dying requires, and with a window that looked down on to the driveway below, where I had parked my car, facing away from the building.

Jimmy was in a high-backed chair, in a dressing gown worn over striped pyjamas. His feet, in slippers, were puffy from fluid retention. More than anything else, though, his colour told me that Shakira Crowe hadn't been kidding when she told me not to hang about. He was jaundiced, a shade of yellow that made me think of a weather warning that might go to amber at any moment.

'I should have known,' he whispered. 'Be sure your sins will find you out, and if they don't, Bob Skinner will. Have you come to arrest me, son?'

I sighed. 'If I had, it looks as if I'd need an ambulance. Where is it, the cancer?'

'It never went away, Bob,' he admitted. 'It metastasised,' he pronounced the word with difficulty, 'into my lungs and liver. It's the liver that'll finish me, they say, very soon. I'll just drift off, they've promised. But look at me. Can you imagine what seeing me like this would do to Chrissie?'

'Truthfully?' I said. 'It would distress her, there's no doubt about that, but in a couple of months I doubt that she'd have remembered. I'm not arguing with your decision, though; it was made out of compassion. I'm not here to take you back either. It's all over, Jimmy. Michael Lennon's going to jail for killing Brass, and Carmel is untouchable after so many years. By the way, what did you and Alf do with the rolling pin?' I asked casually.

'Alf took it home,' he replied, with the best pass he could make at a rueful smile. 'He used it in his kitchen until he died. You really have done the job, haven't you?'

I nodded. 'Did you not think I would when you set me loose on this thing? Of course you did, Jimmy; it was your way of making amends. When I said I'd listen to Brass, not just frighten him off, you knew I'd have to follow up on what he told me. I know everything now, even stuff that you and Alf had no idea about.'

'Such as?'

'Such as that Carmel used you and Alf, the two of you, to help her get away with murdering her lover.'

'She what?' He gasped, and coughed.

'Matthew Ampersand and she were together in Cambridge. She gave him the push, came back to Heatherston and married Barley Meads for his farm and his money. If the truth had come out that it was her the poor fool saw with Matthew, not Briony, she'd have lost the lot. Whatever she may have said to me now – and I'm sure it'll have been much the same as she said to you and Alf – I know fucking well that the murder was premeditated. That woman never took a step in her life that wasn't planned in advance, apart from one, maybe: shagging her boyfriend's older brother.'

'She took us for fools?' he whispered, incredulous. 'No. That can't be true.'

'It can and it is. Look, Jimmy, I know everything I need or want to, but for one thing. Why? Why did you and Alf do such a thing?'

'I can only speak for me,' he said, 'but the answer is guilt, pure and simple. When my sister Grayling told me what Ampersand had done to young Joanna, and that it was being covered up by the church, I was furious. I went straight to Easterlee, looking for Barley to apologise to him for what had happened with Briony. He wasn't there and so I spoke to Carmel. When she called me later on, in a panic, telling me that she'd gone up to remonstrate with Ampersand and he'd wound up dead . . . I thought that it was all on my shoulders. So I told her to get out of there and leave it to me; I didn't even think about it, just did it. Then I called Alf, and between us we decided that if we made sure the body was never found, there would be no harm done.

'Alf knew about the old Traprain quarry pond and said that would be the perfect place. When he was reported missing, as he would be, I would be able to keep enquiries well away from there. That's not how it wound up, of course; when the body was found, it became a case of saving our own skins. We never set out to fit Meads up for it, but the way we'd dumped Ampersand and the stuff we'd used, he fitted the bill. I wasn't sure, but Alf said he was such a swine, he deserved it. So he got it, and the business died with him; for thirty years, until that man Brass turned up.'

'I know, and then you tried to use me to get rid of him, by any means I chose, I imagine.'

He nodded. 'When I saw in the paper that he was dead,' he wheezed, 'for a while I thought you had done it.'

'Thanks for that,' I growled.

'I'm sorry, son. I should have faced him myself, but I just wasn't brave enough.' He tried to straighten himself in his chair, but failed. 'I am now, though. Are you going to tell Maggie Steele, or young McGuire? Her rather than him, please. He always frightened me, that one.'

'I'm telling neither, Jimmy. I'm going away from this place – not that I was ever here, you understand – and you will never see me again.'

'Thanks for that, son,' he murmured, with a pathetic look in his eye that made me want to run from the room.

I might have done just that but for one last act. 'I'm not leaving you to die alone, though, Jimmy. There's been too much between us for that. Joanna's downstairs, your niece. Chrissie's being looked after, and she'll stay with you for as long as is necessary.'

His eyes filled with tears, and mine may have been a little moist too.

I squeezed his bony shoulder and turned to leave. I thought there was no more to be said, but I was wrong. He called after me: 'Bob, you will look after Bowser, won't you? Chrissie can't stand the bloody animal.'

Discover more gripping novels
in the Bob Skinner series . . .

When millionaire Leo Speight is found poisoned at his
Ayrshire mansion, Police Scotland has a tough case on its hands.
Speight was a champion boxer with national hero status.
A long list of lovers and friends stand to benefit from his
estate. Did one of them decide to speed things up? Or was
jealousy or rivalry the motive?

The Security Service wants to stay close to the investigation
and they have just the man to send in: ex-Chief Constable
Bob Skinner. Combining forces with DI Lottie Mann and
DS Dan Provan of Serious Crimes, Skinner's determined to
see Speight's murderer put away for a long time. But there's
a twist even Bob Skinner couldn't see coming . . .

Available now to buy and download in eBook.

Quintin Jardine

Deathly high stakes in the corridors of power

STATE SECRETS

A BOB SKINNER MYSTERY

Former Chief Constable Bob Skinner is long out of the police force but trouble has a habit of following him around. So it is that he finds himself in the Palace of Westminster as a shocking act befalls the nation.

Hours before the Prime Minister is due to make a controversial statement, she is discovered in her office with a letter opener driven through her skull.

Is the act political? Personal? Or even one of terror?

Skinner is swiftly enlisted by the Security Service to lead the investigation. Reunited with Met Police Commander Neil McIlhenney, he has forty-eight hours to crack the case – before the press unleash their wrath.

There are many in the tangled web of government with cause to act. But the outcome will be one that not even Skinner himself could predict . . .

Available now to buy and download in eBook.

THRILLINGLY GOOD BOOKS
FROM CRIMINALLY
GOOD WRITERS

CRIME FILES BRINGS YOU THE LATEST RELEASES FROM
TOP CRIME AND THRILLER AUTHORS.

SIGN UP ONLINE FOR OUR MONTHLY NEWSLETTER AND BE THE FIRST
TO KNOW ABOUT OUR COMPETITIONS, NEW BOOKS AND MORE.

VISIT OUR WEBSITE: WWW.CRIMEFILES.CO.UK
LIKE US ON FACEBOOK: FACEBOOK.COM/CRIMEFILES
FOLLOW US ON TWITTER: @CRIMEFILESBOOKS